# HOWL IN THE KNIGHT

## JULIUS A.M. BROWN

DIVERTIR
PUBLISHING

*Salem, NH*

# HOWL IN THE KNIGHT

*Julius A.M. Brown*

Copyright © 2025 Julius A.M. Brown



*Cover design by Kenneth Tupper*

*Published by*
*Divertir Publishing LLC*
*PO Box 232*
*North Salem, NH 03073*
*http://www.divertirpublishing.com/*

ISBN-13: 978-1-938888-33-5
ISBN-10: 1-938888-33-2

Library of Congress Control Number: 2025940625

Printed in the United States of America

# TABLE OF CONTENTS

# CHAPTER 1

R UN RUN RUN," I yelled as Larry and I dashed by Aaron, who was standing on the corner beneath a streetlight checking his phone. He was dressed in a skin tight white t-shirt, tight jeans, and a $300 pair of casual athletic shoes. How did I know they cost that much? Because he told me when he called my $20 sneakers cheap. Screw Aaron—forty bucks for a pair of shoes is highway robbery. Besides, the rain had probably ruined his shoes, while my sneakers were good to go.

Aaron looked up from his phone as we passed him. He didn't seem to understand why we were running, not until he looked from us to the thing that was chasing us. Several hundred pounds of muscle in the form of an eight-foot tall and severely ticked-off cyclops in a cheap business suit came charging behind us.

"FOUR FUCKING ACES!" the one-eyed giant bellowed as he came at us with the grace and abandon of a runaway train.

"Fallen Night!" Aaron swore. One moment he was a dozen feet behind us, and the next he was a dozen feet ahead of us. Freaking vampire speed. "What the hell did you do?" he asked over his shoulder.

A mail box, the big blue kind that you see as often as phone booths, came flying through the rain. It hit the side of the building a few yards ahead of us and tumbled to the ground ahead of Larry and me. Larry stepped around it. I jumped over it just as the spot on the brick wall that it had struck gave way. A falling brick and some smaller debris hit me in the head, but I shook it off and kept running.

"It wasn't me, it was Larry," I yelled.

The guy running just a few feet ahead of me looked back at me like I had just told him his mother smelled of elderberries. Larry Lipowski was a foot shorter than my 6'2" frame, but his legs were pumping much faster than mine were. He had curly red hair, freckles for days, and was wearing a nice-looking green leisure suit. He had taken off the jacket and was currently using it to hold a pile of money to his chest. As fast as we were running, and with as many obstacles that we had to avoid, I figured he would just drop the cash gradually if not all at once. Larry never dropped a single coin, and he had quite a few dollars' worth of them in the pile.

"It's not my fault. I didn't do anything wrong!" Larry protested.

"FOUR FUCKING ACES!" the cyclops yelled again.

"Why does he keep yelling that?" I asked Larry.

"I have no idea what he's talking about." Larry shrugged.

We rounded another corner and ran through the fence opening into the parking lot. There were only half a dozen cars in the lot. The Rust Bucket, my rusty old dodge truck, was parked right in the middle of the lot and facing the opposite direction. All we had to do was get in and haul out of here.

I looked over my shoulder and watched the cyclops leap over the fence. He flew through the air, over my head, and landed a few dozen feet in front of Larry. His wingtips slid across the ground as he spun to face Larry and me as we skidded to a stop.

"FOUR FUCKING ACES! I'M GONNA KILL YOU, LARRY," roared the cyclops.

Larry turned to face me, and then as casually as if he were asking me to pass him the salt at dinner, he said, "Sir Michael White, Knight of Innocence, Defender of the land of Baltimore Maryland and its peoples. I, Larry Lipowski, ask that you defend me from this brute. I am an innocent and a citizen of the merry land of Baltimore, while Chester is a hired thug from out of town." Then he walked behind me and addressed the cyclops. "Chester, any problem you have with me you can take up with the knight."

I looked back at Larry and said, "You called me because you were too drunk to drive! You said you would buy me dinner."

That's when Chester took the front of my flannel shirt in one meaty hand and lifted me up to his face. His breath was surprisingly minty fresh when he said, "Four fucking aces."

"Okay," I said. "So, Larry had four aces?"

"Four aces and a king," Larry said. "I won that pot fair and square!"

"So, what's the problem…umm…Chester?" I asked.

"He wins every week. Every fucking week because he cheats," Chester said.

"Preposterous!" Larry said.

"Chester, he's half leprechaun you know. There is a word for that, but I can't think of it. Anyway, he probably wins because of that whole 'Luck of the Irish' thing," I said calmly.

"Exactly my boy. Luck of the Irish! If I could tattoo it on my nuts I would," Larry said.

"He had four fucking aces!" Chester said. "He cheated!"

"A winning hand fair and square," Larry said. "Four other players, and you single me out just because I'm smaller and weaker than you are."

"Chester, having a good hand doesn't mean he cheated," I said. "You can't just bully people into admitting to accusations." I looked Chester hard in the eye. The cyclops may have been holding me two feet off the ground like a sack of potatoes, but I don't back down from bullies on principle.

"We took the aces out of the deck before Larry arrived," growled the cyclops.

I turned my head to look at Larry. The little cheat smiled and said, "Oh…well how was I supposed to know that?"

I turned back to Chester and huffed, "If he gives the money back, will you let him go?"

"I'm going to get the money back after I kill him," Chester said.

"Chester, you really should reconsider," I told him.

"I'm going to kill him," he said.

"Then I'm going to stop you," I said. Chester looked at me and laughed. He laughed so hard I bobbed up and down while he held me. Larry gulped so loudly that they could have heard it on the moon.

"You're gonna stop me? Humans really are stupid, but you sure are funny, too. Tell you what, how about I give you a free punch?" the cyclops said. Chester lifted his chin and tapped it with the fingers of his right hand. "Why don't you put one right here, Mr. Knight."

My eyes rolled as I cocked back my right arm for a punch. "Impact!" I snarled as I threw a straight right punch. Magic gathered to my call, and when my fist hit Chester he went down under the weight of my blow. I followed through with the punch breaking his jaw and sending him sprawling onto the ground. He dropped me as he fell. My feet touched the ground, and I jumped backwards with my hands up for a fight.

"Holy shit," Aaron said from beside my truck.

"Holy shit," Larry said.

"Holy shit," Chester said with what should have been a broken jaw.

I grabbed Larry, and we ran to my truck. Aaron climbed in on the passenger side as I shoved Larry into the middle from the driver's side. We took off into the Baltimore night and left Chester behind us on the ground in the rain. Aaron kept looking behind us as I drove. Larry started counting his ill-gotten gains. Once we were five blocks away, I couldn't hold back anymore.

"Larry Lipowski, you're half human and half leprechaun. You're Jewish, you have curly red hair, and you have freckles. Did you have to bring together every freaking stereotype about both of your heritages by cheating at poker?" I asked.

Aaron looked down at Larry and said, "Seriously man, the only joke you can dodge is being a soulless ginger."

Larry chuckled. "I lost that thing in a game of blackjack sixteen years ago."

Aaron, Larry, and I all broke into laughter. We couldn't help it. Larry Lipowski was a soulless, ginger, Jewish leprechaun that just cheated at poker and hid behind the city's knight. It was just too much.

"You know you're buying us both dinner for this, right?" Aaron asked.

Larry stopped laughing.

# CHAPTER 2

WE GOT A booth at Kate's Bar and dried off as best we could. It had been raining for a solid week, and I had yet to invest in an umbrella. We made sure Kate knew that our meal was on Larry's dime and took a booth in the back along the far wall. A pretty young waitress that couldn't have been more than twenty climbed into the booth to sit next to Aaron while she took our orders. Her breasts were basically spilling out of her low-cut top while she smiled at Aaron and leaned up against him. She had full pink lips and hair with enough bounce to star in the remake of Flubber. I watched as she flirted with Aaron, who paid her no attention. He was fixated on his phone. Then she leaned over the table and flirted with Larry while she took his order. Larry, for his part, reached over and pulled not one but four coins from behind her ear. I was sitting next to Larry with my back to the wall patiently waiting to order my food. When the waitress finished with Larry, she hopped up to leave.

"Excuse me, miss," I said.

"No," she said as she kept walking away.

"Beg your pardon, miss," Aaron said as he looked up from his phone.

The waitress, Stacey from what her name tag said, turned around with a smile on her face that could have lit up the city. "What can I do for you, sweetie?" she asked him.

"My friend would like to order," Aaron said sweetly.

"Sorry, sweetie, but we don't serve perverts," she said.

"I'm a pervert?" I asked.

"Don't act all innocent, asshole. You've been staring at me like I was your rightful property since you came in," Stacey said.

Aaron looked her over from head to toe, and she smiled while he did it. Her t-shirt was two sizes too small and cut low enough so that it was basically just cupping her breasts. Her shorts were the same size as her underwear. Even her apron was folded and tied so that it didn't obstruct her patrons' view of anything.

"Miss, my friend would have to buy you clothing and somehow manage to put them on you before anyone looking at you could be called a pervert," Aaron said. Stacey's mouth dropped. My best friend the vampire continued, "Two cheese steaks with extra mayo and onions, triple fries with no salt for each, a pitcher of Mountain Dew, and a pitcher of beer. And if I think you messed with it in any way, being fired will be the least of your problems."

Stacey stomped away screaming for the bouncer. Some people in the bar looked over at us. Others ignored the situation. Aaron went back to his phone. The bouncer, Bruce, came over to see us. Bruce was six feet tall and weighed in at two-hundred-fifty pounds of muscle. He was bald, sported a few tattoos, and oddly enough he was wearing a gun on his hip. That was new.

"Stacey says you threatened her, Aaron," Bruce said.

"She called Michael a pervert," Aaron replied. He liked Bruce, but tonight the big man was apparently not important enough for Aaron to look up from his phone.

Bruce looked at me and shook his head. "Sorry man, she's human. She hasn't exactly figured out this place is filled with preternatural creatures. Hard to believe that if shit goes fubar in here, she just called the one guy that is sworn to protect her a pervert," the big man said.

"It's all good man. What's with the piece?" I asked.

"Kate said we had to bring heat or not come into work. I don't ask questions. I just hope I won't have to use it. I'll put in your usual order, Michael. Enjoy your night, fellas," Bruce said. He walked away just as someone else came to join us.

An old man in a trench coat and fedora walked over to us. He was dripping wet as he shrugged out of his coat to sit next to Aaron. Priest Gregory Greyshadow was wearing his clergy blacks and sporting a shoulder holster with a black revolver. He waved to a waitress that wasn't Stacey, and she came over to take his order of beer, a burger, and fries with extra salt. Basically, a bunch of food a sixty-year-old man shouldn't be eating.

"Larry, word on the street is that Bob's poker crew is after your head. They hired some muscle to come after you," Greyshadow said.

Larry went pale. I patted Larry on the shoulder and said, "Don't worry, padre. I laid his muscle out in the street. He won't be messing with Larry anymore."

"Yeah, I heard about that. Chester isn't Bob's hired muscle. Chester is the guy that got first crack at the little cheat. He told Bob how you cold cocked him with a single punch, so Bob hired the Bridge Boys," Greyshadow said.

"The Bridge Boys!" Larry screamed.

"The Bridge Boys?" I asked.

"The Bridge Boys! Because being a parrot helps move along conversation oh so well," snapped Aaron, still not looking up from his texting.

"Yep. You ripped off the wrong poker game, Larry," the priest said.

"I'm so fucked," Larry said. "The Bridge Boys are crazy. They…they…"

"Always collect their toll," Greyshadow said.

Larry sunk down into his seat. I heard Aaron say, "Larry is gonna die," under his breath.

"Okay, so who are the Bridge Boys?" I asked.

"Kid, I thought you had learned at least some of the major players in the city's underworld by now. How the hell do you call yourself a gum shoe?" Greyshadow asked.

"I don't. I call myself a *part time* private investigator. Emphasis on the '*part time.*' Now, who are the Bridge Boys?"

"The Bridge Boys are four big shots in the game here in Baltimore and in a lot of the surrounding states. They take out contracts every once in a while if someone offers them enough money," Greyshadow said.

Our food arrived by way of another waitress that wasn't Stacey. This waitress was named Georgia, and she wasn't flaunting her body for tips. She could have, and she would have emptied a few wallets. Georgia was not human. I know this because human girls treat me like Stacey did. Georgia smiled at me and poured my first glass of beer from my pitcher. When she walked away, she winked at me over her shoulder.

We said grace, because it doesn't hurt to be thankful for the little things in life.

"So, they're human?" I asked.

Aaron laughed. "No, the Bridge Boys aren't human. Think about it. The Bridge Boys always get their toll."

As I pondered Aaron's words, the door to the bar swung open, and two men in several layers of castoff clothing came inside. One limped while supporting himself with a wooden crutch. The crutch was held together with duct tape. The other man walked with a surprising spring in his step.

"Beer," said the spring-stepping man. "Lots of beer!"

I went back to pondering and eating. I knew Aaron wasn't going to give me any hints, and Priest Greyshadow was too deep into the sinful bliss of his meal to be bothered. Larry just looked at his food and muttered something about a last meal. Larry didn't know it, but I wasn't about to let anyone hurt him. Still, letting him sweat might teach him a lesson about cheating and using people.

I was halfway through my second cheese steak when the sound of glass breaking tore me from my food. The bum with the spring in his step was leaning over the counter and yelling at one of the female bartenders.

"I said beer! What is this piss you keep giving me?" he yelled.

"It's beer," she yelled back.

"I've had seven and don't have a buzz. Give me something stronger!" he yelled.

"Cash first, asshole," she yelled back defiantly.

"Calm down, Eddy. You got enough cash to keep us in booze for the rest of the night if you want," said the bum with the crutch.

"Shut up, Johnny." The first man leapt over the bar, shoved the bartender to the ground, and started grabbing bottles of liquor. He turned them up one after the other.

Bruce ran over to the bar and right up to the guy. He grabbed the old vagrant and started dragging him away. They had gone three steps when the old guy tensed up, and Bruce came to a sudden stop.

The big man looked down at the smaller man and said, "Come on, man, don't make me hurt you." The bum reached for another bottle, and Bruce snatched it from his hands. The bum snatched it back with such speed and force that when he pulled the bottle away from Bruce he flung it across the room. It hit a patron in the head and shattered against the poor guy's skull.

"Shit," Aaron said. He leapt over Priest Gregory and ran to tend to the injured man.

"Alright, buddy I tried to do this the easy way," Bruce said. He hit the guy with a right hook that would have knocked me for a loop.

The old man staggered back a step. Then he straightened. Bruce had a good hundred pounds on the old man and was almost a foot taller. None of that mattered to Eddy. He hit Bruce with a right hook of his own that sent the bouncer stumbling backward spinning like a top. He fell over behind the bar, and everyone went silent. I had seen Bruce throw out drunks before, and some of them were preternatural beings. I had never seen anyone just drop him like that.

The old vagrant grabbed another bottle of whisky and turned to his friend. "Drinks are free, Johnny boy!"

The sound of a shotgun chambering a round caught Eddy's attention. Kate may have weighed only 140 pounds, but she was a woman that would defend her bar and staff from a dragon if one came calling. Kate stood 5'8" tall, and while the rest of her staff wore black tee shirts she wore red. Her right arm was covered in tattoos from the back of her hand all the way to where her shirt sleeve ended. Possibly further, but she never wore tank tops. Her left eye had an eye patch over it, and she wore make up of dark colors on her sun-kissed skin. If you compared Kate to the female staff in the bar, it was like comparing a cover model to some little girls playing dress up. Kate was hot and she knew it. She was also dangerous, and everyone else knew it.

Eddy turned to face her and licked his lips. "Hey, Miss Kate," he said. "How about you and I have a little fun?"

"Eddy, are you drunk?" Kate asked.

"No!" he yelled.

"Come on, Eddy. We can go find some tail outside," Johnny said.

"No!" Eddy growled. "Not tonight. Tonight, I am going to drink as much as I want and fuck whoever I want. And I want her! Come here, little girl," he said as he took a step toward Kate.

Kate's shotgun roared in answer to his invitation. Eddy flew backward as buck shot emptied into his chest. Blood splattered on the floor, bar, ceiling, and on Kate. She put her empty gun on the counter behind the bar and stepped over Eddy to check on Bruce. Her stride didn't slow when she stepped over the body she left on the ground. Kate was stone cold.

As Kate bent down to check on Bruce, Eddy stood up. He had holes all over his chest. He growled and then screamed in pain. He rounded on Bruce and Kate. I heard Kate swear, and then a gun barked several times. Eddy jerked back, but he did not go down.

Eddy wasn't human.

I jumped over Larry and sprinted over to the bar. When I leapt over the bar, I saw Kate holding an empty pistol that she had taken off Bruce. Eddy rounded on me when I landed, and he tried to hit me with a back hand swing from his right arm. I had already dropped too low for that to work. I hit him in the gut with my shoulder and hoisted him into the air. I grabbed him by the shoulder and groin and flung him back across the bar. He hit the ground hard, and I hurtled the bar to go after him.

Eddy got to his feet just as I got to him. He growled at me, and I got my first good look at Eddy. He was filthy. Dirt and grime were matted in his wild hair. He had to be at least fifty years old and the veteran of a few fights from the scars on his face. Then there was his beard. It was an epic grizzled beard that you would expect to see on a dwarf. Strangely, his beard was gray on the ends, but the closer you got to his face the more color the hair took on until his face was framed in a mane of dark brown hair.

Eddy charged me like a wild man. His hands came in at my throat, but I grabbed both of his wrists. Eddy kept coming, and I found myself being forced back. Eddy was not a big guy. I am. I stand 6'2" tall and weigh in at 275 pounds of mostly muscle. None of that seemed to matter to Eddy. My boots hit the bottom runner of the bar, and that was the only thing that kept me from being pushed through the whole building.

Eddy hauled back his right arm and sent a punch at my face. I ducked, grabbed that arm with my left hand, and stepped in with my right foot leading. I hit Eddy in the gut with my right and then in the chest with the same fist. He stepped back from the blows but didn't back down. So, I hit him in the throat, twisted his right arm under my left, and hit him in the face with a right hook.

Eddy growled and hoisted me up with his twisted right arm. The amount of strength it takes to do something like that just reaffirmed that Eddy was not human. His left arm came over his head in an arching blow that looked more like an exaggerated volleyball spike than a punch. I shoved off of his lifting arm and quickly stepped to my left to avoid the blow. Eddy's fist went through the bar top and halfway down to the floor.

Before he could recover, I grabbed Eddy and yanked him across the floor in a spinning rush. We circled a few times, and I pushed him out toward the door of the bar before he could gather his wits. When he finally caught his footing he came back at me screaming. I took a step toward him and threw a straight right into his chest.

"Impact," I said under my breath so that no one would hear. For the second time that night magic gathered to my call, and when I hit Eddy in the chest, I hit him with the strength of a giant. Eddy went flying out the swinging doors, over the porch, and out into the gravel parking lot. I heard shuffling behind me and spun to see Johnny hobbling past me.

"I'm sorry man. I'm real sorry. I won't let him come back in. Please don't call the cops," Johnny said. He hurried out the door and into the rain.

I stood there for a few minutes just in case Eddy decided to come back inside. I was unarmed, so that punch was the best I could give, and I could only do it one more time today. When Eddy didn't come back inside, I breathed a sigh of relief.

The bar was quiet. Slowly the sounds of forks touching plates came back into the room. The jukebox stopped sounding like white noise, I could hear people drinking, and conversations about what had just happened started up.

A strong hand grabbed my shoulder and spun me around violently. Kate stared at me without meeting my eyes. It was a strange thing. Kate was perhaps the only person in the world that would look at me without even glancing at my eyes. It felt like she knew what could happen, that she knew God had 'blessed' me with the ability to experience the trials and hardships a person had experience in their lifetime. It always relieved me that she did not look me in the eye, because Kate scared the living hell out of me.

"Sir Knight, you have my thanks," she told me.

"It's not a problem," I said.

"No, Sir Knight, it is a problem. That man will want you dead. You hurt him, and you hurt his pride," she said.

I looked back over her shoulder at the heavy bar that the man had broken through like it was made of off-brand Legos. "Comes with the territory," I said coolly.

"No, Sir Knight. Not this territory. Trust me on this when I say people like him do not live here, and it is for the best," Kate said. She turned to leave but said to me over her shoulder, "He will only get stronger."

Aaron walked up to me while shaking his head. "Did you know he wasn't human?" the vampire asked.

"I guessed. Vampire?" I asked.

"No," he said. "I have to catch a flight tomorrow morning. I will be gone for two weeks. I'm taking Emory with me."

I looked at my friend and narrowed my eyes. "Something to do with you being on your phone all night?"

"Yeah. I was texting with my father. He wants me home. He wants to talk to me about something important." Aaron sighed.

"Wait, your dad? Your dad is a vampire, too?" I asked.

"No. My biological father is dead. The vampire that sired me sired me as his son. He had no idea I would be…well…a misfit. He checks up on me now and again. He offers me virgins sometimes to tempt me into eating people. I don't, but he just shrugs and asks me to play the piano for him," Aaron said.

"So, your sire has no problem with you being gay, but he does have a problem with you not wanting to eat humans?" I asked.

"Yeah. He's fine with me being gay. He's older than the term. Men having sex with men and women having sex with women doesn't bother him. His problem is that I don't eat people like a good little blood sucking immortal. He says we are the top of the food chain, and I shouldn't stroke the ego of my food. You humans might get the idea that you aren't cattle," he said.

As I let the creepiness of that bit of knowledge seep into my brain, the rest of the bar gathered itself up. Kate was okay and Bruce was coming around. Aaron and I went back to our booth. Larry was paying the tab.

"How is your hand?" Aaron asked. I lifted my left palm to show him the long scar that ran down the center of my palm. The scab had recently fallen off, leaving me with a reddish-brown mark to show for my efforts saving the city. Aaron examined it and nodded in approval of my healing.

"Why are you taking Emory?" I asked. "And how are you catching a flight in the *morning*?"

"I will be in a titanium coffin with a magnetic locking system that only opens from the inside after being activated. Once I am on my father's private jet I will be fine. I am taking Emory because the last time I refused to bring my lover to meet my father he took it as an insult. He killed an entire village in his frustration," Aaron said.

I changed the subject. "The Bridge Boys are trolls, aren't they?" I asked. I prayed that I was wrong. I needed to be wrong. I had never wanted to be right in my whole life as badly as I wanted to be wrong right now.

"Yep," Aaron said.

Great. Homicidal hoboes and trolls. Fairy tale life for the win!

# Chapter 3

WE ALL HEADED out into the parking lot. It was still raining, and it was starting to get cold. Larry looked like he was going to fall over and die. I had let the poor guy suffer enough. "Come on, Larry, let's go," I said.

Larry looked up at me wide-eyed and skeptical. "Are you going to take me to the Bridge Boys?" he asked.

"No, Larry. I don't turn people over to things that want to hurt them. I'm going to keep you safe until we figure things out. You can stay at my place tonight. I have work tomorrow, so Priest Gregory will keep you safe for a bit if it's cool with him," I said.

"Sure kid. Bring him by the church. He can help clean the pews."

"Seriously? You're going to keep the Bridge Boys from killing me?" Larry asked.

"It's kind of my job Larry, and you kind of involved me anyway, so here we are," I told the little man.

Larry grabbed me and hugged me. He came up to the top of my stomach, so it was awkward, but I hugged him too. Priest Greyshadow and Aaron got into Aaron's Mercedes and took off into the night. I drove Larry back to my place. Larry wanted to stop by his place and get a few things. I told him it was better to do that tomorrow and that I would go alone. I live in a small apartment in a not too bad side of town. I have two neighbors above me and one beside me. My upstairs neighbors pretty much leave me alone unless they need something fixed. It pays to be a carpenter sometimes.

I set Larry up on the couch. I gave him a pillow, some blankets, and some shorts to sleep in. He had to pull the drawstring all the way out to get them to fit, but they would serve for the night. I was going to offer him something to drink, but he was out the moment his head touched the pillow. That was for the best because I was beat.

I walked over to my front door and ran my hand across the circle Eden had etched into the wood. I spoke the words she had taught me, and I felt the magic of my home come to life as the outside world was closed out. Eden said that before Kerri-Lynn had come to visit me it was impossible for my apartment to maintain a defensive ward. Kerri-Lynn had made my apartment a home. She and I had created love here. We had made memories. We had fought, we had laughed, and we had loved so hard that it had transformed a rented space into a loving home. It had only taken a couple days.

I checked my watch and saw it was only a few minutes before 11p.m. I could get a few good hours of sleep in, so I stowed my gear, set my sword on the bed beside me, and closed my eyes.

Muffled sounds from my closet yanked me from the light sleep I had found. I looked over at the open door to my closet. There was a plastic storage bin on the floor. It was wrapped with duct tape and bungee cords. It rocked back and forward every few seconds. I had forgotten I had been sleeping with headphones on so that I could ignore the storage bin. I lived alone so I could just tune it out, but since I was supposed to be protecting Larry, I had to be able to hear if someone broke in.

The bin started rocking more frequently. Shaking my head, I got up, picked up the storage bin, and set it on my bed. I removed the four bungee cords that were the second layer of security for the bin. Then I grabbed my silver knife and cut away the duct tape that was the first layer of security. Before I opened the bin, I pulled my .50 caliber Desert Eagle from its holster at the head of my bed.  Slowly, I lifted the lid of the storage bin and pointed my gun inside.

Inside the storage bin was a black and brown teddy bear. He had a button for a right eye and a purple and green marble as a left eye. The marble was the original. He had on overalls that had been fine looking a year ago. Now they had blood all over them. My blood. There was a plastic sword and shield next to the bear. Oh, and the bear was tied up with shoestrings. He also had duct tape over his mouth. I put my gun on the side of the bear's face and pulled back the hammer.

"If I untie you, are you going to try to kill me again?" I asked.

The bear's marble eye turned so that the green pupil looked directly at me. Then the little teddy bear turned its head from side to side.

"Can we have a conversation that isn't about how you want me dead?" I asked.

The teddy bear nodded.

"Good," I said. I pulled my gun from the bear's head and put it back in its holster. I undid the bindings on my old teddy bear, and he sat up.

I let him remove the tape from around his mouth on his own. He growled in pain as he pulled the tape off of his mouth. "Dammit, that shit hurts," he said. "Did you have to gag me?"

"Yeah. You wouldn't let me sleep," I reminded him.

"Oh? Well pardon *me* for disturbing *your* rest," he said.

He seemed kind of angry. This was the only conversation we'd had since he first tried to kill me a few months ago that didn't involve a stream of obscenities, death threats, and curses upon myself and my unborn children. So, this was going well.

"I have questions," I told him.

"Oh, I'm sure you do. But I don't care! I don't know how you summoned me back here, but when I figure it out I am going to get the hell away from you. But if I can't figure it out, I am going to kill you and be done with it," the teddy bear said as he climbed out of the storage bin. He was a little over a foot tall and threatening me like he wasn't all stuffed with fluff.

"Look, Horace," I said.

"That's not my name!" he yelled at me.

"Okay…Well, what is your name?"

He glared at me and folded his arms. "You'd love to get your filthy mitts on my true name, would you?"

Names are a big deal. Your true name is the name that resonates most with the core of your being. It is the very essence of who and what you are. To know your own true name was a sign of power. To possess the true name of another was to possess power over them. There were three people in the world that knew my true name: my mother, my grandmother, and Kerri-Lynn.

I shook my head no. "I don't want your true name. I want a name that I can call you. I have always called you Horace because I thought it was your name. What should I call you?"

The teddy bear narrowed his eye at me. "You don't want my true name?"

"No. I just want to know why you want to kill me. I thought…well…this sounds stupid, but I'm talking to a teddy bear so what the heck. I thought we were friends," I said with a shrug.

Horace, the bear that my grandpa had given me as a baby, looked up at me. His mouth hung open at my words. His arms uncrossed, and he lifted them up to me for a hug. My life has been a train wreck. Every person I met before I became a knight hated me with the exception of my family and Kerri-Lynn. Roughly ninety-two percent of the people I have met since becoming a knight have hated me. I have been accused of being a demon, a rapist, and Judas reborn. So, when an obviously magical stuffed animal from my childhood offers me a hug I am going to take it!

I knelt down to hug Horace, my long-forgotten friend. Horace jumped up to embrace me by wrapping his arms around my neck. Then he started to strangle me with a strength that no child's toy should possess. I fell back on the floor gagging and trying to pry the little bastard from my neck. I felt claws digging into my skin.

"Friends? You think we're fucking friends? A friend would have let me stay with my family. A friend would have let me have my fucking rest. I protected you for ten damned years and little snot buckets like you for more than a hundred years! I want to go home! Just die already and let me go!" he yelled.

I reached up onto my bed for my gun with my right hand, but I couldn't reach it. I fished around on the mattress for a second until my hand wrapped around the hilt of my sword. I drove the hilt of the sheathed blade down and drilled it into Horace's face. He fell away and rolled across the floor. I got my legs under me, swooned, and fell with my back against the bed. My left hand touched my neck, and I felt cuts along my throat. None were deep enough to outright kill me, but when I pulled my hand away it was covered in blood.

Horace was back on his feet, and he roared at me with a sound that would have made a grizzly bear turn tail and run. I couldn't run because I could barely keep my body upright. I took my sheath in my left hand and drew the blade with my right hand. The growling sneer on Horace's face fell away, and his one eye went wide.

"Is that one of the Twelve?" he asked. Then he fell over in a boneless heap as someone pounded on my front door. I just stared at him for a moment and shook my head. I sheathed my sword and went to answer my front door after I grabbed my gun.

I looked through the peephole and saw my upstairs neighbor Mr. Wilson in his wife's robe standing in the rain. I opened the door and tried to greet him cheerily. "Hi, Mr. Wilson," I said.

Mr. Wilson was a short and scrawny man. If it wasn't for his wife's satin mini robe, I was sure I would see his ribs under his pale skin. He was bald except for a ream of lush brown hair around his scalp. He was an angular man with a large hawkish nose. "Black, I am reporting you to the landlord. You know the rules, no loud parties!" he said. Mr. Wilson was not an evil man or a racist. He was just mean-spirited and not good with people.

"Mr. Wilson, my last name is White. I'm a black man, not that it matters. Also, I am not having a party." I opened my door so that he could see my sparsely furnished apartment. My couch where Larry was sleeping soundly. My weight bench sat with the chair propped up in case I had company over. My spool also had a nice tablecloth on it.

"Who's that on the couch?" he asked.

"My accountant. He fell asleep getting my taxes ready," I told him.

"What was that scream thingy that came from down here?" Wilson demanded.

"Mr. Wilson, I was asleep until you knocked on my door. I have no idea what you are talking about," I lied.

"Why is there blood on your neck?" the persistent man asked.

"Cut myself shaving," I said.

"In your sleep?"

"Yep…I sleepwalk…and shave. Sleep shaving."

Mr. Wilson narrowed his eyes. He took one last look around my apartment and said, "I'm watching you Bla…err…White!" Then he stomped off in his borrowed robe and blue bunny slippers.

I locked my door back up, spoke the words that would reset the wards Eden had placed on my threshold, and checked on Larry. He was out like a light. I guess he was either exhausted or the heaviest sleeper of all time.

I walked back to my room to find Horace on my bed. He was kneeling over my sword and rubbing his paws along the length of the unsheathed blade. I was going to raise my gun at him, but he spoke up before I could.

"This is one of the Twelve Swords of the Apostles," he said. "My charge is a knight?" He looked up at me and I nodded. "Michael White is a Knight of the Crucifixion, just like his grandfather. We have a lot to discuss."

He patted the bed next to himself. I closed the door and sat down to have a heart to heart with my teddy bear. He kept looking over my sword while I put away my gun.

"It's late, so I won't take long explaining this," he told me. "Ask me questions at the end, okay?"

I nodded.

"I am not a teddy bear, and my name is not Horace. I am an ursa, and my name is Texaferis. We are an ancient and powerful race long since removed from this world. Removed except for our duty to protect the young of humankind. Thus, idols were created as conduits for our souls and strength, the latest incarnation being what you call teddy bears. When a child is given a teddy bear by someone that truly loves them and wants to see them safe, that teddy bear becomes the conduit for an ursa. Until that child loses their innocence of the world the ursa protects them, in secret of course, from all of the supernatural foes that may try to harm them or spirit them away, from all the things they believe in but the adults around them have long shrugged off as fiction, and from all the things that the ignorance of the world ignores. Any questions?"

I had a lot, but he was right. It was late. I was tired, and I had a day full of work and trolls ahead of me. So, I asked a stupid question.

"Can I call you Horace?" I asked.

My teddy bear chuckled. "Gods, you haven't changed. Yeah kid, you can call me Horace."

"Let's talk in the morning. Cool?" I asked.

"Cool kid," he said.

Horace grabbed my pillow and slept at the foot of the bed. I set an alarm and laid my head down on the pillow that was Kerri-Lynn's. I wasn't so stupid that I hadn't washed it since she left. But I was love struck enough that I could imagine that it still smelled like her.

# CHAPTER 4

**M**Y ALARM WENT off, so I rolled out of bed. It was 2:30 a.m. and I did not want to get up. I wanted to sleep until morning, but I had a personal issue that I had to work on.

I got dressed in a hoodie and sweatpants. I wrote a note for Larry and taped it to the front door. After checking my wards, I got into my truck and drove out to Druid Hill Park. I stretched and thought about the night before. Aaron had jogged past me while I ran at top speed. Larry had outpaced me from the moment we started running. Chester was in cheap dress shoes with no traction and still kept pace with me easily. It wasn't that I was slow, but I sure wasn't as fast as I could have been. So, I needed to fix that. I walked over to Druid Lake and started jogging. The lake was one and a half miles around. If I jogged for the first lap and sprinted the second lap, I could slowly build my speed and stamina.

It wouldn't be a quick fix, and it wasn't going to save my life today or tomorrow. Intelligence, power, strength, and wisdom were all things that a person needed time to gain. A person needed time to build and to understand. I needed to be faster, so I had to work at it. It wasn't just going to happen. So here I was, the only idiot in Baltimore awake at three in the morning, jogging in the rain.

The fog was thick as it rolled off of the lake. The rain added misery and weight to my run as it slowly soaked my clothing. It wasn't a cold morning, but it wasn't a warm one either. I decided I would bring a towel and a change of clothes tomorrow. It was going to be miserable driving home in soaking wet clothes.

I finished my first lap and was about to start sprinting when a black Lincoln Town Car drove past me. It did a U-turn and drove back toward me. The car slowed to a stop on the curb a good twenty yards ahead of me. A young man in a gray chauffeur's outfit, complete with cap and high boots, stepped out of the car with a black umbrella held delicately above his head.

The chauffeur haled me silently as he walked around to the back passenger side door. I slowed down as I approached. Cautiously I put my hands into my pockets so that I could feel the knives I was carrying. The young man opened the passenger side back door as I approached and held the umbrella out for his passenger. Once the man exited the car, the chauffeur closed the door and took up a position just behind his passenger. As they walked toward me, the Chauffeur held the umbrella so that the passenger was shielded from the rain while he was left to the elements. We stopped just short of each other, a few feet separating us so that they wouldn't seem threatening, and I would feel more comfortable being approached by two strangers on a dark morning.

The passenger was a man of average height and build. He was older than me by at least two decades, with a full head of silver hair that he had combed back to look as professional as any old guy with money. He wore a tailored gray suit with a silver shirt and gray tie. His long black coat ended just under his knees, and his polished black shoes did not make a sound as he approached. When the chauffeur stepped beside him and bowed, he took the handle of the umbrella in his gray gloved left hand. The chauffeur relinquished the umbrella, folded his arms behind his back, and retreated several steps behind the older man. I guess this was supposed to give us the illusion of privacy.

"Hello young man," the older man said. "I know this is probably an odd situation. Here you are, a black man, minding his own business when some white man with his own chauffeur flags you down on a cold, foggy morning before the sun comes up."

I shrugged. "Nah, it happens all the time. The last time it was Ed McMahon with a check."

He chuckled at that. His smile was not perfectly bright white, but his teeth were an odd color similar to white but not quite there. His teeth were even, and his smile exuded a calm confidence in himself. He held out his right hand to show that he wasn't holding anything and said, "Well I don't have a check for you today. I just have a question, if you don't mind sparing a moment on a curious old man."

"Not at all, as long as you aren't asking for my wallet or if I know where to score drugs," I said.

"Young man, if I want drugs I will just go see my doctor. They may be more expensive, but a prescription means fewer headaches in the end. Get it? Prescription! Headaches!" he said as he laughed at his own joke.

I joined him a moment later because it was just that funny. We laughed for a bit before he held up his hand while trying to catch his breath. We both sobered before he started speaking again.

"I am curious to know why you are out here running in this weather. You could join a gym and use a treadmill. Why out here in the darkness, fog, and rain?"

It was an easy question to answer. "I can't afford a gym membership. Even if I could, I want to train my body to run when I need to. When you actually need to run, the ground won't always be dry and flat. The weather isn't always going to be seventy degrees, and the light won't always be favorable. If I want to train myself to run, then I need to actually run out here like I will need to in the future."

The older man shrugged and nodded. "Why so early? No one else is out here this early, but that could just be because of the rain."

"I read once that if you do something every day for thirty days it becomes second nature. If I get up this early and run, not only will I get better at running, but I can go home and sleep until it's time to get up for work. I figure a little exertion and recovery will do me some good."

"I drive by here every morning around this time, and I have never seen you out here. Is this the first of your thirty days?" he asked. I nodded. "I know this is forward, and feel free to say no, but could I run with you? Not today, of course, but for the rest of your thirty days at least?"

I started to say something, but he cut me off. "I'm sorry. It's just that, well, I'm getting old. My family has me chauffeured around all the time, makes me watch every single thing I eat, and they are absolute hawks about it. They got me a personal trainer, but she barely lets me build up a sweat before she tells me to take a 'cool down.' I used to run all the time, but everyone in my family is too busy and would probably ruin it for me. All I am asking is to run with you so I can assure my family that I'm safe if they find out," he said as he hitched his thumb over his shoulder at his chauffeur.

I thought about it for a minute. He was just an old guy that wanted to have someone to run with. It was harmless. Then again, he could have been a serial killer, or worse, a politician! In the end, I figured having someone to chat with would keep me from thinking about how my clothes were soaked, how I was broke, how my neighbor was constantly snooping on me, or any of the other problems I had.

"Okay, sure," I said. "I plan to get here just before 3a.m. every morning. I'm going to jog the first lap around the lake and sprint the second one. If you think you can keep up then I will be glad to have you along."

He pursed his lips as he thought it over. "I can keep up for the first lap, but maybe not the second. But I can call it quits after that if it's okay with you."

"That will be fine."

He held out his hand and said, "It's a deal."

I shook his hand and said, "My name is Michael, by the way."

"Thaddaeus," he said. "I will see you tomorrow morning, Mr. Michael."

He retreated to his car while his chauffeur and I exchanged numbers. The young man was quick to text me so that he could make it back to the car before Thaddaeus had to open the door for himself. I watched him drive off and just shrugged as I got back to finishing my run.

I was right about how miserable it was driving home in soaked clothing. I toweled off once I was back inside my apartment and collapsed on the bed to get a couple hours of shut eye.

# CHAPTER 5

**M**ORNING CAME TOO soon. I woke up with a hundred questions for Horace. I could have woken him up, but I thought about all the things I wanted to know. If he answered a third of them I could have been there all day long, so I let him sleep. I had to get to work.

Larry was still passed out when I dropped sweatpants and a t-shirt on his head. Since that didn't wake him I shook him. That didn't work either. I let the poor guy sleep while I took a quick shower. My hot water was still broken, so the ice-cold shower woke me right up. By the time I was clean, Larry was up.

I forgot to warn him about the lack of hot water when he walked into the bathroom. When he opened the door steam bellowed out of the bathroom. I could feel the heat from his shower radiating into my living room.

"You might want to get your water heater looked at. I couldn't get the water to cool down.  It wasn't bad but it left the bathroom a little toasty to get dressed in," Larry said.

I ran into the bathroom and turned on the shower. The water was ice cold. The same with the sink. I just shook my head and went back to the living room where Larry was getting dressed. My clothes were way too big for him, but they would do until I went by his place.

"Okay Larry, you asked for me to protect you and I will, but since you lied to me in the first place I am charging you. Its one-hundred bucks a day for me to keep the heat off of you," I said.

"One-hundred dollars?" he asked.

"A day. If you want to call it quits I understand, but that's the fee," I said.

"Aren't you sworn to protect me?" he asked.

"I am sworn to protect the innocent and those who are targeted by evil. You cheated some other gamblers, and they hired goons to come after you. You don't get a knight, you get a bodyguard," I told him.

"What's the difference?"

I lifted the sports bag that I used to hide my sword when I am pretending to be an average citizen. I dropped my sword inside and zipped up the bag. "One carries a sword and the other carries…" I didn't finish the statement. I lifted my shirt so that he could see the black Desert Eagle in all of its .50 caliber glory on my right hip. Today it was loaded with iron shells. I had the chrome Desert Eagle that Kerri had given me in my bag just in case.

We got in the Rust Bucket and drove down to the Basilica of the National Shrine of the Assumption of the Blessed Virgin Mary, better known as the Baltimore Basilica. Priest Gregory was waiting for us and was ready to take Larry into his care for a few hours. Priest Gregory was a devout believer of the word of God. But he didn't like to sweat the small stuff like cleaning the church, so if I needed to stash someone for a while he was happy to put them to work. Priest Gregory was outside with another gentleman. I pulled up so that Larry could get out and the new gentleman could get in.

"Morning Drew," I said.

"Morning Michael," Drew said. Drew Thompson was in his early thirties, Caucasian, and built like he had once been very athletic. He had size to him but no substance, like the life had been drained from him. He was bald and his face was drawn. His beard was scraggly, and his teeth were bad. Drew weighed about one-hundred-forty pounds of fading muscle. His green and black flannel shirt hid his track marks and his most recent attempt at suicide.

Drew was homeless. He had been a college student when the market nearly tanked. With a college diploma and almost one-hundred thousand dollars in student loans, he had set out into the world to make his fortune. Sadly, like so many others in this day and age, the world crapped upon him and left him for dead. I had found him in an alley a few months ago trying to cut his wrist with a broken liquor bottle. I had my sword with me and used it to speak to him with the power of Truth. Now he was living between a homeless shelter and the church. He had even gotten a job with a small but up-and-coming construction company.

"What's for lunch, man?" I asked.

Drew held up his lunch pail. "PB&J. I have an extra for you."

I shook my head. "Nah, that's all you man. When lunch rolls around enjoy it," I said.

I drove across the city to Highlandtown Elementary School. It needed a new roof, and a lot of people needed jobs, so the contractor sub-contracted some workers including White Knight Construction. White Knight Construction had only two employees, but they are pretty hard working. When we pulled into the parking lot, I let Drew get out before I slipped my gun into the secret holster under the dashboard and hopped into the truck bed to gear up for the job. I opened the toolbox on the back of my truck and stowed my sword bag, pulled out my tool belt and hardhat, and then pulled out ones that I had bought for Drew. When I handed them to him, he immediately noticed his name and the company's name on a patch on the back of the belt.

"What're these," he asked.

"They're your tool belt and your hardhat. They came in through UPS yesterday while we were working," I said as I handed him his own tools to fill out the belt. When I hopped down from the truck bed he wrapped me in a hug. I returned it. "Come on. Let's get to work."

I was excited to be working on improving a school. We had started yesterday, and I had pretty much stripped a quarter of the old roof myself. Today when we showed up to stand in line to clock in, I was looking forward to a hard day of work in the profession I loved. But I was held up because my time card was missing. I checked the slots twice and then a third time. I even looked behind all the other cards.

I looked over and saw the foreman walking over. He was a big guy in every visible way. Tall, heavy with muscle, and he walked like he had a purpose. "Hey Mr. Anderson," I called to him.

He didn't slow down when he saw me waving. He walked right up to me and stopped with his arms folded in front of him. "White, I need you off of my work site," he said.

Something vile ran down my spine. I looked around at the other workers. They were all different nationalities, representatives of many different religions, both genders, and they were all looking at me with hate in their eyes. I got a sinking feeling in the pit of my stomach as I asked, "Why?"

"Look, White, let's not make a scene, okay. The crew watched you yesterday. They say you swung that pickaxe like a mad man, you kept leering at the females on site, and you kept picking fights," said Mr. Anderson.

I thought about the day before. I had worked on my own, which I didn't think about at the time. I probably did swing my pickaxe a little harder and more constantly than anyone else here. I was used to swinging a sword after all. It had gotten hot, so I had taken off my shirt. Several of the women had noticed that and moved away from me. I don't think I look good with my clothes off…or with them on for that matter. Several fights had been picked, but it was always another worker coming over and yelling at me. Some of them had taken offense to the speed at which I was working. Some had even gone so far as to threaten to push me off the roof. I had reported it, but I didn't give it a second thought. It was just how people reacted to me.

"Mr. Anderson, I didn't do anything wrong, and you know that. Heck, yesterday you said you wished you had ten more of me," I told him.

Mr. Anderson shook his head. "Get your shit and leave, White. You and your employee," he said.

Now I was worried. Drew needed this job. He had been rejected by every job he had taken in his adult life. Being rejected now could be the straw that kicked him off of his upward path and back into the gutter. I put up my hands as I waved them back and forth. "Hold on. Hold on. Hold on! Mr. Anderson, be reasonable. I will go, but don't let Drew go. He didn't do anything wrong."

Mr. Anderson looked at Drew over my shoulder. He knew Drew's situation because I had to disclose any potential problems my employees would have had with drug tests. I had paid a penalty to the hiring company so that my crew could take on the subcontract. I was in the hole because of it, and that was fine as long as I could help out Drew. If they kicked him off the job, then I would have failed all around. People don't like me. It's something I deal with on a daily basis, and I am fine with it. But Drew did not have to carry my burden.

Mr. Anderson took a long deep breath and puffed out a long sigh. "Fine White. He stays but you go. Got it?"

I nodded. I walked back over to Drew and said, "I have to go. You stay. Finish the workday, and I will pick you up at quitting time."

"I don't want to stay where we aren't wanted," he said.

"I'm not wanted. You stay. Its good honest work for good honest pay," I told him. "If you need anything just call my cell or the office. I am going to head over there and see about our next job."

Drew looked down at the floor and nodded. He seemed scared. I patted his shoulder and said, "I am counting on you Drew. Represent!" I retracted my hand and made a fist. Drew lifted his head, and he had a smile on his face. He made a fist, and we rapped our knuckles together. "Go see Mr. Anderson to get your time card. Quitting time is 6 P.M. so I will be here then. Work hard."

Drew went to get his time card, and I headed back out to the parking lot. There were three guys standing by my truck. Two of them were my height, and one was a foot shorter than me. The shorter guy was standing in the middle of the tall lean guy and the tall fat guy. I wasn't in the mood for what their eyes told me they wanted to happen.

"Excuse me, fellas, I am heading out," I said not too cheerfully.

The short guy stepped forward. "Yeah, man, you can leave. We just want to have a word with you first." It's always the short guy.

"You acted like hot shit yesterday," the lean guy said.

"You got some of our crew fired. Boss said they weren't pulling their weight," the fat guy said.

I thought about it. There had been a group that had been taking it too slow and too steady. When they went to lunch, I decided to help them out and did most of their section. I wasn't being mean or showing off. I just didn't have any food and had plenty of energy. So why not help out some guys that were falling behind? I had asked if they minded, and they said it was fine.

"Look guys, I didn't mean to get your friends fired. I just wanted to help out," I said.

"Oh, he just wanted to help! See guys, this is all a misunderstanding," the short guy said while looking back and forth between his friends. "Well, that's cool man. Since you want to help, just give me all the money in your wallet. Our friends have bills to pay."

I looked evenly at the shorter man and then at his nodding friends. I shook my head and sighed. "You guys do not want to do this."

"Do what? We aren't doing anything, man. Not unless you don't give up your cash and those nice tools of yours," the short guy said. The lean guy and the fat guy began to space themselves out. I looked over my shoulder and saw Mr. Anderson standing in the doorway. He shrugged, turned around, and walked back into the building. I shrugged, too, because I really did not want to fight these guys.

I heard work boots shuffling forward like they weren't sure they should be moving. I turned back to face the three men just as the fat guy hit me in the face. Now I get into fist fights with supernatural beings on an almost daily basis. I can take a hit, and this one was nowhere near the top one hundred punches I have taken in my life, so I could shrug it off. The problem is that in the real world, in a real fight, shrugging it off doesn't mean you stand there and act like nothing happened. Shrugging it off means that one hit isn't going to do any lasting damage, but you still have to deal with the fact that something hit you. You have to deal with leverage, gravity, and luck. None of which were on my side.

The fat guy followed through with his punch, so I went stumbling backwards under the weight of his fist. It was still drizzling, and the moisture on the ground was just enough to cause the parking lot to be as slick as ice, so I slipped. Then my old nemesis showed up to take up cause with my three assailants. Gravity came out of nowhere and body slammed me into the parking lot.

I rolled over onto my stomach and got up to my knees. They started stomping on me. Heavy work boots slammed repeatedly against my back, legs, and head. If I was a normal man, they would have had me at a major disadvantage. As it stood they had me at just a rough disadvantage. I took their hits and pushed up to one knee. A work boot slammed into the left side of my face at the same time as a separate work boot slammed into the back of my head. Pain shot through my skull, and I started to fall. I gritted my rattling teeth and pushed off with my legs into a forward jog.

I got ahead of my attackers and turned to face them. I could feel blood flowing from my mouth where the boot had hit me, and my right eye was swollen from the punch. I watched them approach and said, "Last chance to walk away, guys." They all laughed and came at me with violence in their eyes.

When I became a knight, I was a skinny guy that couldn't fight his way out of an already opened wet paper bag. I couldn't take a punch, I couldn't give one, and I had no survival instincts in a fight. My grandpa, The Knight of Justice, fixed that right fast and in a hurry. He invited every uncle and male cousin I had over the age of fifteen to our house and had me fight them five on one for three hours a day for a month. I learned how to fight, and I learned how to fight multiple people at once.

I let them get close, and when they did I exploded into action. The lean guy got to me first, so I came forward when he tried to punch me. I lifted my arm to block and stepped into the blow. It halted his attack, but my counter-attack hit perfectly. When I stepped into his punch, I grabbed him by the head and pulled down. At the same time, I raised my knee to meet his forehead. He screamed in pain then started to fall. I grabbed the arm he had used to punch at me with the arm I had used to block, grabbed the waist of his pants with my free right hand, and barreled ahead. We collided with the short man, and I bore down with my left shoulder, practically throwing myself at the ground. My momentum plus the additional weight of the lean guy was too much for the short guy, so we went down in a heap with the short guy on the bottom. I drilled in with my shoulder when we crashed down, and then I rolled over them and on to my feet.

The fat guy had just rounded on me. I turned to look him in the eyes to let him know that I would not hesitate to defend myself. He squared his shoulders and stepped up to me. His fist came up in a hard right hook. I knocked that punch away with a swing of my left arm and brought around my own right hook. He blocked it, but I saw the shock in his eyes when the weight of my blocked punch knocked him back a couple of steps. He came at me with the intent of wrapping me in a bear hug. I came forward fast with a straight left like I was a southpaw. I hit him in the face, and he staggered backward. That's when I hit him with an uppercut that I am sure rattled his teeth. His right eye, like mine, was swollen shut when he fell over.

I looked at my three attackers lying there on the ground. I could have laid into them even more, but I didn't. I got into my truck and peeled out of the parking lot. When I was a few blocks away I pulled over and killed the engine. I clenched my hands into fists and started pounding on the steering wheel and dashboard. I hated fighting people for no reason. Those guys were angry at me because they saw me as a problem. Why couldn't their lazy friends work harder, or why couldn't they help them out? Why did they have to come after me? Why? I ask that question every day of my life, and the answer is always the same. Silence.

I sat there for half an hour on the verge of something, but I don't know what it was. I started to sweat. My windows fogged, and I felt something welling up within me. Anger? Rage? Hatred? I couldn't pinpoint it. I couldn't focus. I pounded the steering wheel again with my hands and even my head. I scratched the palm of my left hand then slammed my fist into my door. Then, of course, with everything building up to a boil inside me, my phone had to ring. The theme to *Cops* came blaring from my pocket. Without thinking about it I pulled out my cell phone and yelled into it.

"What do you want now?" I asked. Of course, I knew who was on the other end of the phone. I'm a simple guy. I match my ringtones to the people that they are for. When Aaron calls, the theme to *Buffy the Vampire Slayer* plays. When Eden, my witch friend, calls, the tune of *Bewitched* hits my ears. So, when the theme from *Cops* played, it could only be one man on the other end.

"The same thing I always want White, answers," Captain Garrett Clay said. Over the past year, Detective Clay had been promoted to Captain. The only blemish to his rise was that, despite the hefty lawsuit my lawyers had raised on the Baltimore Police Department, he insisted on having me as a consultant on any and all cases that showed the tell-tale signs of the supernatural.

"What is it now? Did you find a mailbox thrown against a brick wall— because I can explain that," I said.

"We have three dead bodies with their guts ripped out," he said.

I sat up straight and looked around me. The windows were completely fogged. I let the anger over what had happened earlier settle in the back of my mind and cracked my door. Some rain hit my arm and turned to steam. "Where do you need me?" I asked calmly.

"Duncan near Fayette in Butchers Hill. You know it?" he asked me.

"Yeah…I'm just down the street," I said.

There was an awkward pause before Captain Clay said, "Get here now. This shit is bad, and the vultures are circling."

By vultures Captain Clay was referring to the clean-up crews and throw-away divisions. They will never admit to it, but every police department in the world has divisions that they use just to bury undesirable cases. Those cases could be anything, such as a scandal with a city official that is popular among officers, a drug cartel that rats out other cartels, or a five-year old psychopath. Then there are the cases like the ones Captain Clay insisted on tackling—missing persons, mysterious deaths, and eyewitness accounts of impossible events. Most anyone would want such things swept under the rug. Then again, most people didn't have a Knight of the Crucifixion on speed dial.

"There in five," I said. I fired up the Rust Bucket and headed off to take a look at some dead bodies.

# CHAPTER 6

THERE WERE POLICE cruisers all around the vacant lot that took up a quarter of a city block. Most were from the vulture groups that would want to sweep whatever had happened under a rug. The rest, three cars, were from Captain Clay's Special Investigation unit. Of course, there were reporters everywhere and plenty of onlookers. Whatever this was, it wasn't going to be quietly removed from the public eye.

When I pulled up, I stripped off anything that could be recognized by a vanilla mortal as a weapon. I have learned that cops and non-cops with guns do not mix. I fished around in my cab for the I.D. badge that Captain Clay had given me. I found it next to one of my hidden guns. I clipped it on and put on my best 'I'm here to help' smile. The cops that saw me coming were all in suits or plain clothes. I watched as their hands moved into position to draw their weapons and told myself to remain calm. I walked up to the nearest officer, a man who had seen me around at least fifteen crime scenes in the last seven months but had never given me his name even though I asked for it. I held up my plastic badge and said, "Michael White, White Knight Investigations. I'm here as a consultant." He scrutinized my badge for a few minutes before letting his partner do the same.

"Dammit, Phil, let him in," shouted Captain Clay. Phil and his partner stepped aside, but each gave me a quick once over. I walked past the police line and was waved over by Captain Clay.

When I first met Garrett Clay, he was the poster boy for a movie about the successful life of a bully after high school. He was tall, muscular, and dead set on having things his way. That's how I had seen him and judged him. I'm a knight, and it's not my job to judge people. Garrett Clay was all those things, but he was so much more. He was a man that was scared of what he felt was myth and legend. He was a man that wanted to honor his oath to serve and protect. Most importantly, he was a man that put others before himself.

I learned that first hand when he took a bullet that was meant for me. That bullet had bounced around inside his body so violently that it had injured his spine. Because of that, Captain Clay was now in a wheelchair.

"Thanks for coming, Michael," he said. He held out his hand when I reached him, and when we traded grips I was reminded that he was still the man I had met before. His hand had the strength of a man twice his size and half his age.

He could have crushed my hand, but he didn't because people who know how and when to use their strengths don't waste time with petty displays.

"Not a problem. It's not like I have a real job or anything," I said. I was still upset about being kicked off of the construction site, but I needed to move on.

"The way I see it, this is the only job that matters, so let's get to work," he told me.

Detective Clay didn't wait for me to respond. He rolled forward and I fell in next to him. He had gloves on, and I noticed that his wheelchair didn't have handles on the back. Clay had taken a bullet that was meant for me, and though he was temporarily confined to his wheelchair, he was determined to keep his independence. He drove this point home when we came to a curb and he rocked one of his front wheels up onto it then repeated the action until all four were on the higher ground.

"How's rehab coming?" I asked.

"Fucking perfect. I can walk a whole five damn steps before I fall over like my body is nothing but dead weight," he said.

"It's better than not having the possibility of walking again," I countered.

"It would be a hell of a lot better if I had those tattoos of yours," he said.

"I can arrange it if you have a solid $50 million in gold nuggets and gems and a bottle of hundred-year-old whisky," I told him.

"Seriously?"

"Scotch might work too, but I'm not sure," I shrugged.

"Damn, that's not covered by my insurance or worker's comp," he said.

We came to the middle of the lot, and he stood…er…sat…next to something covered in a blue tarp. "When we got word of this, I thought it was on your side of the fence. It reminds me of that ghoul thing a few months ago, but I don't think it's exactly that." He reached down and pulled the tarp off of the ground.

I have fought demons and vampires. Magical creatures from our world and beyond the veil are a constant in my life. Death and destruction are nothing new to me. But when I looked down at the blood and gore that only vaguely resembled a human body I nearly lost my mind. My hands grabbed my mouth and swallowed back bile. The more I swallowed the more my throat kept forcing bile back up. It took a minute and a lot of mental discipline, but I managed to force my stomach under control. I wiped my hand on my jeans and looked down at the body.

The woman had not been young, but she had been beautiful like all women are. Her long red hair was matted with dirt and blood. Her face was worn and beaten from a hard life, but you could see a spark of hope in her lifeless orbs. Her intestines were on the outside of her body. They were mangled and chewed with bits and pieces scattered around. Her left leg was missing, and I could see where something savagely ripped it free of the body.

I pushed the blood and gore aside in my mind and forced myself to look for details. I couldn't tell her age, but she had sunken eyes. Her clothing was a hodgepodge of t-shirts, sweatpants, a jacket that was too big for her, and a coat that was too small. I could see burn marks around her lips, and her fingers were scraped and torn. She had been homeless.

Captain Clay had watched me taking it all in. "You know her?" he asked.

I shook my head. "No, but I have seen her before. I volunteer at the soup kitchen every now and then. I have seen her there serving and eating. I think her name was Molly…or Mary…no Marcy! Marcy! Yeah, Marcy," I said.

"So, you did know her," Clay said.

"No. I knew her name. Knowing someone's name doesn't mean you know them. I have no idea what her last name was, if she liked cats or dogs, or if she had a family," I said. "I know she was homeless, spoke English, and didn't mind eating after everyone else was fed."

"Can you tell anything, you know, from the body?" asked Captain Clay.

By now most of his unit and a few vultures had gathered around. They didn't trust me, but they wanted answers. Everyone wants answers to the questions that have been in their minds since before they were potty trained. Are monsters real? Why are we inherently afraid of the dark? Why does something seem bigger than me when it scares me? They wanted to know, and believe it or not, like me or not, I am the guy that was stationed in Baltimore to answer them as best I can.

"You said there were three bodies," I said.

Captain Clay pointed to two more tarps on the ground. I visited them both and found similar scenes. One was of an aged homeless man that, if the dog tags were any indication, had served his country. Whether in war or general service I may never know, but he had fought here. His hands were bloody and clenched into fists. His chest was ripped open, and his ribs were broken. I could see them along with his lungs and heart, both of which were shredded. He too wore the uniform of the cast off and the unwanted. His military jacket with the patches marking him as a sergeant in the U.S. Army was worn and battered, but like those that wore it the jacket had held up to the weather and the world. The final body was of a young woman around my age. She was in the fetal position with her hands wrapped around her belly defensively. The left side of her body had been ripped open. Any of the several wounds on her body could have proved fatal, but I was sure it was the massive throat wound had killed her. Her eyes were closed, and her face was painted in a macabre grimace. The clothing she wore was newer in era than the other two victims but just as old and worn.

I found a place to stand centered among the three bodies. I stood still and lowered my head. I let the sound of the rain block out everything else. The chatter of nonbelieving officers and onlookers faded. The sickly feeling in my stomach went away. The anger from my earlier fight drained from me. I opened my mind's eye and allowed the world, the real world, to come into view. I can't *see* magic. To me seeing magic is like seeing air. You can when it's actively carrying something like dirt or ashes, but then you are seeing what the air is moving, not the air. When magic is still it is invisible, and you have to feel it. So, when I open my mind's eye, I allow myself to feel the presence of magic. But all I felt was the rain. It was light and annoying, but that was all I felt. I had thought I would feel power or something tainted. Instead, all I felt was rain.

"Well?" Captain Clay asked.

"Nothing. There's nothing here," I said. I started looking around, but I couldn't find anything out of the ordinary.

The whispers started. I could hear officers complaining about the hack that the Captain kept hiring. I could hear them laughing and I could see the vultures getting ready to sweep these people under the rug. They wanted them to go away, to be invisible in death as in life. I looked around at the gathered people and could feel them writing this off as just another event that they need not be concerned with.

It pissed me off. My left hand started to itch. I gritted my teeth and clenched my hands into fists. "Idiots," I growled. "Uncaring, self-serving, ignorant children!" I felt the temperature rise and smelled burning pitch for some reason. Then none of that mattered, because I looked over at the body of the young woman. Something about her nagged at me, but I couldn't figure out what it was. I walked over to her and knelt.

"Hey, asshole, don't touch the evidence," one officer yelled.

I ignored him. She wasn't evidence, she was a person. A person that deserved respect in life and in death. Maybe that respect had been denied to her in life, but I would be damned if I was going to let that happen to her now. I looked upon her with my mind's eye and my ears perked up.

"Get an ambulance over here!" I screamed.

I jumped up and ran to my truck. I vaulted up into the bed and opened my toolbox. People were already murmuring and screaming at me. I pulled out my sports bag and pulled my sword from it. I didn't unsheathe the blade, but I did sprint back over to the girl. An officer tried to stop me from getting to her, but I politely shoved him out of my way. I dropped into a baseball slide and came to a stop at the woman's side. I drew my blade a few inches from its sheath and laid it across her still form.

"God it's me again," I said as my hands started working. "I know I am not your favorite person, but I need some guidance, please!"

I was peeling away layers of bloody cloth and fabric when the officer I shoved grabbed my shoulder and dragged me back. He had his gun out, not his cuffs.

Some officers were yelling for him to stand down. Others were yelling for him to "clock the bastard good." Captain Clay was yelling for everyone to "calm the fuck down." The officer hadn't raised his gun from his side yet, and I didn't have time for this crap. I gritted my teeth and swung my arm up into his nuts. He turned red, blue, and then purple all in the span of half a second. He fired his pistol once into the ground then fell over. I scrambled back over to the girl as officers swarmed me.

Guns were drawn, obscenities were yelled, and more than once I thought my life was at an end. As onlookers cried out for blood and patience, as rain blurred our vision, as fear and hatred started to win the day, a baby's first cry shook everyone in the area to the core of their being. Faith, magic, power, or whatever you want to call it, because it is all the same, washed over us. I pulled a child into the world amidst lowering guns, lowering tempers, and rising hopes.

# Chapter 7

I HATE THE rain. The ambulance took a whole twenty minutes to arrive. The storm opened up before they got to us, but I had a few emergency blankets in my truck. The baby girl was warm and dry if nothing else. I let the EMTs have their way with my truck's cab when they arrived. They didn't want to move her until they were sure she was stable and comfortable.

One of the EMTs came up to me when they were ready to take the baby and said, "You couldn't find any dirtier blankets?" He shoved past me, and they took the baby off to the hospital.

Captain Clay waved me over to his car when the ambulance left. He looked me in the eyes and said, "They want you arrested for assaulting an officer. I'm not letting anyone arrest you, though."

"Is that going to go over well with your squad?" I asked.

He looked at me with a sad expression on his face. "Every cop in Baltimore wants you behind bars. Did you know last month there was a crew on you 24/7?"

That rocked me back on my heels. Last month had been relatively quiet for me as far as being a knight, but I did have a few occasions to whip out my sword. Had the police seen me throwing down with magical folk?

Captain Clay continued, "A few hundred-man hours in surveillance of a guy that spent his days fixing stairs at nursing homes and taking his neighbors grocery shopping. I read the report. A few times they wanted to bring you in on possible drug charges, and one guy said you fit the description of a mugger. Tell me something kid. Why do people hate you?"

It was a blunt question that I had asked myself all of my life. The last twenty-four hours alone had reinforced it. I didn't have an answer. I just shrugged and said, "Guess I have one of those faces that only a mother can love."

Clay laughed. "That's for damned sure!" We both had a good laugh then. I liked Captain Clay, and it felt good to know that one of the good guys outside of The Church had my back.

"I still need answers kid. I'll be digging on my side of the fence. Keep me posted on your end," Captain Clay told me. I nodded and we shook hands again.

I got back in my truck and just sat there for a moment. The sound of the rain tapping against my truck relaxed me, and I may have nodded off for a bit. If I did it was because I had so much on my mind. I had to keep Larry safe, there was a magical teddy bear at my apartment, I had lost the first professional construction job I had gotten in months, and now there was something out there ripping people apart in my city. I opened my eyes and stretched. Looking at my phone showed I had lost just an hour. There was still plenty of time to save the world before dinner.

First up was Larry. I had promised him I would get him some clothes and other stuff from his apartment. I drove a few miles down the road to some upscale luxury apartments near East Eutaw Street. Larry's place was called Chesapeake Commons. Taking one look at the three-story building with its fancy gate and its easy access to the light rail, I knew that I could never afford this place. It kind of irked me that I was struggling to afford the rent in my rinky-dink place, but Larry, who was a liar, a cheater, and a thief, was living here. I smelled something rotten burning again but didn't see anything when I looked around. I headed inside with the keys that Larry had given me. He lived in a third-floor loft, and when I opened the door to the place I instantly wanted to kill Larry.

The place had been furnished by someone with amazing taste. I am a do-it-yourself guy, but I don't know anything about furniture. All of Larry's stuff was a mix of brown and cherry wood furnishings. He had artwork that looked like it belonged in museums, there was a grand piano that looked older than this country, and his kitchen had every luxury appliance I had ever heard off.

I owned a spool.

Larry had told me where to find his luggage. I went about my business of gathering up some of Larry's clothes—mostly shirts and jeans, but two suits just in case. I grabbed some of his toiletries so he wouldn't feel completely out of sorts at my place. Then of course I grabbed his laptop. I don't have internet, but I am sure he had something he could entertain himself with offline. When I was done I had two suitcases, a computer bag, and two clothing travel bags to carry home.

I stepped out of the apartment and headed down to my truck. I had parked in the parking lot beside the apartment complex. There were plenty of cars there. I honestly don't know much about cars. I can't identify them just by the way they look, and I couldn't tell you the difference between an American made or a foreign model. What I could do was identify a car that would cost way more than any other car in the parking lot. Especially when it was parked right next to my truck.

There was a tall man in a tailored business suit looking my truck over. He was bald, thin, and completely unremarkable. He looked up at me as I approached, and I could see my own reflection in his sunglasses. He smiled as I neared, and I saw that his teeth were far too wide and far too even to be human. I acted like I didn't notice.

"Hello! Are you the owner of this truck?" the toothy stranger asked in an elegant and polite voice.

"Yep," I said. I was ready to toss everything at him and go for my gun if he tried anything. I kept approaching and angled myself for the door of the Rust Bucket.

"So, you are Michael White?" the stranger asked.

"That depends. Who's asking?"

He stepped toward me, and I stopped walking. When he reached into his suit I dropped everything and pulled my gun. My black Desert Eagle came up fast in my right, and I had the safety off as I balanced it with my left. I had iron shells in the magazine, and one was in the chamber. Iron and cold iron were usually an answer to supernatural beings being able to recover from just about anything. One squeeze of the trigger and this thing would be dead.

The stranger pulled out a business card and handed it over to me like I was a customer looking for a new car and not a guy with a huge gun pointed at his face. I eased my gun down, clicked on the safety, and took the card. I read it aloud. "Hung T. Roll, Investment Banker."

"At your service, Mr. White. Tell me, when was the last time you reevaluated your investment portfolio?" he asked me.

"When did I do what to who now?" I asked.

"Oh, I am so sorry, Mr. White. I have gotten a little ahead of myself. 'Don't make an enemy, make a client.' It's what my father always tells me," he said.

"Well, I guess that's a good thing, Mr. Roll," I said, slipping my gun away but not fastening the holster shut.

"Mr. Roll is my father. Please call me Hung," he laughed. "Alright, business before business, Mr. White, so let's get down to it. I am here for Mr. Larry Lipowski. If you would be so kind as to hand him over, I will kill him as expediently as possible, and we can get to reevaluating your investments. I can promise you that we can get your money working for you instead of for your bank."

I looked down at the business card. I looked back up to Hung. I looked down at the business card. "*Hung T. Roll.*" My eyes went wide in realization, and I yelled, "Holy crap, you're a troll!"

Hung's lips moved out wider than I could believe as he smiled at me. The edges of his smile literally touched his ears. I will admit that I was a little creeped out. My mind raced, and I tried to remember everything I could about trolls. Before I could even begin to recall any information, Hung spoke to me.

"Mr. White, I know that you wish to protect Mr. Lipowski, but in this matter I am afraid that protecting him is doing a disservice to your office," the troll investment banker said.

"A disservice to my office?" I asked.

"Mr. White, you are a Knight of the Order of the Crucifixion, sworn to protect the mortal and supernatural world from nefarious doings. Mr. Lipowski is not the victim of some villainous plot. He is the perpetrator of a crime against other supernatural beings that wish to balance the scales so to speak. In that regard, I must say that you seem to be overstepping your authority. Now I am no lawyer, but this seems somewhat illegal to me, as you are interfering in an age-old form of justice in the supernatural world," the troll said.

He had a point. Larry was half leprechaun which made him a supernatural being. The Knights of the Order and the Templars protected the mortal world as well as the supernatural. Both worlds had their own guardians, rules, and whatnot. If he was wholly supernatural, I would think about letting it stand. But Larry was also half human, which made him a card-carrying citizen of the human race. He was mortal…kind of…so he was privileged to my protection. There was a more important factor to this, however.

I handed Hung T. Roll his business card back. "Larry is my friend, Mr. Roll. If you want him then you are going to have to go through me," I said. I had already put my right hand on my gun and clicked off the safety once more.

Hung T. Roll took his card back and frowned. He put it back in his pocket and let out a long sigh. "I would have loved to have you on my client list, Mr. White," he said. He took off his sun glasses and tucked them away in his pocket. Yellow bloodshot eyes looked upon me with a resolve for violence.

I drew my gun faster than I had the first time. Before I had it leveled, Hung's left arm came forward in a limp-wristed slap to my chest. His fingertips barely touched me, but I went flying sidelong into the windshield of the car that I was standing in front of. My upper body went through the glass, and I can only thank God himself that my throat wasn't shredded then and there. The car alarm went off. I lay there with my head buried in the driver's seat and my torso on the dashboard. The steering wheel was on the floor and my gun was still in my hand.

"Ow," I said.

Something strong took hold of my ankle and pulled me up through the glass and debris. Hung held me upside down at the end of his left arm. He tossed me in the air the same way men do when they want to get a better grip on a broom or mop. He clutched the middle of my calf and lifted me higher. He lifted me until we were face to face. I looked up and saw that his arm had stretched out of the sleeve of his expensive suit to a length that was closer to my height than the length of an arm.

"Now, Mr. White," the troll said. His voice was deeper and throatier. He didn't sound like a human anymore. He was starting to show himself more as well. I looked up at his arm again and saw his muscles squirming beneath his skin suit. "I am a reasonable troll, and I can understand your concern for your friend. Let me explain something to you…"

I shot him in the face. Point blank. Iron and smoke discharged from the barrel of my gun right into his forehead. Hung's entire head bent back to high five his spine. I grinned as I began to drop to the ground.

The grip on my leg tightened. Hung slowly lifted his head back up to look at me. There was a smoking hole the size of a baseball right through his forehead. But it was the absolute look of madness in his eyes that terrified me. I lifted my gun to fire again, but his right hand closed around mine and he crushed my hand. He didn't break it, he crushed it. The bones in my hand shattered. I heard my gun clank to the ground over the sound of my own screaming.

Hung lifted me into the air and slammed me down on the roof of the already damaged car. I felt metal crunch and fold all around me. He then ripped me free of the car and whipped me around to smash into the driver's side of the car. More glass rained down on me to cut up my face. Hung didn't stop there—he decided to ruin the passenger side the same way and finally the trunk. I had felt my ribs break somewhere between the roof and trunk. Blood was running freely from dozens of wounds along my entire body. I was in severe pain, and there was nothing I could do against the troll.

"I think it's time we brought our business to a conclusion, Mr. White," the troll said.

Hung the troll lifted me into the air above his head and began to swing me down toward the parking lot. I gritted my teeth in anticipation of my head smashing open like a melon. I felt the pull of gravity as my body stretched toward the ground. I opened my eyes to see that Hung had stopped his swing midway to the ground. There was a ringing in my ear that I couldn't quite place until Hung pulled a cell phone out of his pocket. He looked at the screen, sighed, and then dropped me to the ground. His arm shrunk back to a more human length and the hole that I put in his head closed up.

"I am sorry, Mr. White, but I have to cut our meeting short. You see, my ambition was to finish this up on my lunch hour. I am due back at the office for an important meeting in just ten minutes," the troll in human form said.

I blinked. A lot. Hung the troll just stared at me in blank patience. He was being awfully polite about not killing me. "Oh…ah…it's no problem. You can *not* kill me anytime you want?" I asked more than said.

Hung smiled as he pulled out his sunglasses. He walked over to me and slipped a business card into my uncrushed hand. Then he started away while saying, "Remember, Mr. White, I can get your money working for you better than anyone! Also, I suggest you give up Mr. Lipowski to my brother. He is more volatile than I am, and I would hate for him to kill a possible client like yourself over something so… mundane."

I watched him get into his yellow Lamborghini and drive off in a squeal of rubber. Hung T. Roll, one of the Bridge Boys, had beaten me bloody and spared me because he had a business meeting with an important client. I lay there on the ground letting the rain wash the blood off my body. Just when I thought the worst part had passed, a young black woman came outside screaming about her car. This was turning out to be one swell day.

# Chapter 8

I SAW YOU wreck my car," the angry woman yelled as I sat up. She had been yelling about her poor destroyed car for a few minutes now.

"If you saw what happened, then why aren't you asking how it was possible for him to swing me around like that," I grumbled.

"What?" she asked.

"You saw him use me like a hammer on your car, and you aren't asking how that happened? You didn't see anything, lady," I said. I stood and started gathering Larry's stuff.

"You wrecked my car mother fucker! Where are you going?" she yelled.

"To my truck. I have someone that will fix your car. Just let me pick up this stuff," I said.

"It's totaled asshole!" she screamed. She ran by me as I was limping over to my gun and grabbed it. Holding my gun in one hand, she aimed it at me with her finger on the trigger. Looking at her, she wasn't a big woman as far as muscle or size. Heck, she was soaking wet and would probably weigh in at under one-hundred pounds. If she shot at me, it was likely she would kill herself trying to hold my gun in one hand.

"Now hold on, lady," I said as I threw my hands up defensively.

"You wrecked my car!" she said.

"I told you I would get it fixed!"

"It's totaled!" she yelled.

I pointed to my truck. "My cell phone is in there. My cousin is my mechanic. Let me gather up this stuff and call him. He will fix your car. If he can't, I will pay for it," I said.

She thought about it for what seemed like a long time. Finally, she said, "Give me your keys so you can't drive off."

I opened my truck and then gave her the keys. I gathered up all of Larry's bags and got them out of the rain. Then I climbed into my truck and sent a text message. The message I got in reply said, "two hours." I showed her the text and she nodded.

She took my gun and keys and went back inside her apartment. I kicked back while we waited and tried to let my body heal. The runic tattoos all over my body allow me to heal at an accelerated rate from just about anything that doesn't kill me. All I have to do to maintain that superhuman ability is keep myself well-nourished and in good physical condition. Too bad I am usually underfed. Lucky for me I had eaten enough to at least get my crushed hand and ribs repaired. I set an alarm on my phone and went to sleep.

My alarm went off just as the young woman came back outside to yell at me once more. Like clockwork, a black flatbed truck rolled into the parking lot. The side of the truck said "Frank's Towing and Repair" in white letters trimmed in neon green and purple. The truck pulled right up so that the bed was in front of the wrecked car.

Out into the rain stepped a man in gray, greasy, and torn sleeveless coveralls. He was a little taller than me with the musculature of someone that had been fit all of his life. His light skin resembled mine but a little darker. His black hair was done into braids and pulled back into a ponytail that ran down to his waist. He was wearing mirrored sunglasses and carrying a tool belt that he was fitting to his waist as he walked. When I stepped out to shake his hand, he slapped my hand away and pulled me into a hug that would have made a bear's ribs crack.

"Blood of my blood!" he said just before pushing me out to arm's length. "What's good with you, little cousin?"

"Hey, Drey! I'm good. Just had a little problem with a troll," I said.

My cousin Drey looked back at the car then frowned at me. "You okay?" he asked. When I nodded he sucked his teeth and grunted. "Did you use the ring?"

I looked down at the ring on my right hand. "Didn't get a chance to. It's working great, though," I told him.

"Just be careful with it. It will let you hit with the strength of a giant but only three times a day. Don't try doing it any more than that. This isn't like your shield. It doesn't run out of power, it's just going to malfunction, and I don't know how badly," he told me.

"Is this him?" the young woman asked as she waved around my gun and keys. I ducked back, but Drey just looked at her like he was bored. "Is this the man you called to fix my totaled car? It's been hours! What did you do, drive from another state?"

"Virginia, ma'am," my cousin said with a smile and a nod.

"Well as you can see my car is totaled. So, are you going to give me money to fix it, or do I need to call the cops?" she asked.

My cousin smiled at her. Drey turned and walked over to her car. He put his hand on the crushed hood and gently traced across the damage. He stopped in one spot and patted the car. Then he pressed down on the hood, clenched his fingers like he was grabbing something, and slowly pulled his hand up. The hood of the car groaned and popped, metal straightened with a screech, and the hood snapped into place.

The young woman stood with her mouth hanging open. My cousin turned to her, smiled, and handed her a business card. "I have an associate in town that lets me use his garage. If you allow me, I can have your car ready for you no later than tomorrow afternoon," Drey said. As she took the business card he took my keys and gun from her.

She stammered. "Uh…ummm…sure. Thank—" She started to say 'thank you,' but I slapped my hand over her mouth. She screamed and shoved me away. "What the hell?"

"Sorry, it's just that you shouldn't thank him. It's not professional. He has to fix the car first," I said.

She gawked at me then threw her hands up. "Whatever. Just fix my car, and this asshole said he was paying for it," she said.

"Yes ma'am," my cousin said.

The young lady walked away, and Drey stopped smiling. He turned to me and said through clenched teeth, "Why didn't you let her thank me?"

"Because when you thank a fairy for their work they become hostile," I said.

My cousin Drey was the oldest of my cousins. He was nearly thirty and had always looked out for me. I had always thought that it was because he loved me, but after I learned the truth about faeries, I wondered if it was because he loved me or because I was *his*. Drey, short for Dreyalkain, is a gremlin. His mother, my aunt, is human, but his dad is a fae named Grizzallkain. I call him Uncle Grizz. He had worked for my grandpa for a time as a mechanic and had fallen in love with my aunt Sharon. Drey had inherited his dad's skill with all things metal or mechanical. He, like Larry, was half human and half fairy. I wish I could remember the name for them.

Drey pulled off his shades and looked at me with his cascading green and blue eyes. Those eyes reminded me that Drey was never entirely human. He was of the magical and of the mortal world. I did find it odd that he was showing me his real eyes though.

"You shouldn't let your glamour fall," I told him.

Drey grunted and handed me my gun and keys. Then he started hooking the car up to the lift. "I can't help it. It took a lot to fix that hood. I wouldn't have done much to the girl if she thanked me," he said.

"The last time someone thanked you, I remember gramps smacking you over the head and telling you to give back the guy's teeth," I said.

"They were gold with diamond studs on them! What the hell was I supposed to do? He said *thank you*! He owed me!" Drey snapped. I could see his teeth growing sharp, his dark hair was frizzing up, and he seemed taller.

"Drey, cuz! What the heck?" I asked.

Drey looked around. He touched his mouth and then looked at his hands. "Shit, it's the rain. I gotta get moving. Look cousin, if you need me call," he said.

Drey hoisted the car onto the wrecker, secured it, and took off. He left me standing in the rain wondering what the heck was going on. I looked up at the sky and wondered if the rain was ticking everyone off as much as it was ticking me off.

It was almost lunch time, and I was soaked. I drove home and found Horace reading through my book on monsters and supernatural beings. He had several other books on folklore and mythology sitting on my table opened to various chapters.

"Studying for finals?" I asked.

Horace looked up at me and shrugged. "I'm trying to find something that will tell me why I'm back here. I was dismissed when you outgrew your innocence. Almost five years ago I found myself back in your bear, and I have been trapped here ever since."

I swallowed hard. "So, me losing my innocence set you free?"

"Yes."

"Um…okay. So, what would happen if I became an innocent again?" I asked.

The teddy bear scrunched up his face. "How the hell would you do that? You can't just hit your head and forget that you aren't an innocent little boy anymore. It's not like God granted you a second childhood or…" Horace stopped talking and turned to look at me. "Innocent doesn't always mean young."

"Nope. It could mean naïve or not guilty," I said.

Horace looked at the bag I was carrying. "What sword do you have?"

I reached into my bag and pulled out my sword. I didn't want to tell him, but lying wasn't going to help. "The Sword of Innocence," I said.

Horace looked at the sword with wide eyes. "Do you know who had that sword before you?"

"Yeah," I said.

"Judas Iscariot," the old teddy bear said. "He was chosen by Jesus, trusted by him, loved by him. And he betrayed him."

It was an old story. One that most people already knew. What they don't know is that the Apostles were also the chosen Knights of Jesus. Judas was the first and only man to ever wield the Sword of Innocence before it found its way to me. It's ironic that Jesus chose the greatest sinner in history to protect innocence.

"Kid, I thought you had some baggage before with that curse, but this is just ridiculous," Horace said. "Well as long as you are the Knight of Innocence I guess my job isn't done." He started packing the books back up now that his mystery was solved.

"The curse of Ignorance is Bliss sucks, but everyone deals with it in their own way I guess," I said.

Horace put another book on his stack and turned to look at me again. "Not that one. The curse that's on you. You know, the one that…" Horace trailed off and bolted to his feet. "You don't know about the curse?" he yelled.

"What curse?" I asked.

Horace slumped back down. "You were cursed, kid. The day you were born. A very powerful demon cursed you when he couldn't kill your grandfather."

"Some demon cursed me instead of cursing my grandpa?"

"You were the youngest of your family. The most vulnerable. How do you hurt someone that has spent his life trying to protect people?"

I thought about that for a moment. I shrugged when I couldn't figure out an answer.

"You make it so that no matter how hard he tries, no matter how much he sacrifices, no matter how much faith he has, and no matter how much hope he has, he will never be able to keep the people he loves safe. You were meant to be a reminder of that. I didn't think you would live a year when you were cursed," Horace said.

"You thought I would die? I was cursed? How? When?" I slumped onto the couch next to my teddy bear with my sword across my lap.

"Your grandfather was coming to the hospital. He had bought me for you. A demon was there in the maternity ward. They fought, and with the demon's last breath he cursed you. You never thought it was strange that people instinctively don't like you or that people will break their own necks to hurt you?"

"I always thought I smelled bad or that I was just ugly," I said.

"Well, you do smell bad, and you are pretty ugly. But that's all you male humans," Horace said.

"That's kind of mean."

"Look, if all the cards are on the table, kid, I am a racist, a drunkard, and you can't leave me around Barbie dolls."

"What the heck, Horace?"

He shrugged. "I also steal stuff." He pulled open a seam on his chest and pulled out a pack of cigarettes and a lighter. He tapped the pack, pulled out a cigarette, and put it between his lips. Then I got to watch this beloved toy from my childhood light up a cigarette with an orange Bic lighter. "I also smoke."

"No!" I snatched the cigarette from him and tapped it out. "You're a freaking teddy bear! You can't smoke!"

Horace glared at me. "News flash kid—I smoke, I drink, and I fuck! I'm not just some stuffed teddy bear. I'm an ursa. You want cute and cuddly I can do that, but this is the real world, kid. It's an act. I have needs, and right now I need my smokes," he said. He held out his paw for the cigarette. I hesitated, but then I shook my head and handed it to him. He lit up again as I stood up. "Where are you going?"

"It's been a heck of a day and I'm hungry. You?"

"I can eat," Horace said as he dropped to the floor and followed me into the kitchen.

"Wait, I was asking to be polite. Can you actually eat?"

"Yes, I can eat, and before you ask, no I don't need to eat but I enjoy it."

"What about afterwards? Do you poop?"

"Do I shit? No kid, I don't shit. That would be weird."

"Then where does it all go?"

"Kid, I am a magical fucking teddy bear. Its fucking magic."

We made cold cut sandwiches while I told Horace about my day. He complained that I was a punk for not liking spicy mustard and expressed his distaste for vegetables on sandwiches. We ended up with four ham sandwiches with lettuce, spicy mustard, and tomato. I grabbed a Mountain Dew, Horace grabbed a beer, and we sat down at the table to eat.

"I'm gonna look up trolls in the monster manual after we eat," I said.

"You should pick up the other books and not just the overview manual." Horace told me.

"What?"

"Yeah. Your book is an overview of the Church's Paranormal Encyclopedia. Didn't you ever wonder why you only had one and your grandfather has almost thirty books?"

"I thought they were just encyclopedias that he kept in his den. I didn't know they went along with the monster manual!"

"No one told you?"

"Most of the Church hates me."

"That's the curse. Why aren't you asking me more about it?"

"Can you help me get rid of it?"

"Two of the most powerful wizards in the United States, a paladin, and an angel couldn't break it. I'm in the body of a child's toy. What do you think?"

"Then there's no point worrying about it. It makes people dislike me. I smell bad and I'm ugly. Moving on."

Horace nodded. "The bridge boys are bad news, kid. I'm surprised you survived meeting one of them."

"You know about them?"

"Yeah, big enforcers in the magical underworld. They work for a guy named Fraul."

"Who's he?"

Horace took a pull from his beer and mulled it over. "Think of the biggest, baddest crime boss out there. He has the brains, charisma, guts, drive, and purpose to do what he wants when he wants. Now make him a troll. Take Frank Lucas' foresight, Al Capone's ruthlessness, and the charisma of Morgan Freeman. That's Fraul."

"Am I going to have to deal with him after I deal with his boys?"

"One step at a time, Michael. You should get the other books and then read up on trolls."

I began to nod in agreement when my phone rang to the tune of *Inspector Gadget*. The call was on the business line for White Knight Investigations. There was a private number on the screen. Normally when someone called that line it was to ask me if I could help find out if their significant other was cheating on them. It was good money, but it reminded me why I was only a part-time private investigator.

I answered, "White Knight Investigations, Michael White speaking."

A female voice came back across the phone. "Hello, Mr. White, my name is Lydia Black."

I could already hear her story. She would want me to find out if Mr. Black was cheating with Mrs. Green next door. "Hello, Mrs. Black. How can I help you?" I asked.

"Mr. White, I am calling on behalf of my husband. He would like to hire you for a job. He is driving at the moment and prefers not to talk on the phone. Could we meet you at your office at 3 p.m.?"

I looked at my watch. It was just past 1 p.m. so I had time. "Of course we can, Mrs. Black. May I ask you what this pertains to?"

"Some things are better discussed in person, Mr. White. But I do need something from you right now."

"What is it?"

Her voice came back to me as though the phone was further from her mouth. "Mr. White, I have you on speaker phone. I would like you to invite myself, my husband, and our companions into your territory under the Laws of Avalon."

The Laws of Avalon were no joke. They were written by several powerful beings, some of which could claim godhood from what I was told. The laws governed the civil interactions between beings and were recognized by most of the supernatural community. I knew the rules...mostly...I had a book on them. The Church recognized them, and as a Knight of the Crucifixion I was obligated to abide by them. Since this was my territory, by inviting someone into it I was offering them safe passage, my protection, and in some respects I would be taking responsibility for their actions under the Laws.

"Mrs. Black, I extend an invitation to you, your husband, and your companions to join me in my territory of the city of Baltimore, Maryland. You have my word that I will provide you with my aid and protection so long as you abide by the Laws of Avalon," I said.

The voice that came back over the line was male. It was calm and deep, and each word carried a weight of authority. "We accept your invitation, Mr. White. We will arrive at 3 p.m. sharp. Goodbye."

The line went dead. I shrugged and picked up another sandwich. Horace was staring at me. "What?" I asked.

"You just gave people that you don't know free passage into your territory! What the hell is wrong with you?" screamed my teddy bear.

"Dude, if they are bad ass enough to come into town and cause trouble, they would do it whether I offered them safe passage or not. This way if they start trouble I can kick their butts without fear of retribution from any signatories of the Laws," I said.

Horace started to argue but stopped himself. He opened his mouth again and closed it. Then he smiled and said, "You got your law degree."

"Yep."

"Did you pass the bar?"

"Never took it. I wanted to work with my hands. It just feels right to build, fix, and restore things."

"Jesus was a carpenter, you know."

I smiled about that old fact. Horace and I ate in silence after that. Jesus was a carpenter, but I wasn't about to start comparing myself to him. It always bothered me that I probably had more in common with Judas than with Jesus. That was probably true for most people.

When we finished with lunch I made a phone call. When someone picked up on the other end I gave them an elaborate password, and they gave me another phone number. When I called that one and gave them another elaborate password the speaker put me on hold.

"My name is Priest Abernathy. Who is this?" came a stern male voice over the line.

"Sir Michael White, Knight of the Crucifixion, wielder of the Sword of Innocence," I said.

There was a pause. "The sword of Judas," the voice said.

I sighed. "Yeah, that one. I just need something brought to me in Baltimore."

"What do you want, Judas?"

"Well first off my name is Michael, not Judas. Second, I need a full set of the Paranormal Encyclopedia that all knights are given."

"What happened to yours?"

"I never received one. All I got was the overview book."

There was another long pause. "My records don't show you as having one, so we can issue you one without investigation or cost. I will have it to you in one month."

"No. That doesn't work. I need it now."

There was another pause. This time I heard voices whispering to each other. "I can send you a set tonight, but they will have to be delivered by Templars."

I silently swore. The Templars were Knights like me, but they were a man-made order that served the Church exclusively. The Knights of the Crucifixion were Templars but with more range and freedom to act. We were part of The Church, but in the end we served God and all that he created. I was lucky enough to not have any Templars in my territory, and inviting them in was the last thing I wanted to do.

"Haven't you ever heard of FedEx?" I asked.

"Sir Michael, I am not about to send forty books filled with mystical spells, incantations, spiritual history, and demonic lore through FedEx, UPS, or the United States Postal Service. Now do you want them or not?"

"Yes! Yes I want them. Have the Templars contact me when they arrive. Remember that I need them ASAP."

"I will. Goodbye."

Abernathy hung up the phone, and I reflected on how much I hated contacting any member of the Church besides my grandpa or Priest Greyshadow. I joined Horace on the couch and handed him a soda.

"There are forty books in the encyclopedia now," I told him.

He nodded. "After you get the books we can go over trolls. I will tell you this much though—they aren't Fairies. They are Folk of Lore."

"What?"

"Folk of Lore. It's just what it sounds like."

"Folklore? Like the normal word, folklore?"

"Not so normal. It's like fairy is a catch-all term for all of the magical creatures of Second Earth. Folk of Lore are beings who don't exactly fit neatly into the categories like dragon, god, fairy, or human."

I choked on part of my sandwich, but it went down after I coughed a bit. "Did you say dragon?"

"Focus. We are talking about Folk of Lore, specifically trolls. Tolkien is probably your most common reference for them. He wrote about them. Dwarves, elves, and the like. Trolls aren't fairies, but they share some traits. Cold iron might hurt them, but there is no guarantee. Magic will hurt them, but even then they can heal from anything that doesn't outright kill them," he said.

"Great. So, all those games that said fire was the weakness of trolls were wrong?" I asked.

"Fire might work. Well, maybe magical fire," Horace told me.

"Okay. I'm heading to the office. Want to tag along?" I asked him.

"The second you aren't alone I'll be nothing but a stuffed bear again. I can hear and see, but I won't be able to help you or talk to you."

"So, in other words, I'm on my own?"

"Yep."

"Great. I get to be the superhero that walks around with his teddy bear," I said with a shrug.

I changed into some clean clothes. I chose a red and white short sleeved flannel and a brand-new pair of blue jeans. Keri-Lynn had bought them for me before she left. I put on my Orioles baseball cap to finish off my look. Horace hopped into my bag, and we took off to my office.

## CHAPTER 9

BEFORE I EVER rolled into town, Gregory Greyshadow had walked the beat of Mobtown's mystical streets. The priest had been Baltimore's paranormal gumshoe, but more than that he had defied the powers that be. Humans running roughshod over fairies, ghouls, and vampires tend to die at a young age. He hadn't. But even a man as tough as Priest Greyshadow has his limitations. A pacemaker, diabetes, and seeing more horrible things in a few years than most people see all of their lives will weigh on a man. So, when I walked into town and was introduced to him by no less than an actual angel he decided to clock out. Now I walk his beat, and he sits in the shadows offering me anything he can to help me.

The coolest gift I have ever gotten, outside of my sword, was a set of keys. I parked in my usual space outside of a standalone brick building in West Baltimore. The sign on the door said, "White Knight Construction and Investigations." This had been Greyshadow's office and his home. Now it was mine.

My office was on a corner with a laundromat next door, row houses as far as the eye can see across both streets, and a pizza place directly opposite the front door. When it was Greyshadow's place they delivered. They refuse to deliver to me because we are in a bad neighborhood, but they are open all night so I can always just walk across the street.

I walked in and hit the lights. The front of the building was a typical office setup. There were couches lining both of the side walls, a round table with stacked magazines and paperback novels in the center of the room, and a vending machine on each side of the door. One was for snacks and the other for drinks. A large, sturdy desk cut from a single piece of ancient redwood was in front of the back wall. In front of it there were two comfortable chairs. Behind it was a newish office chair on wheels. A bookshelf sat off to the left behind the desk against the wall. It was filled with old file boxes and a few novels. There were two coat racks, one next to the snack machine and one in the corner next to the desk.

In the opposite corner was a door leading to the back of the building. Back there was a room with a fully stocked bar, a loft, and a wall with fourteen big screen TVs. Greyshadow had put it all together. The only thing I could rightly say I added was the Dungeons and Dragons calendar on the wall. Well also the carpet in the office, but Greyshadow had paid for it.

I put my bag down on the desk. Horace unzipped it and climbed out. While he looked around I walked over to my coat rack and put my cap on a hook. Three

53

other garments were there. One was a black fedora which I put on. The second was a long black trench coat…or was it a duster? It had been a gift from Greyshadow when I got my private investigators license. The last thing on the coat rack was a jean jacket with white fur around the collar and cuffs. That had been a gift from Keri-Lynn, and I had not worn it since she left Baltimore…and me.

"Nice place," Horace said.

I touched the collar of the jacket and shrugged to wipe something from my eye. "Yeah," I said in reply.

"How do you want to play it, kid?" Horace asked.

I picked him up and set him strategically atop the bookshelf with *The Song of Fire and Ice* to prop him up. "You watch and keep track of everything that goes on. We'll compare notes afterward. Sound good?" I asked.

"Sounds good kid. Just remember that I can't help you out. You sure you've got this?" Horace asked.

I showed him my Desert Eagle in its holster on my waist. I opened my bag and pulled out its chrome twin before opening a drawer on my desk. Inside was a silver snub-nosed revolver with a dark brown grip loaded and ready. I set the chrome eagle in a special holster under the middle of the desk and then sat down to wait.

I propped my feet on the desk and tipped my fedora down, so I looked kind of cool. Then I fell asleep. I'm not ashamed to admit it. I woke up when one of my books hit me in the head. I looked up at Horace, and he nodded toward the door. I could see the lights from a large vehicle creeping up. I heard doors closing and grabbed my sports bag from the desk. I slid my sword out and set it against my desk in easy reach. If some supernatural being wanted to start a brawl with me, I would feel more confident in my chances with a magical sword powered by God's will than with any gun I owned.

Through the tented windows of my office, I counted five figures. The door opened, and an older black man dressed in a black suit stepped in. He was followed by a black woman in a pants suit. She was a midget…dwarf…little person…crap baskets, I don't know how to say it correctly. She was under four feet tall. Her dark hair was styled in natural twists and curls. Next was a tall black man in his late twenties wearing dark jeans, a black tee shirt, and a dark brown cowboy hat. He also had a gun belt with a silver revolver on his right hip. The next man through the door was an older white guy with long steel and black hair pulled into a ponytail. He sported a nicely trimmed goatee and wore black slacks with a gray silk shirt. He had a shoulder rig with a semi-automatic pistol in the holster.

The last person to enter was a tall Caucasian woman with long red hair. She was wearing dark jeans, a stylish blue short sleeved button-down shirt, and spurred cowboy boots. A leather gun belt holstered a colt .45 revolver on her right hip. Her body wasn't skinny or fat but thick with muscles from head to toe. It was like a super model had walked in with thick toned hips, a solid waste, and breasts that were bigger than my head. I had never seen her blue eyes look so sad.

"Faith?" I said as I bolted to my feet.

"Howdy, Michael," the young woman said.

I looked around at the group once more. Each of them was in excellent physical condition, they all moved with athletic grace, and each one was scanning the room the way a predator does when it enters unknown territory. They had spread out, whether by design or instinct I could not be sure, but the first man that entered had taken point and was flanked by the short woman and the young black man on his right. Faith and the older white guy were on his left. Each was spread five feet from the other and five feet back. I knew of animals that hunted in that 'V' formation.

"Werewolves," I said.

"Perceptive," the short woman said.

"He knows the bitch," said the older white man. "Every idiot knows werewolves travel in packs."

"Faith, who are these people, and why are you here?" I asked.

"Mr. White," the black man standing in the point position said. He walked around my table and up to my desk. He held out his hand to me and said, "My name is Kodiak Black."

I shook his hand. His grip was strong. I glanced back over his friends and noticed something strange. Out of everyone in the room he was the least important to me. He was right in front of me, and I still hadn't looked him over. I was shaking his hand and looking at everyone but him.

On a whim I opened my mind's eye. I immediately felt the magic permeating the room. It felt primal, raw, and wild. Uncut power scraped against my body like claws against a tree. I focused on each of Kodiak's companions and could feel the beast stirring within them. Each one gave off an aura of a different magnitude. Faith's was the weakest. The two men were nearly equal, and it seemed to me the magic they were each giving off seethed toward one another. The little woman's was the strongest. She was on par with Faith's dad Jedidiah Kane, the alpha of the Virginia Pack. I was just about to close my mind's eye when I realized that I still wasn't looking at the man in front of me.

When I focused on Kodiak Black I found something I didn't expect. I found absolutely nothing. All things give off a hint of magic because magic is in all things. In all things there is that spark of creation, the very essence of existence. In Kodiak Black I felt nothing. In fact, the more I tried to feel him the harder it was. I kept picking up on the other people around me, on my sword, and even on Horace behind me. But Kodiak Black was a wasteland of nonexistence. My head started hurting, so I closed my mind's eye.

I met Kodiak's gray eyes and saw a cold void behind them. As unimposing as this man seemed, my instincts told me that he was the most dangerous person in the room. We both retracted our hands at the same time.

"How can I help you, Mr. Black," I asked.

"You spoke with my wife, Lydia, earlier today," he said as he motioned to the short woman. She smiled at me and nodded politely. "Mr. White, I have something of the utmost importance to discuss with you, but before I do that I need to know you can be trusted to be discreet."

"My clients have had me dig through their personal lives, finances, and…"

He cut me off. "How many clients have been of the supernatural world?"

"None. My supernatural cases are usually assigned by the Church," I said.

"Tell them how you fought my dad, Michael," Faith said.

The older white man turned to her and snarled, "Shut your mouth, bitch."

Faith, the headstrong daughter of the Alpha of the Virginia Pack, lowered her head and shut her mouth. I let my eyes focus on Mr. Ponytail, and when he turned his head back toward me I lifted my shirt so that he could plainly see my gun. The room was quiet as I calmly tucked my shirt into the hem of my pants so that it wouldn't be in the way of my draw. I felt the slight shift in the room as everyone except Faith and Kodiak got ready for a fight. Ponytail grinned at me.

"I don't know you. I don't care to know you. But if you snap at that girl one more time, call her out of her name one more time, or just make me think she doesn't like you, I'll put a bullet in your forehead," I promised.

The older werewolf growled at me and took a threatening step forward. I popped the security strap off of my holster. He cracked the joints in his neck.

"Marshal," Kodiak said. The older werewolf turned to look at him. "You are a guest here, as we all are. I am sure that Mr. White will not be offering us violence unless we invite it by insulting his friend, for example."

Marshal turned to face me once again and pointedly took a step back. I clipped the security strap back on my holster.

Lydia cleared her throat causing both Kodiak and me to turn our attention to her. "Perhaps we should observe proper etiquette," she said.

"Of course, even in times like this we should observe our manners," Kodiak said. "Mr. White, I have already introduced my wife, and you know Miss Kane. The gentleman to my left is Marshal Thatcher, third in my pack. The young man to my right is my son West Black, Alpha of the North Carolina Pack."

"It's a pleasure to meet you all. Thatcher, get the hell out of my office," I said. Thatcher growled at me. "Kodiak, I don't deal with bullies. You want my help, then you get this asshole out of my office."

"Kodiak," growled Thatcher, but Kodiak cut him off. Not with words or a look. He just lifted his left hand and turned the wedding band on it as though he meant to take it off. Thatcher stopped growling. He took a long hard look at me and then lowered his gaze, turned on his heels, and walked out into the rain.

Kodiak lowered his hands to his sides and blew out a breath. "Mr. White, may I be direct with you?" he asked. I nodded. "Mr. White, I am not in any condition or mood to properly sit down for a discussion of business. In truth, I want to do nothing more than give my pack the order to descend upon your city and tear it apart from the ground up. But as I am a man of practicalities, I understand that such action would only benefit a small few. I am here, Mr. White, because I need help, and you are the only man in the world that can help me."

I took in Kodiak's words. It wasn't often that anyone was this direct with me. But even in being direct, I could feel that he was hiding something. "What pack are you the alpha of, Mr. Black?" I asked.

Kodiak smiled at me. I don't want to say it was wolfish, but darn it was. "A truth for a truth, Mr. White?"

It was an odd saying. It was an old saying. Truth for truth was a mutual exchange of power between two beings. If I agreed he would answer my question, but in return he could ask me one of equal importance, and I was bound to answer truthfully. There was no magic behind the deal that I knew of, so I could always just lie. But breaking your word had a power all its own. To lie, to welch on an ancient deal, would be inviting karma, fortune, chance, fate, or any number of cosmic balancing forces to take a shot at me. Anything could happen from stubbing my toe to my gun misfiring the next time I holstered it.

I stood straight and said, "Truth for truth Kodiak Black. What is your truth? What pack are you the alpha of?"

"I am the Alpha of the New York Pack," Kodiak said. "Now what is your truth Michael White? What is the most important thing in this world to you?"

I was rocked back by his question. I had expected him to ask me a secret about the Church or something important. I reached down and pulled my sheathed sword up so that he could see it. Kodiak frowned at the blade. I set it on the table and opened a small pocket on the side of the sheath. There was a photo hidden there. I pulled it out and slid it to the end of the desk. Kodiak walked over and took up the photo. He looked at it and then up at me.

I met his puzzled expression and said, "That is a picture of my entire family at my grandmother's birthday a few years back. Family is what is most important to me. That is my truth."

Kodiak sat my photo down carefully. He motioned for West to come to him. West walked over as he pulled a manila folder from his vest. Kodiak took the folder and held it out to me. "Mr. White, eleven days ago someone kidnapped my brother, Everett Black. Will you help find him?"

# CHAPTER 10

I TOOK THE folder and quickly thumbed through it. I wasn't reading it, but I can commit anything I see to memory. Word sequences, numbers, or pictures. I can basically recall anything I have ever seen. I don't have an eidetic or photographic memory because I have to remember it in perfect order. I can flip through a book, but I can't tell you what is on page thirty-five unless I think about pages one through thirty-four first. I also can't do it with things I have heard or felt. Just with things I have seen.

There were pictures of a devastated house riddled with bullet holes and holes from something much larger and more destructive. There were bodies everywhere…that's not right…there were pieces of bodies everywhere. I had seen horror movies that were less gruesome. All of that to take one man alive.

"I'm assuming your brother is a werewolf. I've fought your kind before. Movies and TV don't give you half the credit you deserve for being supernatural powerhouses. So, Mr. Black, I have to ask, who or what can kidnap a werewolf?"

It was true. Werewolves were always portrayed as being the weakest of the monsters. In truth they were near the top of the food chain in the magical community as far as creatures that live in the mortal world go. I had filled three young werewolves with buck shot and watched them shrug it off like mosquito bites.

"I hate to be flippant, Mr. White, but if I knew who or what took my brother I wouldn't need you," he said. There was no change in his voice. No rise in timber or quickening of speech. But everyone in the room stiffened at his words.

"Okay, so why can't you just track him by scent? I know you wolves can find any member of your pack at any time."

West spoke up. "Have you been outside lately? It's raining. We can't track by scent in the rain."

I looked down at the folder in my hand and pulled out a picture. A man that looked taller and more muscular than Kodiak looked back at me. Other than his height and musculature, he was the spitting image of Kodiak with a heavy beard. I set the folder down and rolled my neck to clear my head.

"You think he's here in Baltimore?" I asked.

"Without a doubt. If he were anywhere else in this world I would know," Kodiak said.

"Alright. Mr. Black, I would like to help you, but as it stands I am more in the dark than you are. Something kidnapped your brother, brought him to Baltimore,

59

and is holding him here without the resources backing at least three packs being able to find him. I feel like something is missing from this situation, and without answers that you probably do not want to give I can't help you," I said.

"If I gave you those answers you would help me?" asked Kodiak.

I thought about that for a moment. I looked over his entourage again and answered a question with a question. "What would you like me to do, Mr. Black?"

"I want you to find my brother, or I want you to allow me to bring my entire pack into your city and stay out of my way," Kodiak said with a terrifying calm in his voice.

"That's not happening. This city is under my protection, and you are not bringing a bunch of frenzied werewolves into it," I said.

"There are already frenzied werewolves in your city," Lydia said. I looked over at her, and the small woman continued. "Whoever kidnapped Everett has used him to change at least a few people in your city into werewolves. I would suggest you agree to help us now, Mr. White, before it is too late."

"What do you mean by that?" I asked.

"It's three days before the full moon, Mr. White. Every person that has been bitten since the last full moon will turn when the full moon rises. Then you will have a bunch of frenzied and wild werewolves rampaging through your city. The only thing that will be able to stop them is a werewolf more dominant than all of them," lectured Lydia.

I looked at Kodiak and found that wolfish grin on his face once more. "So, either I find your brother, or you won't corral the werewolves?" I asked.

"Correct," he said.

"Well, Mr. Black, you seem to have me over a barrel. I guess you expect me to let you ride shotgun in my truck while I look for your brother?"

"I don't want to step on your toes, Mr. White. I brought Miss Kane because you and she seem to get along. She will represent me and my interests. I do ask, however, that when you locate my brother you contact me. My son West or I will assist you with controlling him after his rescue."

"Controlling him?"

"My brother isn't always the poster boy for control, Mr. White. He was taken by force, injured, and is likely being tortured. If he is panicked then he will have to be managed by a more dominant wolf. There are few wolves in the world more dominant than he is."

"Alright…I'm guessing you can cover my fee?"

Kodiak reached into his jacket pocket and pulled out an envelope. He set it on the desk and slid it toward me. I picked it up and opened it. Inside was five grand in hundred-dollar bills.

"You require a retainer of $500.00 to be paid upfront, and it is nonrefundable should the client decide they are unhappy with your results. You charge a fee of $100.00 an hour. You charge expenses to the client, and you do not accept checks," said Kodiak.

"There's five grand in here," I said. "That's ten times my retainer."

"Mr. White, this is my brother. I am paying you to not take any other case in the foreseeable future. I want him found. I need him found," Kodiak said.

"I already have a case, Mr. Black," I said.

"I won't ask you to abandon it, but I must insist that my situation take priority," he said. I nodded. Larry wasn't paying me crap, and this was $5000.00 on top of my hourly fee. Tonight, I was eating steak. Screw that, tonight I was eating!

"I have two requests," I said. Kodiak lifted his eyebrows. "The first is that your son make himself available to me for the duration of this investigation. Get a hotel and be ready to go when I call you."

Kodiak and West exchanged looks. "I was going to do that anyway," the younger werewolf said.

"Good. The second request is that you, Kodiak, leave town with all of your other werewolves."

Kodiak's eyes flashed. They didn't narrow or grow wide or become intense. They flashed. Gray light sparked from them, and the lights flickered. Car alarms went off outside, and I could swear that I heard thunder rumble in the distance.

"I am not leaving, Mr. White," Kodiak said.

"Yes you are. If you want me on this case then you need to leave town. No offense, but you're the scariest person I have ever met. I won't be able to focus on anything while you are in my city," I said.

Kodiak fixed me with a glare that could freeze a tidal wave. He started to speak, but Lydia cut him off. "We will leave," she said. Kodiak turned to her so fast that I felt the air in the room stir. "Kodiak, you haven't slept in days. You want Everett back like we all do. The difference is that you are willing to kill everyone in this city for him. You know that you need to step back. Let's not make this harder on everyone involved and let the knight do his job."

Kodiak nodded slowly to his wife. He turned back to me and took a deep breath before speaking. "If we meet these requests, will you help me, Mr. White?"

"That and I need some questions answered. After that I will be glad to help," I said.

Kodiak stuck his hand out to me and said "Done." We shook on it. He then turned on his heels and walked to the door. "I am going outside to make arrangements for my son and for Miss Kane," he said.

"Faith stays with me. She is my friend and under my protection whenever she comes to Baltimore," I said.

"Mr. White, that is not happening," said Kodiak.

"With all due respect, Mr. Black, this isn't a debate. Faith is my friend, and she is going to stay with me," I said.

"Miss Kane has been with her pack since she was a child. This will be the first time she has been outside of the influence of a pack, which a werewolf needs to function in modern society. My son can help her cope, Mr. White. You cannot," Kodiak said.

His words hit me like a hammer. I started to bow my head and agree, but something stopped me. Something deep inside me rose to the surface. I had been beaten up by a troll, choked by a teddy bear, and fired for working too hard! I was sick and tired of being told that doing what I felt was right was wrong. I didn't know these werewolves, and I didn't give one flying flip as to what they thought was best for Faith. She was my friend, and I was going to keep her safe.

"Faith. Is. Mine," I said.

Kodiak and West both narrowed their eyes at me, and West shook his head. "Faith is a lone wolf right now. She cannot be left on her own."

"She isn't on her own. She is with me, and she is mine to protect. The end," I said.

Lydia smiled. "Not a challenge. An affirmation," she said.

Kodiak nodded. "I will make arrangements for West. My wife will answer any questions you have," Kodiak said. He opened the door then stepped out with Faith and West following behind him. That left me alone with Lydia Black.

I motioned for Mrs. Black to take a seat. She did and I took mine. Before I could even settle comfortably into my chair she spoke up. "You might as well ask me that question first," she said with a smile.

I started to open my mouth, but I held my tongue. I wanted to ask, but it seemed so rude. I thought about any way I could possibly approach the elephant in the room without destroying any hope I had of a pleasant conversation.

"How does someone like you become a werewolf?" I asked.

Lydia smiled at me. It wasn't a pleasant smile. It was a tolerant smile, the kind of smile you give to the parents of the kid that is afraid of the escalator but insists on riding it. "That isn't the question. What you meant to ask was how does a midget get turned into a werewolf," she said.

"Okay, let's go with that," I said. I was more than happy to take the coward's way out on this one.

"What do you know about slavery in America, Mr. White?" Lydia asked.

"I have a public-school education supported by two college degrees that are not in history." I smiled.

"So not a damn thing worth mentioning," she laughed. "Alright. I was a slave. I was born on a plantation in North Carolina. You have no idea what it's like to be considered less than human, Mr. White. It wasn't like the movies. Movies are made by people that on some level need the audience to like what they see. Yes, they want people to feel and think about what they see, but in the end they want to sell tickets. I saw other slaves murdered in ways that would make horror movie lovers sleep with night lights. I once saw a man flayed for being lazy. He had been working in the field all day under the hot sun and asked if he could get some water. They whipped him, flayed his bottom lip, and dumped salted water on him. When he screamed, they flayed part of his arm."

I cringed at the thought of it. I didn't know anything about slavery beyond what the movies portrayed and what teachers were willing to talk about. Lydia talked about it like seeing someone flayed was as common then as seeing a man wearing boots is now.

"That man was the most productive slave on the plantation. He was six feet tall, almost solid muscle, and never sick a day in his life. If they would do that to him, what do you think they would do to a little girl with dwarfism?" she asked me.

I didn't want to think about that.

"They put me to work in the big house. They had me clean and fold laundry. They had me wash dishes. And they had me play with the little girls of the house. They were all older and bigger than me, so they loved having a living baby doll. Except for the fact that I was black. So, they shaved my head and put a wig of straight blonde hair on my head. They painted me white, and they made me pretend that I wasn't a slave. It was as if everything those girls did was to reinforce to me that I would never be anything beyond property—nothing more than a negro baby doll. But the worst part, the absolute worst part, was what happened when one of the men got a hold of me," Lydia said.

I started to say something, but she held up a hand. "I'll spare you the details. One day a pair of young black men in fine gray suits came riding up on horses. The Master and his people didn't know how to act or what to do. Black men on horseback. The white folk had a fit. All the two black men wanted was a place to rest for the night. The field bosses started to shoe them off when the larger of the two announced that they had money to pay for a room. The Master told them they could stay the night. They were given blankets and pointed to the barn. A hired field hand tried to rob them that night. The larger of the young black men killed him. The Master and the other white folks didn't take too kindly to that. He ordered that the smaller one be whipped and the larger one be lynched."

"They gathered up all the slaves," she continued. There was a strange accent creeping into her voice. "Massa said he wanted us all to see what happened when a nigga gets uppity and lay hands on a white man. They dragged the two strangers out to the whippin' posts with their hands tied. Before they could hitch them up, the smaller stranger said he was done with men. Said he was done with the way men segregate themselves from each other. Said he was done with all of it. Massa told him to shut his mouth and went to slap him. The stranger snapped the ropes around his wrists like they were made of wet noodles. He caught Massa's hand and grabbed his shoulder with his other hand. Then he ripped Massa's arm off. The other stranger broke free, and they both started to change. Blood seeped from their skin. Their arms and legs broke and reset themselves. Their clothing ripped and exploded as muscles swelled and tightened. Fingernails became claws and teeth turned to fangs. Fur covered their bodies, and when their screams finally stopped two giant wolf monsters stood there among us."

Lydia had long ago stopped looking at me. She turned back to look me in the eye and spoke with a growl. "They started killin' the white folk. Not all of them. They rounded up the ones they liked, said they had been watching all of us. They offered us both, black folks and white folk, the chance to be free. They offered us power, strength, and eternal youth. There were twelve white folks left alive, and all of them took the offer. Of the eighty slaves on the plantation, only six took the offer. That was eighteen people they tried to change into werewolves. Four survived the transformation. I was one of them."

"The two strangers were Everett and Kodiak, weren't they?" I asked.

Lydia nodded. "Everett is bigger than Kodiak, but Kodiak is the oldest." She nodded again.

We sat in silence for a bit. That story had been personal. Origin stories always are, and they all tend to suck. Mine did, and according to Horace it was worse than I thought it was.

"Now that that is out of the way, please ask me anything you would like, Mr. White. I will answer if it is pertinent to the investigation or if I feel like it," Lydia said. She had replaced her frown with that disarming smile of hers.

"Okay, second question: what are you? I mean in your pack. My knowledge of werewolves is limited to…well, the movies," I said.

"Fair enough. The movies and books portray werewolves as an extension of the normal wolf hierarchy. In some ways this is true, but the major falsehood is that it is a male-dominated society. Women are not subservient, nor does being born male place you above anyone in the pack hierarchy. I am Kodiak's mate and wife. Some wolves separate their human and werewolf relationships. Kodiak and I do not," she told me.

"Okay, so what are you to the pack? Second? Beta?" I asked.

"No. Everett is Kodiak's second. I am what the pack calls a den mother. I take all the pups and train them how to be werewolves." Lydia smiled.

"So, you are a nanny?"

"No," she laughed. "A 'pup' is any new werewolf regardless of age."

"So, you teach the new wolves to…" I prompted her.

"The initial change brings on a sort of second childhood. There is a sense of invincibility and unaccountability with becoming a werewolf. I bring new wolves back to reality. I teach them the two stages of transformation, how to fight, and how to hunt. I then teach them what is expected of them and what is acceptable. I teach them to follow our rules which have kept us classified as a fictional monster for centuries," she said. "If they can't learn, or refuse to learn, I kill them. Every pack has a den mother."

My jaw dropped at her casual mentioning that she killed werewolves for not following her rules. "So, what if they do learn and then decide to break the rules anyway?"

"Then it falls on their alpha to kill them," she said.

"That's it? You just kill them? No talks, no warnings, and no remorse?"

Lydia raised her eyebrow at me and said, "Mr. White, we aren't soulless monsters, but we are still monsters. Our rules prohibit us from acting like the monsters that horror stories have made us out to be. We fix our problems in-house and don't leave them for anyone else to clean up. Yes, we kill those that do not conform. No one has time to deal with the kind of trouble a single rogue werewolf can cause even if we are immortal," she said. "What is your next question, little boy?"

I let that slight slide. "So, the two transformations are into wolves and giant man wolf things, right?"

"I teach them the feral form and the wolf form transformations," she said.

"Feral form?"

Lydia held up her hand, and I watched as her fingernails began to elongate. Their natural coloring didn't change, but her red fingernail polish began to shed as her fingernails sharpened into claws. "The feral form is exactly as it sounds. Werewolves in human form have above average strength, speed, and other physical capabilities. When we change into our feral form, we are basically feral humans. In this state we have superhuman abilities, and our physical appearance is more primal. In my feral form, for example, I am 5'8" and can bench press seven-hundred pounds," she said. Her hand returned to normal, and she pulled a bottle of nail polish from her purse to touch up her once again human nails.

"I'm guessing the wolf form is just that?" I asked.

"Yes. We are more akin to the dire wolves of the old tales than the wolves of today. Larger, stronger, and built like a tank. We heal from mundane wounds almost instantaneously, and we shrug off magic as we do in any form. Magically enhanced physical assaults can still harm us, but not to the degree that they would other beings," she said in a matter-of-fact tone.

I was starting to get a picture of what I could be up against. It wasn't looking good, and I still had a few more questions. "How do you become a werewolf?" I asked.

"There have been three ways. The first is to be cursed, but the last being that we know of that could do that is long dead. So that leaves us with two ways. The most prominent way is to be attacked and savaged by a fully transformed werewolf to the point of near death. If you survive then the change will be upon you. If you survive your first full moon then you are a werewolf. That is how it was for hundreds of years," she said.

"And the last way?" I asked.

"Only recently, within the last seventy years, we have found a way to give birth," she said.

"Well congratulations. We humans have been doing it for centuries." I smiled.

"We are human, Mr. White. Metahuman, but still human. We have sex and get pregnant. Unfortunately, the full moon forces us to transform. A pregnant werewolf always loses the baby when she transforms," Lydia said.

I watched her move her hand to her belly. She only touched it with her fingertips, and I could see the pain she was hiding. "But West is your son, right?" I asked.

"Yes! He is my oldest child. Recently we found a way to keep from transforming during the full moon. Because of this, our women can know the joys of giving birth." She smiled.

"The pain you mean," I said.

"Yes the pain, but the joy as well. To create life is something you will never know, Mr. White. The magic involved is beyond anything you have ever felt," she said. Her eyes roamed over to the hilt of my sword. "Or maybe it is exactly like the power you wield in that sword."

"How do you keep from transforming?" I asked.

"That is not pertinent to the investigation, Mr. White," she said with a smile.

"Okay. Who or what do you think took your brother-in-law?" I asked.

"I have no idea, Mr. White. It would have to be something powerful, something exceptionally powerful to be sure. Have you read any of the old stories, Mr. White? The Brothers Grim for example?" she asked me.

"Yes. Some are just old storied made up to scare kids, but others are warnings," I said.

"The Big Bad Wolf in those tales is very real and very dangerous, Mr. White. Any werewolf can be destructive, but whoever took Everett is toying with a force of nature. He is a natural disaster waiting to happen. Mr. White, for your sake and for the sake of this world I hope you never have to see The Big Bad Wolf," she said.

"Mrs. Black, thank you," I said. I stood up and she hopped down out of the chair. She was so small, but I had the feeling that she could kill me easily if she wanted to. "I will be in touch, and I will find your brother-in-law."

Lydia smiled, thanked me, and turned to leave. When she got to the door I called after her. "One more question. Why did you call me a little boy?"

She turned back around to me and smiled. "I have heard of you, Michael White. The Knight of Innocence. Wielder of the sword of Judas. Grandson of Franklin White, a Paladin. They say you wear children's clothes, shirts with cartoon characters on them, while you fight monsters. You proclaim yourself the protector of Baltimore, and you never walk away from a fight. You leave death and destruction in your wake every time you dress up to play superhero. I know a child when I see one, Mr. White. Don't take this the wrong way, but there are plenty of grown-ups in the world but few adults. You aren't an adult. You are just a little boy with a man's body and a magic sword," she said.

"Then why come to me?" I asked.

"Because adults don't save the day in the fairy tales. Little boys and girls do. I know for a fact that you have a knack for saving people, so I told my husband that you were the man for the job," she said. "Is there anything else?"

I shook my head. Lydia turned and walked outside. After what she had just told me, I felt silly about asking my teddy bear to talk to me about it, but that was what I was about to do. That was until Faith walked back into the office, soaking wet from the rain, and slammed the door behind her. She looked at me with a mixture of emotions—anger, fear, and regret mostly. Without a word Faith dropped her duffle bag, leapt at me, and wrapped me in a hug. Then she started crying into my neck.

# CHAPTER 11

I HELD FAITH tight for a long time. I had never seen her cry, and I was worried about her. That and I don't think the jaws of life could have pried me free of her embrace. Seriously, werewolves are strong, and I don't think Faith has ever hugged anyone that she could crush before I came along. So, I cherished the little bit of air I could take in and held my friend until she stopped unintentionally squeezing the life from me.

"Michael, I am so sorry about this," she said.

"What are you sorry about?" I asked.

"I was visiting West's pack when Kodiak called him! He brought me to Kodiak, and he made me tell Kodiak everything about you! I'm sorry! I didn't know he would bring this mess to your doorstep!" she told me. She stepped back from me as though she expected me to tell her to get out or something.

"Why were you visiting West's pack?" I asked.

"Me and Daddy have been butting heads lately. I challenged his third for position in the pack and he denied me. So, I decided to join another pack. I'm a grown woman now, not some little pup," she declared as she folded her arms over her chest and pouted.

"Says the girl that still looks like she is just turning sixteen," I said. I smiled at her, and her pout faded.

"I'm older than you," she said.

"I know. But I can buy a beer without getting carded," I teased. I turned to the window and watched as the other werewolves drove off. "Let me pack up, and then we can roll out."

"We gonna go find Everett right now?" she asked me.

"No. I have another obligation, but we will get started right after that," I said. "First we are going to go recruit some help."

Faith made herself busy with her phone while I packed up. I figured that since I was on the clock as a P.I. I would look the part. I grabbed the duster or trench coat, whichever it was, and put it on. On a whim, I grabbed the snub-nosed revolver and stuffed it into the pocket of the coat.

Once I had all my gear together, we got into the Rust Bucket and headed to a nicer side of town. Traffic was good, so the trip didn't take long. We pulled up to a three-story Victorian that always stood out to me. Something about it reminded me of my grandparent's home in Virginia. They looked nothing alike,

69

but something about it just screamed happy home. There was a white picket fence that had a fresh coat of paint courtesy of yours truly in exchange for the wards on my apartment.

It also had a new swinging gate, also courtesy of yours truly, because I allegedly broke the other one. I may have touched something in the house that I was specifically told not to touch, and it may have accidentally released a contained imp that then tried to eat my face. During the struggle, I may have panicked, screamed "face hugger," and ran for my life. But that is only one version of the story. In my version I sound way more manly and did not trip, fall through the gate, and accidentally kill the imp by impaling it on a shard of the broken gate. Because that would just be silly and dumb luck. I am a knight, and I valiantly defeated a foe. Anyone who says otherwise is an evil liar.

We got out, and Faith sniffed the air. "What is this place?" she asked.

"It's my friend's place. I'm getting her to help us out," I said.

"Michael, it's raining, so the fact that I smell magic rolling off the ground out here tells me this place is filled with it."

"I guess so. It is a wizard's house," I said.

Faith stepped back. "I'm not going into a witches house."

"Wizard...not witch. But are you sure? She is pretty nice."

"I'm not even supposed to be here, and I'm not going into a witch's house unless I am transformed and invited. Even then I won't feel right in there with all this magic."

I shrugged. "Suit yourself. Stay with the truck and yell if you need something. We will be out in a minute or two."

I walked up by myself and knocked on the front door. When the door opened, I was greeted by a woman in a yellow sun dress and a white sweater. She had oven mitts under her arms and a frown on her face. Eden Freedman was just under five feet tall and as always dressed as the stereotypical happy homemaker, from the yellow headband to the matching bunny slippers.

"Hello, Mr. White," she said. "I didn't call you, and I haven't had any problems that needed your attention. So, either you are in trouble, or you need help with something."

"Can't I just come by to see my friend?" I asked.

"Not without calling first. I'm a widow. A young man showing up out of the blue at supper time raises questions, starts gossip, and is just plain inconsiderate. You aren't an inconsiderate young man that wants people to gossip about me or question my virtues, are you, Mr. White?"

"Nope, I'm just a private dick with a missing person and a few dead bodies in need of a bit of wizardly assistance," I told her.

Eden stepped aside and waived me in. "Please do come in, Mr. White."

We sat in the parlor room and Eden, being the perfect homemaker she was, insisted on serving coffee, tea, and cake while we talked. I had tea and she had coffee. She served it in a beautiful China set that made me feel both welcome and fancy. So, I stuck my pinky out while I drank.

"Before we get down to business, can you take a look at something for me?" I asked. Eden nodded, and I pulled Horace out of my bag. I handed him over, and she looked at me curiously before taking it.

"Do you keep your diapers in that bag, too?" she asked.

"Nope, I keep them in the truck. What can you tell me about it?"

Eden turned the bear over in her hands a few times. "It's an old teddy bear, it's got your name sewn into the overalls, and it smells like menthols," she said with a shrug.

"Well duh, it's a teddy bear. I knew that much." I signed.

"And you are aware that it smells like menthols? Been smoking behind daycare, Michael?" she asked.

"No! He is the one that's been smoking, not me," I argued.

"Your teddy bear…has been smoking?" she asked skeptically.

"Yes, because he isn't a teddy bear. He is a magical, totem, spirit, bear thing," I said.

Eden looked over the bear again and then back to me. Then she whispered a few words. Her eyes flashed for an instant, and then she looked over my bear again. For about two minutes I sat there quietly as she examined every inch of my teddy bear. Then she sat him on the table between us.

"Michael, there is nothing at all magical about this bear. It's a stuffed toy. Not a totem, nothing demonic, nothing angelic, nothing supernatural at all," she said.

"That can't be right. He talks to me, he ate a sandwich, and he drank a beer. He lit a cigarette in my apartment and smoked it!" I argued.

Eden nodded. "Alright. Michael, are you feeling okay?"

"Fine, just frustrated," I groaned.

Eden nodded again. She got up and walked over to a side table. She opened the drawer and brought me a pen and paper. "Write your name ten times, Church Boy. First and last only. Don't ask questions, just do it."

I took the pen and paper then wrote my name 10 times like she had instructed. The moment I was done she snatched the paper. She looked at it for a bit and folded the paper before placing it in her apron pocket.

"What was that about?" I asked.

"Didn't I tell you not to ask questions?" she said with a smile. "Now put your teddy bear away and tell me who your new little playmate is that's waiting outside?" she asked.

"You know she's an adult, right?" I picked up Horace and put him away.

Eden nodded. "You're right. I don't know her, so I shouldn't dismiss her like that."

"Exactly!" I said.

"So, Michael, who is your new babysitter?" she smirked.

"I walked into that, didn't I?"

"Toddled, but yes."

"Her name is Faith Kane. She is a friend from Virginia here on—"

Eden choked on her coffee and spilled some into the saucer she held under her cup. She set them down and took a moment to compose herself. "Did you say Kane from Virginia? As in the Virginia Werewolf Pack? That Kane?"

"Umm, yeah. You know them?" I asked.

"Michael are you being serious right now?" she asked. Her voice was harder than it usually was when she entertained me, and her face had dropped the southern socialite look that I associated with being in her home.

"Yeah," I said.

"They are one of the most notable werewolf packs on the east coast. Maybe the North Carolina pack is more notable, but that's because their alpha is maybe the second most powerful werewolf in the country. Maybe the world. Either way, Jedidiah Kane is an old power unto himself."

"Yeah, I met him once. He punched me so hard that I had an out-of-body experience. Saw it from every possible angle," I said.

Eden tilted her head. "He hit you and you had an out of body experience?"

I shrugged, "Yeah, it was weird."

"Have you ever had any other out of body experiences?" she asked.

I thought about it for a while. Nothing came to mind. Then again, few things had ever hit me that hard. "No. Why?"

Eden shook her head. "No reason. But back to the point. Why is a werewolf in Baltimore and outside of my home?"

"Oh. She came here with my new client, Kodiak Black. I invited him here, and he hired me to find his missing brother. I was hoping you could—"

I didn't get to finish my explanation as Eden reached over and grabbed my ear. She twisted it as she started walking. I was forced to follow as she dragged me through her home.

"Does Aaron know you invited Kodiak Black into Baltimore?" she asked.

"No, he's out of town!" I yelled as I tried to keep up with her as she walked and I hunched over at an odd angle.

"So, your best friend leaves town, and you decide to fucking replace him with a werewolf?" she yelled back.

"Huh?"

Eden tugged my ear hard, and I went skipping forward right out her front door into the rain. I caught the porch railing as I stumbled down the brick stairs. She threw my hat and coat to me. I didn't catch them and had to pick them up.

"So, you aren't going to help me find Everette Black?" I asked.

Eden, small and cherubic in her features, seemed a towering behemoth as she stood in her doorway. "No member of the International Council of Wizards is about to get mixed up with helping you after you invited Kodiak Black and his werewolves into Baltimore! Now you listen to me, Michael White. You need to tell Aaron about this, and you need to do it now! He is the only one that can help you fix this mess."

"But he's out of town! I need help now, and you're the only wizard I know powerful enough to help me. Come on Eden, lives are at stake," I argued.

Eden grabbed her head in apparent frustration then yelled, "Of course they are! Lives are always at stake when you deal with extra-mortal beings. The point is that you don't have to make things worse by inviting a pack of werewolves into Baltimore!"

"What was I supposed to do? Ask them to do a ZOOM call?" I countered.

Eden's eyes went wide. With a word in a language I didn't know, she flicked her hand at me. The air around me began to whirl, lifting water and throwing it in all directions. A small tornado formed around me and lifted me into the air. I was carried past the white picket fence, where the tornado vanished. I fell to the sidewalk, landing on my butt.

"Does this mean you won't help me?" I yelled.

"A mage would have to be insane to help you with this, church boy!" she yelled back.

"Hey, what about my bag?" I asked. Another tornado came surging across the lawn, and it dropped my sports bag in my lap. "Thank you!"

I got into the Rust Bucket where Faith was waiting for me. "So did you get some help?" she asked.

"Yes and no," I told her. "She isn't going to help, but she gave me an idea."

"What's the idea?"

"First we are going to pick up a couple of guys and get some food. Then we are going to find someone to help us out."

"Who?"

I started my truck and took off down the road. "We are going to find a mad mage."

# CHAPTER 12

WE HEADED TO the construction site to pick up Drew. The construction site was emptying when we got there. Drew was waiting on me right next to where we had originally parked. He had his gear in his hand and a drawn expression on his face. I pulled up and rolled down my window to talk to him.

"Hey, Drew, how was your day, man?" I asked.

"Good. We got the roof fully stripped and started the work on the replacement," he said.

"Awesome! Come on, I'll buy you dinner, and you can tell me about it," I said.

Drew shifted away from me and said, "Thanks, but not tonight Michael. I was kind of wondering if you would drop me at Code Blue?"

Code Blue was a homeless shelter on Fallsway. It was on the way to the church, and I didn't mind dropping Drew off. But I was worried why he was turning down a meal with me. "Anything wrong man?" I asked.

"Nah. Just the foreman was looking for more guys, and I know a few people," he told me.

"Sure. If they do well, maybe I will put them on my payroll for the next job. Just let me know. Let's roll," I said.

Drew walked around and opened the passenger door. He was greeted by a curvy werewolf girl with breasts large enough to make a man forget his manners. Which Drew did as he stared at Faith's chest.

"Drew, this is my friend Faith. Faith, this is Drew, my friend and employee," I said.

"Howdy, Drew," Faith said as she scooted in closer to me.

"Hello Miss," Drew stuttered as he climbed in.

It was a quick ride to Code Blue. When Drew got out, I told him to leave his gear and that I would pick him and anyone else up in the morning. Drew thanked me and headed inside. It did my heart good to see Drew doing well.

We drove to the church where Priest Greyshadow was waiting outside. Larry was with him, and he looked like he had a hard day. I got out of the truck and looked him over. His hair was disheveled, his clothes were filthy, and his hands were bandaged in several places. All in all, he looked nothing like Larry should look.

"What happened? Trolls?" I asked.

"He tried to kill me!" said Larry.

Priest Greyshadow gave me the biggest smile I had ever seen on his face and said, "I think this is the first time your friend here has actually worked in his entire life. He cleaned one whole row of pews today. He cut his hand open four times, developed seven blisters, and almost overdosed on Pine-Sol, but he did it."

"He tried to kill me," Larry said again as he grabbed hold of me. He must have grabbed too tightly because he jumped back and began shaking his hands as he yelled, "Oww!"

I couldn't help but smile. I turned my attention back to Priest Greyshadow and said, "Thanks. Mind if I bring him back tomorrow?"

"Sorry, kid, doctor's appointment. Getting the yearly done," he said. I eyed my mentor for a moment. He hated doctors and avoided them at all costs. He must have noticed the gears turning in my head because he held up his hands in a 'what else can I do' pose and said, "The church's women's group is making me go."

I nodded and left it at that.

"You're wearing the coat and hat. Got a case?" he asked me.

"Yep," I said.

It was his turn to look at me like I was keeping secrets, which I was. "Hush hush stuff? Supernatural?" he asked.

I nodded once.

"Kid, you have good instincts. Trust them. If you need a gun hand or a prayer let me know."

"Thanks, Padre. Oh, by the way, is this a duster or a trench coat?" I asked.

Priest Greyshadow laughed out loud. "Eden will kill me if I tell you, but she had it made special for you," he said.

"I thought you got it for me?" I said.

"I did. I needed a leather worker, and she knew one. It's tailored for you. When I told him that I wanted a trench coat he told me that dusters were popular with kids these days. Eden and I both agreed to keep it professional. It's a trench coat, kid. That's what a real Gum Shoe wears. The buttons are actually runes of protection. Eden made them herself."

"Seriously? Eden made the buttons?" I asked.

"For some reason she likes you, kid," he laughed.

I laughed as well. "Well, we're going to roll. Take care, Padre."

"Stay alive, knight," he told me.

We shook hands, and then Larry and I walked down to the Rust Bucket. Faith looked at Larry through the window and figured that she would take the outside seat, so she hopped out. A night breeze blew by us, and it would have been so cool if my coat whipped out in front of me. It just hung lifelessly to my legs.

Faith cocked her head and sneered at Larry. "Not fully human? Changeling, fetch, or scion?" she growled angrily.

"That's the word! Oh crap! Scion! He's a scion!" I said as I stepped in front of Larry.

A scion was the offspring of a human and a magical being. Some had powers and some did not. A changeling was a fairy switched at birth with a human child. This could be for any number of reasons, ranging from saving the human child from disease with fairy magic to wanting to eat it and not pay for the meal. Worse was the fetch. A fetch was a magical construct of a child. It would grow to be loved by the parents of the missing child only to suddenly die.

Faith's expression softened with the knowledge that Larry was not left by a thief or an evil construct. He could still be evil, but at least it didn't involve kids. She gave him a smile.

"Faith Kane, this is Larry Lipowski. Larry, this is Faith," I said.

"Kane...like the Virginia Pack?" Larry asked.

Larry's head only came up to the middle of Faith's chest. She bent down so that they were eye to eye and said, "Woof."

Larry went pale. I put my arm around him to usher him past Faith and into the truck. I looked at Faith as I held the door open. She smiled at me and said, "Bark," as she got in. We hit the road, and I filled Larry in on what had happened.

"So Hung is off my back?" he asked.

"Why do you say that?" I asked.

"Trolls collect on the first attempt. It's in their nature, and something about them makes people go along with it. They either do it the first time or not at all. That's why the Bridge Boys work together," said Larry.

"Maybe. How many more Bridge Boys are there?" I asked.

"There are four total, so that leaves three," he said.

Great! There were still three damage resistant, super strong, and super violent trolls out there gunning for Larry. Plus, now I had this werewolf business to deal with. "Who wants food?" I asked.

"I could eat," Larry said.

"What are we eating?" Faith asked.

"Takeout. I have to get Larry behind closed doors," I said.

I had Larry call ahead to Kates's so that chef Orgoth could get our meals ready. Nine cheese steaks, nine double orders of fries, and the four cases of soda I got from the grocery store set me back $100.00. When we got to my place we ate. Faith and I each put away three cheese steaks, and Larry wisely kept his food out of our reach. I stepped outside while they finished dinner. Once I got into my truck and locked the doors, Horace climbed out of the bag. I handed him a cheese steak, fries, and soda.

"Thanks kid," he said.

Horace started eating while I texted Aaron. *"Hey Aaron. Picked up a new case. Eden thinks you can help with it. Working for a werewolf named Kodiak Black. You know him? Hit me back when you get a minute."*

With that part done, I started asking questions while I waited to hear back from my best friend.

"What do you think about all of this?" I asked.

"First off, you should fuck the werewolf chick," he told me.

"What the heck?" I asked.

"She wants you! The slight glances, the teasing of your friend, and what girl built like that just cries into a guy's neck? None! That girl isn't a crier. She's a screamer, and your name is on the edge of her lips, kid. Let me watch," he said.

"What the heck?" I repeated. "First of all, she looks sixteen. Second she is my friend, and third if and when I do have sex you do not get to watch!" I said.

"Yes, I do," Horace said.

"No, you do not!" I told him.

"Yes I do. In fact, I can get you laid. Girls dig guys with teddy bears," he said.

"No, they don't," I snapped.

"Sure they do. Guys with teddy bears are sensitive, boyish, and in need. Women like that kind of shit. You are a freaking gun toting, monster fighting, sword swinging knight with a magical teddy bear. You are the bad boy that they can never bring home to meet their parents with a soft side that only they can tend to…with sex," he told me.

I stared at Horace for a long time. He finished his sandwich and started licking his paws. I just sat there digesting what he had just told me. My teddy bear wanted to watch me have sex with a werewolf. There was a bad joke here, but there was also a plot for a porno movie.

"I need an adult," I said.

"No, you need to get laid. You haven't had sex since Kerri-Lynn left. It's good for you, kid," Horace said.

The mention of Kerri-Lynn hurt me more than it should have been able to. "Drop it," I said.

Horace shook his head, but he did not continue. He drank some of his soda and said, "You need to get moving. Hit the streets and get some info. Your witch friend would be good, but if the missing werewolf is in the city he didn't come in through normal channels. You know anyone on the shadier side of the street?"

"I do. But I can't take Larry," I said.

"Leave him here. Your wards are good enough to protect him. Do you have a spare phone?" Horace asked.

"Yeah, I have a few burner phones in my room," I said.

"Set me up with one and your number. I will be in your room. If anyone comes knocking I will text you," he said.

"Sounds like we have a plan," I said.

My phone buzzed with a text from Aaron. It said, *"Yeah, kind of. I know OF him. Why?"*

I replied, *"Contacted my office with a case to find a missing werewolf. Kodiak Black thinks the werewolf is in Baltimore."*

I set Horace up on my bed with a burner phone. I set Larry up in the living room with a shotgun filled with cold iron buck shot. I set my wards, and then Faith and I took to the streets.

# CHAPTER 13

I TOOK US to the hood. It's a cliché thing to say, but in a city plagued by drugs and violence you typically can find a hood. There were abandoned buildings, rundown houses, and vagrants on every other corner. The night life in Baltimore was filled with depravity and sin when the cameras were rolling. But the real night life of Baltimore was filled with more. There was magic running wild in this town.

The particular hood I was looking for wasn't one you just randomly walked through. It wasn't one where you would find crack and marijuana being sold by kids. Nor was it a place the police would frequently drive through to keep the peace. Sure, a cop car would come through every once in a while, but only if the cop driving was in the know or unlucky. This hood was the place for the magical beings of Baltimore to inhabit, and woe to any unsuspecting being that wandered in unprepared for the game.

I kept driving through intersections only to stop and look up. Faith caught on to my strangeness after the fourth intersection. She started looking out her window as well. After the seventh intersection she finally gave up.

"What the hell are you looking for? The street signs are on the corners, not in the air," she informed me.

"I'm not looking for street signs, I am looking for sneakers," I told her. I hung a right and took us further down Washington Boulevard.

"I thought we were looking for Everett. You're shoe shopping?" Faith asked.

I pulled up to another intersection and looked up. "No. I'm looking for shoes hanging from power lines," I said.

"Why?" she asked.

"Do you know what it typically means when you see shoes hanging from power lines?" I asked her.

"No. Why the hell would you hang shoes from a power line?" she asked.

"Typically, it means that you can buy drugs nearby," I said.

Faith looked out of her window and pointed out a pair of white sneakers hanging on the next set of power lines. "So now you're gonna buy drugs?"

"Nope. White sneakers aren't what we are looking for," I said. I turned again and smiled when I saw them. I pointed up to the power lines at a pair of red sneakers. "Red is what we want."

"Why red ones?" she asked.

"Red sneakers mean that someone around here is looking to trade power for power, knowledge for knowledge," I said.

"Who does that?" she asked.

"Street mages," I said.

We parked and got out of the truck. I was packing my black Desert Eagle, the snub-nose, and my sword was strapped across my back. Faith had her revolver and the whole werewolf thing going for her. She had thrown on a stylish leather jacket for the weather and I had my coat. I grabbed a plastic bag off the seat and locked up the truck. The rain was still coming down lightly as we walked down the street.

"What the hell is a street mage?" she asked me.

I thought about how to explain it to her. "Do you know how magic works in people? Or rather, how magic is expressed?" I asked.

"Yeah, you turn into a werewolf, or you do other stuff that normal people can't," she said.

"Right but wrong," I said. "Magic isn't any one thing. It's in everything. The ability to wield magic is what we are talking about."

"I don't get it," she said.

We turned into an alley, and I was quick to watch the shadows. "Alright, let's say you and I both have a small talent for wielding magic. How do we measure it? Do you know?" I asked.

She shook her head.

"One way is to teach a person a simple spell and have them perform it as many times as they can, but the most used way is to let the person write their name," I said.

"What does that do? Anyone can write their name," she said.

"Not true. They could be illiterate. But when a person writes their name, they do it with their own style, their own handwriting. Magic always expresses itself when we create something, and that includes writing our name. That's why no two people have the same handwriting. Someone with a small talent will have a mediocre style of handwriting. A major talent will have a lavish and magnificent style," I said.

We came out of the alley and onto another street. We kept walking, and I noted that there was no one else on the streets tonight. Faith looked all around us. She sniffed the air time and again only to get angrier and angrier.

"What's wrong?" I asked.

"I can't get a scent," she said. "And I still don't get this magic stuff," she said.

"Well don't worry about that part. A street mage is a mage that learned their magical trade on the street instead of from a master of the art. Most of them don't even understand their power. Worse off, most of them discovered their power too late and had no way to express it before it got bad," I said.

"What do you mean," she asked.

"Well, a person has to release their magic before it builds up too much for them to contain it. Kind of like having a full cup, only instead of water we are talking about magic."

"So, either they drink it, or it overflows?"

We turned down another street. "Yes. The problem is when you don't have a way to express all of that magic. It just keeps building and building. At some point you hopefully find a way to express yourself like this," I said as I pointed to a huge mural on the side of the building next to us.

It was a rendition of Black Jesus on drums, Hispanic Jesus on guitar, and White Jesus on keyboard. Even at night in the rain and darkness the mural seemed more than just a tag. It had depth and not just shading. It was as if the artist had plucked a three-dimensional thought of these three saviors having a jam session from their head and transferred it completely to this wall with the use of spray-paint.

"It's beautiful," said Faith.

"Because magic, creation, is beautiful. The greatest artists of our world were probably mages and never knew it. Magic expresses itself mostly as art. Any art from calligraphy to dance," I said.

Faith looked at me with a sad expression on her face. "And if it doesn't? If the magic just keeps building up?" she asked.

"Then you get people like me!" a voice said from across the street.

Faith spun around. She growled as she dropped low, ready to spring the twenty feet across the street to where the voice had come from. I had my hand in my pocket and was clenching the snub-nose. There was a man across the street from us standing beneath a streetlight that hadn't been working a moment ago. He was a Caucasian man with a long-grizzled beard. He was taller than me but rail thin. He wore a black raincoat over an oversized fleece shirt and a Baltimore Ravens t-shirt. Ragged jeans and worn shoes finished off his outfit. He stood in the rain with the wind blowing his raincoat behind him like a cloak. My coat just hung lifelessly as usual.

We squared off on opposite sides of the street. The rain created an awkward mist around our legs. Faith continued to growl, so I put a comforting hand on her shoulder. She stopped growling but never looked away from the man.

"Well, well, well, well," the man said. "Sir Michael White, defender of the great city of Baltimore. Welcome to the land of alleys and gutters. Welcome to the domain of the unheard, unseen, and unwanted. Welcome to the dumpster of this merry land. Welcome to the Hood of the Second City!"

"Hello to you too, Willy. How are you?" I asked.

"Cold. Wet. Poor. Hungry," he said. "Also, I am a little scared of that girl. She looks like she wants to hurt me."

"Michael, do you know him?" Faith asked. "I can't smell too well in the rain, but he doesn't smell right."

"Well, he is a mage," I said.

"Mage or not he doesn't smell right," she told me.

I narrowed my eyes. Willy was a homeless man that had a lot of power. By a lot of power, I mean he was one of the most powerful casters I had ever met, though I only knew a handful. Eden was a powerful wizard with decades, maybe centuries of training behind her. Willy, on the other hand, was a mad mage driven insane by his gift. I didn't know how old he was, and until now I had no idea that his insane brand of magic might be identifiable by other magical beings. That, however, was a question for another day.

"I know him, and he is pretty helpful. Aren't you Willy?" I called to him.

Willy looked left and right. He then lifted his right hand and stuck his index finger into his nose. He started rooting around in his nostril as he spoke to me. "What can I do for you tonight, oh great defender of the downtrodden?"

"Is there somewhere we can go and talk? I would rather we did business out of the open," I told him.

Willy pulled his finger from his nose and wiped it on his coat. He turned to his right and started walking. I nudged Faith and told her to stay close to me. We walked further down the street to an old one-story building. It was burned out but still standing. The roof was mostly intact, and some of the windows had survived. The front door was just a gate of rusted bars with no lock, but a thick metal chain was wrapped between the movable bars and the stationary bars.

Willy pulled the chain off the gate and walked inside. We followed. The inside of the building was decorated in hobo chic. There was a bed of piled cardboard boxes and a beaten-up mattress in the corner. Lawn and patio chairs made a comfortable living room. A barrel filled with burnable items sat beneath a hole in the roof. A stolen park picnic table was set up as a dinner table with a beaten and dented charcoal grill sitting off to the side as a kitchen. And what bachelor pad isn't complete without a spool for a coffee table? Willy's spool was cleaner than mine, but mine had a nice tablecloth on it.

The ceiling, walls, and floor of the building displayed more spray paint art. There were pictures of angels, animals, fairies, police cars, storms, and witches. Each one was a work of art worthy of the namesakes of the Ninja Turtles. Then there were the runes and sigils painted all around and over the artwork. Willy had defaced his own art with magical wards, and even without opening my mind I could feel their power.

"Welcome to my humble abode," Willy said.

"This place is beautiful, sort of," Faith said.

"Willy, I need some information. Can you help me out?" I asked.

"Well that depends!" Willy said. "I have plenty of information, but what do you have to trade?"

I tossed Willy the plastic bag I was carrying. He caught it and pulled it open. He snatched the 18-inch sandwich out of the bag and started ripping the aluminum foil off of it. He bit into the cheese steak inside and closed his eyes as he experienced true bliss. I let him get in a few more bites before I tried to strike a deal.

"So can you help me out, Willy?"

Willy's eyes popped open, and he shook his head in the negative. "A single sandwich, though surely crafted by one gifted by the gods, is not worth the information you seek," he told me.

"He isn't gonna help us?" Faith asked.

"Willy, how do you know what information I seek?"

"Oh, Knight of Innocence, you walk in circles that others dare not. You consort with the witch, the vampire, and the priest, but rarely do you learn. The wise listen and the streets talk. The streets have told me that you are looking for Everett Black. They have also told me that any information regarding werewolves in this city is more valuable than this sandwich," Willy said as he held up the cheese steak. He stealthily took another bite while glaring at me.

"Willy, there are fries and a soda in that bag, too," I said.

Willy looked into the bag by sticking his head into it. He pulled his head out with a mouth full of fries and started chewing while he spoke. "A deal has been struck! For a combo meal is always a bargain. Is there ketchup?"

"Bottom of the bag."

As Willy plopped down to eat his meal Faith whispered to me, "So now he is going to help us because you gave him a sandwich?"

"He is going to help us because *he was hungry* and I gave him a sandwich. Look around you. This isn't the Ritz, and no one comes down here to hand out food or blankets. A kind gesture, even with the intent to get something in return, is often appreciated by those that have nothing," I said.

I moved closer to Willy, and the street mage looked up from his feast. "I need to know all that you know about Everett Black, Willy. Do you know who took him or why? Do you know where he is?"

"You are a black man with the name of White in search of another black man with the name of Black. I am a white man with the name of Willy. White wants Black. Willy knows White wants Black. Willy doesn't know where Black is. Black doesn't know where Black is. But you know who knows?" asked Willy.

"Who?" I asked.

"G.I. Joe! That real American hero! He fights for freedom wherever there's trouble!" Willy said.

"Willy, I appreciate the reference to a truly awesome cartoon, but—" I started to say, but Willy cut me off.

"Over land and sea and air!" Willy shouted.

"This guy is crazy," Faith said.

I stared at Willy for a moment and then went over the folder Kodiak Black had handed me in my mind. Everett Black was taken from his home by force. The pictures in the file had shown a home that looked like a war zone. There had been holes in the walls with debris everywhere. The file said that grenades and rockets were used to attack his home, and after all of that he had been taken alive. When you take someone you have to move them, and the only way to do that is by land, by sea, or by air.

"Crap!" I said.

Faith turned to me. "What?" she asked.

"They don't know how he was taken from the pack. We don't know! And I'm guessing you don't know either, do you Willy?"

"Oh no, no, no. I know two things that you don't know. First, I know that I need to go to the bathroom. Second, I know that this rain is a bitch," he said. He looked up at the opening in his ceiling and then at Faith. He shrugged and said, "But not like you. You are a bitch but not in that way."

Faith snarled at Willy. "What do you know about me, old man?" she asked.

Willy looked at Faith while he chewed a mouth full of fries. He swallowed then blinked, and when his eyes opened he was a different man. Willy no longer looked at us with the eyes of a homeless lunatic. His eyes were more akin to Priest Greyshadow, Kodiak Black, and my Grandpa Franklin White. Willy's eyes were the eyes of a man that had seen some horrible shit, had done some horrible shit, and was ready to do even more horrible shit at the drop of a hat. When he spoke to Faith he still sounded like a mad mage, but his words carried the weight of experience earned through trial.

"I know that you are a werewolf that has left her pack. I see no bonds connecting you to an alpha, and I know that lone wolves tend to die when the moon calls. I know that you have smelled danger, but that is a very small aroma in a world of scents, wolf pup. There is much you can do but much you need to learn. In short, she who has not smelt it has not dealt with it."

It got quiet in the room. I saw Faith's body twitch, and her already tight clothing looked a lot tighter. She started to shake, and I could hear a low growl starting in her chest. It didn't sound like a sound that a human could make. Her long hair seemed to get longer before my eyes. I started to reach for Faith so that I could try to calm her down. Just before my hand touched her shoulder her upper body bulged with added muscle. I stepped back reflexively, and Faith lurched forward.

Willy belched. It was loud, spittle flew from his mouth, and when he was done his eyes glazed over as he rubbed his stomach with both hands. "Yummy, yummy, yummy," said the mad mage.

Faith stood upright in shock. Her extra muscle fell away, and her hair shortened. Faith started to shake again, but this time from laughter instead of a building growl. She folded over as she laughed and slapped her knee. "Willy, you really are a loony wizard, aren't you?" she asked.

In reply Willy farted. Faith cringed and stormed off to the door. I started to follow her.

"Thanks Willy," I said. "If you happen to come across anything else please let me know."

"Oh, Innocent Knight, there is one more thing you should know," Willy said. I looked back at him. "The Bridge Boys always get their toll."

I nodded and walked out into the rain to stand next to Faith. "You okay?" I asked.

She nodded.

"I don't mean about what happened in there," I said.

"Shut up Michael," she said.

"If you need…" I started.

"Shut up!' she said, and she shoved me with one arm. I went rushing down the sidewalk. I scrambled just to keep my feet under me, but in the end I fell over and rolled for a few feet. As I climbed back to my feet, I realized that in my need to be there for my friend I had forgotten that I was dealing with a super strong and temperamental monster.

"Are we done here?" she asked me.

"Yeah," I said. "Let's get out of here."

The walk back to my truck was a symphony of falling rain. Faith was angry and didn't want to talk about it. I could respect that. We all have our demons. It just worried me that hers had claws and fangs. When we reached the truck I moved to the driver's side. I had just put the key into the lock when something leapt down from the bed of my truck to tackle me.

Faith screamed as I tumbled away with my assailant. Hands scrambled for purchase around my throat and eyes as we rolled through the watery street. I wasn't fighting just yet, but I was trying to put some distance between me and whatever was rolling around with me. When I stopped face down on the ground I pushed up as powerfully as I could with my arms. I expected my attacker to force my head back down, and that is exactly what happened. What they didn't expect was for me to reach up with one arm to grab their shoulder and to push off with my legs. Our combined strength flipped us over onto my attacker's back. I slammed my elbow down into where their ribs should have been then rolled away.

I got to my feet and took in the situation. My attacker was dressed in rain-soaked rags. He was older than me and looked like he was in dire need of a sandwich. He scrambled to his feet to face me. I saw his rotten teeth bared beneath a long and ragged beard. There was another man squaring off with Faith. He hadn't gotten the drop on her, but he had come at her while she was distracted by worrying about me. He stood between her and my truck.

"Faith you okay?" I asked.

"Yep. Just about to kill this asshole," she said.

"Faith, we don't kill humans."

"Michael, you dumbass, they aren't human. They're werewolves!"

Fear raced up my spine as that realization settled in on me. I didn't want to shoot with Faith standing just behind my target, so I turned and ran across the street toward an area that had once been an alleyway between two buildings. One of the buildings had collapsed from fire, or maybe it had been demolished. Either way it was an empty lot with room to throw down.

"Faith, follow me!" I yelled.

The werewolf girl spun on her heels and darted away from the other werewolves before they could react. She was beside me in an instant, and then she slowed down to match my speed. We leapt a two-foot wall of brick that separated the lot from the street. On came the two werewolves. They couldn't resist with our backs turned and us running from them. It was just like in the movies. Unlike the movies we did not let them catch up. We both skidded to a stop while spinning and drawing our revolvers. We fired and filled the night with the sound of gun shots. The man Faith shot at fell back like he had hit a wall while the one I shot fell forward.

My snub nose was empty. I don't know how many times Faith had shot. I saw her reach in her pocket for more bullets when someone started clapping. I looked past the dead werewolves to find four more people standing between us and my truck. Two I recognized as the homeless guys from the bar last night. Eddy still looked like a jerk, and Johnny was walking without crutches. The other two were new—a man that looked like he was strung out on something and a woman that looked even worse.

"Crap, I didn't think they would find them so fast, Johnny," Eddy said as he walked over onto the lot.

"Do we really have to do this, Eddy?" Johnny asked.

"Yes!" Eddy roared. "That piece of shit needs to die!"

Faith looked at me with a raised eyebrow. "Just so you know they are werewolves too."

"Gee, you think?" I snapped back. I wasn't going to let her know I had just figured it out.

"Hey, you assholes, get up!" Eddy yelled.

The two guys we had shot started squirming on the ground. They apparently weren't as dead as I thought. They worked their way back to their feet and looked none the worse for wear.

"See! What did I tell you! Fucking immortality and eternal youth! Bullets can't even kill us!" Eddy preached.

"Just let me find some silver bullets," I mumbled.

All the werewolves, including Faith, looked at me. Four of them were a good fifty feet away, and they still heard me over the fall of the rain. Eddy looked around at his friends then squared up his shoulders before grinning at me.

"Well, I guess that means you don't have any right now, right?" he asked. He didn't wait for an answer before he charged me yelling, "Kill him!"

I had gotten distracted, so of course I completely forgot about reloading. Luckily Faith hadn't. She leveled her gun and fired six shots before the werewolves could close on us. She emptied her six-shooter into the poor bastard she had shot the first time and the one that I had shot as well. Still, she wasn't packing silver ammo, so eventually they would get back up again.

Faith holstered her gun and bared her teeth. She took a deep breath and jutted her head forward as she roared in defiance. The other werewolves skidded to a stop. All eyes went to Faith as her roar faded into a growl. Eddy and his buddies looked from me to Faith with confusion in their eyes. Two of them backed off a few steps, but Eddy and another turned their attention fully to Faith. They went at her without giving me a second thought. One of the ones on the ground scrambled up to go at her as well.

Johnny and the other two came at me. I pocketed my revolver as I drew my black Desert Eagle. Johnny leapt at me before I could level the gun and punched me in the gut. I stumbled backward as I doubled over. I fell onto my back but managed to hold onto my gun. When they closed on me I swung my arm up and started firing wildly at them. I struggled for breath as I kept squeezing the trigger of my gun. I managed to get air back into my lungs just as I clicked on empty. I scrambled up to a crouching position and found the werewolves shielding themselves with their arms but otherwise unharmed. I had missed with every single shot.

"Okay, plan B," I said as I drew the Sword of Innocence from its sheath. I held the sword out to my right side in a one-handed grip. The light of the street-lamps reflected off of the blade, and the werewolves took in the sight of my sword. I could feel the power of the weapon thrumming in my hands, but that power was still at rest. "Seriously? Six evil werewolves are trying to kill us, and you don't glow? You aren't going to cut through the night? Not even a spark of white fire? How did I end up with the temperamental sword?"

Johnny growled and charged at me again. I still didn't have a full set of lungs, but I had to get into the fight. I met his charge with a forward thrust that brought me to my feet. He skidded to a stop and fell onto his back to avoid the blade. Before I could angle the sword to go after him the other two werewolves came leaping at me.

One of them landed a punch in my ribs and it knocked me back. They attacked with reckless abandon, and as they landed blow after blow I realized two things. The first was that I was in trouble. The second was that they didn't know how to fight. They were just flailing wildly. That punch to my ribs was awkward, and the werewolf's knuckles barely grazed me. Another punch to my gut missed by a mile. They kept stumbling into their attacks, and if they had taken a second to coordinate they could have taken me out without much effort. As it was, a flurry of clumsy fists fell over me, and I had to rush backward to avoid them.

As I threw up blocks with my left arm and worked my sword in short slashes with my right to keep the werewolves at bay I took another punch to the ribs. At some point I expected claws, but instead of using claws or fangs they were just throwing wild punches. I caught a glimpse of Faith's fight out of the corner of my eye. Eddy and his buddies had swarmed her. They were throwing punches and kicks. It was three against one, so of course some of the blows were landing. I had to get over there to help her.

The werewolf on my left kicked at my left leg. I dashed to my right to avoid the blow. Their punches had more power behind them than an emaciated human should have been able to produce, so I attributed it to werewolf strength. A kick from them would have been more than I could have handled. I had caught the third werewolf off guard with my sudden rush to the side, so I thought to keep running until I could jump into the fray with Faith. Johnny came skidding in front of me to put a stop to that idea. I could hear the other werewolves coming behind me. I brought my sword across in a slash at Johnny's throat. He ducked under the attack, and I kicked him in the face. I felt his nose crunch under my steel-toed boot.

As Johnny fell away I spun around to bring my sword around in a back hand slash. The second werewolf dropped to the ground to avoid the blade, but the third wasn't fast enough. My sword cut across his stomach, and blood gushed from the wound. He fell to his knees as he screamed.

"You cut him!" screamed the second werewolf. He looked at me like I was the monster here. I watched as he scrambled away from me.

His friend was bleeding, but he had enough energy to scramble away as well. I turned back to Johnny and found his face a bloody mess. I stepped toward him, and he rolled away from me. I looked over at Faith's fight where Eddy and the other werewolves were being out matched. Faith had dropped one and was backing the remaining two away with punches that knocked them away by feet when she connected.

"Why are you attacking us?" I asked Johnny.

"Cause Eddy said to!" he whined. He literally whined like an animal.

I looked back at the two other werewolves that I was fighting and realized that they didn't want to attack me. They didn't want to fight at all. Eddy had commanded them, and they had obeyed.

I looked down at Johnny and said, "Your friend isn't cut deep enough to kill him. Get him some help. Leave!"

Johnny got up and ran to his injured friend. He and the other unscathed werewolf helped the one I had cut to his feet. They ran off at a brisk pace that made me think werewolf number three was going to be fine. I turned back to Faith and decided that Eddy was not going to be fine. I ran over to Faith's fight. I circled out to the side so that they didn't see me coming. When I got close enough I darted behind Eddy and yelled, "Hey asshole!" He turned around just in time to see my right fist coming across. "Impact," I yelled just before I connected with his jaw.

The sound of bones breaking drowned out the sound of rain falling. Teeth, lots of teeth, went flying from his mouth. Eddy flipped over and spun around in the air before hitting the ground. Faith and the other two werewolves looked at me with looks of shock on their faces.

I leveled my sword so that they could take in the view of its fine edge. "Take this asshole and leave, unless you want some of what he just got," I said.

The female werewolf reached down to help Eddy to his feet, but he was out cold. The other male werewolf came to help her, and they carried him off into the night. Faith growled at them and tried to lunge at them, but I grabbed her around the waist.

"Hold it Faith. We need to leave," I said.

Faith spun to face me. "Why? They attacked us! They need to die!" she snarled.

"Because you're bleeding!" I said.

Faith looked down at herself. She put her hand on her right side and found it covered in blood when she lifted it to her face. Her expression turned to one of puzzlement. "I never felt his claws," she said. I hustled her back to the Rust Bucket just as the sirens started in the distance. I got her into the truck and gave her my shirt to press against her wound. When I pulled off I fished my phone out of my jacket to call Larry. There were several missed calls on my phone from the past three minutes. There was also a text.

The text read: "People are banging on the door and demanding that you open it. The scion is scared shitless and has no idea how to use a shotgun. Humans are dumb. You are dumb. Bring me some tequila, and do you have Wi-Fi?"

# CHAPTER 14

THE SOUND OF sirens was in the distance as we melded into the night's traffic. I looked down at Faith's abdomen. She had pulled her shirt up to press my tee shirt to her side. I was driving shirtless, which wasn't a problem because it was hot in the cab of my truck. I mean really hot. There was steam everywhere.

"Michael, will you turn the heat down? Lord the windows are fogging up," Faith panted.

"The heat's off. Are you generating heat by healing or something?" I asked.

"Michael. did you just ask me if I was in heat?" Faith asked.

I stuttered through a few responses before shaking my head and saying, "No ma'am."

Faith laughed at me. "You are too easy. Michael."

I shrugged and laughed at myself. The temperature began to drop as my head started to clear. I looked down at Faith's wound and saw blood clotting around its edges. I touched my own ribs and wondered if I healed as fast as she did. If my healing was on par with a werewolf's then I might just make it through this mess. My hand was mostly healed from my fight with Hung T. Roll, but it still ached, and my weapons still didn't feel right in my hand. As it stood Eddy was going to be fine in a day or so, and he was going to be ticked.

"We have trouble at my place. Can you reload my gun?" I asked her.

The words had barely left my mouth when she snatched up my Desert Eagle, ejected the magazine, slapped a new one in, and chambered a round. "Damn, I love this gun!"

"There's another one in my bag," I said.

She pulled out my second Desert Eagle and checked the magazine and chamber. She put the gun in its clip-on holster and handed it to me. "You are gonna need these if we have another fight. And try hitting something this time," she told me.

"I hit the guy the first time," I grumbled.

"No, you didn't. I shot him when you missed," Faith said.

Somewhere in the back of my mind I knew it was true. I replayed the fight in my head and keenly felt that old fear of harming another human being. I fought monsters, and it was easy to get my head into the space of being a hero. The problem was that heroes didn't kill people. I had slayed demons and killed monsters, but I just couldn't bring myself to kill a human. It went against everything I had ever believed. I'm a Christian…not the best…not the worst, maybe. I am not supposed to kill my fellow man or woman.

I slipped the second holster onto my hip as I pulled onto my street. I drove into my gravel parking lot and jumped out to face two men in long coats. The wind had their coats flapping around them like medieval cloaks. As I pulled mine on it clung to me lifelessly. I made no attempt to hide either of my sidearms.

Both men faced me squarely. One was short but wide with muscle. He was older than me by a good deal. The other was tall but not as tall as me. He wasn't as muscular as his friend, but he looked capable. He looked like he was around my age. They each had a sword strapped to their bodies. The smaller man had a broadsword strapped across his back, and the taller man had a long sword on his right hip. As they pulled back their coats I saw that each had a gun strapped on their hips as well.

I knew right away what they were but not who they were. "You two must be with the Templars," I said.

The shorter one nodded. "That we are. Who the hell are you, boy?"

I took a long look at him. He was 5'5" and about fifty pounds heavier than me. From the looks of him it was all muscle. His mid length hair was dark and matted by the rain. He had a thick black beard with a swath of gray on the right of his chin. A scar tore down the center of his forehead, slit his left nostril, and the top of his lip. He stood calmly, but his posture worried me. His hands were limp at his sides and his feet looked flat to the ground. I had seen my grandpa stand like that, and my grandpa could kick my butt from now until the second coming if he wanted to.

"I'm Michael White," I said. The taller man eased his hand onto the handle of his gun at the mention of my name. "Sir Michael White, Knight of the Order of the Crucifixion."

"Wielder of the sword of Judas," sneered the tall man.

"Wielder of the Sword of Innocence," I corrected him. "The sword once carried by Judas."

"So, you admit it," he said.

"Admit what? My name?" I asked.

The older man held his arm out to calm down the younger man. "Easy now, Lincoln. He is a Knight of the Order, and the grandson of Franklin White at that. We came here to do a job, not start a fight," the older man said.

Lincoln spit off to the side and said, "Sir, you have to be kidding me. Why the hell is a member of the Black Guard running errands for Judas?"

My ears perked up at the younger knight's statement. I saw a flash of irritation cross the older knight's face. He shook his head tiredly before waving his arm at an air-tight storage bin that was sitting in front of my door.

"We came here to deliver these texts to you," the older man said. "Your roommate said that he had a 'fully automatic shotgun with armor piercing bullets.' He also said you were going to attack us with your pack of werewolves." He raised an eyebrow at me.

"He has a shotgun because some trolls want to kill him. I just have one werewolf with me. She's in the truck," I said as I hooked my thumb over my shoulder towards the Rust Bucket.

The older man narrowed his eyes warily before slowly nodding. The younger man gritted his teeth and looked past me to the opened door of my truck. His eyes narrowed, and I saw him reach around his back. His arm came forward clumsily like he was having trouble rotating his shoulder. He jerked his arm up, and he was holding a revolver that looked too big for his hands. The barrel was longer than normal, and the cylinder was huge. It looked like it could hold shotgun shells. It must have been a long night because it barely registered that he was pointing it directly at me.

Lincoln grunted as he thumbed back the hammer. I came to my senses and had to force myself not to move. If I did then Faith would get hit instead of me. The older man grabbed Lincoln's gun hand, punched him in the gut, and spun him around. In the time it took me to cross my arms over my chest the older man had pinned Lincoln on the ground with his gun hand behind his back and a hand on the back of his head.

"What the…" Lincoln started to say, but the older man pulled his head up and smashed it back against the ground.

Lincoln screamed in pain as the older man wrenched the gun from his hand. He popped the cylinder out and dropped six long bullets to the ground. Then he stood and looked down at Lincoln before kicking him in the side. "Get up and wait in the car," he told the younger man.

Lincoln stood up, dusted himself off, and glared at me while he wiped blood from his face. He looked a lot younger than I had thought in that moment. The older man shoved the unloaded gun into Lincoln's chest and repeated his orders. Lincoln took the weapon and did as he was told. He walked over to the sidewalk and got into the passenger side of a black sedan.

That left me alone in the rain with the older man. He walked over to me and looked me up and down. I had almost a foot on him but so did Lincoln. He nodded once and then held out his hand. I took it and we shook. But he didn't let me go when I pulled away.

"Do you know what the Black Guard is?" he asked me.

"Yeah," I said angrily. "You're the Church's assassins."

He shook his head in the negative. "No. We are the Church's police. We keep the peace just like you and your fellow Knights of the Order. Only we fight the good guys when they go bad."

"You kill anyone the Church wants dead," I said.

He nodded. "Peace isn't always created with a pen, boy. Anyway, my name is Sir Liam Keegan. It would be best if you kept this little incident to yourself, as I will be keeping the fact you are harboring a werewolf in Baltimore to myself. Have a good night, Sir Michael," he said as he let me go.

Keegan walked over to the sedan, but I called after him before he opened the door. "Why would anyone care that I have a werewolf in Baltimore?" I asked.

Keegan looked at me over his shoulder and said, "Because a knight harboring a werewolf won't be looked on favorably by many of our superiors. Tell your grandfather that I said hello." With that he got into the car and drove off.

I watched them leave. When I was sure they were gone, I told Larry to open the door. Then I went and got Faith out of the truck. She had lost a lot of blood. I picked her up and carried her as she argued with me. I set her down on the couch and got Larry to help me drag in the storage bin. I grabbed my gear out of the truck, and Larry gathered up all six of those huge bullets. Then I locked us inside behind my wards.

I knelt next to Faith and reached to inspect her wound. The moment I touched her she grabbed my arm and growled at me. Amber eyes stared at me while she snarled through bared fangs. She squeezed my wrist, and I had to strike her arm to free myself. I backed away from her, and she scrambled off of her back into a crouched position. Faith growled again as she readied herself to pounce.

"Faith, you have to calm down. You are bleeding and I am trying to help," I said. I kept my eyes on her, but out of the corner of my eye I could see Larry standing by the kitchen clenching my shotgun.

Faith pushed off with her legs and collapsed to the ground in a heap. I ran over to her, but she snarled at me. Ignoring her I reached down and hauled her back onto the couch. She struggled but I pinned her down. Then she shoved me so hard that she threw me over the back of the couch. I hit the ground face first.

"Should I shoot her?" Larry asked. He was holding the shotgun with the butt end directly in front of his face as he aimed at Faith.

"No!" I yelled at him. "Put that thing down and get one of the first aid kits from the kitchen."

Larry ran off to get the first aid kit. I pulled my phone out and dialed a newly added number. It rang twice before a male voice answered, "Did you find my uncle?"

"No, West. What I did find was a bunch of werewolves," I said.

"A pack," West Black said.

"Huh?" I asked.

"A pack. A 'bunch' or group of werewolves is called a pack. Why are you calling me if you haven't found my uncle?"

"Faith is hurt. One of the werewolves clawed her beneath her arm along her rib cage," I told him.

"You said she was under your protection," he growled.

"And she is," I said. "I protected her and brought her home to safety. The problem is that she isn't healing and won't let me help her. She is too freaking strong to hold down, so how the heck do I help her?"

"She needs a pack! I told you that. She was born into a pack, she has never been on her own, and she has never had to rely on just herself to deal with being a werewolf. She can heal as long as there is no silver in her wound, but without a pack it will be painful and take longer than it should. Her best bet is to return to her human form," he told me.

"She's already in her human form!" I yelled into the phone.

There was silence on the line for a solid minute. When West spoke again I could hear something powerful lurking behind his very human-sounding voice. "You are telling me that you took a packless werewolf into a fight in her human form? What kind of fool are you?"

"I didn't take her into a fight. We got jumped," I countered.

Faith growled. I looked up to see her climbing over the couch. Blood was soaking through her shirt turning it from blue to purple. It was on her arms and staining her pants, too. She looked horrible. Worse than that, she looked hungry.

"Michael," she croaked. "Get…away…please," she told me.

"Put me on speaker!" said West.

"Don't werewolves have super hearing?" I asked.

"Do it!" roared West.

I hit the speaker button. "You're on speaker!"

Faith's clawed hand came down at my throat. I could feel her claws digging in when West Black's voice thundered through my home.

"Faith Kane!" roared the North Carolina Alpha. "Hold!"

Faith stopped moving. Her body was frozen with her eyes wide and her claws digging into my flesh just enough to scare me a whole lot. She snarled and pressed her claws deeper as if she were trying to prove to herself that she could.

"Faith Kane, you will not kill that human. You will not kill or eat anyone that offers you no harm," said West.

Faith roared, and her roar was met with a roar that shook the floor beneath my back. Faith recoiled, letting my throat go in the process, and snarled at the phone in my hand. I dropped the phone and scrambled away.

"You are a dominant, but you will submit to me, Faith. You will obey me," West said in that very human sounding voice of his.

"I am not yours!" growled Faith.

"Who is more dominant?" West asked.

Faith roared, and again she was met with a roar that drowned out her own. She snarled and shook in frustration. Then she did something strange. Faith tilted her head so that her neck was fully exposed above my phone.

"Do you submit?" West asked.

"Yes," she growled through gritted teeth.

"Remove your clothing and transform to your wolf form. You will not bite. You will not claw. You will harm no one," West instructed her.

Faith growled as she rolled back over the couch. Her gun belt went flying toward my bedroom. Her pants and boots went toward my front door. Her shirt came flying over the couch to land at my feet. Her bra followed, and her panties landed on my weight bench. Faith groaned and then she screamed. She thrashed on the ground knocking my spool away from her and my couch back toward me. I heard bones breaking and a sound like meat being pulled apart.

"What the heck?" I asked.

"Faith, you will be silent as you change," West said. The room went quiet. I no longer heard bones breaking or flesh ripping. "You may want to get her some food, Mr. White. A lot of food. Raw meat would be best."

"Okay," I said. I grabbed the envelope with all the cash in it out of my room. I came back to grab Larry and found him stripping out of his boxers. I snatched up his clothing, my phone, and our coats. Then I hauled him out to the truck. Before closing the door, I caught a glimpse of Faith somewhere between being a human and a wolf. Her outer skin was gone, just gone! She was nothing but new flesh, raw muscle, and bone. Her face was elongated, and her jaw was unhinged. Her hands were balled into fists with bones rupturing through her knuckles. Her eyes scared me the most. They were filled with pain. "Larry, find me an all-night butcher shop. West, what the heck is happening in my apartment?"

"Who the hell is Larry?" asked West.

"Half Leprechaun. Client. Not a threat. Moving on," I said.

"You have never seen a werewolf transform?" he asked me.

"I have seen Faith do it in a matter of seconds, and it never hurt her," I said.

"Faith was a daughter of the Virginia pack. There are forty-seven werewolves in that pack. A pack absorbs the pain of the change. A pack lends its strength to each other. A pack offers control to a werewolf. This girl has never made the change without the safety net of the pack to protect her. It will likely take her half an hour to change, if she survives it," West said.

"If?" I asked. "What do you mean?"

"Exactly what I said. The change is not easy, Mr. White. It's not like in the movies where a werewolf just gets up and starts walking in its new body. The change can kill the first time, and anytime that the person isn't willing to fight through it. Faith has never had to fight through it," he told me.

"I need to help her," I said.

"We can't go back there!" yelled Larry.

"No. You need to find her food. If she lives she will need to eat. The more food you give her, the easier her recovery and the next change will be," said West.

"How much meat should I get? Three or four pounds of hamburger?" I asked.

"About how much do you think she weighs?" asked West.

"Um…I am never supposed to verbally associate an actual number to a woman's weight," I replied.

"That may be the smartest thing you have said today. However much you think she weighs I would buy that much in red meat," said West.

"What?" I yelled.

"For the first change. For the next she will just need a full stomach. Her body will gradually adjust to the change, and she will start to naturally recover from it," West said.

"Fine. I will call you when I get back home," I said as I hung up my phone. "Larry did you find me a butcher?"

"Not on this side of town. I found a Walmart," the still nude Leprechaun said.

"Okay, so next question. Why are you naked?" I asked.

"I don't know! One minute I was holding the first aid kit, and then the guy on your phone told Faith to take off her clothes. The next thing I know I am stripping as fast as I can," Larry said with a shrug.

"Okay, do you mind getting dressed?" I asked.

"Not at all," he told me. When he didn't start getting dressed, I motioned to his clothes, and he took the hint.

We went to Walmart. We grabbed about two-hundred-forty pounds of hamburger and steak. Then we stood in the checkout line for fifteen minutes. It's always odd when there are twenty-five registers, only three are open, and you can see a minimum of thirteen employees walking around doing absolutely nothing. Then I had the pleasure of giving the cashier $1197.07 to cover my order. After a quick stop for gas, which cost me $42.61, we made it back to the apartment.

I called West, and he picked up on the first ring. "What is your address?" he asked.

"I am not giving my address to the son of the scariest man I have ever met," I said.

"So, you still insist on doing this on your own?" he asked.

"Yes! My friend, my city, my problem! Now what do I do?" I replied.

"You feed her. I commanded her not to harm you, but she may try if she is too far gone. Don't die, Mr. White," he said before hanging up on me.

"Okay Larry, I am going to leave the door open. Don't come in. If it looks bad, get in the truck and go to the church. Priest Greyshadow will know what to do," I said. I handed him my truck keys, and we walked up to my door. I took a deep breath, and then with several bags of raw meat in one hand and my sword in the other I had Larry unlock and open my apartment door. Then I stepped into my home to either help or kill my friend.

# Chapter 15

FAITH WAS STILL on the living room floor. She had completed her transformation, but she wasn't breathing. I eased my sword ahead of me as I made my way over to her. The closer I got to her the more idiotic I felt. Faith in her human shape was faster and stronger than me. If she was alive then I was a dead man. Holy sword or not she would kill me before I could even think of defending myself. But I had to do this if she was to survive.

I eased along the wall until I was in front of her. There on my floor was a wolf as long as my couch. She wasn't moving, and if she was breathing it wasn't noticeable. I took a cautious step toward her, and light stirred on my sword. It wasn't the light from my apartment. This light was a soft blue, like the kind you would wrap an infant in. It only stirred on the center of my blade, never moving toward the edge. I had never seen it do that before. Faith's eyes opened and locked on me. Her normally blue eyes were gone. Dark black pupils surrounded by amber looked back at me. She growled and slowly began to rise.

I threw the first bag of meat toward her, and it landed with a wet splat. Larry had unpacked everything in the truck as I drove. Each bag was just a sack of open meat. Faith got her footing and crouched like she was going to jump at me. I threw a second bag of meat at her. The giant wolf stopped growling long enough to sniff the air, and her eyes focused on the bags in front of her. She eased over to one, sniffed it, and shoved her face into it.

Happy wet chomping and slurping sounds followed. In less than a minute Faith had emptied that bag and moved on to the second. I watched as she finished that bag as well, and I smiled when she lifted her head to look at me. But I stopped smiling when she growled. It made me remember that she was starving and that I was holding a lot of raw meat. I tossed all of the bags I had to her, and she tore into them.

"What's going on?" Larry asked.

"Bring me the other bags," I said. He brought the bags to me, and I told him to lock himself in the bathroom with the shotgun.

I locked up the apartment and sat down against the wall to watch Faith eat the rest of her meal. I angled my sword so that if Faith decided that I looked tastier than beef and steak she would skewer herself charging at me. I should have locked myself in the bathroom with Larry, but there was some part of me that was thinking of survival in the long term. Here and now, I could look at a werewolf and familiarize myself with them. Faith was the only transformed werewolf I had ever seen, so I just had to hope that she was at least average for a werewolf.

Faith was covered in fiery red fur from head to tail. From paw to head she was about four and a half feet tall. From head to tail she was about five feet long. Her weight had to be north of three-hundred pounds of what looked like solid muscle. I watched her move to another bag of meat and took note of her claws. They were about three inches long and as thick as my thumb. Interestingly enough they weren't straight but slightly curved, almost hooked like a raptor's. Then there were the fangs. They were as long as house keys, and they looked like they could rip through just about anything I could throw in front of them.

Faith kept eating and I kept watching. If I had to fight one werewolf I could probably manage it. I was taller and more acclimated to moving around in human created environments. At the very least I could climb on top of something that was out of the werewolf's sphere of reach and shoot it. I could also hit it with a car. In a straight up fight, I would have to rely on magical sword trumping claws. I could win. The problem was that I knew there were six werewolves waiting to turn at the full moon.

The large wolf in my living room devoured the last bag of meat. Faith raised her head to me and bared her teeth. I stiffened and braced for her attack. She didn't growl and she didn't lunge. Without a sound she walked over to the couch, hopped onto it, somehow managed to turn in a small circle a couple of times, and then lay down in that classic curled position that dogs use. I waited. I was still scared and didn't want to make any sudden moves. After about five minutes I could hear her snoring lightly. After another five minutes I decided to get up and retreat to my room.

I pulled the bin filled with encyclopedia into my bedroom. Then I knocked on the bathroom door. Larry answered in typical Larry fashion for the night.

"I have a shotgun!" he shouted.

"I know," I said. "Look, the couch is occupied, so do you want to crash in my room with me?"

"I'm good in here if you have a pillow and a few blankets," Larry said.

I had even better. I had a pillow for him, a blanket, and a sleeping bag. He stretched out in my bathtub with room to spare. With my guests settled in for the night, I went into my bedroom and locked the door behind me. No sooner had I locked the door than Horace stood up on my bed.

"Hey kid. You good?" he asked me.

"No. This is bad. I might be in over my head," I said.

"Sounds like you," he snickered.

"You don't know me!" I snapped.

Horace looked at me and shook his head. "Wrong kid. I know you. I know you better than anyone else in this world. I know you used to tie towels around your neck and pretend that you were Superman. I know that you use to put on your yellow raincoat and pretend to be Dick Tracy. I know that you used to put on two baseball caps, put a bubble pipe in your mouth, and walk around with a magnifying glass to pretend you were Sherlock Holmes. I know that you have a soft spot for anyone that needs help, and I know that you have never given up when things got tough. I know Michael Franklin Joshua White, and I know that he doesn't quit," my teddy bear said.

"I'm tired, Horace," I said as I leaned my head against the door.

"Then rest. But open the bin. I'll read up on trolls and give you an overview in the morning," Horace said.

"Really?" I asked.

"Hey, I'm stuck here until I figure out a way to get home. I might as well do my job. I can't physically protect you from this shit, but I can help you prepare. Think of me as your Bear Friday," he said.

"That's Girl Friday," I told him.

"You can't be picky, kid. You let the hot chick turn into a wolf. You can't fuck a wolf, not in this state," he told me dismissively.

"What?" I asked.

"Nothing kid. Get some rest," Horace told me. "Tag out. I'm on watch."

I climbed into my bed and pulled the covers up over my head. There was a werewolf in my living room, a leprechaun in my bathtub, and a teddy bear in my bedroom reading the encyclopedia cryptidia. Somewhere there was a horror writer laughing at me.

My alarm went off at 2:30 a.m., and I rolled out of bed. Horace was on the floor with my encyclopedias and a bottle of beer that he did not have when I went to sleep. I started getting ready for my run while he ignored me.

"Isn't it a bit early to be drinking?" I asked him.

"It's only early if you went to bed. I didn't, so shut up," he countered.

I couldn't argue his point. I threw two knives into my pockets, put on a hoodie, and marched out into the rain to go for my run. Thaddaeus was at the park waiting for me. He even brought me a bottle of water. His chauffeur stayed behind with our vehicles as we started our jog.

"So, Michael, what do you do for a living?"

"I'm a carpenter, but right now I'm out of work. What about you, Mr…"

He chuckled. "I told you my name is Thaddaeus."

"Sorry, it's just weird calling someone so much older than me by their first name. No offense."

"None taken young man. Now what do you do for money if you aren't building houses and repairing schools?"

"Well…I'm also a part time detective."

Thaddaeus stopped to take a drink from his water bottle. I had a pull from mine too. With our whistles wet we returned to our jog.

"So, a part-time detective? What's that like?"

"It sucks! Either I'm going through people's garbage for lingerie receipts or I'm waiting outside of a motel with a camera trying to get pictures of a cheating spouse."

"Are there really that many men that cheat on their wives?"

"And vice versa."

"Is that all you do? Catch people…What's the phrase? Uh…Stepping out?"

"Well, every once in a while I get to do something worthwhile. Something like find a missing person or protect someone."

"Anyone famous or anything like that?"

"Right now, I am looking for a missing person that's pretty important to his family. I'm also playing bodyguard to a buddy of mine."

"Finding and protecting people, huh? Well, people are probably scared to mess with a big black guy like you." Thaddaeus stopped running and held up his hands. "I'm sorry, that didn't come out the way it was in my head. That probably sounded pretty racist."

I started laughing. "It's okay, Thaddaeus. I know what you meant, kind of." We started jogging again. "I wasn't always the big black guy. I used to be the skinny pale guy."

Our jogging lap had come to an end as we reached the point where we originally started running. Thaddaeus' chauffeur was standing there with an umbrella ready for his boss.

"How about tomorrow you tell me about who you are trying to help now?"

"Sounds good to me, Thaddaeus. See you tomorrow."

"You bet! Maybe this rain will have finally stopped by then."

As Thaddaeus retreated into his nice dry vehicle I took off at top speed. I sprinted for a fourth of the mile and jogged the rest. My throat was dry and burning when I got back to my truck. I drank the rest of my water bottle and then drove home. I crept into my apartment and back to my room. Horace was there studying. I didn't bother him. I just fell on the bed and passed out.

# CHAPTER 16

WHEN MY ALARM went off I sat up. Then I pulled my clock off of the nightstand, ripped it out of the wall socket, and threw it across the room. My head fell back to my pillow.

"Kid, get up!" said Horace.

"No!" I said.

"Get the fuck up, Michael. I have shit to tell you, and the moment your buddies get up I am not going to be able to," Horace argued.

"Fine," I growled.

Horace handed me an encyclopedia and climbed onto the bed. He opened the book to the first page of the entry for trolls. Then he pointed to the first line of the entry. I read it aloud.

*"We haven't killed one."*

I read it again in my head. Then I realized that what I was reading was a testament to the amount of trouble I was in. No knight, no paladin, no priest, and no Templar had ever killed a troll and lived to tell about it.

"They are giants with little to no magic beyond the natural gifts that all fairies possess," Horace said. "That means they can contract with a mortal and have the power of glamour. Do you know what that means?"

"Yeah, fairies can create magical contracts with mortals. Most beings can, but when a fairy makes a deal it binds them to the mortal and the mortal to them. In a sense they own part of you, and not even death can break that contract," I said.

"Good. Do you understand glamour?"

"Yeah. They can look human, or actually…" I rubbed my nose then started sneezing. My allergies were horrible in the morning. "They can look like pretty much anything."

"Okay, you understand their magic in the most basic sense of what they can do. Now the bad part," Horace said as he turned the page. He pointed to an illustration of a troll standing next to a human. It was two feet taller than the human in the depiction and almost twice as wide.

"So, they're bigger than me. That's nothing new," I said. I had another sneezing fit, and snot ran from my nose to my pillow.

"Gross kid. Go take some Benadryl," Horace said.

I pulled the pillow cover off and used it to clean my nose. "In a minute. What's the bad part?" I asked.

Horace pointed at another line, and I tried to read it through tearing eyes. When he noticed that I couldn't make out the words he read them aloud. "Trolls are not fairies. They do not have any of the weaknesses that a fairy has. They can lie, and iron doesn't hurt them any more than it hurts you. They eat anything that they can put into their mouth. They can regenerate from anything that does not kill them. It is best to avoid them at all costs."

I pressed my face into my pillow. "So, all the fae bonuses and none of their weaknesses. I hate my life," I said with a muffled voice.

"No point feeling sorry for yourself, kid. You picked this fight," Horace said.

I lifted my now snot covered face and said, "No I didn't!"

"You could have given up the leprechaun, but you decided to fight four trolls instead. That is picking the fight," Horace told me. "Now, I do have some useful information on trolls. They apparently can't resist making bargains, so you could potentially buy them off. Also, they may or may not be able to swim. The book says your best bet is to push them into large bodies of water, but it's not clear why."

"Great, so I can bargain with them or push them into water. Get on the phone and tell them that they are only allowed to attack us at swimming pools!"

"Sarcasm isn't good on you kid. Neither is snot. Go clean yourself up," Horace said as he closed the book. "You'll be fine. It will all work out in the end."

"Is that because if I die you get to be free?" I asked as I got out of bed.

"It'll all work out in the end," shrugged my teddy bear. "Oh, and your phone was buzzing. I think someone texted you."

I checked my phone, and sure enough there was a text from Aaron. *"Question! Was Kodiak Black IN your office, or did he just call you?"*

I responded, *"Both. He called and I told him to meet me at my office. Trying to find Everette Black. Any tips on dealing with werewolves?"*

I opened the door and walked to the kitchen. Once there I took out a bottle of my allergy medicine. I opened it and shoved several pills into my mouth. I had long ago surpassed the chemical-induced lethargy that came with taking allergy medication. I needed it to function like some people need coffee. Next I grabbed a dish towel and began to wash my face in the sink. I sneezed for a while longer and had to keep washing my face because my eyes wouldn't stop burning. As I was scrubbing my face something bumped against my leg…and growled.

I had completely forgotten that a dangerous werewolf was in my living room. I leapt back against the pantry door and started looking for a weapon. My kitchen is small. If I stand in the middle of it, most things are in arms reach. I looked to the knife block, but that was on the other end of the kitchen counter. The red-furred wolf growled as she stalked toward me. There was no room to maneuver without leaping onto the countertops which wouldn't put me out of the werewolf's range.

The wolf lifted up and slammed both of her front paws against the wall to trap me between them. With her muzzle inches from my face, she pealed back her lips to show me her fangs. Her jaws flew open as she came forward. I rushed to the side, but she pressed her full weight against me pinning me to the wall. Then she licked my face. Rank breath and wet slobber assaulted me, and I remembered being tackled by my dogs when I got home from school. Reflexively I reached up and scratched her behind the ears. She licked my face all the harder then.

"I'm guessing this means that you are okay," I said.

Faith dropped back to the floor, turned, and trotted away. I finished cleaning myself up and joined her in the living room. She was stretched out on the floor in front of my couch with her head on her paws. I sat down and just looked at her. Her red fur looked like waves of fire across her body. It was beautiful, and all that beauty hid the fact that she was a monster. If a dog lover ever came across a werewolf they wouldn't know what to do with themselves. They should run away, and they should be terrified, but I bet most would want to walk right up to a werewolf to pat them on the head.

"So, I have to go out and look for Everett Black today. I have to keep Larry safe, too. Want to come along?" I asked.

Faith shifted her head to look at me with one open wolf eye.

"If transforming hurts, I can't imagine you would want to do it again, but I don't want to leave you cooped up in here all day. So do you want to go for a ride, girl?" I asked.

Faith growled at me.

I recoiled back on the couch and patted the air in surrender. "Okay, my bad! You aren't a dog! I'm sorry—just don't eat me!"

Faith got up and growled at me again as she walked around the couch. She walked over to her duffle bag and turned it over. She stuck her head in and rummaged around for a moment. Still growling, she came back over to my side of the couch and dropped two items from her mouth onto my lap. I stared at the items, and I didn't know if I should laugh or not. When the smile touched my lips and Faith growled at me, I decided laughing was not the best course of action.

The first item was a black collar with dull studs all around it. There was a golden heart-shaped name tag on it that read 'My name is Faith. I like to be brushed' on one side. The other item was a rope of braided blue cord mixed with reflective materials. On one end was a loop to hold in your hand, and on the other end was a clasp. Faith had given me a collar and a leash, the perfect disguise for a werewolf.

"You want me to put these on you?" I asked.

In response Faith sat down and held her neck out to me. I picked up the collar and reached over to fit it around her neck. While I felt around her neck

I felt something sharp as it grazed my finger. I took the offending item in hand and pulled it from beneath Faith's fur. It was a tooth, a fang actually, and it was pierced by a golden chain. I pulled it further out and found several fangs decorating the chain in the same fashion. Further down I found a simple golden cross centering the item.

When I first met Faith we had fought each other. She thought I was trying to kill her little brothers, and in truth I was. A family of hunters had been attacked by something that had all but killed them. I had taken it upon myself to kill the monster that had done it. What I found were children that had the speed, strength, and near invulnerability of werewolves. They kicked my butt and wrecked my truck. Just as I had begun to fight back, Faith had appeared to defend her little brothers from the real monster. That real monster being me—a grown man, with guns and a magic sword, that had decided it was okay to kill something just because he had the power to do it.

I ended up fighting a werewolf alpha who easily could have killed me. Instead, he showed me mercy. He called my grandpa to come take me home, fed me, and gave me a jug of moonshine. My grandpa had pointed out to me that each of the werewolves I had met all wore a necklace of fangs centered by a cross. They were Christians, a different version of Christians, but Christians none the less. Just like I was. I learned that night that being different doesn't make you a monster. Your actions made you one. That adventure humbled me.

I said a quick prayer, thanking God for my friend and his lesson. Then I finished putting the collar around Faith's neck. Before I could attach the leash Larry came out of the bathroom. Tucked under his arm was a black umbrella with a hooked redwood handle. He had on a checkered orange and yellow leisure suit with a matching pocket square and a bow tie over a white shirt. I wanted to laugh, but he actually made it work. Faith started making a chuffing sound that must have passed for laughing among werewolves. I say it must have, because just like laughter it was infectious, and I started laughing as well. Larry just glared at us.

"I am going to get dressed, and then we are going to get Drew," I said as I clipped on Faith's leash and tossed it to Larry.

I put on jeans, an orange tee shirt, and my work boots. Of course, I grabbed my sports bag filled with my normal assortment of tools and weapons. On a whim I grabbed my silver-edged survival knife and strapped it to my left ankle. I went to join the others in the living room and found my door open. I rushed outside to find Faith just inches away from my neighbor, Mrs. Faraday. The old woman was sitting in her favorite lawn chair with a beach umbrella protecting her from the rain. She was completely unaware that the creature just inches away from her was not some random dog that I had brought home.

"Larry, why are you guys out here?" I asked.

"Faith was scratching at the door for something, and I wasn't about to say no to something that could eat three of me," Larry argued.

"Faith? Is that her name?" Mrs. Faraday asked. She reached up, because Faith was just that darn tall in her wolf form and scratched the werewolf behind the ears. "You are so pretty. I wish my hair had been as beautiful as yours when I was young."

Faith shifted her head so that Mrs. Faraday could scratch her without having to reach up uncomfortably. My 88-year-old neighbor was petting and scratching a werewolf like she was an actual dog. Faith for her part seemed to be enjoying it.

"Michael, whereever did you find this pretty little girl?" Mrs. Faraday asked.

"Umm…she found me," I said honestly.

"Isn't that always how it is? The pretty ones always find you. First, that wonderful Kerri-Lynn, and now this even prettier one. Maybe if you are lucky she will keep you," Mrs. Faraday said.

The mention of Kerri-Lynn had struck something in me. I felt a pain in my heart that was fresh and raw. She had left me out of necessity, so she could preserve her relationship with her family. I understood it. I just hated it.

Faith had a different reaction. Her face darted forward at Mrs. Faraday and her jaws opened. Before I could even call out a warning Faith started licking Mrs. Faraday. That's when my neighbor started laughing. Mrs. Faraday laughed from somewhere deep within her heart and soul. I could feel the joy radiating off of her, and the pain from my memory of Kerri-Lynn subsided. It wasn't gone, but it wasn't bothering me. I looked over at Larry, and he was grinning from ear to ear.

Mrs. Faraday patted Faith one last time and then gently pushed her toward me. I took Faith's leash from Larry and smiled as my neighbor said, "I didn't mean to keep you young ones from your adventures. I just had to see that pretty girl. Go, go, go. Have a wonderful day all of you, and maybe you can tell my Peter about your adventures when we go to see him next week. Unless you forgot?"

I smiled all the wider. "Never, Mrs. Faraday. I'm taking you next weekend, and I will be happy to share a story or two with Mr. Faraday."

The smile I got from that old woman could have melted the heart of an ice demon. We waved goodbye and got into my truck. Faith hopped into the bed while Larry and I climbed into the cab. As I pulled off, I waved goodbye to Mrs. Faraday one last time.

"You don't actually tell that old lady and her husband about your *adventures*, do you?" Larry asked.

"I do. They are two of the nicest people in the world. I think they believe some of what I say and feel the rest is just to entertain them," I said.

"You tell people about being a knight?"

"Just them. I'm supposed to keep it a secret, but I don't like lying. Besides, it makes them happy. I could trade everything if Mr. and Mrs. Faraday laughed every day like she did this morning,"

"You don't see magic like that every day. Not in adults at least," Larry sighed.

"I know," I agreed.

The rest of our ride to Code Blue was quiet. Drew had five men and two women waiting for us to give them a ride. They were happy to get a chance to work but skeptical about riding with the giant canine in the bed of my truck. Faith curled up at the top of the truck bed so as not to seem threatening. All seven of the extra workers were able to find a comfortable position in the bed while Drew joined Larry and me in the cab.

I was happy to be taking them to work. They needed it, and in truth so did I. Mundane good deeds reminded me that not every problem in the world needed to be solved by guns, magic, or divine intervention. The truth of the matter was that these people just needed to be shown some good old-fashioned human decency. That's when a thought came to me.

Pulling out my cell phone, I hit one of the buttons on my speed dial. I hit the speaker just as a voice said, "Kate's Bar and Grill. This is Ralph speaking. How can I help you?"

"Ralph? Don't you mean Raphael?" I asked.

"Orgoth isn't here, and until he shows up its Ralph like my mother named me. What's up, Michael," one of Kate's best assistant cooks asked.

"Can I place an order to be delivered around noon to a work site?" I asked.

"Sure, if you pay the delivery charge and tip up front," he said.

"Not a problem," I said with a smile.

"Boss, what are you doing?" asked Drew asked.

I ignored him as I gave the address for the delivery and ordered enough food to feed the small crew. I ordered extra just in case and promised I would pay the tab the next time I was in the bar. Ralph was cool with it when he told me that the bill would be $80.00, and I told him to add in his $24.00 tip.

"Boss you didn't have to do that," Drew protested.

"I can't have you guys working all day on empty stomachs," I said as I pulled into a McDonalds. I ordered biscuit sandwiches, coffee, and orange juice for everyone. I also ordered twelve biscuit sandwiches for Faith who had to wait outside. Somehow that came out to another $117.00.

We weren't the first ones to the job site, but we were still early. I opened my toolbox and handed out spare hard hats. Drew was smiling when he put on his hard hat and tool belt. As they walked into the building it felt good to watch people who were just happy to be able to go to work. I wished that I could join them, but I had a job to do myself.

Just as I was about to get back into my truck, the three assholes from yesterday came running up. They each had a heavy tool in hand and bad attitudes written all over their faces. I opened my truck door and pulled out my baseball bat. If they wanted to fight me again, I was going to put a real hurting on them this time. I might not stop there. I could break their legs. I could go in there and rough up the foreman for firing me while I was at it. Steam rolled up around me as they approached, and I thought for a second about grabbing my gun.

Just as they started to call out to me I heard a growl coming from above my head. Faith stood up in the bed of my truck and bared her teeth. All three of the men came to a stop. I couldn't help but grin.

"My, what big teeth she has. That's what you're thinking, right?" I teased. All three of them started taking cautious steps backward. I reached up and patted Faith. "Now I know what you're thinking. You think that as soon as I leave you can hassle the people I just dropped off. Well, if I get a call from one of them before the workday ends, I am going to come back with this girl off of her leash. Just remember that you guys have to keep working here, and even if you run, someone will be kind enough or afraid enough or just hate you enough to tell me where to find you. And when I do, I will make sure that I break every bone in each of your hands. You won't be able to wipe your own asses let alone work in construction again."

All three of them looked at me as I spoke. No, not at me, just above me. I didn't realize it, but I was holding my bat above my head like a club. I was also a lot closer to them then I intended to be. With just a single swing of my arm I could cave the short one's head in. From there it would be easy just to turn on the fat one and bring my bat across his jaw to bust out all of his teeth. Then I could…

I gritted my teeth, and with an effort of will I said, "Leave. You have a job to do. That school needs a new roof." When the three assholes didn't immediately move, I screamed at them, "Get your asses back to work!" Then I took my bat in both hands and stomped my foot down like I was going to strike out at them.

They ran away screaming. I swung my bat in the air in frustration a few times. I yelled and stomped around. It wasn't until I heard Faith whimper that I began to calm down. Those assholes had really pissed me off. I didn't need this today. I took a few deep breaths before walking back to my truck. I patted Faith once more and said, "Thanks." Then I tossed my bat back into the bag, climbed in, and pulled off.

## CHAPTER 17

"WE'RE GOING IN there?" Larry asked. He was holding Faith's leash as we crossed the parking lot to the hospital.

"Yes Larry. In addition to protecting you, I am working a missing person's case. When you have a missing person, you have to consider the worst-case scenario. That being that Everett Black is dead," I said as I open one of the unmarked side doors to the building.

We walked down a dimly lit corridor until we came to a small waiting area. No visitors were present, just two attendants in the little office area behind the front desk. One was sleeping, and the other was diligently minding the counter. I walked up to the desk and stood patiently as the attendants did their best to ignore me.

After two minutes of pretending I wasn't there, the one that was awake looked up from his computer screen and greeted me as best he could. "You could just call you know," he said.

"Cory, if I called I would still have to come down to identify the body, right?" I asked.

He grunted. "Fair enough. What can I do for you, White?"

"I'm checking to see if you have a dead body," I said with a smile.

The young man sat back in his chair and flipped me off. "No shit Sherlock. Why the fuck else would you come to a morgue?"

"I hear some people stop in for a bite to eat," I grumbled.

The young man nearly fell out of his chair, but he caught himself and turned to face his sleeping counterpart. These two men were a contrast. One was older, portly, and inattentive. The other was young, gangly, and alert. One was human and the other was a ghoul. When the older man didn't stir in the least, the young ghoul finally exhaled and slumped back into his chair.

"Are you trying to get me fired or killed? I just want to know where I stand with you, knight," Cory grumbled.

Ghouls are a strange kind of monster. They survived by eating the flesh of the dead. They could eat the flesh of the living, of course, but the dead were plentiful and didn't fight back. Aaron had tipped me off to a nest of them living in Baltimore. Their leader had gotten the brilliant idea they should all take up jobs involving the storage of dead bodies. Because of that, I had met ghouls on several occasions when looking for a missing person. Cory was always partnered with the older human, and the older human was always asleep. This paring made things a lot easier for me.

"I'm not trying to get you fired or killed, Cory. I am just saying that some things eat dead bodies. Do you know of anything here eating dead bodies?" I asked.

"Seriously, do you think I shit where I eat?" Cory asked. "Look, you already know we only eat a John Doe when it's up for cremation."

"Exactly! I am here to see if there is a John Doe here. About six feet tall, black, and muscular," I said.

Cory lifted one eyebrow and asked, "Is this a Black Lives Matter thing? Seriously, knight, I don't care that you fucking humans kill each other based on race. All it is to my kind is white meat killing dark meat."

"You do know I could kill you, right?" I asked.

"You won't. Not with witnesses around. You knights value your secrecy and your oh so precious humanity. When you started coming around, I convinced my boss that we needed security cameras all over the morgue by stealing a few bodies. I ate good for a month and got a nice little incentive for you to not kill me," he bragged as he leaned back in his chair with his hands behind his head.

I nodded. He had a point. I couldn't kill him with camera's watching me. "Hey, do you know my friend Larry?"

Larry walked up to stand next to me. His head was barely above the counter, but Cory could see him. Cory leaned forward in his seat and grinned.

"Shit! It's the leprechaun that the Bridge Boys are looking for. You know they are gonna kill you, right?"

"I hired him to protect me!" Larry said as he hooked his thumb at me.

Cory looked at me and laughed. "So, the knight is gonna die soon? Good, I can get back to sleeping and eating on the clock."

"Do you really think some trolls are going to kill me?" I asked. I thought exactly that, but I wanted to know where I stood on the power scale across the magical community.

"It's the fucking Bridge Boys, you dumb-ass human. There aren't many trolls that can say they have lived for fucking centuries in the human world let alone have enough power to blend in among them. It's a hard as fuck job for most of us to blend in, but my body is built to shift into a harmless looking human's. Trolls don't have that kind of magic most of the time. Those that do are scary, and what is worse than a scary idiot with power?"

I shrugged.

He smiled and said, "A smart asshole with power. They say the Bridge Boys always get their toll, and that's been true longer than our states have been united. You're going to die if you don't hand him over and beg them not to take offense."

"I will keep your opinion in mind. Now about that body," I said.

"Tall, black, athletic…could be a lot of bodies. Anything more specific?" he said in a snarky tone.

"Maybe furry?" I said.

"Furry?" Cory asked skeptically.

"Yeah, furry. Like her," I said. Right on queue Faith slammed her front paws on top of the counter and stood even with my shoulders. She bared her teeth without growling and stared down at Cory.

The ghoul, for his part, did not try to flee or scream. He did turn pail, however, and for an instant I saw the skin on his face grow thin. His eyes slipped deeper into his skull as they turned a dark almost blood red. It only lasted an instant, but it was enough for me to get a glimpse at what a ghoul looked like outside of its human disguise. Cory pulled himself back together before he changed enough for the security footage to be an issue.

"That's a werewolf," he said.

"A werewolf? I hadn't noticed. I thought she was just a really big and really pretty dog," I said.

"That's a fucking werewolf. Werewolves don't live in Baltimore. Why the hell is there a werewolf in Baltimore?" Cory all but screamed.

"Because she is helping me look for another werewolf. Tall, black, athletic, and maybe furry. Any John Does that fit that description recently?" I asked.

Cory gulped, reached for his keyboard, and started typing. He had to look at his screen, but his eyes kept darting between the screen and Faith. He finally stopped typing and focused on the screen. "We've had four Johns this week that partially fit that description," he said.

"Four in the city?" I said.

"The city? No. In this morgue. There are fifteen that match that description across the city right now," he said as he clicked through a few screens.

"Fifteen? That can't be right. That would be every John in the city," I said as I tried to look at his screen.

"Wrong again knight. There are currently twenty-six John Does in the city and nine other identified bodies. We have a few here that don't fit that description too," Cory said.

"There are 35 dead people in the city, and it isn't all over the news?" I asked.

"I wouldn't know. I don't watch TV much. It rots the brain," Cory said.

I thought about having that many dead bodies in just a few days. I was sure that I would have seen something in a paper or heard about a serial killer on the radio. "Show me the bodies."

Cory looked up at me and said, "No way."

"Larry," I said.

"Faith," Larry said.

Faith bared her teeth and leaned forward. Cory got the message and scooted away from her. "Fine, I'll take you back there, but the wolf stays here," he said.

"Fair enough. Larry, stay with Faith. Faith, keep Larry out of trouble," I said as I walked over to the locked door that separated the waiting room from the actual morgue. Faith hopped down and dragged Larry over to a bench. He sat down and she curled up on the floor.

Cory printed something off on the computer and opened the door for me. We walked down another hallway to an exam room. Once we were inside Cory checked his paper. Along the wall were four rows of ten refrigerated cabinets. He walked along the wall tapping six different cabinets as he went. Each cabinet popped open about an inch from the wall. Cory came back to the first cabinet and opened it up.

The man lying on the small bench had died brutally. His skull was partially caved in, and his chest had been shredded into ragged strips of flesh. Part of his shoulder was missing. The medical examiners had already cleaned him up, but just the sight of it was enough to tell me that his death had been a bloody mess. I could accept that. Monsters were real after all, and a monster had done this. What set me back was the look in his eyes. They were open and looking up at me with an expression of resigned acceptance. A look that told me all too clearly that his life had been hard, and he was ready for it to end.

"What was the cause of death?" I asked.

Cory flipped through his printed pages. "Says it was a hit and run," he said with a shrug.

"A hit and run? With all these bite and claw marks?" I asked.

"It says hit and run. All of them died from something similar and are listed as everything from hit and run to natural causes to eaten by rats," the ghoul chuckled. When I narrowed my eyes he just grinned and said, "Ignorance is Bliss, right?"

I ground my teeth at the mention of that ancient curse. Humans had somehow made themselves ignorant of the truth of the world around them. We naturally ignored magic, monsters, and our own instincts when we are alerted to the goings on of the supernatural.

It made us nothing more than lambs waiting to be slaughtered.

I closed up the cabinet and looked at the next one. Another person who should not have been dead. His body was shredded and broken, and track marks were still visible on his arms. The next body showed me what a woman looked like if she was starved down to skin and bone. The next and the next and the next were all the same. Men and women that were killed by some brutal beast that devoured human flesh and bone. Men and women that had been through hardship in life only to have those lives ended by monsters that they probably didn't even believe in.

I insisted on seeing each body, and for a few minutes Cory took a sadistic pleasure in showing them to me. After the ninth body, even the ghoul started to turn shades of green with sickness, and after the tenth he turned red with anger. He growled something about how humans were genocidal vermin. I had to remember that in a city of millions of possible meals Cory and his kind kept their diet to those that were already dead, and they did it by choice. I didn't know what prompted that choice, but it meant that I didn't have to worry about them killing anyone.

Larry and Faith both stood when I walked back into the reception area. Faith whined as I approached, and I rubbed her head absent mindedly. I took her leash, and we all started down the long hallway that would lead us out of the morgue. There were too many dead bodies that had been ravaged by a were-wolf for someone not to have noticed. Once we were outside I pulled out my cell phone and made a call.

"What have you got, White?" Captain Clay asked.

"Why didn't you tell me there were a few dozen killings like the ones you showed me yesterday?" I asked.

"What the hell are you talking about, White?" he asked.

"The morgues are filled with bodies, fresh ones! Someone's been killing people by the dozens, and you cops are covering it up!"

"White, what the hell are you talking about? There are no reports of homicides in the last few days that I haven't read. There were six. My three and three other random ones around the city," Clay argued.

I bit down my anger and looked back at the morgue. "I just came from the morgue. They have dozens of dead bodies that have come in in the past few days."

"Dead bodies don't mean homicides, White. Every cop knows that," Clay said with a sigh.

"What about those reports you read? What do they say about the bodies?" I asked. Clay was quiet for a while. I could hear papers shuffling and keys clicking in the background.

"Every last one of them describes the body as ravaged by a wild animal. BPD is discussing cracking down on dog fighting rings," he said. Then, with a voice filled with exasperation, he added, "Then there are the more than a dozen cases of bodies found dead on the street. Not one of them classified as a homicide."

"Why?" I asked. The rain around me was building into a warm fog.

"I don't know, White. But I am damn sure going to find out," Clay said. He hung up on me leaving me standing in the fog both figuratively and literally.

We all got into the truck, and Larry asked, "So where to next?"

I started up the Rust Bucket and looked around as I thought about that. I had come here looking for one dead body and found dozens. I knew they were all connected because of Everett Black. Now I just had to find him.

"We check by land, sea, and air," I said.

# CHAPTER **18**

THE PUBLIC LIBRARY is an amazing thing! All you need is a library card, and they will let you sit down at a computer for hours. I looked up the flight records of our local airports for the past few weeks. Then I looked up train records. Finally, I looked up shipping records. What I found was that gaining access to transit information is scarily easy. I also didn't find out anything about any private flights, private trains, or private ships transporting anything from New York to Baltimore.

I looked over at Larry who was on the computer next to me. Somehow he had managed to gain access to an online poker site. His right hand rapidly clicked the mouse while he danced a coin across the knuckles of his left hand. I watched as his screen ticked up winnings. He had started out with a thousand bucks, but I could see the amount clicking up by hundreds or thousands with each hand dealt. I stopped trying to track down Everett Black for a moment and watched Larry scale from $200,000.00 to $748,600.00 in the course of an hour.

"Larry, how the heck are you doing that? Every hand they deal to you has a pair of something and two or three aces," I said.

"Luck of the Irish," he said.

"No one is that lucky," I said.

Just then Larry was dealt a hand of a four, a seven, a nine, a two, and a queen. Only the queen and the two were in the same suit, diamonds. The other online gamblers practically doubled their bets when Larry threw back all but the queen. I watched as the dealer dealt out cards once again, and my jaw dropped when Larry was dealt the ten, ace, jack, and king of diamonds. I didn't understand poker, but the probability of that happening had to be almost as high as Larry's final winnings total. I watched as his screen ticked up to $992,400.00. Larry dropped from the game, pulled out his cell phone, and showed me a bank account screen showing the deposited winnings.

"Larry, why the heck did you need to cheat at poker with luck like that?" I asked.

Larry shrugged his shoulders and said, "Is it *really* cheating if you don't get caught?"

"Larry, you did get caught," I said.

"No. I ran away. No one caught me, and as long as they don't I say I won fair and square. It's their word against mine," he said as he stood up. "I'm going to the bathroom."

I turned back to my computer and went back to my research. Larry honestly believed that as long as no one physically caught him he was in the right. I wondered if that's how criminals and politicians felt.

"If no one catches you then it's not wrong…" I said to myself. I looked up the transit records from around the time Everett Black was abducted. I was looking for shady doings and underhanded deals before, but now I was looking for something a little more practical.

My phone buzzed as I got another text from Aaron. *"Just Kodiak or other werewolves too?"*

I texted him back, *"Not Kodiak. Other werewolves. Keep running into them."*

I got back to my search. It took some time, but I found something interesting. When Larry came back I asked him to check behind me.

"So, there was a train late getting into the station. What's the big deal?" he asked.

"That train left the previous station on time with no problems. Plus, look at the online complaints from passengers," I told him.

He scrolled through some of the complaints, and I watched as he scrunched up his eyes. "It's just people complaining about the ride being bumpy, taking too long, and being held up to add a few cars from another train. Then there is one asshole with a whole blog post about how some dumb animal in the added train cars kept him awake with all of its howling." Larry stopped reading and looked up at me with a smile.

I nodded as I said, "And about how it felt like the train was going to tip over the tracks." We cleared our search histories, logged out, and hit the road. We started at Penn Station and downloaded a map of the rails. Where we ended up was East Lombard Street. There were several rail yards in this part of Baltimore. They were separated by distance, terrain that was unfriendly to civilian vehicles, and thick underbrush. The upside was that there were no fences.

Sneaking into a train yard is surprisingly easy. Almost comically easy. We basically just parked on the street and walked right into the first train yard. I'm sure some people noticed us, but the combination of Larry and I looking like hobos combined with Faith just looking like a giant dog kept them all away.

Navigating the train yards was no easy task. The constant light rain had soaked the unpaved ground, so the mud and gravel made our trudge through lines of boxcars and flatbeds far more of an ordeal than I had expected. My work boots were digging into the ground to steady me, but with every step they collected more mud which slowed me down. I had to kick them against the tracks every so often just to keep a good pace. Larry had fallen twice, but not a single drop of mud had tarnished his suit. He also found a wallet with no ID and two hundred bucks in it the first time he fell. Then on his second fall he found a Rolex.

Faith moved around easily even though she kept coming to the end of her leash. On reflex I tugged back when she got too far ahead of me. The first time she growled at me, and I told her to stay close. The next time she bared her teeth, and I tugged her harder.

"I don't care if you are a werewolf. We stick together. We can't move as easily as you in this mess," I told her. Faith snorted at me but slowed her pace.

We came across an open boxcar that stood host to a small family of four. They shied away from us and huddled away from the door. The dad, at least I think he was the dad of the small group of four, stood between us and his family. He brandished what looked to be a railroad spike in his hand.

"What you want?" he said in what sounded like broken English with a Spanish accent. I couldn't see them clearly, but that let me know that they might have been immigrants.

"Easy friend," I said. I held up my hands and backed up. I smiled and motioned for Larry to do the same. Faith just lolled out her tongue. "We aren't here to hurt you. We're looking for something, and we'll keep moving on."

That was when one of the children coughed. I looked into the darkness and took note. He was a scruffy-looking man that looked like he could use a meal. She was a withered woman that needed more time resting and warmer clothing. There was a little girl with a tattered but clean puffy white coat. Then there was another child so small that I couldn't begin to tell how old it was. Dressed in rags and bundled up, I had no idea if it was a boy or girl. All I knew was that it coughed again and kept coughing. I reached into my pocket, and the man rushed to his feet. He came at me but stopped when I held up three crisp Ben Franklins. Slowly we walked towards each other, and I handed him the $300.00.

"Have you heard of Code Blue?" I asked.

He nodded. "The shelter."

"Yeah. Go there and tell them Priest Gregory sent you. But first take that little one to get some medicine," I told him.

"What's your name, senior?"

"Michael White. Yours?"

"Jermon Hernandez."

We shook hands.

Larry and I turned to leave when Jermon called out, "Why? Why do you do this?"

I waved at him without looking back as I said, "Because it's storming, and your kids need warm beds tonight."

Our search had reached its fourth hour and second rail yard. We had walked numerous miles up and down the lines of unused train cars. We had encountered animals and people. We were also filthy. Well, Faith and I were filthy. Larry was still in near pristine condition as he trailed behind us. It was nearing lunch time, and we hadn't turned up a single clue. I had thought I could find something here, but luck wasn't on my side. It was time to call it quits.

"Hey, Michael, what are we looking for here?" Larry asked.

"Clues Larry. Hair fibers, footprints, detailed dastardly plans encrypted on a flash drive, or footprints outlined in blood. Stuff like that," I said.

"How about a boxcar riddled with bullet holes and claw marks," Larry said.

"That would be great, but I'm not that lucky. Even you aren't that lucky," I said.

"Well, I just found a boxcar riddled with bullet holes and claw marks," he said.

I turned around slowly, and sure enough the little leprechaun was standing next to a boxcar that I had overlooked. It had enough holes in the side of it that you would think it was designed that way. Along various parts of the wall of the boxcar at different angles were long slashes torn into the metal. I looked down and saw that several of the wheels were warped. Looking up I could see where part of the roof had been ripped apart and was elevated like something had peeled it backward like the lid of a can of tuna.

"Well maybe you are that lucky," I said. I walked around the boxcar taking in all the damage that had befallen it. This was what we had been looking for. Everett Black had come to Baltimore on a train, and from the looks of it he had fought with his captors. Maybe he had escaped. From the looks of things, it was possible, and I had already seen evidence that something was turning people into werewolves.

I opened my senses to see if there was anything around beyond what I could see with my eyes. Nothing came to light before me. I couldn't sense anything magical or supernatural. All I could feel was the rain coming down and the mud trying to swallow my feet. I reached up and took hold of the sliding door with both hands. It was bent and warped along the track, but with a little elbow grease it moved just enough for us to get inside.

"Faith, you go in first and see if you can get a scent or two. Once you are done give us a signal and we will climb up to take a look," I said as I started to move out of the way. Faith leapt right over me, dropping mud on my head and shoulders as she soared into the boxcar. Her momentum snatched the leash from my hand only after it yanked me forward to smack my chest into the lip of the boxcar. My day was getting better by the second.

I let Faith do a couple circuits of the boxcar before asking, "You good?" Faith gave a bark in response. I cupped my hands to give Larry a boost into the boxcar and then leapt in myself.

Bullet casings covered the floor. Blood painted every surface. In the center of the boxcar was a cage, or rather the remains of a cage. The iron bars had been bent in places and ripped right out of the ceiling and floor framework in others. Someone, likely Everett Black and his captors, had fought here. I looked around for a few moments and then fished a flashlight out of my bag. With all these shells and all of the dried blood, it was obvious people had died here. Was one of them Everett Black?

I angled my light up to the roof and the gaping hole there. The roof looked like part of it had been peeled back. It was partially rolled the way aluminum or ribbon does when stressed. It was the edges that worried me. The edges were even and perfectly straight for a span of twenty feet. There are plenty of monsters with claws sharp enough and strong enough to rip that roof open. But to do it by cutting two perfectly straight lines twenty feet across. Whatever did that was skilled, and skilled meant two things in a monster. Dangerous and intelligent.

Faith's growl reverberated around the boxcar. I turned and found her haunches up and her body low, ready to pounce. She was facing the door, and I didn't bother to ask her what was wrong. If a werewolf was ready to fight something then I needed to be ready too. I killed my light, stowed it, and drew my black Desert Eagle. Clicking off the safety, I racked the slide and grabbed Larry by the arm. I dragged him over to Faith and put him between us.

A single hand gripped the sliding door of the box car. Metal squealed in protest as the warped door was pulled back as easily as I had racked the slide on my gun. A man in a long brown coat, a brown suit, and a black tie stood there easing the door back with his right hand while holding an umbrella in his left. He looked up at the three of us and let his eyes roam between Faith and Larry. He was a tall man with a thick frame. He had a rim of dark hair crowning his head and a chevron mustache to match. Other than that, he was completely unadorned and forgettable. His eyes settled on Larry, and he spoke.

"Come with me, Mr. Lipowski. It's raining, and I have more important business to attend to today."

Feeling ignored as I pointed a loaded gun at this stranger, I felt the need to speak up. "I'm sorry, but 1) Larry isn't going with you, 2) Who the heck are you, and 3) How the heck did you find us?" I asked.

The stranger finally looked at me. "Are you Michael White?" he asked.

"That would be me. Now again, who are you and how did you find us?"

He reached into his jacket pocket and pulled out a card. He flicked it at us, and Larry caught it. "It says 'Gung T. Roll, Architectural Distribution and Supply.' Fuck, he's one of the Bridge Boys!"

"Seriously, T. Roll? You dimwits couldn't come up with anything more creative than ripping off Mr. T. Hedgehog?" I laughed.

Faith stopped growling and stared at me. Gung T. Roll tilted his head to the side like he was puzzled. Larry just shook his head. "I get it, but that was lame. You need to never try to be funny," Larry said.

"Mr. White, will you and your werewolf please go about your own business? This matter does not concern you, and it most certainly does not concern were-wolves."

I rolled my eyes at the troll in human skin. "You should already know that if you want Larry you have to go through me first."

Gung T. Roll sucked his teeth, shrugged his shoulders, and said, "Shouldn't take more than five minutes to dismember and eat you. I was planning on chicken for lunch, but dark meat is dark meat." He took off his coat, neatly folded it, set it aside on the lip of the boxcar, set down his umbrella, and rolled up his sleeves. He pulled off his tie, folded it neatly on his coat, and jumped up into the boxcar. Then he put up his dukes like a gentleman of old.

"Faith, guard Larry," I said. I wasn't about to actually duke it out with a troll. I'm not that stupid. I pulled the trigger of my Desert Eagle. The roar of the gun shook the walls of the boxcar as I put a bullet into Gung's chest. Blood sprayed free of his chest as the bullet crashed into him. Gung went tumbling over the lip of the boxcar, and I saw mud splash into the air as he landed out of my field of vision.

I walked over to the door and looked down. Gung was sprawled out with a hole in his chest. That hole stopped a few inches into his body and was as big as his left pectoral should have been. Beneath the skin and blood was a folded mass of dark brown skin. In the middle of that skin were the smoking bits of my bullet. Gung's eyes opened, and I unloaded six more rounds into him from near point-blank range. Cotton, blood, and flesh flew away to reveal more dark brown skin.

Gung sucked his teeth as I hurried to reload. "Didn't expect you to shoot me. Damn, it's been about seven years since I was shot," he said. He rolled forward onto his feet and leapt back up to the boxcar. I was already backpedaling and had just gotten another magazine into my gun when Gung stepped forward and lifted his boring brown loafer in a stomp kick. His foot hit me in the chest, blast- ing the air from my body. I went flying across the boxcar to slam into the opposite wall where I felt myself press into the metal. I hung there as the boxcar rocked back from my impact only to rock forward and resettle. The motion should have thrown me forward, but I was actually caught in a mold that was the general shape of my back.

I wasn't up there long though. Gung walked over, grabbed me by the front of my shirt, and flung me over his shoulder like an empty soda can. I went flying out of that boxcar and into the side of one that was sitting parallel across the way. I landed in the mud as I tried in desperation to get air back into my lungs. I could hear Faith growling and Larry screaming. I curled into a fetal position and tried to roll onto my hands and knees. My hands began to spasm as they tried to grab hold of something solid to fight with. I couldn't make sense of my surroundings. Why was the world spinning? Why were my ears ringing? Why was I suddenly weightless?

Gung was holding me by my shirt as he looked me up and down. "You didn't break," he said. "Guess I shouldn't be surprised. Hung said he smashed you through a car and you kept fighting. Not much fight in you now, but you didn't break." He reached out with his free hand and took hold of my left leg. "I think I'll start with a drumstick".

Faith crashed into Gung's back, slamming us both into the boxcar. She bit down on the shoulder of the arm he was using to hold me, and I fell back into the mud. I managed to suck in a breath as Gung struggled to get Faith off his back. The three-hundred-pound werewolf had her forepaws planted on his upper back, and her back paws were raking his lower back. She had her full weight on him as she tore into his flesh in three different places.

The problem was that Gung wasn't screaming. He was barely grunting. His right arm reached up toward Faith. It began to stretch, and the skin of his hand tore apart to reveal a hand the size of my chest. It had four long fat fingers and a thumb that ended in shovel-like claws. Faith saw it too, because she bounded away from his grasp. He rounded on her, and as he did a mass of bulky flesh spilled out of his human skin where I had shot him in the stomach. He stood there, half man and half monster. With his business suit and his suit of human skin ruined, Gung T. Roll was slowly becoming Gung the Troll.

"A leprechaun, a knight, and a bitch. I'll kill them all once I scratch my itch," said Gung as he curled his troll hand up under his right arm and started scratching his armpit.

Gung's back was to me now, and I moved my right arm to shoot him. I realized then that I had dropped my gun somewhere. I pushed up to my knees and reached over my shoulder. Grunting, I forced myself up to my feet and started stumbling forward in the mud. Gung must have heard me coming because he started turning toward me. He was still scratching his armpit as he turned while laughing at me. His face had split open to reveal a mouth that was so big that his lip had to roll back to just under his eyes to smile.

"Break the knight, rip off a haunch, so I'll have a bit of lunch. Then I'll beat the bitch until she's broke, and I'll strip her fur to make a coat," he said as he reached up with his still human left hand. He started to grab the skin of his face just below his eye like he intended to rip off the rest of his human mask.

I flung myself forward to shove the barrel of my shotgun into his chest and pulled the trigger. His chest exploded into tatters of human flesh, monster flesh, and bone. But he didn't fall over. He stood there with his left hand still grasping for his face. I started shaking in disbelief as I watched his human hand clutching the side of his face and tearing it away. Then I nearly screamed when those tattered remains of his chest started knitting themselves back together.

I leveled my shotgun at his chest again and fired. Then I fired at him again.

The fourth shot dropped the troll on its back. I unloaded the remaining shells into him as fast as I could rack the weapon. When the shotgun was finally empty I let my shoulders slump. I let go of the gun with my left hand and let it sway in my right hand. I took a deep breath and sighed in relief. Gung T. Roll, Gung the troll, was finally dead.

The dead troll's leg twitched. Its shredded upper body began to pulse and spasm. My feet started moving, and something in the back of my head began screaming that there was a reason trolls were the monsters of so many tales. Faith watched as I started backing away and ran to my side. We both watched as the mutilated troll started putting himself back together.

"Nope, not dealing with this! We're out," I yelled. I turned to run and fell into the mud again. The beating Gung had given me was beyond what I could endure and walk away from. Adrenaline and fear were keeping me conscious, but I wasn't going anywhere under my own power.

Faith dropped her leash in my hand. She barked at me and started nuzzling my arm to get me to move. I got the impression that she was trying to help me up. I wrapped her leash around my hand and tried to pull myself up on her back. Faith picked up my shotgun in her mouth and sprinted away. The problem was that I wasn't on her back.

I jerked forward, and Faith dragged me through the mud as she ran all the way back to my truck. All I could do was hold on and try not to let my face hit too many rocks. We had covered miles in our search for that box car, and Faith didn't slow as she cleared that distance with a speed that I couldn't have matched on my best day. It felt like hours to me as I scraped across glass, rocks, train tracks, and weeds. I was barely conscious when we got to my truck. I wasn't even surprised to see Larry sitting in the cab with the heat on and my gun beside him.

"You dropped your keys on my foot when the troll kicked you. They scratched my shoes and ruined their polish," he complained as he helped Faith hoist me into the passenger seat.

CHAPTER 19

I NEEDED TIME to heal. I fumbled through things in my mind as I tried to plot a course. That troll had found us in the middle of a train yard. That meant one of two things. Either they were tracking Larry somehow or they had followed us. Neither option sat right in my stomach. If they were tracking Larry, why not jump us at the library or hospital. If we were being followed then when did they start following us? They could have come at us at my apartment or the job site. If they were tracking Larry then it wouldn't matter where we went, but if we were being followed then by leaving the troll in the dirt we might have lost the tail.

I pulled out my cell phone and hit one of my speed dials. The phone rang three times, and the pause between each felt like an eternity. The ringing finally stopped, and a pleasant voice came over the speaker.

"Hello, Mr. White, how can I help you today?"

"Hello, Mrs. Freeman, can I hide out at your house for a couple hours or so? Also, can you remove a tracking spell from a leprechaun?"

I could hear her eye twitching when she said, "Mr. White, just what have you gotten yourself into now?"

"I got beat up and need to heal. Shouldn't take long if you have an extra chicken or maybe a couple pies sitting around that I can eat."

"Does this have anything to do with werewolves?"

"Only that one is with me. This is because of trolls."

"Well in that case I just happen to have an afternoon free today. I guess I can babysit you for a few hours."

I rolled my eyes. She just loved to push my buttons. "Thanks," was all I said before I hung up. I pressed a saved location in my phone's GPS and set it in the dashboard holder. "Follow that and wake me when we get there."

Larry nodded his understanding, and I let my head fall to the side so I could rest. I took a quick look in the rear and side view mirrors to make sure no one was following us. Nothing odd or sinister stood out. I did note that there was a cop car in the lane next to us. It was a few cars behind us, but it was odd that a cop would be driving in the slow lane behind three other cars when the middle and far left were both empty. I let my eyes count cars instead of sheep until I fell asleep.

When I woke up we were parked in front of Eden's home. There were several children between the ages of eight and ten just leaving the gate. We walked into the yard behind them, Faith and Larry supporting me every step of the way. We had barely stepped onto the porch when a small black woman in old jeans, a button-down work shirt, and a scarf tied around her head stepped out. She had splotches of paint on her outfit here and there, but other than that she was as meticulously clean as always.

"Hey Eden. Is that pie I smell?" I asked.

"Pie. Muffins. Cupcakes. Chocolate chip cookies. Why is a werewolf in wolf form at my front door instead of in your truck?" she asked with a smile.

"Long story. Food please."

"You are covered in mud."

"Short story. Bed please."

"I'm going to run a bath. You are getting in it. If you track mud into my home I will kill you. If the werewolf isn't house trained I will kill you. If the leprechaun, I assume you are the leprechaun." Larry nodded. "If the leprechaun leads a troll to my house then I will kill you after I kill the troll. And again, for the record, I am not involved in any werewolf business in Baltimore."

"How did you know about the trolls?" I asked.

"The whole city, well the whole magical community of the city, knows about the trolls that are after this leprechaun you have taken it upon yourself to protect."

She led us into her home, and when she closed the door I felt the wards of her home seal away the outside world. I felt a blanket of power all around us, and I knew in my bones that we were safe. I didn't feel the least bit hesitant to hand over my clothes and my weapons before slipping into the hot bath that Eden had drawn for me. After Larry helped me into the tub, she came in and collected my muddy clothing. She did, however, set my sword against the side of the tub.

"Mr. Lipowski, you may rest in the guest bedroom across the hall. I will be in shortly to see if there is indeed a tracking spell on you. I am however going to put your clothing into the wash first, Michael. I will be right back with something for you to eat."

She and Larry walked out, and I let myself slide into the bath. The hot water soothed my wounds, and I had a brief flash back to Kerri-Lynn coming into my bathroom with her phone and singing to me. I started to drift off to that wonderful memory when Eden walked in with a long tray filled with baked goods. The tray rested nicely across the width of the tub. Screw sleep, there was a small bakery worth of cakes, cookies, and pies in front of me.

I started stuffing my face, and Eden laughed to herself. "I guess if you let them eat in the tub then you only have to clean them up once."

I shoved a whole piece of pie into my face and chewed it while trying to argue. "I'm not a child."

"He said with strawberry and cookie crumbs all over his face. You are no different than the little ones that just left."

"Who were they?"

"My students, young magi that are receiving basic instruction before I place them with mentors."

"I didn't know you taught people magic."

"Of course. I am a member of the International Council of Magi. It's my duty and my honor to teach them before they end up hurting themselves or others. If not, we would end up with more street mages and more dead bodies."

"Lots of those in Baltimore right now."

Eden picked up a cookie and held it out to me until I bit it. She smiled and said, "That is not your fault, Mr. White. Eat, get well, and then solve that problem. I will check on you in a few minutes."

Eden turned on her heels and left me alone. I went back to eating in silence. There was so much food, and I was so hungry. My tattoos could heal me from just about anything, but they had drawbacks. The more I healed the more fuel my body needed. Even worse was that the faster I healed the more fuel my body needed. I couldn't control the speed at which I healed unless I wanted to push it all the way to its limits. The worse I was hurt then the faster my tattoos tried to heal me. So here I was stuffing my face because my tattoos were trying to do the two things that needed the most fuel.

When I finished eating, I slid down into the water to relax. The bath water was cool now, but it still felt good on my sore body. I thought about what had happened up until now. Someone had abducted the brother of a werewolf alpha. That same someone, or possibly multiple unknown subjects, had brought him to Baltimore. This person or people have been using this abducted werewolf to turn other people into werewolves and were leaving bodies in their wake. And the icing on the cake was that I couldn't focus on the problem because a bunch of trolls were trying to kill my friend.

I could feel the anger of the situation mounting inside of me. Larry was being hunted by trolls that I was apparently ill equipped to fight let alone kill. People were dying left and right, but no one cared because they were homeless. Here I was in the middle of it all without a single darn clue as to how to fix any of it beyond 'shoot the bad guys and save the good guys.' Lydia Black was right—I was just a little boy playing superhero.

I took a deep breath then exhaled slowly to let all of the anger, confusion, and doubt flow out of me. It was a poor attempt, but the water helped. I was able to nod off for a bit in a nice hot bath.

When I woke up I was clean. Eden, like a maternal ninja, must have snuck in and actually washed me. There was a washcloth slung above the curtain bar that had not been there before. There were also multiple bottles of liquid soaps, shampoos, and conditioners all with non-allergenic labels lined up on the back counter of the tub. To drive her point home, she had dropped a rubber ducky into the bath water. The joke was on her. I preferred toy boats.

I climbed out of the tub to towel off and found my clothes were sitting on the toilet seat lid. They were cleaner than I had ever managed to get them and pressed. They smelled fresh and wonderful. The scent set off my allergies, and I just barely moved my face fast enough not to cover the clean shirt in snot. I found my weapons wiped clean and reloaded inside of my sports bag. My boots were cleaned but not shined. The turn over service was lacking in that department.

I rummaged in my bag until I found my allergy meds and took a few of them. I sneezed for a good ten minutes before the medicine kicked in. Then I cleaned up my face and checked my phone. I had been asleep for a couple of hours. Time was not on my side today. I needed to pick up the work crew soon and then hit the streets again.

I walked across the hall to the guest bedroom. No one was there so I called out to Eden. I called out a second time and she called me down to the living room. I went downstairs and found the wizard sitting cross-legged on an ottoman. Faith was still muddy and was napping on a blanket. Larry was standing in the middle of a circle of chalk wearing only his boxers, bright green boxers with pots of gold all over them.

"Larry, seriously?" I asked as I pointed to his shorts. I couldn't help but laugh at the leprechaun wearing underwear that was at best a cartoonish jab at his magical heritage.

"They're comfortable," he said.

"Get dressed Larry, you're clean," Eden said as she stood up and walked over to her coffee table. She was holding a glass orb in her hand. Eden set it inside of a long wooden box filled with all kinds of wizardly doodads. I walked over and watched as she began to clean and put other items away. "There are no tracking spells on the leprechaun. You can drop him off on a corner and let him take his chances with the Bridge Boys."

"You know I am not going to do that."

"Then how are you going to find Everett Black while a bunch of trolls are hunting you?"

"How do you know about Everett Black?"

"Willy. He may be a street mage, but a mage is a mage. We talk sometimes. I give him cookies and clean clothing, and he gives me information."

"So, any info on my case?"

Eden shook her head. "No. I wish I could help you, Michael, but I tend to keep my nose in wizard business and not in the business of others. Business like hitmen from the church being in town after finishing their business is something I tend to stay out of."

It was my turn to nod. Eden wouldn't get involved directly, but she still had my back. "What's all this?" I asked.

"Magic detection kit. Lots of items to detect lots of different things. Mainly stuff for detecting magic in young children"

"Cool." I noticed a stray piece of white chalk and picked it up to hand it to her. Eden reached out for the chalk but pulled her hand back.

"Church boy, do you think you could draw a circle on the floor," she asked.

I looked down at her hardwood floor and at the circle she had drawn. It was an intricate work of two circles, one inside the other, and connected by triangles.

"Not like that," I said with a shrug.

"Just draw what you can."

I leaned over and began to trace out a circle. Eden reached down and smacked my hand. "Not like that. Get down there and actually try."

"Yes ma'am, Mrs. Freeman," I groaned.

I got down on my hands and knees and began to draw a circle. I use a compass and protractor when I am designing structures in my free time. My free hand isn't that good but it's passable. The circle I made, however, was absolutely horrible. In fact, it was closer to an oval than a circle. I looked at it in comparison to Eden's and shrugged.

"I can do better, honestly," I said.

"Notice something strange about it?" Eden asked.

"Not really. It's just a bad-looking circle."

"Yes, but what color is the chalk?"

"White." My eyes nearly popped out of my head. The chalk was white, but the circle I had drawn was blue. Bright blue! I scraped a few lines on the floor and each one came out bright blue.

"Color changing chalk? Cool!" I said.

"Yes…pretty cool," she said.

I handed the chalk to Eden, and she took it so she could put it away in her case. Then I stood up, pulled out $200.00, and handed it to her. She took the money but squinted at me curiously.

"I don't need to be paid to help you, Michael."

"Good, because I'm not paying you. Those kids, however, deserve ice cream and juice when they come here. If they do well in their studies, of course. Plus, I hear that teachers have to buy their own school supplies."

I gathered up my team, and we headed out to the Rust Bucket. Eden had given us a break, but the clock was ticking. There was one more night before the moon was full, and if I didn't find Everett Black before then werewolves were going to be running wild in my streets. That was going to leave way too much crap to clean up.

# Chapter 20

WE PULLED UP to the work site just as the work crews were pulling out for the night. My crew looked worn and battered. That all changed when they found hot food and cold drinks in the bed of the truck for them. It had cost me another $75.00, but they were happy and that's what mattered. Drew road upfront with Larry and me while Faith and the others road in the bed of the truck. The sun was going down and I had ground to cover, so I didn't even bother trying to get Drew to stay at the church tonight. I dropped him and the crew off in front of Code Blue.

"Might have a bigger crew tomorrow, boss," Drew told me.

"Hey, see if a guy named Jermon Hernandez is inside. If he is, see if he wants a job. Tell him Michael from the train yard wants to hire him."

"Will do, boss."

We rapped knuckles again before I drove off. I wanted to get back out into the streets. I wanted to hunt down whoever was turning people into werewolves and stop them. I wanted to have it out with the last two trolls and make sure Larry was safe. These are the things I wanted. I pulled my gun from its holster and felt its weight in my hand. My Desert Eagle was the gun I used the most, and I was accustomed to holding for a prolonged length of time. I could not hold the gun still in my hand. I wanted to do a lot, but what I needed to do was rest and recover.

I drove us back to my apartment. I told Larry to chill out inside for a bit while I spent some time with Faith. I still had her collar and leash on her, so I guided her to the part of the lot reserved for washing cars. I ran inside and came back with my car washing bucket, some fancy soap that Kerri had left behind, sponges, and a big towel.

Faith growled at me when she figured out that I meant to wash her. "Hey, you aren't the only one that got filthy today. I still have thumbs and Eden washed me. You are getting a bath."

Faith turned and bolted for my front door. She reared up to put both of her front paws on either side of the doorknob and turned it with practiced ease. I chased her into my apartment to find her in the bathroom sitting in my bathtub. It dawned on me that though Faith looked like an animal she wasn't. I had basically just told a grown woman that I was going to wash her outside where everyone could see her. I am such a freaking idiot!

"I'm sorry, Faith. I wasn't thinking at all," I said. I went back out into the rain to get my cleaning supplies. Then I came back in and started the water in the shower.

The water heater was working today, so I scrubbed Faith from top to bottom with nice hot water. She held still the entire time as I ran my hands through her fur to make sure I got every bit of mud off of her. I shampooed her twice and pulled down the detachable shower head to massage her from head to tail while I rinsed her off. Faith had saved my life today, and the least I could do was make sure she was clean.

When I was done I reached to grab the towel to dry her off. Faith grabbed the shower curtain with her mouth and pulled it across the length of the tub. Then she shook herself dry. When she was finished she pulled the curtain back, stepped out of the tub, and stood ready for me to finish the job. I dropped the towel on her and began rubbing her from head to tail as she squirmed beneath me. I had to towel myself off a little, of course, but once we were both dry we headed out to the living room.

Larry had his laptop set up and had somehow managed to figure out the Wi-Fi password for one of my neighbors. That or he had his own internet connection going. Either way he had a movie queued up.

"Vampire in Brooklyn?" I asked.

"A monster we aren't dealing with in a city that doesn't concern us," he countered.

I nodded my approval and sat down on the couch to watch. Faith rummaged through her bag before coming and laying across our laps. She dropped a large brush down beside me and growled until I picked it up. I spent the duration of the movie brushing her. Faith's soft fur, warm body, and the company of she and Larry did me some good. At some point we ordered pizza. It arrived, and of course the driver couldn't break a hundred. I let her keep the additional $50.00 as a tip. She also took time out to pet and praise Faith. We watched another movie, *The Untouchables*, before it was time to call it a night.

Larry headed back to the bathroom while Faith curled up on one of the rugs in the living room. I double checked my wards and locked myself in my room. I did some stretching and changed into a pair of shorts to sleep in. Just as I was about to crawl into bed Horace sat up.

"So how does this work? You just wake up when you feel like it?" I asked.

"I'm usually awake kid. I can only move when you are alone, or at least when no one will notice. Your pals must have just drifted off to sleep. Is that a shoe print on your chest?"

"Yes."

"Wanna talk about it?"

"A troll beat me up."

"You fought another troll and lived?" Horace said with more than a bit of surprise in his voice.

"I managed to disable him just before executing a tactical retreat," I bragged.

"Oh, so you ran away like a little bitch?"

And just like that I was back to wanting to shoot my teddy bear.

"Do you have to be such a jerk?"

"Are we about to talk about your feelings or something? If so, I am just going to warn you now that I'm going to call you a bitch a lot and my throat might get parched. Mind grabbing me a couple of beers?"

I shrugged. This would be a losing battle. It was par for the course but still a losing battle. I went to the kitchen, grabbed two beers and a sports drink, and then locked myself back in my room. Horace had grabbed one of the new encyclopedias and was going through it again. I handed him both beers and flopped down on my bed.

"So, if you were supposed to protect me as a kid why don't I remember it?"

"You probably do. You just rationalized it away as your imagination or playing. That's what Ignorance Is Bliss does. As a kid you were more open to believing more than just what was acceptable. The older you get the harder that curse affects you. That's why you hear people say that old men are set in their ways."

"Is this how all teddy bears work?"

Horace looked over at me and shook his head. "No. The teddy bear has to be given freely to the child out of love. Some nice people donating a bunch of stuffed bears to an orphanage at Christmas time isn't going to call out to a single Ursa. You were lucky, kid. Maybe blessed. Your grandfather loved you from the moment your mom told him she was pregnant. If he hadn't, you would have just had a plain old stuffed bear. You would be dead."

"Because my grandpa killed a demon in the hospital nursery," I asked.

I saw Horace's marble eye narrow. "Yeah. That and other things. Lots of other things."

I sat up in my bed. "What other things?"

"Stuff you don't have to worry about now, kid. You are a grown-up now, so you are safe. But there are some things in this world that only appear to children. Monsters that exclusively terrorize and even kill kids because adults cannot see them. So, if you ever have a kid and that kid says that there is a monster under their bed, then there is a fucking monster under their bed. Get your sword, your gun, and anything else you have because how the hell does every kid that is afraid of monster know they are under the bed or in the closet? How do they all know those monsters have teeth and claws and that they all talk? How? Because they aren't making it up."

I was frozen stiff. I had just been told by a magical teddy bear that children were being terrorized by monsters and that adults didn't believe them. That couldn't be right. We would have noticed something, found evidence, or remembered it ourselves from our childhoods.

"And you just fucking rationalized away what I just told you, didn't you?" Horace asked. "I just told you for a fact that little kids could see monster that you couldn't, and you let Ignorance Is Bliss tell you otherwise. A fucking magical teddy bear that exists solely to protect children from monsters that you cannot see just told you that those monsters exist, and you chose not to believe me."

Holy crap, he was right! Worse, I knew that monsters were real. I knew that magic was real. My best friend is a vampire. A half leprechaun and a werewolf were sleeping in my apartment. A wizard had given me a tray full of baked goods today. A troll had curb-stomped me today, and I had the shoe print on my chest to prove it. Yet here I was, a knight sworn to protect the innocent, and I didn't believe that a monster I hadn't known about existed.

"What can I do?" I asked.

Horace looked away from me and signed. "God picked a good one to wield that sword. You can't do anything, kid. That's my job. The job of my kind. Besides, you have enough on your plate. Get some rest. I'll have some more info for you on trolls in the morning."

I laid back on my bed and pulled the covers up around me. The world seemed like a much bigger and darker place as I tried to close my eyes to get some sleep.

"Hey Horace," I said quietly.

"Yes Michael?"

"Thank you for keeping me safe."

I turned over to go to sleep. I like to imagine that I heard my teddy bear sniffle as he went back to his work. He might have, but it would have been drowned out by him belching.

# Chapter 21

THADDAEUS WAS WAITING for me when I arrived at the park. After a quick stretch we started our jog. We had only been at it for a little over a minute when Thaddaeus asked about my current case. I wasn't about to tell him about leprechauns, trolls, or werewolves, but I could skirt the truth.

"Well, I have two right now. I am playing bodyguard to my friend Larry. He has a hit out on him, but the guys that are trying to collect on him have a pretty strict code. They will only come after him once. If I can keep him safe until each one tries and fails then I'm golden."

"That sounds a little scary, and a little too good to be true if you know what I mean," Thaddaeus chuckled.

"Yeah, I have been wondering about that. My intel isn't exactly the picture of honesty or street smarts."

Magical beings were quirky with some things. Larry had told me that trolls either did something the first time or not at all. The Bridge Boys had a reputation for collecting on the first go round, but there was nothing that I knew of that said they couldn't come back for a second round. That was just a bridge I was going to have to cross when I came to it. Hopefully a troll wouldn't crawl out from under it.

"What about the second case?" Thaddaeus asked.

"I'm trying to find some guy's missing brother. My client says that his brother was abducted, and from the looks of things he was. Whoever has him is using him to push some bad times on innocent people."

"Bad times? Like what? Is he a drug lord like on that one TV show? The one with the teacher that makes drugs because he has cancer and can't afford the treatment?"

"No. It's more like he has a disease that he doesn't want to spread around. These jerks are making him spread it against his will."

"That sounds horrible. Is there a cure?"

"Not that I know of. If there was I don't think the poor guy would have the disease in the first place."

"Good point." It may have been my imagination, but Thaddaeus sounded genuinely sad about that.

We had reached the end of our jog, and Thaddaeus' chauffeur was there waiting on him. We shook hands, said our goodbyes, and agreed to meet the next day. I turned to leave when Thaddaeus asked me a strange question.

"Michael, have you tried talking out your problems?"

I shrugged. "I don't think I can just convince a kidnapper to return a hostage."

"Well maybe not. But maybe you can talk these rogues that want to collect on your friend into giving up?"

That thought had never crossed my mind. Maybe I could talk to one of the Bridge Boys. Horace had told me that trolls liked to make deals. "Thanks, Thaddaeus, that just might be an option!"

We shook hands again before I took off to finish my run. When I got back home I curled up in bed and enjoyed a couple hours of dreamless rest.

When I woke up I reconsidered the whole running before dawn thing. I was missing precious sleep, but the exercise was good for me. A month wasn't going to kill me, so I decided to stick with it. I collected myself and thought through my plan for the day. If I could avoid it I would leave Faith at my place, but I needed her today. I washed my face again, gathered my wits, and prepared to ask my friend to go through hell for me.

Faith was lying on the floor in the living room. She rose to a sitting position when I approached. I knelt down so that I could look her in the eyes. Those dark amber eyes pierced into me. I knew that what I wanted her to do was selfish, but it was my best chance at saving Everett Black.

"West told me that it was going to hurt for you to change back. I hate to ask, but I need you today. Can you change back now?" I asked.

Faith whined at the request and backed away a bit. I had witnessed part of her change two nights ago. I was asking a lot of her.

"I need you, Faith. Is there anything I can do to help you?" I asked.

Faith looked me in the eye and eased up to me until our noses were touching. As I watched her eyes I felt something pull between us. In her eyes I could see my own, but it didn't feel like I was looking at a reflection. I saw her eyes within mine and mine within hers again and so on. I felt wild magic spark somewhere inside of me, and I had the urge to do something, but I didn't know what.

Before I could begin to figure out what I needed to do I felt a rush of wind in my hair as I ran through the woods. I was so young that I should have been crawling, but I needed to run so that's what I did. Long legs pounded the ground next to mine, and I saw a woman with a wide smile running beside me. There was a man running behind me as well. He didn't smile, but when he looked at me I felt his love for me and everyone around me. I kept running and I kept growing. Every step brought new strength to my growing form and new faces to this marathon of life. The woods began to change to cities with wide rivers. Skyscrapers surrounded us, but we kept running. Ten, then twenty, then thirty strong we ran, and we grew. Soon I was the same size as the larger ones, and then there were smaller ones all around me looking to me with wonder and joy.

That wild magic came back to me, and I realized that I was running faster. There was a man in front of me. He was strong, stronger than the mountains and the trees. With every step the sun fell lower, and the moon rose higher into the sky. The man in front of me began to run faster and so did we all. At first we all kept pace with him, but soon each of them fell back while I ran forward. I was the only one that could keep up with him. The sunset began, and I felt his words. I heard his words through that wild magic.

"Run with me! Hunt with me! Fight with me! Be mine and I will protect you. Be mine and I will teach you. Be mine and I will die for you!"

He fell forward and so did I. The moon rose and we ran on four legs. The moon light enveloped the wolf before me, and I heard my voice echo in my soul and in the souls of every member of our pack.

"I will run with you! I will hunt with you! I will fight with you! My father, my alpha! I am yours!"

Every step of Faith's life, every hardship, every triumph, every dream, and every nightmare came flooding into my memory. I felt the pain of her first teeth coming in and the pain of her first transformation without her pack. I felt the embarrassment of her first period and the joy of tossing her little brothers in the creek. I knew what it meant to be Faith Kane.

Then I was in front of her again as plain old Michael. My body began to itch all over, and I mean all over. I itched in places that had never itched before. Under my fingernails, my earlobes, the individual hairs on my arms, and even my teeth! It all itched! Faith snarled a split second before I felt every muscle in my body seize up. I fell over. I started sweating as the temperature in the room shot up to 150 degrees. I tried to scream as I felt the flesh peeling from my bones, but I passed out as my fully exposed body somehow fell into a vat of salt.

When I came to, I could feel my heart beating in my chest like I had just run from the east coast to the west coast and back. Every part of my body had that feeling you get when you sleep on your arm. You know that feeling like a thousand needles are rapidly tapping your skin. My balls felt like that, and I am pretty sure that was the least of whatever had just happened. I tried to sit up, but my body protested by sending alternating flashes of cold and heat down my spine. I just lay there in a literal puddle of my own sweat.

I turned my head to the side to see Faith on her belly. Faith was in her human form, naked, and in a puddle of her own sweat as well. She was breathing as heavily as I was and looking at me with the same look of confusion that I am sure was on my face.

"What just happened?" I asked.

"You wanted to help, but that's impossible. Only a pack can help," she said.

"Huh?" I asked.

"I reached out to my pack on reflex. I don't have one now. There was no one to help manage the pain of the shift. When it happened, I felt you. You took some of the pain, but that's not possible—you aren't pack," Faith said.

We both struggled to our feet. I, being a gentleman, turned my head away from my naked friend. I grabbed my trench coat and tossed it over my shoulder to her. "Put that on, kick Larry out of the bathroom, and you can grab a shower. You can use my room to get dressed. Dress like you did the other day if you don't mind," I told her.

"Did you like the way I was dressed?" she asked.

"Yeah, I guess. I thought you looked nice," I told her.

"Better than how I usually dress?" she asked.

"Nah. The way you usually dress is cool. I don't think anyone in the world can pull that look off except you," I said.

Faith smiled. She ran to the bathroom and kicked Larry out. He and I sat on the couch in complete silence until she was done and dressed. Larry showered after that. He also used my room to get dressed. I was the last to shower and the last to get dressed. I wasn't going to work as a carpenter today since I had been fired from that job. Today I was working as a knight and a part time private investigator, so I dressed the part.

I pulled out two storage bins from my closet and geared up. I wore black wing tips and black dress pants. I tucked a red button-down dress shirt into those pants and tied on a black tie around my neck. I then made sure I had my ring on my right hand and my crucifix around my neck.

For what I had planned I wouldn't be able to walk around with my weapons, so I had to pack them into my sports bag. Of course I packed my sword. Then I put both my Desert Eagles into the bag. I also packed a shotgun, my nunchucks, and the silver knife my mother had given me. I was about to zip up my bag when a thought occurred to me. I reached into my closet to grab one more item and stuffed it into the bag. I also tossed in some spare clothes that were more suited to throwing down in the streets for later.

Dressed and geared up we headed out into the city. It was still drizzling. The first stop was Code Blue to pick up Drew. When I pulled onto Fallsway nothing seemed out of the ordinary, but as we approached the building flashing blue lights filled my vision. There were police cars everywhere. We pulled up short of a barricade and got out to look around. I spotted a few officers that I knew and called out to them. When they saw me they waved me into the building. I left Faith and Larry in the truck.

The inside of Code Blue was a sanctuary for the less fortunate. The place was never the classy hotel for the homeless that many would have you believe our tax dollars are being strangled out of us for. It was always clean, organized, and structured to make sure that anyone that entered this building felt welcomed. Warm beds tended by warmer faces were the norm. They had a stocked kitchen and long tables to accommodate as many mouths as possible. Soft lights were present among the standard florescent lighting to push back the shadows of bad breaks, hard lives, and lost hope. This place was a shelter from the figurative and real monsters of life.

Sometime during the night, it became a nightmare made real. Tables, beds, and all sorts of furniture were ripped apart. Bodies were strewn all over. Some were whole, but most were in pieces. Blood pooled and caked the ground, walls, and every other surface. I could see bits of body parts all around. Fingers missing hands could be spotted in crusted blood, guts scattered like the contents of a ripped grocery bag littered the floor, and swaths of flesh were scattered around like fallen birthday decorations. The smell of blood, feces, rotting flesh, and urine mixed with the ventilated air freshener to create a macabre sweet smell that made me want to throw up. I noticed that several of the officers and probably some of the victims had done so.

I looked over the scene from the entry way. Priest Greyshadow had drilled into me the importance of taking in everything with a clear head. First I had to be detached from the scene in front of me so that I could gather all the information I needed to make logical decisions. I couldn't think about the voices screaming in my head. I pushed the voices back, and for the first time I noticed that Captain Clay was beside me.

"What the heck happened here?" I asked.

"I was going to ask you, Mr. Supernatural," he said. "We have ten identified bodies, but there were fourteen workers here last night. We have a roster of forty-six guests. Twenty were men, fifteen were women, and eleven were children. I say *were* because we haven't assembled enough damned pieces to tell if they were all slaughtered here or not. I can't examine the crime scene myself because I am still in the damned wheelchair, and on top of it all your damned truck is the last thing on camera before the power went out. So, tell me right now why I shouldn't let the officers that aren't in my department throw your ass in jail?" Captain Clay said. His voice grew angrier, darker, and more desperate with every sentence.

"I dropped my employee…my friend Drew off here last night. I had bought him and a few other folks dinner after they worked at a construction site all day," I said.

"So, you were here when this shit happened?" Clay asked.

"No, I dropped them off then went home. It never occurred to me that the werewolves might come here," I said.

Clay didn't say anything. He drummed his fingers along the grips of his wheels. He motioned for the two officers that were standing near us to disperse, and they left to gather more evidence. Clay and I stood alone in silence for a long while. I ran my eyes over the room again and again while pushing the voices farther back in my head. I saw a glob of blood fall to the ground from its perch on a wall. I looked away only to find an eyeball peeking at me from a mound of torn tissue and dried blood. I had to grit my teeth to keep the voices back.

"Werewolves?" Clay asked. "You're telling me that werewolves did this? Does this have anything to do with you fighting over near Fulton Avenue two nights ago?"

"Yeah. How did you know?" I asked.

"Call-ins about gun fire and wild dogs growling loud enough to wake the dead came in. The responding officers didn't find shit except for some crazy old man babbling about knights, dogs, and princesses. I didn't give it a second thought until right now," Clay said.

I didn't respond. I just filed everything away.

"So, did werewolves do this or not?" asked Clay.

I nodded. "The ones I have seen were dressed like homeless people. The crime scene from the other day was probably a werewolf attack as well."

"So, werewolves eat homeless people? That's your theory?" Clay asked.

"No, they aren't eating them. They are turning them into werewolves," I said.

Clay looked up at me with a look that prompted me to continue.

"Homeless people are all over this city. There are thousands of them. How many people see them every day and do not take note of them. How many people ignore them on a daily basis. The only reason we are even discussing them right now is because of two murder scenes. The werewolves that are doing this are raising an actual army right under our noses, and the only reason we know about it is because they got carried away here," I said.

"Unless they didn't get carried away. The only bodies we found were employees. They could be sending a message," Clay said.

"What message?" I asked.

"That they don't need or want us. That we are expendable. The message itself isn't really that hard to get. The question is who the message is for."

My stomach dropped and rolled. "It's for me, isn't it?"

Clay reached into his pocket, pulled out an evidence bag, and handed it to me. In it was a swath of leather with gnarled ends like it had been chewed on. There was a patch attached to the leather. It read Drew Thompson Employee of White Knight Construction. The final three words had a claw mark through them.

He waved over an officer who produced a set of photos. "We found places on the scene where the ground was torn apart with blood pooled into it. If you ask me, they look like claw marks," said Clay.

I looked over the photos and had to agree. "Werewolves. Definitely werewolves," I said. In one of the photos, I saw a puffy white coat covered in blood. The temperature in the room rose by ten degrees.

"How do we detain them?" Clay asked.

"You don't. Not unless the Baltimore Police Department has silver handcuffs, silver lined cells, and silver bullets," I said.

"Our budget barely covers the evidence bags we are going to need for this shit," Clay said.

"Was anyone alive when you got here?" I asked.

"No. We have reports of some people running screaming through the streets around here, but we haven't located anyone fitting a single description," Clay said.

I handed him back the evidence bag and turned to leave. Clay wheeled around in his chair and called out to me, "White, I didn't say you could go!"

I stopped in my march and looked back at him over my shoulder. "I'm not a cop. I'm not one of your officers. I'm a knight. This is your crime scene, but the people that did this, no, the monsters that did this are mine to deal with. So, with all due respect, Captain Clay, I don't take orders from you. My friend is either dead or worse in the hands of a man that hates me. I am going to get him back," I said.

Clay ground his teeth together. I could see the rage in his eyes, but beneath that rage was the understanding that I was right. "Get the job done, White, and don't make me regret not locking your ass up," he said. He was a man of action, and in truth he was more of what this city needed in a protector than I was.

In the end this wasn't a job for the police. Monsters needed to disappear, property could get destroyed in the process, and people needed to die. This was a job for a knight, and in Baltimore Maryland that meant it was my job.

## CHAPTER 22

I SLAMMED THE door to the Rust Bucket and put the pedal to the floor. I swerved through morning traffic at speeds that were more often achieved by tricked out street racing cars. The Rust Bucket could handle my sudden turns, fast breaking, and flooring it every chance that I got. My passengers, however, could not.

"Are you trying to kill us?" yelled Larry.

He was clutching Faith like a drowning man clutched a life preserver. Faith was holding on to the oh-shit bar with one hand and holding Larry like a mother holds a child when she is determined to protect them. The temperature in the truck was sky rocketing again, so I grabbed the temperature control and cranked it down. I must have turned the knob too roughly, because I accidentally ripped it off of the dashboard.

"Michael, what the hell is wrong with you?" Faith demanded.

"What's wrong? There is a crazy half-turned werewolf with a chip on his fucking shoulder raising an army of homeless people to kill me. That's what is fucking wrong!"

I swerved off the road and into a parking lot. I drove right up to the front of the building and parked next to a truck I had never seen before. It was blue with chrome trim. It was the only other vehicle in the lot. I stepped out into the rain, and steam rolled off my body as I walked up to the door of the building.

Faith and Larry followed me. Faith stopped only momentarily to look at the other truck in the lot. She called out to me, "Michael, are you meeting West here?"

"What? No," I said.

"Well, that's his truck," she said.

"Why the hell would he be here?" I asked as I opened the door.

Kate's Bar was generally empty at 6 a.m. I had been here a few times before the sun came up. Usually Orgoth, the ogre chef that thought he was French, was in the back prepping food for the day. Maybe there were a few magical beings getting breakfast or finishing a pool game. The only constant was that Kate would be behind the bar and filled with information. The difference this morning was that Kate was sitting on the bar with her legs to either side of a shirtless werewolf alpha. West Black stood in nothing but his jeans and boots as Kate kissed him like he was the last virile man alive.

I looked down and found scraps of a shirt on the ground. I looked up at West's

145

back and saw claw marks across his skin that were rapidly healing. I started to say something, but Kate's hand shot up with a single finger held out to tell me to hold on for a moment. She dug her fingernails into West's back and pulled him deeper into that kiss.

When she pulled away she did not look up from him. "Sir Knight, please tell me you have urgent business with me and mine. If not then please turn around and leave," she said.

"I do have urgent business with you, Kate. Two nights ago, a homeless guy tried to end one of your employees, rape you, and wreck your bar. Remember how I stopped him? Well now I need to know who he is, where I can find him, who he has connections with, and—most importantly—why the hell you are making out with scary-ass werewolf number three!" I said in my most polite and urgent of voices.

Kate looked up at me for the first time. She pushed West aside and slid down off the bar. When Kate walked her hips rolled and her chest bounced. The heat in the room rose with every one of her steps as her boots clicked out a steady cadence on the hardwood floor. I had barely realized how amazingly sexy she was in a tight tee shirt, tighter jeans, and brown boots when her hand snapped up and collided with the side of my face.

The sound of her palm meeting my cheek echoed off the walls. I felt the temperature in the room drop, and for some reason my body went limp. I fell to the ground, and my body felt like I had just woken up from a long sleep. My limbs felt like wet spaghetti as I struggled onto my butt and elbows. I looked up at Kate as she stared down at me.

"Sir Knight, I do hope you get yourself under control soon before you lose your head," she said as she walked back over to the bar.

I got my feet under me and stood up. West was leaning back with his elbows on the bar. Faith was behind me but didn't offer to help me up. Larry was behind Faith and had no intention of helping with anything. Kate reached behind the bar, pulled out a bottle along with five shot glasses, and began to pour. She slid one to West, took one herself, and left the other three on the bar.

"Drink, and then I will answer your questions," said Kate.

We all walked over to the bar and took up a shot glass. All five of us drank, and when we did something changed. The outside world seemed distant somehow. I looked to the door and opened my mind. I could still feel the world beyond the bar, but it felt like it was a foreign place. I ignored the two werewolves and the leprechaun in the room. I ignored the wild magical energies that had been left by the bar's patrons over years. I turned to Kate and focused on her. I felt a purposeful and solid sense of control from her. It felt like she was a dam holding back a mighty river. But I couldn't tell what that river was composed of.

Kate slammed down her shot glass before she spoke. "First off, whom I 'make out with' is none of your concern, Sir Knight! West is an old friend of mine. Second, normally I would answer any questions you had, but for your rudeness I will only answer two questions today."

As I thought about what she said, West opened his mouth. "Shouldn't you be out looking for my uncle?"

I looked the werewolf in the eye and said, "You don't seem too concerned about me finding him."

West blew a sigh before he spoke. When he did there was no heat to his voice. Every word was just cold truth. "I am. I want him back. But if the full moon rises and you haven't found him, I can assure you that my father will. He will destroy this city block by block until he does."

I thought about the power I had felt in my office when the werewolves first arrived. I hadn't felt Kodiak Black, but to rule over the entourage that he had with him like he did was warning enough. I knew Faith was the weakest of the group, but she was a powerhouse compared to me. West had dominated her over the phone. I didn't want to know what kind of nightmare Kodiak was in his human form, let alone rampaging through my city as a wolf.

I turned back to Kate and thought about what I needed to do to keep Kodiak Black from destroying Baltimore, to keep Larry alive, and to walk away from all of this with my head still attached to my body. My first question was easy.

"I need a meeting with one of the Bridge Boys. Not Hung or Gung. Either of the other two will do. Can you arrange that?" I asked.

Kate pulled a cell phone from her pocket. She moved her thumb rapidly over its screen. When her thumb finally stopped her phone started ringing. After three rings a deep and gruff voice came over the speaker.

"Miss Kate, this had better be important if you are calling me on this number," the unknown speaker said.

"Hello Hoy. I heard that you were interested in getting your hands on Larry Lipowski. Is that true?" Kate asked.

"Why do you ask?"

"His bodyguard wants to speak with one of your crew. I owed you a favor, so I decided giving you a crack at him would balance our scales. Sound good?"

There was a long pause before Hoy said, "Consider our business settled if both the knight and the leprechaun can meet with me at your establishment in one hour. Of course, you will have to host both parties and promise safe conduct."

Kate looked at me for conformation. I nodded. Kate told him, "I can promise safe conduct to you on behalf of all within my domain as long as you offer the same."

"Done. A deal is struck. I offer my word that I will do no harm to you, yours, or anyone else under the protection of your domain," said Hoy just before he hung up.

"Thanks Kate, that helps a lot," I said.

Kate put her phone away and stared at me angrily. "What is your next question, Sir Knight?"

The cold manor in which she asked clued me in on the fact that she was still pissed with me. I had overstepped the boundaries of our friendship when I questioned her personal choices. Kate was not a friend right now. She was a business associate, and I needed to get this job done.

"Where can I find Eddy?" I asked.

Kate slumped back against the bar. "I'm not sure where to find him. I can probably find out, but it will take some time. Give me until the end of your meeting."

I felt the temperature drop in the room again as sweat ran down my face. Feelings of anger, betrayal, and jealousy had all been boiling inside of me. Now that I had a moment to calm down and think, I recognized that something was wrong. I didn't know exactly what, but I knew I felt exhausted. I opened my mouth to apologize to Kate, and a cloud of steam rolled out instead of words.

The next thing I knew West was easing me into a chair. Kate put a glass to my lips, and I greedily drank the offered ice water. I exhaled after finishing the glass, and more steam came out. I looked down at the palms of my hands and noted that they were pinker than usual.

"What the hell was that about?" West asked.

I shook my head as I tried to clear my thoughts. "I'm just overheated I guess. Kate, I want to apologize to you. I have seen so much crap in the past two days that it overwhelmed me. I should never have said anything about your choices. I'm sorry."

Kate walked back to the bar and brought back another glass of ice water. She sat it down on the table and bent down until we were eye to eye. She smiled at me and said, "I accept your apology, Sir Knight. I understand that you were not in a proper frame of mind. I suggest you get your inner demon under control."

Kate walked back to the bar, grabbed West by the hem of his pants, and walked him to the back of the bar. The three of us, Faith, Larry, and myself were left to prepare for the arrival of the third troll on our own. As I laid out my plans, a howl and a scream tore through the building. The sounds of a werewolf and whatever Kate was having amazing sex above our heads will echo in my mind for the rest of my life.

# Chapter 23

THE HOUR PASSED slowly. I got nervous and grabbed my guns before the meeting just in case things went south. Kate came back down to the bar at some point and began to set out shot glasses and drinking glasses at our table. She also brought out pretzels and kept my glass of ice water full. The whole while she was on her phone trying to get answers for me.

Aaron sent me another text. *"I'm coming home. Get them out before I get there!"*

I didn't have time to reply as a man of average height, average build, average complexion, wearing average business attire, and carrying an expensive looking briefcase walked into Kate's just as the hour expired. He looked around as he straightened his blue and white striped tie. Without a word he walked over to the table where I was seated with Faith to my left and Larry to my right. Reaching into his pocket, he pulled out a business card and handed it to me before sitting down. It read 'Hoy T. Roll, Transit Specialist'.

"Transit? Do you mean as in travel or shipping?" I asked.

"Yes," was all he said in response. When I cocked an eyebrow at him he added, "I run several shipping organizations, travel agencies, and provide materials for several transit authorities on the east coast."

"That sounds fancy," Faith said.

"It sounds lucrative," Larry said.

"Before continuing, perhaps we should observe the customary rights of host and guest," the troll transit specialist said.

Kate stepped into view and poured each of us a shot of fine whisky. At least I think it was fine. I pretty much judge booze by how much I can get with ten bucks. If I can't afford it then it must be good. Kate had pulled this bottle from her top shelf and made a point to dust it off and polish the label in front of us.

My friends and I watched as Kate threw back her drink. Hoy followed suit, and we followed their lead. Kate then took a pretzel and ate it. Hoy took a fist full of pretzels and stuffed them into his mouth. Again, my crew followed their lead.

Hoy picked his teeth. "Fine drink. Bread and salt. You are always the peace keeper, aren't you Miss Kate?"

Kate smiled and said, "I run a bar, Hoy. I don't like having to buy new tables and chairs because someone gets too rowdy over absolutely nothing. You are under my protection and so are they. Don't make me have to protect you or them." She turned to me and said, "That goes double for you. Don't be stupid." Kate sat down two more pitchers of ice water before she retreated to the bar.

Thinking about Kate's words, I fished a pair of business cards out of my wallet. I held all three of them side by side and let my brain get a little ahead of my mouth. I looked at Hoy T. Roll and said, "Trolls aren't as stupid as the stories would have us believe."

Hoy didn't smile. His average looking face which sported plain facial hair, an unremarkable nose, and a moderately professional hair style that just screamed to blend into any crowd of forgettable people in the world simply shrugged. "Humans think being big means something must be dumb. They think being smelly means something must be dumb. They think being ugly means something must be dumb. Trolls are big, smelly, and ugly. So, we let you think whatever you want. It's okay to let idiots be themselves."

It took me a moment to realize that not only had he insulted me, but he had also taught me a valuable lesson about old creatures. I nodded and said, "Well, Mr. Roll—"

He cut me off with an upraised hand, "First, Mr. Roll is my father. Call me Hoy. Second, I am here to discuss the surrender of Mr. Larry Lipowski to me immediately. Anything outside of that is moot."

"What the hell are you talking about?" asked Faith.

Hoy looked at her with his average boring looking eyes. He sniffed at her, and his eyes opened a little wider. "You aren't completely human. A Werewolf? In Baltimore? You must be the muscle." He turned back to me and asked, "Are you trying to intimidate me, Mr. White?"

"Are you intimidated, Hoy?" I asked.

"No. I have no quarrel with any werewolves, and I'm not about to begin one."

"Then nope, that thought never crossed my mind. She is just here to be eye candy."

Faith glared at me, and I could only shrug as plans A through C failed miserably. I was counting on Hoy to be at least wary if not afraid of werewolves. But the troll had looked at her and dismissed her as easily as I would dismiss a dog behind a fence.

"Good then. Shall we get down to business?" the troll asked.

I put my hand on Larry's shoulder and said, "Larry cheated his poker buddies out of some money, and they hired you guys to get it back. So how about Larry hands it over and we put all of this behind us."

"No," Larry said.

I bit my bottom lip and turned to look at my friend. I felt like my eyes were ready to pop out of my head at that moment. "Excuse me, Larry, but what the fuck did you just say?"

"I said no. I'm not giving my money back."

"Larry, I am trying to protect you."

"And you have been doing a great job of it up until now. Way to drop the ball, Mr. Knight of the Crucifixion."

"Larry, what the actual fuck?"

"What? I'm a leprechaun! We don't give away gold, and contrary to popular belief we don't grant wishes."

"Larry, it's not gold, its money! U.S. currency! Cold hard cash! It's not gold!" Larry just stared at me like I was an idiot, and I sighed when I realized that I was. "You are planning to trade it for gold, aren't you?"

"The second this is all over."

"Larry, it's not even yours," I argued.

"I won that money fair and square."

"You cheated at a poker game and got caught."

"It's not my fault they took the aces out of the deck!"

"It *is* your fault that you slipped four aces into your hand!"

"You say that like everyone else wasn't cheating."

"They weren't, Larry! That's the point! You were cheating, and they caught you because you were bad at it! Now you need to give the money back so that the nice troll here won't have to hurt you."

Hoy coughed in the typical way people do when they want to interrupt you. We both looked at him and he shrugged. "Bob doesn't want the money back. He hired us to kill Mr. Lipowski."

"If he didn't get the money back, right?" I asked.

"No. He just wants us to kill Mr. Lipowski."

I heard Larry swallow hard. "Umm…okay. Mr. Hoy, there has to be a way to resolve this without Larry dying."

Hoy puffed out a long breath. "Well, Mr. White, to tell you the truth we don't care about this contract. It's more of a favor really. My elder brother, Hung, owed Bob, and this would balance the scales between them. Though I could be persuaded to force Bob to drop the contract."

It wasn't the ideal situation that I had imagined, but it was better than nothing. "Sure. So, what do you want in exchange for getting Bob to drop the contract?"

Hoy looked over the three of us. His eyes settled on me, and they roamed up and down like he was appraising something valuable. He fixed his gaze on the left side of my body and said, "Your left arm."

Having felt overheated so much lately, the cold feeling I got from the blood draining from my body and the icy fear running up my spine should have been relaxing, but you know what? It wasn't!

"My left arm?" I asked.

"Deal!" said Larry.

"What? No! No deal! What the fuck, Larry?" I screamed.

"Your arm for my life? That's the best deal I've ever heard. I get to live, and the problem is solved without me losing the money."

I turned toward the bar and yelled, "Hey Kate, does it break the terms of hospitality if I hurt Larry?"

"No, Sir Knight," she called back.

The appendage in question brought my fist around to hit Larry in the face. He fell off his chair and sprawled on the floor. I hadn't hit him hard, but I wanted him to know that my left arm was not a bargaining tool.

"You punched me in my face," he squeaked.

I ignored him and turned back to face the troll. "I'm sorry, but did you just ask for my left arm?"

Hoy was frowning at me. He licked his lips and spoke like a man ordering off a menu he had seen a thousand times. "Yes. Your left arm looks quite tasty, and I would like to eat it. Preferably roasted over a spit with butter or a light coating of honey."

"Why do you want to eat my left arm?" I asked.

"It's slightly meatier than your right arm. Is it the arm you use to masturbate? That usually explains the extra muscle and the attachment."

"No! Wait. What?"

"I think he's right-handed. You're right-handed, right Michael?" Faith asked.

"Yes, but that's not the point. The point is that I'm not going to let you roast my left arm!"

"I don't see why you care how I prepare it. I could just bite it off and eat it raw, but I guarantee that having it magically or surgically removed is usually the preferred method."

"I don't care how you want to cook it. You can't have my arm!"

"How else would you remove it?" Faith asked.

"In the old days we treated them like chicken legs. We simply pulled them up and back until the bone separates and the meat tears away."

"Stop!" I yelled. Both Faith and Hoy looked at me as though I had interrupted their discussion. Calming myself I said, "You are not getting my arm. Surely there is something else we can offer you other than appendages."

Hoy shrugged. "What else do you have, Mr. White? It was my impression that you were a humble and poor servant of the Christian God. You live in a run down apartment, drive a decrepit truck, and you run a failing business. You have no money. You have no property. You have no real power. So, what do you have to offer?"

Larry was climbing back into his chair now. I wanted to punch him again but resisted the urge. He was an annoying little jerk, but he was a friend that genuinely needed help. I really didn't have much to offer the troll, but I did have something to work with.

"You are basically doing this for free, Mr. Hoy. Only one of your associates gains something from this. I can offer you money but not much. I can offer you a reasonable favor. What this comes down to is what you would like in return for not risking your lives."

Hoy cocked his eyebrow. "Not risking our lives?"

"Larry is under my protection. I am a Knight of the Crucifixion. Whether or not I intimidate you, you do have to realize that once this meeting is over and we are no longer restricted in our actions, I will bring the full force of my power against anyone that pursues this."

There was a sudden flash from the troll's dull and boring eyes. Those unremarkable orbs turned a dark and dirty yellow for just an instant. For the first time during the meeting, he smiled.

"Go on, Sir Knight."

"My best friend is a vampire. I have a wizard on speed dial. A werewolf is staying in my apartment. I have the entire Church backing me in my decisions. Even if you think none of that matters, my grandpa is a Paladin of the First Order. If Hung, Gung, you, or anyone you associate with comes against anyone under my protection, I will not hesitate to end their life."

I watched Hoy's smile as his flat yellowish white teeth began to sharpen. The edges of his smile began to stretch toward his ears. A soft chuckle escaped him. It started off as a human sound but quickly became something monstrous. Larry scooted away from the table as though he would bolt. Faith had been sitting with her legs crossed, but she uncrossed them and draped her arm over the back of the chair. The way she was positioning herself seemed appropriate to use the chair as a club.

Hoy leaned forward. When he spoke, I heard a troll and not a man. "Little human. Made of flesh and made of bone. Bold as brass but breaks like glass. Are you food? Are you meat? Are you here for me to eat?"

The fear that was holding onto my spine clamped down harder. Hoy came forward in a rush. He was so fast that Faith and Larry didn't have time to react. Kate's table went flying across the room. I leapt to my feet and drew both of my guns. Kate screamed as she racked a load into her shotgun.

Then Hoy froze as his phone rang. The ringtone was as plain and as boring as Hoy tried to be. I saw the clawed fingers that I hadn't noticed before dart into the troll's pocket and pull out a cell phone. Hoy held up a single finger before saying, "Pardon me for just a moment."

He walked away while putting the phone to his ear. He spoke in harsh whispers.

His back was to me which allowed me a perfect view as his back muscles pulsed. They expanded to the size of basketballs then deflated back to human proportions. His not so stylish suit jacket began to thin as his conversation became less whispered English and more throaty grunts. When he finally hung up he growled, sighed, and shoved his phone back into his pocket.

When he turned back to face us he was fully in his human guise once more. He walked up to me, picked up his briefcase, and cleared his throat. "Mr. White, it appears that I will have to decline your offer of compensation in exchange for not killing Mr. Lipowski. I, sadly, have more important things to do than concern myself with a cheating leprechaun."

"Okay…so what about your other brother?"

"Oh, Goy. He is still very much your problem, Mr. White, and rest assured that I will let him know that you are willing to end his life," growled the not at all angry sounding troll.

He looked past me and smiled at Kate. "Miss Kate, I am sorry about your table. Please send my secretary the bill for it." Then just like that he turned on his heels and walked away.

Kate walked up to stand behind me, but it was Faith that reached for my arms. She stood to my side and pulled my guns from my hands. My fingers were still pulling at the missing triggers. I realized what I was doing and forced my hands down to my sides. Kate saw what I was doing as well. The safeties were on both of my guns, and that was the only reason I had not shot Hoy T. Roll. If not for the safety features on my guns, I would have broken the pact of safe passage. Hoy hadn't actually attacked me, but I was already pulling the trigger.

Kate put a hand on my shoulder as she leaned in close to my ear and whispered, "Scared, Sir Knight?" Before I could answer, she whispered again, "So was he. Trolls are dangerous old things, but you are a human. You are the most dangerous thing in the world. Do not ever forget that." Then she slipped a piece of paper into my hand and walked away.

Faith returned my guns to me, and I holstered them. I walked away from my friends to clear my head. I did a quick recap of what I had on my list of problems. First, I still had a troll that wanted to kill Larry and now would probably want to kill me even more. Second, Everett Black was still missing. Third, there was a growing army of homeless werewolves that were gathering behind an asshole that wanted to kill me for not letting him kill and rape people. Fourth, I had a packless werewolf to look after. At least I didn't have a whole handful of problems.

My phone buzzed. I pulled it out and looked at the text message from my landlord. It read: "Mr. White, I have been made aware that you have a dog. Your lease is explicit in that you had to let me know if you were going to have pets in your apartment. Your rent is now being increased by $50 per month (pet fee) and you are being fined an additional $500 for not informing me about your pet. This fee is due at the same time as next month's rent. This breach of contract also forfeits your security deposit."

"What? I don't have a dog!" I said. Then I looked over at Faith. She and Larry were at the bar having a shot. Obviously someone, probably Mr. Wilson, had reported Faith to the landlord. Now I had a handful of problems.

I pocketed my phone and looked at the paper Kate had slipped me. There was an address for where Eddy might be. There was also a warning. Just a few words. 'Get your inner demon under control.' She was right—I needed to keep my cool.

I went over to the bar and asked for a shot. Kate shook her head and pushed me another glass of ice water. I shrugged and began to drink.

"I'm gonna go pee before we go," Faith said.

"I'll come with you," Kate said.

When they left, Larry and I were alone. Larry was sitting there with an expensive looking bottle of whisky and a shot glass. He looked at me a few times but quickly looked away when I took note of him. The ice in my glass seemed to be melting too fast as the awkward quiet closed in around us.

"What is it, Larry?" I asked.

He looked around nervously. He opened his mouth a few times but snapped his lips shut before speaking. Finally, he stammered out a few words. "I um…I just…"

Annoyed and anxious to get our mutual apologies over with I snapped at him. "Spit it out, man!"

My water bubbled. I just stared at my glass in surprise. Larry must not have noticed because he basically screamed at me.

"How do you be brave?"

"What?" I stammered. My glass had bubbled again. I took my hand off of it. All of the ice was gone.

"You just stared down a troll. I watched you punch a cyclops, man. Here I am cowering behind you and pointing a shotgun at your girlfriend. When he flipped that table I froze. I couldn't even run away."

"Okay, first Faith isn't my girlfriend. Second, what are you talking about?"

"Michael, I am a freaking coward. I called you because I knew I was in trouble and that you would bail me out. Since the moment you showed up, I have been hiding behind you like a coward."

The now hot water in my glass aside, I was taken back by Larry's question. I had expected an apology for him trying to trade away my arm. This was straight out of left field. There were a bunch of ways I could answer him and come out sounding pretty cool. But I'm not cool. I'm the nerd that has the other nerd's back.

"Larry, I can't tell you how to be brave because I'm not. I can tell you how to be courageous," I said as I sat down on the bar stool next to him.

"What's the difference?"

"Well, brave is what you are after you gain the courage you need. Being courageous is the first step in gaining courage."

Larry furrowed his brow and squinted at me angrily. "Did you just use a word to define itself?"

"I'm not an English major Larry! I'm a hard-boiled part-time detective, that happens to be an out of work carpenter, that also happens to be a knight in the service of Jesus Christ. None of these things require me to be a master linguist!"

"Yeah, but you can't do that. You can't define a word using itself."

"Larry, do you want to learn how to be courageous or not?"

"Okay, sorry. My bad. Go ahead."

"Alright. When you are afraid you have two options. You can let that fear benefit your enemy, or you can let it benefit you. Fear can help you feel strong, or it can help you feel weak. Fear can help you run away faster or stand as solid as a wall. The point is, fear doesn't make the decision for you. You have to take that fear and decide how it fuels you."

"I still don't get it."

"Well, for example, I get scared a lot. I'm a human that deals with monsters that lurk in the deepest darkest fears of humanity. When the fear builds in me, I usually clench my fist or grip my weapon harder to remind me that I can always fight back."

"That's it? You close your hand, and it makes you brave?"

"No. I close my fist to remind myself that I don't have to run away. I say a battle cry when I need to be courageous."

"A battle cry?"

"Yeah, it's like when Mighty Mouse says, 'here I come to save the day,' or when Darkwing Duck says, 'let's get dangerous'."

"What do you say?"

"I have said a lot of things. Last year when I was scared out of my mind and in a situation that was beyond anything I had ever faced, I said something that summed up everything I believe about being courageous. I don't think it will work for you, though."

"Great! I'm doomed to be a coward." Larry threw his hands up in defeat and let his head fall face down onto the bar.

"No. You just need your own battle cry," I said as I patted him on the back. Larry looked up at me hopefully. "Something that says I am Larry Lipowski, I am a leprechaun, and I am not afraid!"

<h1 style="text-align:center">CHAPTER 24</h1>

W E HEADED OUT to my truck. I had a to-go cup of ice water in my hand. Larry climbed in while Faith and I got ready for a fight. I stripped down to my boxers. I threw on my jeans, a dark blue t-shirt, and my boots. I belted my knife and my guns. Finally, I put on my Baltimore Orioles cap.

Faith wasn't modest in the least. She stripped down to her…well, she wasn't wearing a bra or panties. She stood naked in the parking lot and stretched like her clothing had been contorting her in some horrible fashion. Her stomach was rippled with muscle. Her arms and legs were muscular but soft looking. Her entire body had the exact same skin tone from head to toe like she had done a full body tan. Her butt was almost perfectly round and bounced when she moved. I don't know how, but her breasts seemed even bigger with nothing covering them. She pulled out a pair of cut-off jeans and a tiny plaid shirt. She somehow managed to slide the jeans effortlessly over her ample butt and full-figured hips. Then she tied the shirt off just under her breasts and slipped on her gun belt.

"I'm ready," she proclaimed as she checked her revolver. "Kate said West would be down in a few minutes."

"Oh yeah, I almost forgot about him," I said. I walked over to West's very nice-looking truck. It looked brand new, and his tires looked like they hadn't been on the road for too many miles. I pulled out my knife and slashed both of his front tires and one of the rear ones for good measure.

Faith looked at me like I had just spit on her favorite rock star. "What the hell, Michael?"

I didn't answer. I just climbed into The Rust Bucket and started the engine. Faith climbed in and I pulled off. I was pulling onto the road when I saw West Black walk out of Kate's Bar and get a good look at his truck. He looked up from his deflated tires and met my eyes in my rear view. I swear I could see his eyes flash werewolf amber just before he started chasing us. I floored it and left him in my dust. This was my job and my town. I didn't need or want him anywhere around until it was absolutely necessary.

I knew the street the address was on, but Larry insisted on plugging it into his GPS. I expected to find an old corner store or a crack house. Something resembling a home that a few homeless people could crash at during the day. What we found was an abandoned warehouse. I drove by then doubled back. When I finally parked across the street, all I could do was sigh and smack my head against the steering wheel.

"Ummm, why are you doing that?" asked Larry?

I stopped pounding my head and rested it against the wheel. "The bad guys are hiding out in an abandoned warehouse."

"Michael, we live in Baltimore. There are hundreds, maybe thousands, of abandoned warehouses. What's the problem?"

"It's as cliché as you can get. The more cliché a situation seems, the worse it turns out in this business."

"So, we aren't going in?"

"No, *we* aren't. Faith and I are going in. You are staying with the truck," I said as I climbed out and handed him my keys.

"What? Why? You just got through teaching me how to be courageous, and you said he was raising an army. Wouldn't it be better to have me there to help?"

"Larry, have you ever been in a fight?"

"Yes."

"Have you ever won a fight?"

"No."

"Larry, I do need you but as a wheel man. We are going in. If anyone else comes out or in you have to text to warn us. If we aren't back in thirty minutes, you drive to the church and tell Priest Greyshadow what happened. Okay?"

"Got it. Thirty minutes then go get Father Greyshadow," he repeated.

I handed Larry my keys, and then Faith and I got out of the truck. I strapped my sword to my back, checked my guns, and slung my sports bag across my back as well. We ran across the street to check out the warehouse. We made a complete circuit of the building and found nothing out of the ordinary. There were several service and freight doors along the back side of the building. We found a partially opened freight door and slipped inside.

It was dark in the warehouse. The only light came in from broken windows. Rain had found its way into the building and pooled on the warehouse floor. I didn't immediately see any threats, but judging from the outside there were two more floors of possible trouble.

"What's the plan?" Faith asked me.

"Whoever turned Eddy and the rest of the new wolves must have Everett Black. We find Eddy, make him talk, and then rescue Everett. Stay on your guard—we don't know how many people they have turned," I told her.

Faith sniffed the air. "I couldn't smell anything out in the rain, and it's not much better inside with all this water. I can still smell something above us."

"People?" I asked.

"Werewolves," she corrected.

I pointed over to a stairway, and we made our way to them as quietly as possible. The stairs were wet and slick with water, but what worried me was that

I could see blood stains here and there. We ascended quietly with our guns at the ready. I looked over the edge of the landing and found more than a dozen people scattered around. Some were standing and lurching around the area. Others were sprawled out on the floor and jerking from one position to another.

Faith slipped up next to me and took in the scene. "Damn," she said.

"What's up?"

"They are coming back from the change. When a person first becomes a were-wolf, they lose their shit for a few hours. It's like their brains forget how to work their bodies. They should be harmless unless they are hungry."

"And if they are hungry?"

Faith shrugged as she said, "Shoot them before they try to eat you?"

I rolled my eyes before stepping up to the landing. We stalked into the open area of the warehouse with the bodies of half-conscious people all around us. From their cast-off clothing, I could tell that they were homeless. The sight of bruised flesh, dried blood, shredded clothing, and torn skin reinforced the brutality of what was happening. I saw one man on the ground that had scraped his own fingernails off from digging into the concrete floor. A woman had pulled out most of her hair but not just by the roots. Long swaths of torn scalp with hair still attached were discarded on the floor around her. One man was pulling out his own teeth with his bare hands.

"What the hell are they all doing?" I asked.

"It's what happens when the change happens this close to the full moon and you don't have a strong alpha to help you," Faith growled. I looked back at her and saw her eyes had become glowing points of amber light. Her lips were stretched back, and her now canine teeth were bared. A snarl escaped her lips as she surveyed the room.

I looked at Faith and did not see malice or rage. I saw pain. Faith was trembling with anger, but not at the change the people here were undergoing. She was angry because she couldn't help them. Angry that whoever did this to them wasn't helping them. I watched as she took in every person that was harming themselves because they didn't know what was happening to them.

Her eyes stopped on one poor man sitting against a support beam. She walked over to him and knelt down to pull his hands away from his chest. "Michael, can you help him?" Faith asked me.

I saw blood running from open wounds on his chest as I approached. His hands were bloody from ripping open his own chest and pulling his ribs forward. He hadn't broken them, but he had bent them outward. I wanted to throw up at the sight of bones sticking out of him, but I didn't. I'm a knight, darn it, and I don't throw up when people need to be saved.

"Tell me something, Faith. Will they get better?" I asked.

"Yes. They would be better right now if they just had a strong wolf to pull them back from the trauma," she said.

I nodded. Then I drew my sword and knelt down. I placed the tip of my sword against the ground and sighed. "I have never used this on so many people at once. Let's see if it works." I reached inside myself for the faith that guided me. I pulled it to the surface and channeled it into my sword. The power of Truth flowed through me. I opened my mouth to speak, but no words came out.

I had used Truth before. I could call upon my sword to convey an absolute truth to another person. All I had to do was speak, but the words would not come. I knew what I wanted to say, but with the power of Truth you have to believe the words in your heart. I was terrified for these people, and even with Faith's assurance I was not sure they would ever be alright again. After seeing the suffering these people were enduring, my faith just wasn't strong enough.

It was Faith, my friend, that provided me the strength I needed. She placed her hand on my shoulder as I looked around for answers. When I looked at her face, I saw her desperation for me to help the man before her. On impulse, I took her hand and placed it on the grip of my sword between my own hands.

Faith roared! Her roar before had been drowned out by West Black's, but not this time. This time her roar shook the building. My sword erupted with white light, and its radiance touched everyone on that floor. Even the people hidden behind boxes, debris, and furniture were illuminated.

Then the words came.

My voice rang out with more power than it ever had before. "Children of he who created beast and man. Castoffs of this city of man. Beloved brothers and sisters. You are no longer simply man. You are werewolf, and you are still loved. Do not fear the beast, for man has dominion over the beasts throughout the world and those within themselves. Do not fear the claw or the fang, for they are yours to bear. Do not shy away from the pain of the change, for that pain is power and it should be costly. Look to your elders as you are reborn as both man and wolf. Feel now his power and but a fraction of his love for you."

Just as I finished speaking, everyone began to glow with their own white light. The man before me lifted his hands to his chest as the bones began to bend back into his healing body. Looking around, I saw similar things happening all around me. When I turned back to the man I saw tears running down his face and a smile spreading across his lips that conveyed the joy of a child. He looked up at me, and his lips quivered as if he wanted to say something to me but could not find the words.

Faith smiled at me and began to say something. Instead, she paused and said, "What are you doing?"

My ears finally registered the sounds my mouth was making. I was repeating "not my words" over and over again. The words I had spoken with the power of Truth should have been mine, but they weren't. I knew it, and somewhere within me the fact that someone or something had spoken through me scared me. I was so terrified of the power that I had asked for that I flipped my sword back into its sheath and leaned forward to press my hands against the floor.

Something had spoken through me. I had just been used as a conduit for something with enough power to heal everyone around me. Was it God? Jesus? The Holy Ghost? Maybe an angel or a saint? Whatever it was should not have scared me, but I guess an ant gets terrified when sitting on the finger of a human being.

"Michael?"

I looked up to find a shirtless man approaching me. He was tall, muscular, and had swathes of dried blood all over him. I looked him over from head to toe, but I couldn't place him in my mind. Not until he said, "Boss?"

My eyes went wide, and I leapt to my feet to grab him by the shoulders. I looked him in the eyes and examined every inch of his face.

"Drew! You're alive! Thank God!" I said as I hugged him. I pushed him back to arm's length and looked at him again. He looked a little younger, and for the first time since I had met him he looked rested.

"Yeah…alive…" he said. He looked at me, and I recognized the dried tears on his cheeks. He had heard the words and felt the power, but he still did not believe.

"You are alive, and you are going to be fine. I promise. You may be different, but you are still the same Drew Thompson that you were yesterday and every day before that," I told him.

"I know that. I'm just not sure any of us will be alive long," he said.

"Why?" I asked.

"Because of that huge white wolf that attacked us. It was like something out of a nightmare. It ripped people in half. It ate them, Michael. It nearly killed me but…" he trailed off and began to look down at his body. I started feeling his torso, and I noticed the pinkish tent of newly formed skin around his abdominal muscles.

"What the hell is this?" a new voice asked.

I looked over to the stairs leading to the next level. There was a man descending from the upper floor. He was dressed in a long leather trench coat, dark jeans, and a brown shirt. He was bald and sported a goatee of light brown hair. In his right hand he carried a long leather strap. He looked around with his eyes settling on Drew and me.

"What the hell is going on?" When no one answered, he yelled, "Speak!"

One of the freshly healed homeless men yelped and pointed at me. "He healed us. Him, the one with the sword."

The newcomer leapt down the last five steps to land next to another homeless woman. She scampered away into the shadows as he focused on me. "Is that a fact? Well, who the hell are you?" he asked.

I pushed Drew aside and stepped out into a more open area of the floor. I was about fifty feet from this guy, but if he had magical powers or a gun I didn't want anyone in the crossfire. When I was sure no one was between us I answered his question.

"You want to know who I am? I'm a part time gumshoe, a carpenter, and a die-hard fan of the Baltimore Orioles. But besides all that, I am Sir Michael White, Knight of the Crucifixion, wielder of the Sword of Innocence, and defender of Baltimore," I said as I rested my sword across my shoulder.

The stranger sucked his teeth and sneered at me. He lifted his strap and folded it over once. The motion rang bells in the back of my mind. He was holding a belt, not just some random piece of leather. He slapped the belt against his knee a few times before saying, "Sir Michael White? Well, Mike, what the fuck are you doing down here with my mutts?"

"Your mutts? You mean the people you kidnapped?"

He chuckled at my response. "People? They aren't people anymore. Not for long, anyway. Tomorrow night at moon rise these people are going to be werewolves. They are going to be dogs. Mutts. My mutts!"

"Yours? So, you're the wolf running around changing people?" I asked.

"Do I look like some lowly dog to you? I'm no fucking dog. I'm the man that owns these dogs. I'm their master."

I felt my eyes narrow at his words. "These are people. They may be werewolves soon, but they will always be people. You don't own them. They aren't property."

"They're animals and animals are property. Now, Mike, I am in a good mood, since you healed all of my mutts, so I am going to let you leave. Go on. Shoo." He made a shooing motion with his left hand.

"Nope. See, I'm here for Everett Black. Have you heard of him?"

The stranger rolled his tongue around in his mouth. "You're the knight, aren't you?"

"What gave it away? Was it the sword or me literally saying that's who I was less than two minutes ago?"

"Well, this is good. See, I had to find you anyway. You punked my new alpha and made him look bad in front of his pack. I can't have that."

"Punked your new alpha?"

"Eddy. See, first you showed him up in front of a submissive. That hurt his pride, but that didn't bother me. Then you kicked his ass in front of actual dominant wolves. Then you gave them orders and they obeyed you. I can't have that. Only I give my dogs orders, and only I can punish their alpha."

The sound of a revolver's hammer locking turned my attention back to Faith. She stood there with her amber eyes glowing as if flames were roaring from them. Her gun was leveled at the stranger, and her muscles were bulging as though they were ready to burst out of her skin.

"They aren't yours. Say they are one more time and I'll kill you, you lying bastard. A real wolf would take care of his fellow wolves. You left them here to die," she growled.

The stranger smiled at her. "You brought a bitch with you? Is this the one that challenged my new alpha? Cause she needs to die too," he said just before he let out a sharp whistle.

I looked up at the top of the stairs expecting to see someone running down to join the stranger. Instead, I heard loud thuds above us. The building started to shake, and dust began to fall from the ceiling. The thudding became louder, and more dust fell from above. Then the ceiling above Faith gave way. A man dropped through the ceiling to land in front of her and brought a pipe down on her extended arm. Faith screamed as the pipe broke her bones, and her gun fell from her hand. The force of the blow sent the pipe flying from her attacker's hand as well. That didn't stop him from rising up with a hard punch to her stomach.

I moved to help her, but suddenly there was debris falling from above me. Then I felt a hammer-like punch collide with the side of my face. I hit the ground hard, rolling at first because of the strength of the blow, but then to get myself together. I came up on my knees to find four humanoid monsters standing before me. They were dressed in tight ragged clothing that was now covered in dust due to them dropping through the floor to attack us. The three males had their faces outlined by manes and beards of coarse hair. The one female had wild brown hair draping down to her waist.

Young healthy skin stretched over their muscles so tight that I could see the individual fibers. Their clothing was stretched to the limit and ripping from their bulging muscles. I didn't see any fat on them, so they looked like body builders suffering from malnutrition. As they stood upright, I saw that the shortest one was the female, and she was as tall as I was. I recognized them as I watched Eddy flexing his clawed fingers and grinning at me with a mouth full of sharpened fangs. He and four of the werewolves from last night had smashed their way through the ceiling with brute strength. They had obviously reached the stage where they could transform into their feral human form.

I caught sight of Faith. She had regained her footing and was being pressed by the werewolf that had hit her with the pipe. Eddy waved for one of the other werewolves to help her. I didn't have time to call out a warning because Eddy and his two friends came at me with inhuman speed. I pushed up to my feet, spit out a mouth full of blood, and set myself for a fight.

Eddy reached me first and tried to lay me out with a heavy boot to my face. He had outpaced his buddies and over committed to his first attack. Eddy wasn't much of a fighter. I ducked and grabbed his leg. Then I jumped back and dragged him off of his feet. He yelled, "What the fuck," when I spun him around and flung him into the woman that was coming to join in the fight. He hit her like a sack of potatoes, and they went down in a heap.

The third werewolf leapt over them, but I was ready for him too. I reached over my shoulder and took hold of the handle there. I swung my arm up and down when the third werewolf reared back to punch me in the face. His blow fell short when my strike collided with his shoulder. I felt bone break under that blow, and his scream was enough to let me know that my weapon of choice was more than effective. He fell to the ground howling and grabbing his broken shoulder. I calmly rested my Louisville Slugger baseball bat across my shoulder and looked at Eddy as he scrambled to his feet.

"Batter up," I said as I started toward Eddy and his buddy. Eddy flung the woman at me, and she growled as she tried to take my head off with a looping right hook. I stepped back from the blow. She immediately followed up with a looping left hook, and I understood that she had no idea what she was doing. She couldn't fight, or more accurately she wasn't a trained fighter. When she leapt at me with her hands gripped together above her head, I jumped back again to let her hammer blow whiff by me. When her hands hit the ground she cracked the cement floor and crushed a half foot dent into it. In a straight up fight, I could take this woman and Eddy together, but they had superhuman strength which tilted the odds in their favor.

Well, I had a baseball bat! I took a step forward and swung my bat right into her stomach. She lifted off the ground as she doubled over. I didn't wait for her to hit the ground. I raced past her and leveled my bat for a swing at Eddy's head. I swung for the fences, and he leapt away. The leader of the werewolves scrambled across the floor towards the pipe that his friend had dropped earlier. It had landed next to Drew.

"Drew, don't let him get that pipe!" I yelled.

Drew bent down to grab the pipe, but the stranger yelled out, "Sit!"

I watched my friend retract his hand and drop down into a sitting position on the floor. So did every one of new werewolves except for Eddy's group and Faith. They all sat down and held perfectly still. Eddy got to the pipe and turned to face me. He held it over his head like a club as he found his nerve to fight me. I kept charging and let him swing down at me with all of his strength. I threw my bat up to block as I dropped into a baseball slide. His strike bounced harmlessly off of my bat while I kicked my legs out at his shins.

Overbalanced, the werewolf fell over as I pushed back up to my feet. Eddy recovered faster than I expected. He was on his feet, but his legs were shaky. I leapt backward towards him and brought my bat around at his head. Eddy ducked and came back at me with a swing of his pipe to my gut. I threw my hips back, barely avoiding the blow. Eddy's swing threw him completely off balance, and he stumbled to the side.

I took my bat in both hands and brought it around like I was in a home run competition. My swing struck Eddy in the center of his chest, and the resounding crack echoed through the building. I felt bones breaking as I pushed through the blow. Blood gushed from his mouth as he skidded backward under the follow-through of my swing. Eddy fell to the ground and curled into the fetal position to clutch his broken chest.

I wanted to finish him off, but I felt motion to my side and turned to meet the flying form of one of Faith's opponents. I swung my bat defensively to parry his flying tackle, but when I connected and he flopped to the side lazily I realized that he was dead. Looking down at him I saw a cavernous gap between his chin and his collarbone. Inside I could see blood, mucous, muscle, and his spinal column. Faith had ripped out his throat and flung him to the side like a discarded chew toy. I looked around and found her standing over her first assailant. He was pressed against the ground and pushing with all of his might in an attempt to get Faith off of him.

Faith was in her feral state as well. Her hair had grown into a knee length red mane that stood on end like a tensed animal's fur. Her already skin tight shorts were stretched to their limit and ripping in ways that were a testament to their durability. Then there were her breasts. I didn't think they could be bigger. It just wasn't possible, but they were. Before they had been bigger than my head, but now they were twice that size or more. Soft but toned muscle covered her frame from neck to ankle. I could see her claws digging into the pinned werewolve's forearms as she pressed forward to get her blood coated mouth closer to his throat.

Faith had things under control on her end. I turned to the stranger and started walking toward him. "So, about Everett Black."

I stepped past one of the sitting werewolves when the stranger said, "You there, sick him, boy!"

The man to my left leapt at me from his seated position. He was too close for me to get any force behind my bat for a parrying blow. I brought my left hand across so that my open palm slammed him in the chest halting his advance. At the same time, I turned my body to face him and used the force of his leap to slide away from him. I took a look at the man and realized that he was the one Faith had asked me to help.

"Dude, what gives? I just healed you," I argued.

The stranger whistled again. I heard someone scrambling behind me and turned just in time to see a small woman tackle me. She was a waif of a thing clad in garments meant for a much larger person. When she hit me it must have been like running into a brick wall, because I didn't budge and she fell back onto her butt. Another whistle and another man came at my back. The first man pressed in and so did the woman after scrambling back to her feet. I darted out of their immediate reach to face them squarely.

The stranger kept whistling, and all around me once-injured people were getting up to attack me. They weren't super strong yet. They weren't inhumanly fast. They weren't throwing kicks or punches. They were just numerous, and they were blindly following orders.

I took my bat in both hands like I would a staff and slammed a man in his stomach when he got too close. Another woman jumped on my back. I reached over my shoulder to grab hold of her and threw my upper body forward while pulling her in the same direction. She flipped off of my back and crashed hard on the ground. Then someone's knee hit me in the face, and before I could recover someone else tackled me from behind. My bat was yanked from my hand as men and women began to dog pile on top of me. I thrashed left and right but there were too many of them.

I clenched my right hand into a fist and screamed, "Impact!" I pushed up as I swung my fist with the strength of a giant. Men and women went flying out in every direction as I surged to my feet.

Eddy shoulder rushed me and knocked me across the room a good ten yards. I hit the ground hard, but somehow I managed to roll to my feet. Eddy was about to hit with another shoulder rush, but I saw him coming. When he dropped low to hit me, I popped up with my right foot planted and my left leg raised like I was kicking in a door. I hit him square in his jaw with a size fourteen steel toed work boot. Between my strength and the force of his own momentum, Eddy went down like a sack of potatoes.

"Hey, Boss," said Drew. I turned around to see my friend standing there holding my bat. "I'm sorry, Boss."

Drew brought my bat around and hit me in the side of the head. I remember falling but not hitting the ground. I caught a glimpse of a second dog pile as I fell. Faith must have been at its center. Just before I lost consciousness, I felt dozens of punches and kicks raining down on me.

<h1 style="text-align:center">CHAPTER 25</h1>

"WE HAVE GOT to stop meeting like this," a voice said in the darkness. I opened my eyes to find myself looking up at a man I had seen once before. He wore black pants and a gray t-shirt. He had a well-trimmed beard and dark curly hair. As I took in his appearance, he held his hand out for me, and I took it. With surprising strength, he pulled me up to my feet.

Once I was standing I noticed that I was taller than him by almost a foot. The last time I had seen him I was on the ground near death. I clearly remembered him saving my soul from The Devil, and before this very moment I had never thought twice about that. In fact, until this very moment I never remembered that he had saved me.

He smiled at me as he watched the confusion play across my face. "It's okay. You weren't supposed to remember me. I was stepping in for Bill Fred since you were somewhere that he was forbidden to go."

"Okay…and now?" I asked.

"Well, now you have stepped into something that you weren't supposed to be involved in. You are hurt and in a lot of danger. So, the second you were knocked unconscious I brought you here to talk," said the man in gray.

I looked around. We were on an island or something. I could see the night sky in the air above me with thousands of stars in the heavens. There was a grassy beach to my right with a vast ocean of dark water as far as the eye could see. To my left was a forest. I turned to look at it, and the wind stirred the leaves in the trees. I could see the shadows there swirling in the darkness beyond the tree line. I narrowed my eyes as I opened my mind. I felt my body grow heavy instantly as though the earth's gravity was increasing. Then I felt something stir, and I heard a yawn from somewhere.

The man in gray grabbed my face and forcefully turned me to face him. He held my gaze and spoke slowly. "Do not look over there. You and I are talking. All you need is right here. Not over there."

He let my face go, and I asked, "What's in that forest?"

He shook his head. "Nothing that will make your life any easier."

"Okay, this is my subconscious or whatever you want to call it, right?"

"Sure, we can call it that. It has a better name though."

"Fine, whatever. Call it whatever you want. What's in that forest? This place is mine, so I deserve to know what is in there."

"Something that is not important right now."

The man in gray took a deep breath and sighed. He motioned behind me. I turned to find a fallen log that looked quite comfortable. I looked back at him, and he was sitting on a log now. There was a campfire burning in front of me, and I was sure that it had not been there before. Looking around I saw two other logs for a total of four set up in a square around the fire. I turned to sit on the one behind me and found a Baltimore Orioles blanket covering the log. I sat down and instinctively started warming my hands by the fire. I also took a glance back at the forest.

The man in gray waved his hand in front of my face and began snapping his fingers. I turned to face him, and he glared at me. "Don't look. Nothing there is going to help you right now. You need to focus. Just focus. Focus on the task at hand. We don't have much time to talk, so you need to learn to focus right now."

"Okay. So, another time on the forest?"

"Maybe. If you live. You do remember that you are in a den of werewolves, and you are currently getting your ass kicked, right?"

I may not have felt the pain that I knew was being rained down on my body, but I felt the annoyance of how matter-of-factly he mentioned my current situation. I scratched the back of my head as I rolled my eyes. "Look, obviously you have something to say, and like you said time is short. So, I promise to focus if you will just be as straight forward and not cryptic as possible. Deal?"

The man in gray smiled. "That's why I like you, Michael. It makes life a lot easier when people are straight forward," he said. Then he sighed. "Too bad life isn't easy. And neither is carrying that sword."

He pointed to the ground by my feet, and I looked down to find my sword in the grass. I reached for it and took it in hand only to find that I could not lift it. I grabbed the handle with both hands and pulled with all my strength, but it would not budge.

"Okay. What did I do wrong?"

"Did you do anything wrong?"

"Can you at least give me your name so I can call you something other than 'Not Bill Fred'," I grumbled.

"Sure. You can call me J," he said.

"So, Jay, did I screw up when I decided to help Larry?"

"No, it's always good to help people if you can."

"Okay, was it when I threatened to kill a troll?"

"Nah. Though seeing you try to pull that one off will be entertaining."

"Was it when I made a deal with a werewolf?"

Jay reached over and picked up a stick. He stirred the logs of the fire until its flames glowed brighter and hotter than a campfire had any right to. "There was a knight once who made a deal with The Devil. I'm sure you know at least part of the story. I don't think making a deal with a fellow human being is anywhere on that scale, do you?"

I tried to lift my sword again just to see if I could. Of course, it didn't budge. The blade gleamed in the fire light and the word 'Innocence' shined on the blade. I looked up at Jay, and he shrugged without looking at me. He just kept staring into the flames. I looked at him harder as I thought about our conversation.

"You can't tell me what I did wrong?" I asked.

"Right," he answered.

"What is your name?" I asked.

"You can call me J," he answered.

"What is my favorite food?" I asked.

"Cheese steaks," he answered.

"How many times have I been here?" I asked.

"Twice, including this visit. You have been here twice, but that's just you," he answered.

I didn't try to figure out what he had just told me. That was a question for another day. He answered me. He answered every question except one.

"What did I do wrong?" I asked.

"I can't tell you what you did wrong," he answered.

"Why?" I asked.

"Because, to my knowledge, you haven't done anything wrong," he answered.

"Then if I didn't do something wrong, why can't I lift my sword?" I asked.

"Oh, you mean that sword there? The sword that you got when you asked God for help? Why do you think you can't lift it?" he growled.

I looked down at The Sword of Innocence and realized that, even though helping the werewolves wasn't a mission from my boss, it was still a mission. It was still a job. It was still a task that I was undertaking as a mortal man. A task that I thought I could do without the help of God or Jesus.

"It's not what I did. It's what I didn't do. I never asked for help, not until I was already in over my head."

"Exactly," said Jay. "You don't need to pray for every little thing in the world. God wants you to go out and live. But you always have the option of asking for help. What parent wants their child to never call or write? You have a divine gift, and you walk into battle against evil without so much as a prayer for the safety of those that you are trying to save?"

I looked down at my sword and mumbled to myself, "I'm sorry."

Jay stood up and yanked me to my feet. "You're sorry? No one is asking for you to be sorry! No one wants you to apologize or cower or be dependent on divine intervention! Don't regret the problem, fix it!"

I looked back down at my sword. Then I placed my hands together and closed my eyes. "God? Jesus? If you have a moment I have a problem. Evil has come to Baltimore. Some jerk is using a captured werewolf to turn homeless people into werewolves, and I have taken it upon myself to stop them. I am trying to save Everett Black. I am trying to save my employee and friend Drew Thompson. I am also trying to protect my friend Larry from trolls. There are now dozens of innocent people who are in danger. I am not asking you to tip the scales in my favor. I am not asking you to solve my problem. I am asking you to do what you always have. Please guide me. Please lend me your strength so that I may protect those that need it. Please let me help the innocent."

I felt a weight lift off my shoulders. With a sigh I opened my eyes to see Jay smiling at me. He pointed down at The Sword of Innocence. I flexed my fingers and knelt to reach for my sword. When I took hold of the handle and tried to lift it, my sword rose from the ground easily. I held the weapon before me and sighed in relief.

"You are still in a den of werewolves," Jay said.

"Yeah. Anything you can do to help with that?" I asked.

Jay shook his head. "I can't actually help. I am just giving you an opportunity to help yourself."

"Didn't I just pray for help?"

"Everyone you just prayed to tends to help those that help themselves. Try meeting divine intervention half way, Michael."

"I have to meet divine intervention half way? Seriously?"

Jay bowed his head as he laughed aloud at me. "Are you actually complaining that divine forces are going to help you? Is this real right now? All you have to do is try, and that is reason enough for you to complain?"

I shrugged. "I'm in a den of werewolves, unconscious, and I did already pray for help. I think I have gone above and beyond the half way point of getting myself into trouble."

Jay narrowed his eyes at me. "True enough. Three things. That's all Mr. Knight! First, you need to learn to focus. Second, you need to endure. Finally, you need to reflect. Do these three things and you will find your victory. Also stop complaining. It's not becoming of a knight."

"Got it. So how do I get back to my body?"

Jay smiled like I just handed him a million dollars. "I am so glad you asked!" Then he slugged me right in the face. I didn't even see his fist come at me, but I sure did feel it as his knuckles slammed into my nose and mouth.

"Stop complaining!" he yelled as I fell over.

# Chapter 26

I WOKE UP in a lot of pain. That was a good sign. I was pretty sure I had some broken bones, but the more pressing concern was that breathing hurt. I tried to take a deep breath, but my chest refused to cooperate, and I coughed out blood instead. The coughing was accompanied by sharp pains in my stomach and throat.

When I finished coughing I took stock of my situation. Both of my eyes were swollen, which limited my vision to what was directly in front of me. My jaw was sore but not broken. I could move my toes and my fingers, but when I shrugged my shoulders I felt chains wrapped tightly around my upper body. I was seated on the ground with something hard at my back, maybe a cement column. My whole body hurt, but it was healing even if it was slowly.

I opened my eyes to find the stranger sitting on a comfortable looking leather chair. He had my gear on the floor next to him. Across his lap rested my sword. To his right stood Eddy and to his left stood Drew, still holding my baseball bat. From what I could tell we were still in the warehouse.

"I thought you were going to die while they beat you. I had heard that you knights could heal yourselves almost as well as these mutts, but I didn't think I would ever see it happen," the stranger said. He held up my sword by its sheath so that I could see it clearly. "Especially since knights are supposed to carry magical swords. There isn't an ounce of magic in this cheap peace of scrap. So, what exactly are you?"

"Get your hands off of my sword," I said through my clenched jaw. Every syllable hurt and made me want to scream, but I managed to soldier through it.

He tossed my sword to the side like he didn't care. It clanked off the ground and fell through a hole in the floor. I looked around and saw several other holes clustered together. We had to be on the floor above where we were attacked.

"You come armed with guns, a knife, and a baseball bat. How did you heal my dogs?" the stranger asked.

"They aren't your dogs!" Faith yelled from behind me. She was alive! I felt the chains around me tighten when she did, and I realized that we were chained together.

The stranger snapped his fingers. I felt someone move behind me and heard the sound of someone hitting someone else. I felt the chains jerk as Faith growled in response. "Keep your mouth shut, bitch," said a female voice from somewhere behind me.

Faith growled at her in defiance, so I decided to back her up. "They aren't your dogs," I said.

"Oh really?" the stranger asked with a smile. "Drew here is my new beta. He tells me he works for you. Drew, go hit him with that bat."

Drew whimpered and shook his head. He looked like he wanted to fall over and die in that moment. Suddenly he began to growl and stormed over to me like a man on a mission. He wound up and swung the bat right into my chest. The chains absorbed some of the blow, but I felt my ribs break. My lungs emptied as I coughed up blood. Drew backed up with a look of disgust on his face. He mouthed the words 'sorry boss' as he backed up next to the stranger's side.

I coughed up blood and felt like I wanted to pass out. I felt myself slipping away and heard a voice in the back of my head say, "Focus, endure, and reflect." Using all of my will power, I pulled myself back to consciousness. The stranger was talking to me, but I couldn't make out what he was saying. As I looked at him, a figure in the back of the room caught my eyes. There behind the stranger was a single man in a black coat standing next to a large object covered in a tarp. He had a hood pulled up obscuring his head. The only other detail I could make out about him was that he was holding a katana.

Having nothing better to do. I focused on him and opened my mind. That baseball bat to the head must have knocked something loose in my brain, because I could feel power all around me. It felt like waves crashing into each other. I could feel that Drew was the third strongest wolf in the building as far as the magical energy in their bodies. Eddy was next. It was as if their power was connected in some way. Faith's magic was almost nonexistent next to them. The stranger had a bit of magic in him as well, but not a lot. It was the man in the back of the room that troubled me. I couldn't feel anything from him. It was like trying to see something sitting in front of light bulb. Whatever was under that tarp was powerful and giving off the same feeling that I got from the werewolves.

"You have Everett Black under that tarp," I said.

The stranger had been talking, and I had interrupted him. He sneered at me and started to say something. The man with the hood over his head reached over and pulled the tarp away to reveal a large cage, a cage made entirely from silver from the looks of it. The cage had to be worth a fortune. The large black man inside looked like he could bench press a car. He was nude, and if the word masculine had a picture as a standard in the encyclopedia he put it to shame. His muscles had so much tone and definition that I could see the blood pooled around the creases of his skin. His full beard and afro were unkempt. His eyes were glazed over. He looked like he was in some sort of coma while wide awake. What disturbed me the most was that he was in a kneeling position with his legs beneath him. Four silver rods as tall as my shoulder were skewering him. One bar went through each thigh and shin so that he could not unfold his legs. Then one went through each forearm so that his arms were fully extended out to either side.

My brain began to add things up. Everett Black was in a cage, skewered by silver rods, and he seemed to be doped up enough to keep him oblivious to what was going on around him. With all of that, he was still giving off enough magical energy to dwarf everyone in this building. Except for two people.

"Why the hell did you move the tarp?" the stranger asked.

The man in the hood shrugged. "It doesn't matter. You're going to kill them anyway," he said. I thought his voice sounded familiar, but I could not place it. He turned to walk away. As he put distance between himself and Everett, I was able to feel his power. He didn't seem to have power in him. He felt like he was made of power. It wasn't that he was so powerful that I couldn't interpret it. It just felt like his body was made of energy rather than flesh and bone. That energy felt cold and fluid, just like the rain that had been falling in Baltimore since Everett Black first went missing.

The stranger walked back over to us. He knelt in front of me and smiled. "Well, he is right. I am going to have to kill you. Even that pretty little bitch you brought me."

"Don't call her that," I said through clenched and throbbing teeth.

"You don't like that? She is a bitch, you know. A cute one. That red fur of hers probably looks gorgeous when she is on all fours like the animal she is," the stranger said.

"Shut your mouth," I snarled.

He took a deep breath and smiled even wider. "Can you smell it? Do you even know? She's in heat! I really don't want to put a pretty thing like her down before throwing her to a few studs. Too bad, I've never seen such a dominant bitch in my life. She might kill one of them if they mounted her."

"Three strikes, asshole. I am going to teach you some respect," I said.

The stranger stood up and started walking away. "Well, Mike, it's too bad this is the last time I'll see you." He whistled, and the three werewolves fell in behind him. Drew took one look back at me before the four of them disappeared down the stairs. I heard him drop my bat somewhere on the steps.

When they were gone I struggled against the chains. I couldn't move enough to begin to wriggle free. "Faith, do you see anyone else up here?"

"No. I can't smell anyone but you, me, and one other person."

"That's Everett. He's in a cage made of silver and pinned to its bottom by silver spikes."

"And they just left us up here with him? What, did they leave our guns too?"

It's the simple questions that make life complicated. They had in fact left our guns and all of our gear in a pile just ten feet away from me, with the exception of my sword, which the stranger had thrown and my bat which Drew had dropped on the steps. So, what was the catch?

"Michael, do you smell smoke?" Faith asked.

"No," I answered.

"Well, I do, and I smell a lot of it."

I looked around to see if anything was burning. I couldn't see anything, but then the stairs caught my eye. I could see a flicker of light and shadow like one would see with the light given off by a fireplace.

"Oh yay! They set the building on fire!" I yelled.

"So, what do we do?" Faith asked.

I tried the chains again. They had to be locked with something, but since I couldn't see or reach a lock that didn't matter. I felt my finger with my thumb and found my ring in place there. I could use my ring and break the chains if I could punch them, but again I couldn't move my arms. The chains were old and rusted but still strong enough to hold a human being. But what about a werewolf?

"Faith, are you in your feral form?"

"No. Randal said that if I didn't change back he would kill you."

"Randal?"

"Randal Quinn, the one that was giving orders. Weren't you paying attention?"

"No, but you can fill me in later. I need you to change into your feral form and break these chains."

Faith was quiet for a moment. Then she struggled against the chains as I had. "If I change, I can break the chains, but there isn't enough room for me to do it. The chains won't give enough for me to start."

"Don't worry. They will. They are tied to something pretty soft and squishy."

"You mean you? It might crush you."

"Yeah, but I can take it. Just do it as fast as possible."

"Michael, there has to be another way."

"There probably is, but right now it is either you break the chains or we die in a fire!"

"Good point. Okay, I'll try it."

I started to take a deep breath to brace myself for what was going to happen. Before I could the chains snapped tight around my chest and arms. I added my own strength to Faith's as I struggled against the chains. It was all I could do to stay conscious. I wanted to scream as rusted steel cut into my skin, but I didn't. As she growled, I felt my skin tear as the chains tightened. Faith grunted and I felt my spine press against the support column at my back. My ribs began to break, and I felt every crack but still did not scream. I had to endure the pain.

The pain kept mounting, and black spots began to swim in my vision. Just as I was about to scream for her to stop I heard a link pop. Then another followed. Still there was no relief in pressure. Then suddenly the chains constricted even more, and I thought I was going to die. They broke an instant later, and I fell forward onto the ground. I was swooning between conscious pain and unconscious bliss. Faith scrambled around and pulled me back into a sitting position.

"Michael, are you okay?" she asked.

My body hurt so much that if I opened my mouth I wouldn't stop screaming. I opened my eyes and got my first up close look at Faith's feral form. She was beautiful. Her long fiery hair and wild eyes were exotic to say the least. Her features had sharpened, giving her a look of primal beauty.

She slapped me across my face. "Michael!" she yelled.

I spit blood from my mouth and then said, "I'm okay."

Faith helped me to my feet, and we gathered our gear. We checked our guns, and I found all of my other gear just as it was before I was knocked out. I could grab my sword on the way out, but first we had to get Everett Black out of that silver cage.

I limped over to the cage door and pulled on the bars. Of course it was locked. I thought about shooting off the lock, but I had no idea how that would work. My Desert Eagle could blow a whole straight through the locking mechanism for sure, but would it ricochet and possibly kill one of us? I couldn't kick it because it opened out toward us.

"Can you break it open?" I asked Faith.

She walked over to stand in front of the cage. She reached out tentatively and touched the bars with one ringer. She screamed and jumped back. I grabbed her hand and found a blistered welt on her finger. It was a second degree burn to be sure, and all she had done was touch it for an instant.

"Silver. Can't touch it," she said.

"Okay plan C," I said as I balled my right hand into a fist. "Impact!"

I hit the lock with a solid punch. I felt the impact as my fist collided with the metal, but the lock didn't give. Instead, white sparks flew from the point where my fist had landed. I stepped away and recounted everything I had done before being knocked out. I had only used my ring once, so it should have had two charges left.

"Damn, it must be resistant to magic," I said. "We have to get him out."

"Hey look! White found Black!" a voice said from behind us.

Faith and I whirled around to find Willy standing there with a three-foot-tall wizard's hat made of tin foil on his head. He had a tree limb in his hand with strange carvings engraved along its length. Next to him was a disheveled and terrified-looking Larry. Larry was holding my bat and my sword. They were both covered head to toe in feces.

"What the hell are you two doing here, and why are you covered in feces?" I asked.

Larry was convulsing but he answered me, "He broke the windshield of your truck because he thought I was stealing it!"

"I figured saving your truck would get me another sandwich, Mr. Knight," said Willy.

"The only problem is that I wasn't stealing the truck!" Larry yelled.

"I wanted to ask you about that, Mr. Knight. Was the leprechaun stealing your truck?" asked Willy.

"No," I said.

"Damn. Can I have a sandwich anyway?" Willy asked.

"No, because you broke my windshield! How did you do that anyway? It's bulletproof glass!"

Willy lifted his tree limb and waved his arms wildly. "Magic!"

"Of course. Now why are you covered in feces?"

"We came in here to find you to ask about him stealing the truck. There were werewolves, so we needed to sneak past them," said Willy.

"He threw me into a huge pile of crap and made me roll around in it!" Larry screamed.

"Then he rolled around in it?" I asked.

"Yep. Needed to be all camouflagey," Willy said with a smile.

"This is all fascinating, but can we get back to saving Everett and getting out of the burning building?" asked Faith.

"Oh yeah. Kind of lost focus there. I think I might have a concussion or something," I said. I walked over to Larry and held my hand out for my sword. My shit covered compadre handed over my sword, and I instantly felt its power. I slipped it into its sheath and took my bat from Larry. I walked over to the cage while taking a few practice swings. I took a batting stance and swung with all my strength. The locking panel bent inward after the first swing. It took four more swings, but the panel finally bent inward enough to pop free of the adjacent bar. I tossed my bat to Larry to hold and stepped into the cage. I looked to Faith to see if she would be helping me, but the look on her face told me that she was not coming into the cage.

Everett was pinned to the ground by silver rebar. Again, the bad guys had spared no expense in keeping this man locked down. I was close enough now to see him taking shallow breaths, and I honestly could not believe that he was still alive. His blood had stained the wooden floor of the cage red. He looked gaunt, as though they had not been feeding him, but you could still see powerfully fit muscles beneath his slack skin. His imprisonment had done nothing but trim the fat off of him.

I knelt beside him and whispered into his ear. "Everett Black, my name is Michael White. I am a Knight of the Crucifixion. I was sent by your brother Kodiak to save you. I have to pull this silver rebar out of you. It's going to hurt. I'm sorry, but we don't have time for me to figure anything else out. The building is on fire. So again, I am sorry."

Everett didn't reply. I figured he was too out of it to respond, which hopefully meant he was too far gone to feel pain. I reached for the first pole pinning his right thigh and calf to the floor of the cage. I took it in hand and began to pull. When the rebar began to move it made a sickening sound akin to sliding a knife down the length of juicy turkey at Thanksgiving, only wetter. The bloody end of the rebar came free with a sloppy pop, and I tossed it to the ground. Everett didn't make a sound. If that was good or bad I didn't know, and I didn't have time to figure it out. I pulled the rebar from his left thigh and calf then from both of his arms.

Without the support of the silver rebar Everett collapsed to the ground. I was exhausted from my body's rapid healing and the physical exertion of freeing him, so picking him up in a fireman's carry was out of the question. I wasn't going to get any help from Faith while I was in the cage. Both Larry and Willy were covered in feces, so I wasn't about to ask them for help. I was going to have to dig deep to get the job done.

I pulled his right arm over my shoulders lifting him up as best I could. Then I started dragging him out to the cage. I took one step and Everett gasped. He started taking deep labored breaths. I figured the silver had hindered his werewolf healing powers. With the silver rebar removed it looked like he was trying to recover. I kept moving, and on my second step Everett started groaning. He was probably feeling the pain now. On my third step Everett growled and pulled his feet under him. I looked down at his leg and saw the bloody hole closing up. Everett carried some of his own weight with our fourth step. Then with our fifth step, Everett Black lurched forward and shoved me out of the cage.

I hit the ground hard and rolled across the floor. I didn't scramble to my feet because I was too exhausted. I struggled up to my knees and saw Everett on the ground convulsing. He was laying limp on the ground growling so loudly that he almost drowned out the sounds of his bones breaking and resetting themselves. I had partially watched Faith transform earlier, and it had been excruciating and slow. Faith was a lone wolf, but Everett was still part of a pack. His transformation was almost instantaneous. I saw gray and white fur erupt from his body. Where seconds before there had been an injured man, there now stood a gray-white werewolf the size of a smart car.

Everett stood up and looked at me with blank, unintelligent eyes. I climbed to my feet and got ready for a fight. Why? Because being in a burning building wasn't enough. Saving the victim wasn't enough. Being exhausted and injured wasn't enough. No, I had to fight a freaking werewolf that both the bad guys and the good guys considered dangerous.

"I had better get hazard pay for this," I said as Everett Black stalked from the cage with his fangs bared at me.

# CHAPTER 27

**B**OTH FAITH AND Larry were backing away as the wolf exited the silver cage. I watched Everett stumble a bit as he moved, and his left shoulder touched a bar of the cage. Smoke began to lift from where his fur touched the silver. Everett growled but kept coming toward me. His head was low, and his eyes never wavered from me.

I could barely stand straight, and there was a giant wolf stalking toward me. I slapped my face with both hands then shook my head vigorously. "Larry, bat!" Larry tossed me my bat and I caught it. I stood ready to swing for the fences and said, "Alright Everett, if you want to fight then game on!"

Everett leapt at me, and when he did I realized something. He was the size of a small car, not unheard of in dogs, but he was also a mass of solid muscle. He had to weigh over three-hundred pounds. There was no way my baseball bat was going to turn that much moving mass away from me before it crushed me. I dove forward in an ungraceful attempt to save my life. I didn't roll up to my feet or even away from Everett. I just kind of sprawled out face down under him as he leapt past me.

I rolled over onto my back just as Everett landed and pivoted around to charge me. He was so fast that I didn't register the movement until he was about to sink his fangs into me. Faith hit him from my right side in a charging tackle. She wrapped her arms around Everett's neck and pushed him off to my left just before his jaws snapped shut on my throat. The sound of claws skidding across the ground and boots pounding like pistons filled my ears as I watched Faith drive Everett away.

They came to a stop, and Faith had her arms wrapped around Everett's throat. She started choking him and rearing back to keep him off of his front paws. I lurched to my feet so that I could get into the fight, and as I did Everett snapped his head forward to bite Faith's leg. He yanked his head back up causing her to lose her balance and her grip on his neck. Faith began falling to the ground, but Everett reared his body up and flung her into the air. She hit the ceiling and then crashed down onto the floor. Then Everett leaned down to her limp form and opened his jaws.

I tossed Larry my bat and drew my guns. "Get Faith up and get out of here. I'll lead him away," I told him. With my black Desert Eagle in my right hand, I put three shots into the large werewolf. It rounded on me, and I started running. "Here boy! Come get me!"

Everett came after me with speed that I couldn't match. But I had a plan. I dropped into a slide and dropped through one of the holes in the floor that the werewolves had used to get the jump on us earlier. The giant wolf jumped in behind me, and when he did I leveled my left arm and fired my chrome Desert Eagle. He was too close for me to miss, so when I fired the explosive rounds that I kept loaded in my chrome gun they blasted him with enough force to flip him around and away from me.

I landed on my feet and dropped into a roll to absorb my momentum. Everett hit the ground in a heap but thrashed back to his paws. He growled and came at me like a mad dog in a dark alley. I leapt to the side just as he reached me, and when he adjusted to come after me I shoved my chrome eagle into his shoulder and fired. Blood, bone, flesh, and fur went flying from his shoulder and he crashed to the ground.

I started back pedaling but stopped when the pain caught up to me. I staggered to the side and realized that my pants were on fire. I dropped to the ground and rolled to smother the flames, but I rolled into more fire. I leapt up and found a clear spot to fall down and roll around until the flames died. I looked around and realized that I was surrounded by fire. Smoke burned my eyes and filled my lungs as the building around me burned.

I could see the stairs and could see Faith and Larry running down them. Faith must have still been in fighting shape or close to it because she leapt over Larry, clearing almost ten steps to land on the ground, and charged back into the fight. Larry charged up behind her while waving my bat above his head.

Everett got back up, and I could see the hole I had put in his shoulder was almost completely healed. It looked as though I had just shaved off his fur. He came at me again, and I leveled both guns at him. I fired two normal rounds, and he dodged to the left. That's when Faith darted in and slugged him with a left hook to the side of his head. The sound was as loud as my gun, and I saw Everett lurch awkwardly to the side. He recovered almost immediately and snapped at Faith. She was already moving away, and I was already charging his flank.

I put two more explosive rounds into his chest and back leg. The big wolf just growled and rolled with the blows. He turned and leapt at me again, so I shot him in the chest with an explosive round. The blast slowed him down but not enough to matter. He collided with me, and we both went down. Everett scrambled at me with snapping jaws and raking claws. I lost some skin on my arms, chest, and legs, but I kept the presence of mind to keep scrambling away.

I threw up a few blocks and even fired both guns into his neck and torso. The normal rounds just annoyed him, and he was shrugging off the explosive ones even faster than before. I shot Everett in the side of the head with an explosive round and blew off part of his ear. He growled and raked across with his left paw.

He caught my left hand, and his claws dug in. My gun went flying from my grip along with a good bit of my flesh. I cried out and emptied the magazine of my black Desert Eagle into his gut. It enraged him, and he rushed to his feet just so he could pounce at me.

When he jumped Faith grabbed him around his torso. She couldn't halt all of his momentum, but she kept him from landing on me. Everett bucked and thrashed in an attempt to throw her off. I heard Faith growling in challenge as she struggled to get her feet under her. Everett was throwing her left and right mercilessly, but just for an instant she got her feet on the ground, and that's when she sprang into action. Faith roared and arched her back with all of her strength. She fell backward and slammed Everett into a patch of burning floor. It barely stunned him as he rolled and scrapped at the ground with his claws. Faith lifted him again and repeated the process not once but twice.

On the third suplex, Everett arched his back and managed to break Faith's hold on impact with the ground. I thought I heard bones break, but it didn't matter. He accepted the injury just to get free. Then he snapped his jaws down on Faith's arm and slammed a paw on her back. He yanked up and Faith screamed as the larger werewolf tried to rip her arm off.

I got to my feet and charged through the flames with my right hand cocked for a punch. I screamed, "Impact," as I hit Everett Black square in his jaw. With the force of a giant's punch, I sent the big werewolf flying across the room as I fell down next to Faith. She was grabbing her arm and screaming, but she still had an arm to scream about.

Again, Everett Black landed in fire, and once again he did not care. Everett stood up and stalked back toward us. "Faith, get up," I said. I could barely get up on my knees without my body protesting that I needed to stay down.

"He's too fucking strong. Nothing hurts him," Faith said.

"Can you take him if you transform?" I asked.

"No," she said in a tone that brokered no argument. "It would take too long anyway. I thought we could take him, but I've never fought a wolf this strong."

At her admittance Everett charged at her. We both tried to get out of the way, but he was just too fast. He was too strong and too savage for us to overcome him. I hated it. I hated Faith being in danger. I hated having to fight someone I was trying to save. Most of all, I hated being so weak that every magical being in the world could out class me. It made me so angry that my blood felt like it was boiling.

I pulled myself in front of Faith and slugged Everett with my injured left hand. I didn't realize it, but when I made a fist my hand was covered in patches of fire. I felt the knuckles of my fist pop and my blood spattered over Everett's face. Red hot flames erupted on his fur as my blood landed on him. For the first time in our fight, Everett Black yelped as though something we did had actually hurt him.

Everett backed off and slammed his face into the floor to extinguish the flames. Every swing of his head smothered some flames and left cracks in the ground. I looked down at my left hand, and even though I could see that my hand was on fire I didn't feel like screaming. It didn't hurt. In fact, it felt incredible. I could feel the fire pulsing out of my hand. It wasn't until a few drops of blood fell to the ground and ignited that I realized my hand was only burning where my blood touched my flesh. I could see the blood running along my hand and forearm from where Everett's claw had cut me, right along the scar I got from that hell-cursed dagger.

I didn't have time to consider what that might mean, because Everett growled and came forward with frenzied murder in his eyes. This time I had a weapon. I had a fist wreathed in magical fire. I could feel the grin spreading across my face as I balled my burning hand back into a fist and got ready to punch him again. That was the exact moment that the flames died away.

"Oh, you have got to be kidding me!" I yelled.

Everett jumped at me with claws and fangs ready to tear into me. That's when Willy dropped from another hole in the ceiling. He came down swinging his stick in a two-handed chop. He hit Everett in the back while screaming "KABLAM!"

There was a flash of pale light, and Everett crumbled to the floor. Then the floor gave way, sending both Everett and Willy falling to the bottom floor. Smoke billowed out from the new hole. Faith ran up to me and tried to look into the hole, but she had to pull back from the smoke.

Larry came over to us looking none the worse for the wear. "What do we do?" he asked as he handed me my gun.

I looked around at the burning building and at my no longer burning hand. I was too tired to address his question in any creative way, so I said, "We jump down and keep fighting the super werewolf until we either win or he kills us."

"What?" was all Larry said before Faith picked him up by the belt of his pants and leapt through the hole. I heard them splash into the stagnant water below then pushed myself up to my feet. I ejected the spent magazines and slapped home backups of normal bullets. Then I dropped into the hole.

I fell through ash and smoke. Heat washed over my body, and it hurt to breathe the thinning air. I hit the ground with a splash and rolled through the stagnant water. I rolled to my feet, and the sounds of battle filled my ears. Larry was swinging my bat like a mad man. He was hitting the ground more than he was hitting Everett, but he was trying. Faith was pounding away at Everett with blows that would have crushed any heavy weight boxer. Everett was shrugging off their assault like a tank being hit by bullets.

Willy was holding his tree limb like a rifle, and red blasts of fire were flying from it to slam into the big wolf. Each blast had Everett recoiling like he had been slapped in the face. It was the only reason he wasn't still steam rolling us. The flames all around us were intense, and the steam from the burning water was starting to obscure my vision. We needed to end this fight immediately. So, I holstered my guns, drew my sword, and started forward.

I reached for strength that wasn't there, and instead of sprinting into battle I limped. I raised my sword before me and prayed that even if its blade wasn't glowing it would have enough magic to compete with Everett. I was just a few steps away when I stumbled and fell to my knees. I tried to stand but couldn't. I was too exhausted to get back up. I struggled, but the more I fought to get to my feet the harder it was to just remain upright.

"God, if you can hear me, I just need a little more help. Just whatever you've got available that can handle a super powered raging werewolf," I prayed.

One of the metal loading bay doors exploded off its track and came crashing down into the stagnant water just inches from where I was struggling to stay upright. Debris, displaced water, and dust filled the air only to be vacuumed out due to the change in pressure. As the dust cleared and the daylight poured in, a lone figure surveyed the area from the loading dock.

With a cigar between her lips, wizardly staff in hand, umbrella on her wrist, a dress with the ABCs printed haphazardly on it with bobby socks to match, and I kid you not a pink raincoat with matching hat and rain boots, Eden stepped into the building.

"Eden!" I yelled.

"Idiot!" she yelled back. Then she got in on the action. With a wave of her free hand, she sent Faith and Larry sliding away from Everette Black. Then she said something in an African dialect I didn't know, pulled her cigar from her lips, and blew smoke and frost at the enraged werewolf. The water around him churned, sloshed, and then froze into place around his paws.

"You can't throw magic at werewolves because they just shrug it off. You have to use spells around them to affect them. It's just like a physical attack, Church Boy. No matter how hard you hit them, if it's not with silver or a magical weapon they just shrug it off. Bullet holes heal, limbs will grow back, they just get angrier and stronger," Eden said as she started making a circular motion with her staff.

Everette jerked his lupine head towards Eden with a growl. He ripped his paw out of the ice and slammed it down, cratering the frozen area to his left side closest to the offending wizard. I heard the ice cracking as the unstoppable werewolf began to angle himself towards his new target. Suddenly all of the ice cracked, as did the concrete floor beneath him and the ceiling above him. A section of the ceiling pulled free and plummeted to crash onto Everette Black. It exploded into pieces on the back of the werewolf.

Eden was chanting something and slowly, ever so slowly, Everette was being forced to the ground. I watched as the water around the frozen area moved away as though it were being pressed down then out. Looking up at the new hole in the ceiling I realized that Eden was somehow weighing everything down.

"I can't hold him forever, Church Boy. I've almost doubled the gravity around him, and he is still fighting. If you have any cards left to play do it now. Otherwise, I am going to have to crush him so we can run away while he heals," Eden said through strained teeth.

I tried to get up but fell forward and caught myself by slamming my hands down. Looking into the fire-lit water I could see my sword still clutched in my right hand. The fire light danced on its blade. Then white light began to shine from my sword. I forced myself back up to my knees and held my sword out before me. Its white glow warred for dominance with the fire light, and Everett looked at me once more with those unintelligent eyes. "Everett Black," I roared at the top of my lungs. "I am Michael White, Knight of Innocence and defender of this city. I am here to help you. I am here to return you to your family. Your brother asked me to save you, so here I am. I want to take you to your nephew, West Black. Calm down and know that you are safe. You are among friends."

The light of my sword died away as I fell forward onto the murky floor. I could barely keep my head above the water. I watched as Everett shook his head slowly and then vigorously. He growled as his body contorted and his fur retreated into his skin. In seconds Everett Black was back to being a naked man that was just struggling to stand against the power of Eden Freeman.

She let her spell fade so that gravity returned to normal, and Everette gradually stood upright. He looked at me and offered a nod as he said, "Please, take me to my nephew."

I gave him a thumbs up.

Then Willy ran up and hit him in the back of the head with what I now realized was his wizard's staff. Everett's eyes rolled back into his head, and he fell into the water. Willy held his staff over his head with both hands and started pumping it in triumph. "I defeated the werewolf," he proclaimed as he turned around in circles. Then he looked at me and smiled. "That's gotta be worth a sandwich."

# CHAPTER 28

IT WAS STILL raining outside. Faith, still in her feral form, was able to carry both Everett and me to my truck. She had us each slung over her shoulder. She dropped Everett into the bed of the truck and set me down so she could clear the broken glass out of the cab. "There are emergency blankets behind the seat in the cab," I yelled to Faith. She retrieved one for Everett and covered him up. Willy sat down next to me and started whistling.

"Thanks for the help Willy…even though you broke my windshield," I said.

"Not a problem, Sir Knight. Anything for a sandwich," he said.

"Willy, I never offered you a sandwich," I chuckled.

"No, but you are going to get me one, right?" he asked.

"Sure. A sandwich, fries, and a soda. You deserve it. You and your staff came in pretty clutch," I chuckled.

"Staff? This thing?" he asked. "This isn't a staff. This is a big ass stick. I use it to smack raccoons and rats that try to steal my stuff." I just stared at the mad mage in the tinfoil wizard's hat. What else could I do? Willy was powerful but insane. He was a first-class mage that could be bought for the price of a sandwich.

Eden and Larry walked up together. Well, they walked up at the same time and were close enough to have a conversation in normal tones. Larry was still covered in feces, and Eden wasn't about to let herself get dirty, at least not that kind of dirty. Eden shooed Larry away as she stood in front of me.

"Mr. White," she said in that too prim and too proper tone she used when she wanted to make me feel like a small child being addressed by a teacher.

"Mrs. Freeman," I said in my best 'I have no idea what this is about' voice.

"Sir Knight, you are the only person in my life that I know of that would pick a fight with a shift sick werewolf," she said.

"Shift sick?" I asked.

"Moon struck, lycanthropy madness, rabid. It has lots of names. It means that the werewolf is out of control or in their more primal mind."

"I didn't exactly pick that fight. But I did learn a lot from it," I said.

"Like what?" Eden asked.

"Players in the game. Two…no…three that I didn't know about. We may have to deal with two of them before we can take down the big bad this time," I said.

"We? No, no, no, Mr. White. There is no 'we' in this," she said as she shook her head in the negative.

185

"But you came to help me," I protested.

Eden held up her hand and shook her finger from left to right, "No. I came to help him." She pointed at Willy. "As a member of the International Council of Wizards, it is my obligation and privilege to protect local practitioners from mundane forces, supernatural forces, their own stupidity, and idiots messing around in vampire and werewolf conflicts."

"What vampire conflict. This is just werewolves," I said.

Eden signed and pinched the bridge of her nose. "Have you called Aaron?"

"No," I said. "I texted him."

"What the hell is wrong with your generation?" Eden screamed. "I told you to tell Aaron, and you decided the best way to do that was to text him? Why didn't you call him? These werewolves aren't supposed to be here, and you are just gallivanting around with them like they own the city! What is wrong with you!"

"Eden, it's my job," I said.

"Your job is to keep the peace, not to pit vampires against werewolves," Eden argued.

"Look, just because Faith is hanging with me doesn't mean I am replacing Aaron or you. When he gets back we'll get a pizza and some bad movies and make a night of it," I said.

Eden's eye started twitching. "You cannot be this dumb. Aaron is not going to take this like some spat between friends. You invited his mortal enemies into his territory."

"Vampires and werewolves are mortal enemies? Seriously, I thought that was just in the movies," I told her.

Eden was about to say something else, but Faith called for us to get into the truck. I couldn't move, but Larry and Willy both moved toward the cab of my truck.

"Stop! You two are covered in shit. You ride in the bed," I yelled.

Larry started to complain, but Willy grabbed him and tossed him into the bed of the truck. "You don't argue with the guy that is buying the sandwiches," Willy told him as he climbed into the truck bed. Willy stood up, pointed ahead with his 'big ass stick', and yelled "Onward to sandwiches!"

Faith came over and pulled me to my feet. "Give me your keys," she said.

"Larry has them," I reminded her.

"Larry, give me the keys," she yelled.

Larry tossed her the keys to the Rust Bucket, and she strapped me into the passenger seat. Eden sat in the middle. Faith pulled out of the alley and drove by the approaching firetruck. I could see police head lights coming from the opposite direction in the passenger side mirror. Air and rain flew in through the hole where the windshield use to be. We were drenched, filthy, and freezing, but we were alive. We had rescued Everett Black, and the bad guys were gone. I looked out into the stormy sky and sighed.

"Hey Eden, how did you find us anyway?" I asked.

"Willy came to see me two nights ago and told me he was helping you out. I guess I put the dumb idea of asking a street mage for help into your head, so I decided to make sure Willy didn't get into too much trouble. I got him a burner phone and told him to call me if he or you were in trouble," she told us.

"You don't drive, and I doubt you took the bus, so how did you get here?" I asked.

"I got a LYFT," she said.

"From whom?" I asked.

"Oh no, we are not doing this," Eden grumped. "I took a taxi."

"But you said—"

"I should have let the fucking werewolf kill you," Eden cursed. "Take me home!"

We did. Faith got out so I didn't have to move. Before Eden got out she turned to me and said, "When this is all over, you and I need to have a talk."

"Am I in trouble, Mrs. Freeman?" I said in a mocking voice.

Eden somberly nodded, "Always Michael. It's your most annoying quality, but I'm starting to think that you can't help it. Fix this mess, then we will talk."

"Yes ma'am," I said. Eden climbed out of my truck and walked swiftly to her house. We waited until she was inside before we drove off.

I told Faith how to get back to Kate's Bar. West's truck was still out there but with brand new tires. We had barely parked when West Black came storming out of the bar. I reached into my glove box, grabbed a magazine of explosive rounds for my Desert Eagle, and slammed it into my gun. I set the gun on my lap because I could barely lift it, but I had it angled to hit anything that opened the driver's side door in the chest. I could see the beast in West's eyes as he neared. He started to growl, and I felt the cab of my truck shake. I felt the temperature rise as I realized I was in for another fight. The cab of the truck began to fill with steam, but I could see West Black as clear as day, and I could fill him with every bullet I had as long as Faith didn't move forward or jump.

I clicked off the safety and chambered a round. West was just a few strides away, and the Rust Bucket was rattling under the force of his growl.

"West," gasped a faint voice.

The growling stopped, and West angled his head to look at the bed of my truck. He broke into a run and vaulted into the back of the Rust Bucket. I heard Larry scrambling to get out of the way. I also heard Willy complaining about wet dogs. I clicked the safety back on and holstered my gun.

Faith helped me into the bar while West helped his uncle. Kate was not letting Larry or Willy into the bar without hosing them off first. That job fell to two of the regular bouncers. Once inside of Kate's, Chef Orgoth set to the task of feeding two starving werewolves, one famished leprechaun, one hungry Wizard, and one Knight that was running on empty. Steak sandwiches, burgers, chicken, fries, and onion rings were brought out as appetizers. Fine French cuisine was brought out next.

As I ate my fourth cheese steak, third burger, and my second bowl of some sort of soup by trying to cram it all into my mouth at once, I began to feel my strength returning. My visible wounds were already healing, but the pain wasn't going anywhere. We ate in silence as West watched over us. He had his cell phone out and was talking in hushed tones. I didn't bother trying to hear what he was saying, because there was still food on the table, and I had broken bones to mend.

As my stomach began to fill and my survival instincts began to dial back from eleven my head began to clear. I pulled out my cell phone and texted Drey. With that part out of the way, I thought about what had just happened. I had saved Everett Black, but when I looked outside and saw that it was still raining I knew my job wasn't over. Someone connected to the divine had visited me in a time of need. This wasn't just a freelance job anymore. I was on the clock, the divine payroll if you will.

I started texting as furiously as I was eating. I sent messages to three different parties. I went back and forth with each of them for about an hour while still shoving food into my mouth. It wasn't until the door flung open and a water-logged Drey walked in that I took note of the world around me.

Drey's eyes scanned the room, and when he locked eyes on me he made a beeline for the table where I was eating what would soon be my last meal. There was a table meant to seat sixteen or more between us that he would have to go around to get to me. Drey grabbed the edge of that table and shoved it across the room like it weighed nothing at all. "What the hell did you do to the truck?" he yelled as he approached.

West stepped in front of him and stopped him with an upraised hand to Drey's chest. Drey looked down at the hand on his chest, and then into the eyes of the man that currently owned that hand. He and West were about the same height. West was more muscular, but Drey didn't seem to care.

My cousin smiled and spoke very slowly. "Get your hand off of me, werewolf."

West matched his tone when he answered. "You need to back off, scion." He punctuated his answer with a shove that slid my cousin back a few inches.

Drey pressed forward and began to force West back. The werewolf seemed surprised but only for an instant. West braced and halted Drey once again. It was Drey's turn to seem surprised. My cousin grabbed West's arm and pulled back. He pulled West past him and threw him across the room. Drey didn't skip a beat as he turned back to me with murder in his eyes.

West went flying across the room but rolled when he hit the ground. He came up on his feet and started barreling back toward Drey. My older cousin heard him coming and turned to face the charging werewolf. Kate halted everything when she racked her shotgun. Everyone in the bar froze except for Willy, who kept eating, and Drey.

My cousin raised his left hand toward Kate and spread his fingers. Kate's shotgun flew free of her hands and slammed into Drey's palm. He shouldered the weapon and looked over at Kate. With a smile he said, "Sorry ma'am, but this is about who has a bigger dick, not a bigger gun." Drey dropped every shell from the shotgun and set it on the floor carefully. Then he held up both hands and flexed his fingers in the universal 'come get some' gesture as he walked toward West. "Come on, werewolf. I was just going to kill my little cousin, but I don't mind ripping your head off too."

West cracked his knuckles by bawling his fists. Then he started toward my cousin again. Both men were smiling and just itching for a fight. I didn't like West, and Drey was going to kill me, so I was fine letting them fight it out. But if that happened one of them would die, and I would either have to explain to my family how I sat by while a werewolf killed my cousin or explain to West's parents how he died while in my city. Life is full of hard choices.

"Drey! West! Hold it! Stop!" I yelled. Both men halted, but neither took their eyes from each other.

I got up and walked over to them. I tried to stand between them, but Drey grabbed my shirt and pulled me close. "Blood of my blood, what the hell did you do to the truck?" he asked.

"A wizard blew out the windshield, and it's raining so the cab is soaked," I grunted.

Drey turned his head to look me in the eyes. They weren't human eyes this time. They were those strange cascading eyes that the fae have. Gritting his teeth he asked, "Do you want me to fix it?"

I grinned and nodded. It's the way things had been since the dawn of time. I would break something and Drey would fix it. Toys when we were toddlers, our bikes when we were kids, and now my truck. I was prone to destruction, and Drey was a gremlin. He could fix just about anything.

Drey took in a deep breath and exhaled slowly. "Little cousin, it would be my pleasure to fix our grandfather's truck that he taught me to drive in, took me fishing in, and used to provide for our family for more years than you have been alive."

"Thanks, cousin!" I said.

A look of concern came over Drey's face. "Cousin, you better get back to stuffing your face. Your nose looks like it's broken."

"My nose isn't bro—" Drey slammed his forehead into my nose, and I yelled in pain. I felt it break, and hot blood began running down my face.

He threw me on the ground and then picked up Kate's shotgun and all of the shells. He reloaded it and walked over to the bar. He handed Kate her weapon and then pulled out a wad of hundred-dollar bills. He set three down on the bar and said, "In case I offended you or yours, Miss Kate. My elders have instilled in me far better manners than what I have shown." He bowed to her then turned to walk out. He glanced back at West and said, "Another day, werewolf."

"Any time, scion," West countered.

"Don't forget the rest of the text," I yelled through my hands as I clenched my broken nose.

When Drey was gone West walked over, pulled me up to my feet, and growled in my face. "Who the hell was that?"

"My cousin," I said as I wiped blood from my face with my shirt.

"What kind of fairy is he?" West snapped.

"If you want to know that, then go ask him. I'm not telling my cousin's secrets," I said. I pulled away from West and walked back over to the table filled with now less food because everyone was still eating. I grabbed another burger and began stuffing my mouth. I was three bites in when I noticed how quiet the room was.

I looked up from my food to see that all three werewolves were staring at me. "What are you all looking at? Haven't you seen a grown man eat like a pig before?" They all went back to eating, and I continued to stuff my face until my phone started buzzing. I looked at the screen and excused myself from the table. I went outside to stand in the rain. Drey was working on my truck. He was too involved to notice me.

I put my phone to my ear and answered it in the most respectful tone I could use. "Hello, Grandpa."

"I just got your text," the man on the other end of the phone said. His voice was hard and measured, like most old service men. What set him apart was that his tone was that of an exasperated parent. "It was buried in a mountain of texts from your cousin. What did you do to the truck?"

"I let a wizard blast in the windshield and then drove it in the rain," I said.

I heard him grunt in deep thought across the line. He let out a heavy sigh and said, "You been keeping your oil clean and topped off?"

"Yes sir," I replied.

"You change the filter in the last four month?"

"Yes sir."

"Keeping your tire pressure even?"

"Yes sir."

"Good. Did he punch you for messing up the truck?"

"He head butted me."

"Must have been like ramming his head into the side of a building," he said with a roar of deep throaty laughter.

I chuckled myself. My grandpa kept laughing for a bit then coughed. He coughed for even longer, and the smile drained from my face. "You okay, gramps?" I asked.

"I'm fine. Just a dry throat," he said through coughs. He kept coughing, but when it subsided he returned to that familiar measured tone. "You had questions about the business?"

"Yes sir. It's raining here. It has been for almost two weeks," I said.

"Michael, unless you think you are in for another twenty-six days and nights of rain, I think you will be okay," my grandpa said.

"I checked the weather reports for every day since the rain started. Every reliable source has called for either clear sunny skies or cloudy with no chance of rain," I said.

There was a pause as my grandpa chewed over the information. "Not many magical beings that could do that unless we are talking about aspects or demigods. Maybe three that I can think of. Is it a hard rain or a drizzle?"

"Drizzle. Constant and annoying," I said.

"You notice any new players on the board?" he asked.

"One guy in particular. Hooded and carrying a katana. He felt like he was made of rushing water," I said.

"Well, I guess the rumors were true. The Fairy Courts have a new herald," my grandpa said.

"He's a fairy?" I asked.

"No, a mortal just like us. Remember that to interact with the mortal world, the most powerful of the Fairies must have a herald, someone that connects them to the mortal world. He is the herald for the Princess of Water. I had heard that she had a new herald, but I haven't seen him. Supposedly he took to the power like he was born to wield it," he said.

"He could make it rain like this?" I asked.

"No, but his mistress could. As long as he is in town she can do pretty much anything other than outright kill someone," he said.

"Gramps, if I had to fight this herald, what advice could you give me?" I asked.

"You should avoid it. That's my advice. But if you must then use cold iron. Anything else besides cold iron and magic will just pass right through him," my grandpa said.

"So pretty much my sword and cold iron?" I asked.

"You can also hit him with your truck. They'd never expect that," laughed my grandpa.

My phone beeped to let me know I had an incoming call. "Gotta run gramps, works on the other line."

"Stay alive, slick. And stop busting up your truck before you give Drey a heart attack."

"Yes Sir."

I clicked over to speak to the new caller, and though I had planned on being composed I let my temper slip.

"Hoy, you are a real bastard. Did you know that?"

"Mr. White, most trolls are bastards. My brothers and I can honestly say that we know and are cared for by our father. What do you want?"

"To bargain."

"I already told you that I would accept your left arm."

"No, that's not going to cut it. I am not going to give you my arm or Larry. But you are going to take this bargain."

The troll laughed. It was a human laugh when it started, but it turned dark and gravely as it went on. "Come to bargain, little man. What do you have to offer me?"

"A chance for the last of your brothers to kill me and collect Larry."

"My brother will take his turn when he is ready, knight."

"Yeah, but Larry won't be in town. Hell, he may not even be in this country."

There was a long pause. When Hoy spoke again he did not sound human. "What have you done?"

"All I have heard about you Bridge Boys is that you always get your toll. You can't collect if you can't find Larry. I called up the Church. Consider Larry to be part of the magical version of the witness protection program. They are going to take him, hide him, and keep moving him every time they think one of you is within a hundred miles of him."

I could hear Hoy's teeth grinding. "Do you have any idea what that would do to our reputation?"

"Yes, and I will brag to every single person I can find about how the Bridge Boys can't collect when a knight gets involved."

"What do you want?"

I was grinning from ear to ear when I said, "Just three things. Where, when, and how. I want to know where, when, and how Randal Quinn is planning to transport himself and his pack out of Baltimore."

"And what makes you think I know or even give a damn about that?"

I grinned. "I am betting that, when it comes to the supernatural, nothing illegal moves into, out of, or through Baltimore without you getting your cut. So tell me, Mr. Hoy T. Roll, Transit Specialist, when and where in the city am I going to be standing before I turn Larry over to witness protection?"

I heard a sound akin to the one I make when I pound my head against my desk, but I bet Hoy used his fists to make it.

"You will be at Locust Point on the Patapsco River. There is a pier there where Nicholson Street crosses Hulk Street and the train tracks break off. There is going to be a ship there at moonrise, just before the werewolves have their first change. Moonrise tomorrow will be just before 9 p.m."

"Well, by 10 p.m. either I will be dead, in which case the Church will take custody of Larry—but hey, you can probably bribe them with info on how I died and who killed me. That, or I will be sending all of my new werewolf buddies and fellow Church members home after explaining that Larry doesn't need witness protection. It will just be the three of us in an old-fashioned throw down for Larry's life."

Silence again. For a moment I thought Hoy had hung up, but then he said in a low and serious tone, "At 10 p.m. under the full moon's light, a troll named Goy will face you, knight. His cell phone wont ring, your wolf friend won't fight, he won't offer a deal for your arm left or right. He will simply pull off his human mask and go about his favorite task. He will howl and laugh a bloody fit as he smashes you into bloody broken bits." Then he hung up.

I looked at my screen and remembered the text I got earlier from Aaron. I reread it and texted back, *"Got a plan to beat the bad guy. Gonna cut him off at the pass tomorrow night. He is trying to leave by ship down the Patapsco River."*

I went back inside to find that everyone had moved around. Larry was at the bar chatting with Kate. West and Everett were talking alone in a corner. Willy was asleep on a bench while clutching what looked to be a bag full of leftovers.

Faith was sitting by herself. Something was off about her. Her legs were twitching, and she kept glancing around at everyone. More than once she ran her hand through her hair. She looked up at me, smiled, and then looked away. She straightened her hair again and looked back at me with an utterly bored expression.

I walked over to the bar and took a deep breath before speaking. "Miss Kate. I am sorry about earlier. Will you forgive my actions?"

She gave me a half smile. "You are forgiven, Sir Knight. You returned an old friend to safety. Even though you then let your cousin and West trade blows beneath my roof."

"Sorry about that, too."

"I take it you will be needing something, Sir Knight?"

I fished around in my pocket and pulled out a small item. "Anything that can use this?"

She picked up the item and examined it. "Is that all?"

I shrugged because I had a plan that was pretty darn stupid. Why not go all out? "Can you get me a sniper rifle?"

"No."

"How about a good scope and a tripod for an AR-15?"

"That I can do. Anything else?"

"An AR-15?"

Kate laughed. "I also assume you would like these items to be legally purchased."

"Yep."

She shook her head and covered her mouth while she laughed at me. "Only you, Sir Michael. I'll make some calls." She pulled out her phone and started to walk away.

"Kate, one more thing," I said. She turned to regard me, and I put a ten-dollar bill on the bar. She in turn pulled out a large jar and put the money inside.

"A hint and a guess as to what I am. I am the 3rd sibling of my family, and the only one to bare children," she said.

"I didn't know you had kids," I said.

"Your guess, Sir Knight?" she asked.

I pondered that for a whole minute before my tired mind told my mouth to say, "One of the Norns?"

Kate shook her head, put the jar away, and walked to the back of the bar. "A far closer guess than last time. Try another time, Sir Michael."

One guess a month. That left me some time to get my head together. Right now, though, I needed to get organized. I turned back to the room full of metahumans. Again I took a deep breath, but this time it wasn't to face a bad situation. I yelled, "Listen up!" Everyone turned to face me. Even Willy sat up, but he clutched his leftovers even tighter. I walked forward and called everyone in. Once we were all gathered up, I told them my plan. Once they all stopped laughing at me I told them the plan again. Then West grabbed me by the front of my shirt and lifted me into the air.

"This goes against your deal with my father," he said.

"No, it doesn't. He is more than welcome to come to the party. But everyone has to be out by 10 p.m. Think of it as closing time. I don't care where you go, but you can't stay there."

"And where exactly is there?" he asked as he lowered me to the ground.

"Oh, I am not telling until it's time to move. If you go there early and they smell you they will turn tail, run, and the bad guys get away."

"So just us? Three werewolves, a leprechaun, a crazy wizard, and a knight against a pack of newly turned werewolves, a pack master, and the new herald of one of the fairy princesses."

"Yes. What's a pack master?"

"Randal Quinn," Everett said. "He can control werewolves. Pack masters used to be our mortal enemies. We thought we had eradicated them before the revolution began in the Americas. Now I know that we were wrong."

"So, he can control you guys?"

"No. Not as long as I am here," West said. "My uncle was injured and poisoned by silver. He won't be controlled this time. I am too dominant to be controlled by another other than my father. Faith will be safe once I bring her into my pack."

"I'm not joining your pack, West," Faith said.

West turned to her. "You have been running around as a lone wolf for too long. The full moon will rise tomorrow night. Do you honestly think you can handle another transformation without a pack to mitigate the pain?"

"I don't need your damned pack. I don't need anyone. I transformed just fine this morning. I'm not joining, and you can't force me to."

"The pack master will control you if I don't protect you."

"No, he won't. She already shrugged him off in the warehouse," I said.

West looked at me and then back at Faith. "Is that true?"

Faith grinned at me for an instant and then turned to West. She looked him in the eyes and stood tall. "Yeah. He said I was the most dominant bitch he had ever seen."

West pursed his lips as he looked Faith up and down. "Very well, Faith Kane. Well done."

"Great. Now that we have that settled there is just one more thing we need to figure out," I said.

"What's that?" asked Larry.

"Why hasn't anyone gotten Everett a pair of pants?"

Everyone looked at Everett's naked frame and then back at me. In unison they all shrugged. I was just glad Aaron wasn't here to point out that I was the only person uncomfortable around the naked werewolf.

# CHAPTER 29

DREY HAD FIXED my windshield by the time we were done in the bar. He hugged me, gave me a smack to the back of my head, and took his leave. Hopefully to do the favor I had asked of him. West took Everett with him when he drove off. Kate was staying because, after all, it was her bar. She did let me know a package would be arriving at my house the next day. She collected $2000.00 from me to cover my special order and the food I had ordered to go. Willy had retreated into the city with his precious leftovers. That left me, Faith, and Larry alone in the parking lot.

"So, what do we do now?" Larry asked.

I shrugged. "We go home and rest. Tomorrow night we fight a bunch of werewolves. The best thing we can do until then is let our bodies and minds recover from everything else that has happened."

We got into the Rust Bucket, and I found that Drey had fixed more than just my windshield. All the vents were replaced, I had a new radio console with a touch screen, and he had even replaced the steering wheel with one of those fancy ones that had all the controls hidden around it. This was almost as good as getting a brand-new truck.

That's when I found his note. It was on the dashboard underneath a rock that he had set there. It read, "Blood of my blood, I love you. Stop messing up the Rust Bucket. It deserves to be treated with respect. You do not let liquid get all over the inside of your truck. To help with this, I took out all of your cup holders."

My eyes darted around the cab of the truck, and sure enough every single cup holder was gone. It was a little devious but nothing that would prevent me from enjoying my repaired ride. I started the truck, and that's when the true evil of my cousin shined through. First, it was the new control panel. Everything on the touch screen was in a language I didn't recognize. The radio stations were all set and locked on what sounded like the 'tortured cats' station. Second, the controls on the steering wheel were not connected. Finally, I noticed he had adjusted all of my mirrors. It's the little things that hurt the most.

After getting my truck into some semblance of order, I drove us back to my place. We had a bag of steak sandwiches from Kate's to get us through the night. After dividing them up, Larry offered to queue up another movie. We decided on that classic American tale of life after death, Beetlejuice. With a battle for our lives looming over us, we needed something to ease the tension.

197

Larry sat on the floor while I took a spot on the couch. Faith sat opposite me but put her feet in my lap. As we watched the ghost with the most, Faith kept shifting on the couch. At one point she moved to sit next to me. Then she stretched out with her head in my lap. She finally settled for sitting on the opposite end of the couch while curled into a ball.

About halfway through the movie I decided to call it a night. I excused myself to my room and locked the door. Horace sat up and motioned for me to come over to the bed. I sat down beside him, and he stood up. Then he reached over and smacked the back of my head.

"This is a stupid idea," my teddy bear yelled in a whisper.

"Do you have any better ideas?" I asked.

"No, but that's because I don't give two fucks about a bunch of werewolves that are leaving the city. Your job is done, and don't even get me fucking started on the leprechaun again!"

"So do you think the plan for the troll will work?"

Horace stormed down to the foot of my bed and sat in the corner where the foot board met the wall. He pulled out the old phone I had given him and began flipping through the screen. "What's the leprechaun's internet password? You're going to die tomorrow, so I might as well enjoy your world's porn now."

I thought about what my teddy bear had just said. I looked at him for a moment as he tried to crack Larry's password. He must have figured it out, because he started to unbutton his overalls. He was pulling them down when he suddenly stopped and then slowly looked up at me.

"Do you mind?"

"How exactly are you going to…"

He threw a pillow at me. "Get out and give me some damn privacy!"

"But how are you going to…"

"Don't fucking worry about it, kid! It's none of your damn business!"

"But you aren't anatomically…you can't be!"

"Get out!"

Horace got up and leapt at me with his paws bared. I got out of the way by running to the door and running across the hall to the bathroom. I closed the door and tried to get the thought of my teddy bear doing something that no teddy bear should do out of my head. I climbed into the shower and went over my plan in my head as the water ran down my body. It could work. We had the advantage in experience and timing. We could handle the werewolves. It was the last Bridge Boy, Goy, that worried me. So far I had been beaten by two trolls, intimidated by another, and now I was going to fight one that I had all but promised to kill. I was going to have to bring my 'A' game for this fight.

I was so focused on the battle ahead of me that I didn't notice what was behind me. Soft arms wrapped around my body, and two hands settled on my chest. I started to turn, but the arms held me fast as something large and soft pressed against my back. Before I could scream or thrash, a soft voice echoed in my ear.

"Larry is asleep. I put the little guy on the couch and covered him up. Do you mind if I sleep with you tonight?" Faith asked.

"With me? Yeah that would be fine," I whispered.

Then she kissed the nape of my neck. She rested her mouth on my collar and let her teeth settle against my skin. The water ran over us as I realized how small she felt against my back, how strong her arms were to hold me, and how good it felt to be touched by another person. I turned to her and pulled her close. With my back to the wall below the shower head, I held her in my arms, and she held me. We took the soap and washed each other, never fully letting go and only separating when we needed to. I washed and played in her hair twice before we stumbled out of the shower. Toweling off was especially hard because we only had one towel, and we both had our hands full already.

We managed to stumble across the hallway without waking up Larry. As I backed her into my bedroom, she leapt and wrapped her legs around my waist. Our boy and girl parts were pressed together without joining, but we were close, and it felt so good. I held her butt and the small of her back as she snuggled against me. Her arms lifted up, and she grabbed the pull-up bar above my door. I was still rubbing my face in her hair when she lifted us off the ground.

I felt the muscles in her legs swell around me. Her breasts ballooned in size against my chest. I was being held aloft as Faith stretched her neck up so that her face was next to mine. She put her lips right next to my ear and growled. When I yanked my head back her amber gold eyes looked back at mine. Her lips were fuller, thicker around her sharpened teeth. Her hair was growing longer. I wanted nothing more than to bury my face in her hair and never leave.

I reached up and took hold of the pull-up bar. Together we began to lift and lower ourselves as we just gazed at each other. We took deep breaths, and every once in a while she snapped her teeth at me. When we finally lowered ourselves to the ground she was heavier but still light enough that I could carry her to my bed. I did just that right after I closed the door. Just as we scrambled onto the bed, I caught a glimpse of Horace at the foot of the bed. He was propped up and looking at us. I kicked at him, but Faith pulled me to her just before my foot collided with my teddy bear. I tried again, but Faith pulled me closer to her like I weighed nothing at all.

We kissed for the first time since she got into the shower. In that kiss I felt a woman and a beast warring for control. She wanted it to be soft, but she was hungry and pressed in so hard that it forced my head down onto the pillow. She climbed atop me and kissed me harder. I put my hand on the small of her back and spun. I rolled her over and positioned her beneath me. Her dominant nature forced her to sit up in challenge, and when she did I grabbed her hair. I pulled her head back and went to bite her exposed neck.

Faith surged up and pushed me over so that our heads were now at the foot of the bed, and she was on top of me. She growled as she grabbed my throat and dug her claws into my skin with one hand while grabbing my manhood with the other. Her thumb forced my chin up, and she leaned in to bite my neck while positioning my manhood between her legs. Her lips brushed my skin, and she inhaled deeply. Her lips traced across my exposed neck and my manhood traced across her lower lips as Faith breathed me in. She pressed her mouth against my neck and growled louder than she had that night.

Her growl died away. Faith held me there with her claws digging into one side of my neck, my manhood in her free hand pressed against her womanhood, and her mouth against my exposed neck. I wanted her so badly that I could already feel myself inside of her. Her lips swept across my neck, and she shivered. Both of her hands tightened on the two parts of my body that they were holding. I took a deep breath and could smell the beast within her. She smelled like dirt, trees, and wild flowers. She smelled like a world that would kill me because of my allergies, and that made me want her even more!

"Your scent," she whispered. "You smell like…like that pillow at the head of your bed."

I didn't reply. I didn't move. Neither did Faith. We just laid there with my throat and cock in her hands. The wetness of her sex dripped onto me but grew cold between us. I don't know how long we lay like that, but it was long enough for me to remember what Kerri had said.

*"You are mine, even if we can't be together. I love you, and any girl you find after me is on borrowed time,"* was what she said when she walked out of my life.

Faith said that I smelled like her.

"What did I smell like before?" I finally asked.

"Books, snot, sweat, anxiety, metal, and plastic, like a nerd or a toy store. You smelled sickly and harmless, like a little boy," she said.

"Well, that makes me feel manly."

"Oh, you smelled manly. Every time you fought, you smelled like there was hot iron running in your veins and a fire in your chest. You still smelled like a little boy, but you smelled like a man with a boy's spirit."

I was afraid to ask but I had to know—because I am an idiot I had to know. "And what do I smell like now?"

"Like candy lip gloss and fancy hair product. Like cookies, ice cream, and chocolate. Like comic books and toy trucks. Like a boy and a girl at the same time."

"Yeah. Sounds about right," I croaked. That was how Kerri-Lynn was. The perfect girly girl with a tomboy attitude. She was more nerd than I was and cooler than any action movie heroine that the movie industry could come up with.

"Who is she? You aren't married."

"No. She is…was my best friend. She was my only friend for so long that I can't remember a day without her in my life as a kid."

"Did you sleep with her?"

"Yes."

"You love her."

"Yes."

"Does she love you?"

I didn't know how to answer that. Part of me screamed "no" in rage. Another part of me cried "yes" in desperation. "She can't," I said. "She's normal. A human, and she can't be part of my life."

We lay there in silence again. This time she spoke first.

"Do you think you could ever love anyone else?"

I thought about Kerri-Lynn and felt my heart thump in my chest. I would always love her. Would loving another woman be possible? Would it be wrong?

"Maybe. I never considered it."

"Not once?"

"No. I don't think ahead like that. I think about rent and gas. I try not to think about girls. They have cooties."

Faith laughed at that. She let me go and sat astride me. In her feral form she was all muscles and long hair. I saw the hair had grown in her armpits as well as around her crotch. All fire red and all of it beautiful. She looked like she could wrestle a giant. When she smiled, I could see her sharper and thicker teeth. A person that didn't understand beauty would not have seen her as I did. A mundane person would have seen a monster. I saw a beauty that spoke to the need of a strong partner and the strength of women. I sat up slowly and brought my lips to hers. We kissed and she did not pull away.

She pushed me back down on the bed with a flick of her wrist. I tried to sit back up, but she placed a hand on my chest to pin me down. I tried in earnest to sit back up, but it felt like I was pushing against the weight of a car. I could only force myself an inch or two off of the mattress. She held me there like I was a struggling child.

"Maybe we shouldn't do this tonight," she said. "Not with the battle ahead of us tomorrow night."

"Why?" I asked.

"We just talked about why," she said.

I fell back against the bed. She was right of course. I just wanted her so badly.

"Besides, I would wear you out. You wouldn't be in any condition to walk, let alone fight tomorrow," she gloated.

Before I could say anything she snatched up Horace and put him to my face. "You still sleep with a teddy bear? That's adorable!"

I could feel the blood rushing from my penis to my face as I groaned.

"He was going to get quite a show. Oh well, maybe after we take care of those poor folks tomorrow and the moon passes," she said as she began to shrink back into her fully human form. Her hair receded, and she still looked beautiful.

I tried to sit up again, and this time she let me. Just so she could shove my teddy bear into my arms. She took me by the arm and guided me back to the head of the bed. We lay there face to face with Horace between us. He was facing her. She pulled me in close so that we were pressed together with my teddy bear between us. Then she pulled the covers up over us.

"Since you still need your bear, how's about I keep y'all both close tonight?" she said in that backwoods drawl of hers.

"Okay," was all I could say.

"What's his name?" she asked.

"Huh?"

"Your teddy bear. What's his name?"

"Oh, Horace."

She crinkled her freckled nose. "Kind of a strange name for a little teddy, isn't it. Shouldn't it be Mr. Bear, or Bear Bear, or something like that?"

"It's Horace," I said a little too forcefully.

Faith smiled. "Okay. His name is Horace." She tilted her head down and kissed Horace on the forehead. "Good night Horace. Tonight you get to sleep right here, but after the full moon passes I get your friend all to myself."

I started to say something, but Faith's lips came up to mine, and she kissed me with a patient passion that froze my tongue. She parted our lips with her finger and shushed me.

"We need to sleep. Good night boys."

She cuddled up to me and buried her face in my chest. That left my head right next to her hair. I couldn't help but rub my face against it before I fell asleep. If I could dream I am not sure if I would have dreamed of Faith or of Kerri-Lynn. I'm not sure I want to know the answer to that at all.

# Chapter 30

I WOKE UP before my alarm went off, which was a good sign. I was getting used to my new regimen. Faith was still in my bed and still nude under the covers. The problem with this was that she was not snuggled up with me. She was snuggled up with Horace, and he was grinning. Her arms were wrapped around him, and she had his head nestled between her breasts.

I reached out to pull him from her grasp. He smacked my hand. I reached for him again, and he smacked my hand again. I glared at him, and he began to wedge his head even deeper into her breasts.

"You can't do that!" I yelled in a whisper.

"She put me here!" Horace whisper yelled in return.

"Get over here."

"Go on your run."

"No, you can't do this."

"I'm not doing anything. She put me here. She's holding me. She's happy, and you need to mind your own damn business!"

"I'm not letting you do whatever you are planning to her."

"I'm planning to hold still and let her sleep as long as she wants. Don't fuck this up for me. Go run off a fucking pier and drown!"

I reached for Horace again but with both hands. He started fighting with me, but I managed to get a hold of both of his arms. I started pulling him free of Faith's sleeping person so that I could throw him into the bottom of my hamper for the day. He was struggling, but I was bigger and stronger than him.

"Faith, wake up!" Horace yelled.

Horace's arms went limp in my hands. Faith yawned and opened her eyes. I froze because I am an idiot. Faith looked down to see my hands on Horace's arms which, of course, meant they were currently between her breasts. Her sleepy eyes looked up at me, and I had no idea how to begin to read her face.

"What are you doing? It's too early to fool around," she said.

"I…I'm going for a run," I stammered.

Faith looked down to my hands. "You need your teddy bear for that?"

"N…no…I…umm."

Faith brushed my hands away and snuggled Horace closer. She turned over so her back was to me and wiggled into a comfortable semi fetal position. "Enjoy your run. Mr. Bear and I are going back to sleep."

I lay there for a minute wondering what had just happened. That's when a little brown arm stretched up and reached above Faith's sleeping body. The little balled paw hung in the air just long enough to grab my attention before its middle digit stuck up. Defeated and dismissed, I rolled out of bed to go on my run.

Today Thaddaeus asked me how I went from a scrawny little nerd to a big scary black guy. He didn't use those words this time. I told him part of the truth. I wasn't about to tell him about being a knight.

"I spent four years working out every day. At first it was just endurance training and physical conditioning. That along with a full college workload. Then my last two years of training were spent in martial arts and sword fighting."

"Sword fighting? You mean like fencing?"

"No. Joe taught me a bit, but just to work on my footing and balance. After I had a solid foundation with that, he taught me how to block and parry with a long sword. Then, once I had that down, he showed me how to attack. After that it was instruct, adjust, spar, and correct. Every lesson started with a demonstration and a practical adjustment for my weapon and body type. Then we spared, and then he would correct my errors."

We were almost to the end of our jog by the time I was done explaining how Joe had beaten everything I knew about swords into me.

"And all of this happened in college?"

"Nah. I was doing all correspondence courses. The physical conditioning took place all over North America, parts of Africa, and parts of Europe. The martial arts training was in Japan with Han Nakamura. The sword fighting was in Chicago in a place called Average Joe's Gym."

"Average Joe's…" he said thoughtfully. "Sounds, well, average. Anyone else train there? Maybe some famous actors or something?"

"Nah, no one famous. Everyone in my business ends up going there though. No one can train you to fight with a sword like Joe," I said with a smile. I had to smile. Joe had taught me the sword, and he had taught me about faith. He was the reason I wore a baseball hat when I went into battle and the reason I never felt a need to meet my boss.

We reached the end of our jog, and before taking off on my run I needed to prepare for the worst. As Thaddaeus said his goodbye I held up a hand to stop him. "Thaddaeus, things are coming to a head tonight with both of my cases. If I am not here tomorrow, then it's because I either didn't make it or I am too hurt to run. Either way this could be our last run together. I'm sorry."

Thaddaeus chewed my words over before he responded. "It's that bad? Is there someone you can ask for help? Maybe the police?"

"Nope. Not the cops at least. They can't handle what I deal with." I shrugged.

"Interesting to know. Well, I know you will be okay. You seem like a capable and competent young man. You have my number. How about you call me when you are good enough to run again?" Thaddaeus said as he slapped my shoulder. He held out his hand and smiled at me.

With everything that loomed before me, a vote of confidence was just what I needed. I traded grips with him and pulled him into a hug. "Thanks Thaddaeus. I needed that."

"Sure. Can't wait to run with you again, Michael," he said as he stepped off to get into his car.

I watched him walk off as my phone started buzzing. It was another text from Aaron, *"On the river. Got it."*

I put my phone away, turned, and tried to sprint around the lake once more. This time I made it half way before I had to slow to a jog. I was getting better, but not fast enough. If I lived through tonight, I would up my regimen. Hell, if I lived through this I would ask Aaron to be my nutritionist, because eating cheese steaks and fries every day couldn't be good for me.

<h1 style="text-align:center">CHAPTER 31</h1>

I CRAWLED BACK into bed with Faith, and she snuggled up to me again. I slept with her in my arms until my alarm went off again. We turned it off and slept in. I was about to fight werewolves and a troll. I was going to sleep in today!

We finally woke up when someone knocked on my front door. I motioned for Faith to stay in bed and grabbed my gun. Larry, of course, was still asleep on the couch. It turned out I didn't need my gun. It was just an early morning delivery from UPS. I signed for five packages and locked up the apartment again.

I carried everything into my room and found Faith, still naked and still with Horace in her lap, on her cell phone. "I'm not sure, sir. No, I didn't witness any of it. He is right here. Hold on." I watched her mute her phone before looking up at me. "Kodiak wants to talk to you."

I took her phone and unmuted it. "This is Michael."

Kodiak Black's voice came over the phone with a wave of power. I felt his words pull at me, and I could do nothing but focus on him. "Mr. White, I will be direct. First, let me thank you for finding my brother. I will have the rest of your payment tomorrow, and you can bill me for any expenses or hazard pay. What I need to know now is if anyone has died as a result of my brother's actions."

"Yes," I answered without hesitation. I wanted to say more, but my tongue wouldn't move.

"Thank you, Mr. White. I will see you tonight. Please stay alive until I arrive."

Kodiak hung up, and it felt like the pressure in the room dropped. Faith was looking at the floor, and I slumped onto the bed beside her. I gave her back her phone, and we just sat there for a while.

"Michael, you heal quick, right?" Faith asked.

"Yeah."

"How? You're just a human, right?"

I pulled my hoodie off and showed her the runic tattoos all over my upper body. "Magical tattoos. They can heal me from almost anything. They work fast, but they drain my stamina and strength."

"Damn it," Faith swore as she stood up.

"What's wrong?"

"Tonight, I am going to need to transform, and the last time I did I drained power from you. I don't know why or how, but for that moment you were pack. If it happens tonight, you aren't going to be in any condition to fight."

"I was fine last time."

"Michael, we were rolling around for an hour while I changed."

"An hour?" Had I really lost track of time for that long yesterday? "Wait, it only took half an hour for you to change into a wolf."

"Changing into a wolf is harder, but once you are a wolf you heal fast. Changing into a human is easier but just as painful. Plus, you don't heal as fast as a human. When the moon comes out it's worse. The moon change is more painful, and it takes a lot out of you."

I thought about it for a moment. If the moon was the problem maybe I could skip over it. "What if you just transformed early?" I asked.

"I don't want to be a wolf around that man! Did you see what he did to those poor wolves that didn't have control of themselves? It's like…like they were slaves or something." Faith smacked her right fist into her left palm. She was furious.

"He didn't control you before," I reminded her.

"Before I was pissed. Before I had to protect you. Before…before I wasn't scared. This isn't some fairy tale where the good guys always win."

I stood up and walked over to her. I turned her to face me and held her chin so that she had to look me in the eyes. "Tonight, the good guys will win. Tonight, we are going to get that bastard that forced being werewolves on those people. Tonight, you will transform and fight at my side. Faith Kane, my friend, tonight you get to see a fairy tale ending. We win, the bad guy loses, and we all go home to celebrate."

Then I flashed my winning smile at her. Faith's eyes narrowed, then her brow softened, and then she rolled her eyes. She shook her head from side to side and started laughing. "There are dozens of bad guys, Michael."

"Nope. There are dozens of victims. There are only two bad guys. The pack master and the dude with the katana. Plus, I have an idea on how to take him out of the picture."

"Victims? Wait, are you planning to save all those people?"

"Yeah. What did you think I was going to do?"

Faith stared at me with wide eyes. She started to say something but stopped. She ran her fingers through her hair and then started to speak again but stopped. She blew out an exasperated breath and then shook her head from side to side.

"What's the problem?" I asked.

"Michael, you do know that werewolves aren't allowed in Baltimore, right?"

I suddenly felt like I had missed something over the past few days. Everyone seemed genuinely surprised there was a werewolf hanging around me. I thought they just didn't like werewolves.

"Umm…no…why?"

"Baltimore was claimed as vampire territory in the war."

"Umm…what war?"

"The werewolf and vampire war? The church got both groups to stand down from fighting here because of all the supernatural people that frequent Baltimore. There are a bunch of cities like New York, Chicago, and Los Angeles that were divided up. Kodiak had to get you to invite us. But those new wolves were made here. That's against the agreement."

I felt my stomach turn as I dove head first into this crap hole. "So, what are the consequences for them being changed while in Baltimore?"

"Michael, they have to die. Kodiak is going to kill them."

## Chapter 32

G O! DRIVE AROUND the block for four hours, see a movie, get Larry a hooker, I don't care," I said as I shoved Faith and Larry out the door with my truck keys and $600.00. I had woken Larry up after Faith got dressed. Knowing they would be safe for today, at least, I needed to address a lot of things in a short amount of time.

"But I thought we were resting today," Larry said.

"Plans changed. Be back in four hours. Larry, if you get a hooker please don't get her involved in this, because I am in enough shit!"

I slammed the door and stormed toward my room yelling, "Horace!" My teddy bear was sitting on the bed with a smug expression on his face. "Did you know?"

"That werewolves weren't allowed in Baltimore without the express permission from the city's knight? Or did I know that you were a fucking idiot? The answer to both is yes," he said.

"Why didn't you tell me?" I asked.

"You should have known. You're a fucking knight. You didn't just find a magical sword and become a knight. You squired for..." he trailed off as his jaw dropped open. "You never squired for anyone, did you? You just found a magical sword and started acting like a superhero?"

"I trained with my grandpa, and..."

"But you didn't squire for him! You didn't go to seminary. You didn't study the various arrangements, secret wars, or even the most recent history of the magical world, did you?"

I didn't answer. I just stood there remembering one of my God given talents. Horace couldn't read my mind, but he knew exactly what I had done.

"You fanned through a bunch of books and papers that your grandfather gave you to read but didn't actually read them, did you?"

"I technically know everything there is to know about everything that was given to me to read."

"You're an idiot. You don't even know how to do your job because you decided to skip actually learning it."

"I know my job! I just went over everything about treaties, arrangements, and wars in my head, and I don't recall anything about any deals between vampires and werewolves."

211

Horace folded his arms and tapped his foot. "You said you read everything your grandfather gave you. What about all the stuff the church gave you?"

"That would be the monster manual."

"Michael, how many books were in your grandfather's den?"

"Including the encyclopedias? Somewhere between two or three hundred."

"How many books did your grandfather give you to read?"

"Seven."

"You are missing over two hundred books worth of knowledge on how to do your job."

I fell onto my bed and covered my face with my hands. I had messed up, and to an extent it was my fault, but it was also the Church's fault for screwing with me. Now I had two problems. I had to save a bunch of werewolves from a guy that basically wanted them to be his pets or slaves, and I had to save them from the scariest werewolf alive because he wanted to kill them. And then I had to fight a troll.

"Are you just gonna lay there and wallow in self-doubt?" asked Horace.

"Well, it is an option," I said.

"Not for you. Like I said, Michael, I know you better than anyone. Someone screwed you over, and now that has put people's lives in danger. You won't stand for it, so why even waste time?"

I sat up and fished my phone out of my pocket. "You're right. I better get started fixing this."

"Who you gonna call first?"

"Greyshadow."

I called Gregory Greyshadow and calmly explained to him what had happened.

"You invited werewolves into Baltimore? Are you a fucking idiot? Do you have any idea how much fucking trouble this is going to be? At least tell me that no one has seen you with a werewolf," Greyshadow yelled.

"Not many people have, but more than zero," I replied.

"You're an idiot. Alright, you get to pick. I can call the Church or the Lord Commander of the Eastern United States. You have to call the other," Greyshadow said.

"The Lord Commander? Are you serious? This is that serious?"

"Michael, you may not have done it personally, but by allowing a human to be changed here in Baltimore a major treaty in the magical community has been violated. We have to go to the top on this one."

I chewed it over in my mind for a second as I watched Horace prowl around the packages. I didn't want to speak with any bureaucrats from the Church, but I hadn't planned on telling the Lord Commander until after this was over. It's better to finish the job before telling your boss that you may have screwed things up. At least then I would have something to show for my efforts.

"I'll call the commander," I said.

"You are braver than me, kid. Do you think you can save these people?" Greyshadow asked.

"I have to. It's my job." I shrugged.

"Actually, it's not. Not when it comes to werewolves in Baltimore. So why do you do it, kid?"

"I don't know. All I know is that people are in need, and I need to get ready."

"You're going to figure it out one day, kid. When you do, let me know. I'm calling the Church. Enjoy your talk with the Lord Commander."

Greyshadow hung up leaving me alone with my teddy bear and a sense of dread. I recalled the protocol for contacting the Lord Commander for official business. Normally one would have to contact the regional command office and then they would give you a number to call. That number would be to a go between that would then contact the official to set up a meeting or phone call. The problem was that the go between could be the first in a line of up to five people depending on how tight security was these days. It could take hours or days depending on which jerk answered the first call. I didn't have that kind of time.

Lucky for me, or unlucky in this case, I had an express line as a Knight of the Order. I dialed a single number and waited. On the fifth ring the Lord Commander of the Eastern United States answered.

"Slick, this phone is for official Church business only. Tell me you have a good reason for calling me directly on this line instead of on my cell."

"Howdy, Gramps. Have I got a story to tell you," I said.

I told him everything in detail. Like a true leader, he listened to me and allowed me to explain myself without critique. He absorbed it all, and when I was done he took a moment to digest my report. Like a parent, he let me sit in silence as he decided what to do and what to do with me. Having your grandpa as your commanding officer was a double-edged sword. I knew he wasn't going to overreact over any mistake I made or unfairly punish me. The other edge of that sword was that whatever punishment he came up with would be the most severe possible because he could not be seen as playing favorites or cutting me slack.

"You have really done it this time, Sir Michael," he said.

"I figured that gramps, err, Sir," I said.

"First off, you need to fix this situation tonight. I like your plan, but do you think you can pull it off? It seems like it has a few gaping holes in it."

"There are a few holes in it, but that's just because I am not telling you everything," I told him.

My grandpa's voice came back with a bit of an edge. "Do you honestly think that keeping me in the dark is the best thing for you to be doing right now, Sir Michael?"

"No Sir, but I have to. I am dealing with some factors that I barely understand. If I could tell you I would."

"I don't like it, but in this business I understand how sharing knowledge can change things and how the slightest change can sway a battle. I want it on the record that I do not agree with your decision, but that I trust your judgement."

"Thank you, Sir."

"Alright, Sir Michael, I trust you to finish this, now official, mission. After that three things are going to happen. First of all, you are going to turn in your official report detailing every single thing that happened since you first encountered anyone in Baltimore that may or may not have been a werewolf. I want names, dates, and times. If anyone pissed on a mailbox I want to know where, when, and how it smelled to you. Do you understand?"

"Yes Sir."

"Second, I want you to familiarize yourself with every single aspect of the supernatural history and goings on of Baltimore. You are its Knight. The city deserves better than what we have collectively let happen. I will order the books myself, and if they are not all delivered by next week I want you to call me. If a single book is missing from the list I am going to send you then you let me know. This shunning of you has gone on long enough."

He paused there and let out a deep sigh. I knew this had to be stressful, but that was pretty dramatic for my grandpa.

"Finally, Sir Michael, I am calling a meeting of the Church. The entire Church. Every active sword bearer, cleric, knight, and priest. Other than you, there are two other sword bearers that have not been brought in by ceremony. We are going to fix that and figure out how to fix this at the same time."

"Gramps, are you serious? Every single member of the Church?"

"It will take time, but yes. It's time that you and the others were brought into the Order properly. Sir Michael, there are things going on that may never concern you, but you need to be prepared. I need you to do better. I need you to be better than what you have shown."

"I will do my best, Sir," I said.

"No. I need you to be better. Faster, smarter, and stronger. Got it?"

"Yes Sir."

"Good. Now go save those poor people, Slick. Go do your job," my grandpa said.

"Yes sir, Grandpa!"

"Stay alive. Love you, Slick."

"Love you too, Gramps."

We both hung up. Horace was standing with his arms crossed on top of one of the packages. "Feel better, kid?"

"I feel like I am ready to kill something. There is going to be a meeting of the council about this."

"I heard, but we have other problems right now," my teddy bear said.

"Like what?"

"Well, for one, how many items did Kate order for you?"

"Four."

"And how many boxes are here?"

I counted just to make sure this wasn't a joke. "Why are there five boxes?"

"You tell me, Mr. Hero."

I checked all five packages and froze when I saw that one was from Kerri-Lynn. I sat on the bed with it, and Horace climbed up next to me. I didn't have time to consider all the different things it could be. I took my silver knife and opened the box. Inside I found a letter that read:

'Hey Hero,

I am sorry we haven't talked since I left you high and dry in Baltimore. My family has gone through some difficult times since my father and brothers came to your place. I don't want to say everything in a letter, but I will say a few things.

First off, don't go thinking that everything is over between us. This is a break, plain and simple. We are not done, Michael.

Second, I talked to your grandfather and your cousin. Since you insist on wearing that stupid Orioles baseball cap into battle instead of the actual head gear you are supposed to wear, how about I help you meet common sense half way? Your cousin said he could work with this if I got it for you.

Finally, never forget this. My family may not like you, but I love you. Always have and always will. Don't write because I will never see the letter. But it's 2017, Michael, you can call me you dork.

Love,

Kerri'

I blinked away tears so that I could look further into the box. Inside was a metal construction hat. At first I thought it was just painted in the black and orange of the Baltimore Orioles, but when I pulled it out I found their decal on it as well. The helmet was perfect for both of my jobs. Being metal, my cousin or my uncle could possibly enchant it to protect me. Once again, Kerri-Lynn had gone above and beyond. I couldn't believe her.

I don't know how long I just stared at that hard hat. Horace had opened the other boxes and was pulling on my leg when I snapped out of my trance.

"Come on, kid. We need to start prepping."

We assembled a brand-new AR-15 from the contents of the second box.

From a third box we attached a combination retractable bipod and forward grip. Then from the third box we mounted a scope with a laser sight. It took us a good hour to adjust it in the confines of my hallway while aiming down at the front door. We used a laser sighting dummy bullet to make sure the gun was as close to accurate as we could get in such a short amount of time.

"Some adjustments will have to be made on site," Horace said.

"I know. Hopefully we won't need it, but if push comes to shove…who am I kidding? I want to put a bullet in this assholes head," I said.

"Hopefully you won't get the chance," my bear said. "Oh, do you have a tactical suit for tonight?"

We finished with the rifle, and I sent Faith a text. After that I called Priest Greyshadow and asked him for a favor. Then we opened up the fifth package. Horace nearly fell off the bed when he saw the new snub-nosed revolver that was inside. He watched as I pulled five bullets out of my dresser to go with the one I had shown Kate.

"Where did you get those?"

"From someone else that I want to put a bullet in," I told him.

We readied my gear for the fight. Magazines were loaded, armor was checked and polished. Every one of my weapons was cleaned and checked. Finally, I sharpened and polished my sword. The polish was important but not the sharpening. The blade never dulled from what I could tell. I packed everything I needed to set up before the fight and finished just in time for Faith and Larry to make it back.

Faith held up a decorative box from the mall and looked at me as if this was out of the ordinary. "So, why did you send us to Build-A-Bear Workshop?"

I walked right by her with two bags of gear on my shoulders. I took the box and my keys without explaining anything. I left her and Larry behind as I took a quick trip to Best Buy and then out to what would be the scene of tonight's battle. It took me a few hours to set up, but using as much stealth as I could, I managed to lay my plans for tonight.

When I got home, I laid down to rest before I had to get ready. One of two things was going to happen tonight. Either I was going to die, or I was going to live. After the latter, I would just probably wish I was dead.

## CHAPTER 33

I CAME OUT of my room dressed for battle. Well, first I cleaned the snot off of my face. But then I came out of my room dressed for battle. I wore my black steel-toed work boots with a mix of neon green and standard black laces. I wore steel elbow pads and fitted bracers made of leather and iron that buckled into place on my arms. Dark blue jeans with steel greaves and steel knee pads would protect my knees and legs tonight. I was wearing layers on my chest. An undershirt, Kevlar, a shirt of titanium rings, and a Silver Surfer t-shirt over it all.

Why the Silver Surfer? To intimidate the werewolves, duh!

I wasn't trying to blend in like I normally did, so I wasn't carrying a sports bag. I had my modified tool belt on with both of my guns strapped on. My black Desert Eagle sat on my right hip, while my chrome one sat on my left hip. My silver survival knife was behind my chrome Desert Eagle. I also had a standard claw hammer on my right hip. The work gloves that Drey made for me were tucked into my belt. They were fitted, and the knuckles were padded and topped with ridged iron plates.

Larry was dressed for battle too. He had my baseball bat and a football helmet. He had bought an entire Boston Celtics uniform and warm up suit from the mall. Faith may have insisted that he purchase it, but he looked like he was ready for a fight—or at least a pickup game at the Y.

Faith was nude. She wasn't wearing anything beyond her necklace of teeth with the cross in the center. I did not stare at her. I really didn't. Much.

"Why aren't you dressed?" I asked.

"Michael, I am going to be in my feral form before the fight starts, and when the moon comes up I am going to be a wolf. I don't have time for clothes," she told me.

"Good point." I went into the kitchen and grabbed a bottle of allergy medicine. My nose was stopped up, and knowing my luck I would probably end up being allergic to werewolves tonight. I walked back to my living room, grabbed my trench coat, and put it on. Or at least I tried to. It didn't fit right over my armor. I tossed it to Faith. "Cover up for now. We need to make a stop."

We piled into the Rust Bucket and drove to the office. I went inside while Faith and Larry went across the street to get some pizza. Inside, Bill Fred the angel was sitting on one of my couches drinking a beer. It was a Budweiser. Bill Fred was basically my angelic handler. He took his marching orders from

God or Jesus or someone else in upper management. His appearance right now could only mean one thing.

"So, this is an official mission now?" I asked.

"Of course. Innocents are in danger, and the Knight of Innocence is called to protect them," he said. "You should wear the cloak."

"No," I said.

"It was just a suggestion." He shrugged.

"I left it at home," I said.

He looked down at his watch and nodded. "With traffic the way it is, you should have just enough time to go back and get it. You already took a huge detour for that." He pointed to the coat rack with my jacket from Kerri-Lynn on it.

"So, you just read my mind now?"

"No. One of the higher ups said you would want that tonight, so I have been waiting here."

Now I was curious. "Which higher up and for how long?"

"Someone higher than me and just long enough to grab a beer."

"And this higher up thinks I should wear the cloak?"

"It couldn't hurt."

I just shook my head. I walked over and grabbed my jacket. It fit perfectly. The light blue denim would fend off claws from normal animals but not werewolves. The fur cuffs and collar felt familiar to me. This was a jacket made to work in. I could stand in a storm while building a house in this jacket or stand on a battlefield while cutting down demons.

When I turned back to Bill Fred he was gone. His empty beer bottle was in my recycling bin. Faith and Larry came in then, each carrying four boxes of pizza. They handed me a bill for $110.00. I herded them outside and into the Rust Bucket. Then I drove back to my apartment, grabbed my cloak, and drove us to the meeting place near Locust Point on the Patapsco River.

Larry and I split a double pepperoni, double cheese pizza. Faith ate six triple all meat pizzas. I tried to reach for a slice of hers, but she growled at me and shoved the slice that I had been reaching for into her mouth. We ate in silence as the sun went down and the sky grew dark. Willy was the first to show up besides us. I split a pizza with him as well. Though he could have fit into the truck's cab with us, he chose to sit in the bed.

Fog was starting to roll in off the river, and the stars in the sky were dim. Faith spotted Everett and West coming toward us from down river. I fixed a cheap version of a Bluetooth headset into my ear. When we got out to meet them I had to avert my eyes. Like Faith, they were naked. In their feral forms they were both taller, a little hairier, and their dicks came down almost to their knees. I really did not need to see that. Faith had transformed now and stood next to me in her feral form. I suddenly felt like the shortest, skinniest kid on the dodge-ball field again.

"You could all wear clothes you know," I snapped. "How do you expect to fight with all that swinging around?" I waved my arms towards everyone's private parts to emphasize that I had a problem with werewolf nudity regardless of gender.

"Michael, I told you that I was going to be a wolf. I won't have my breasts swinging around then," Faith reassured me.

West folded his now corded arms over his overly muscled chest. "We could handle this alone, Mr. White. There is still time for my father's pack to enter your city."

"Because they are waiting just outside of it, right? Yeah, I know that, jerk. What I didn't know was that you were planning to kill those poor people that your uncle changed. That is not happening."

West stepped toward me, and I stepped toward him. We stared at each other, but I did not look at his eyes. I focused instead on his mouth.

"They have to die, Mr. White. It doesn't matter how or why they were turned. Werewolves created in Baltimore must be executed. These are our laws, our way of life, and you have no say in that."

"This is my city, right? I am its guardian. I get a say, Mr. Black, and I say that they get to live."

West and I were in each other's faces now. He began to show his teeth, and I felt the temperature around us rise. Faith shoved her hands between us and forced us apart.

"We don't need you two having a dick measuring contest right now," she said.

"Mr. Knight would lose right now. Maybe. Mr. Knight, don't drop your pants yet. I wanna make a bet with the leprechaun," yelled Willy.

"You brought the street mage? Isn't he…insane?" Everett asked.

"Yeah, but he was the only one that could actually hurt you. I brought him as insurance. You know, like on the off chance that one of you goes nuts and tries to do something stupid like killing a person for turning into a werewolf while living in Baltimore," I chuckled.

"You overstep your bounds, Mr. White," West said.

My cell phone alarm went off. It was time to work. "We can settle this after we stop the pack master," I said.

I belted my sword onto my left hip just in front of my chrome Desert Eagle. Then I fixed my scarlet cloak with its golden trim on my shoulders. The two clasps fixed perfectly to the two pockets on the chest of my jacket. Then I slung my shield over my shoulder by its carry strap. Once I was ready, I went over the plan one more time. Then the five of us ran off into the night.

There were no streetlamps, so we were running by starlight. Basically, it was pitch black beyond the ten yards of vision that I had. Everett and West led the way with Faith right behind them, because of course werewolves could see in the dark. Willy was running beside me in high-step like an actor from a 1920's physical fitness film. Then he started pulling away from me, and I realized that Willy had no problem seeing in the dark as well. I started to pull out my flashlight because I was falling behind the pack so to speak.

"Are you wearing a tool belt filled with weapons?" West asked.

"Yes," I said as I slipped a long black flashlight out of a sheath on the left side of my belt.

"Between that and your armor, a werewolf is going to hear you coming a mile away," he said.

"Well forgive me for being a weak human that needs a freaking arsenal to take on a pack of supernatural predators," I snapped.

"I will, as long as you don't turn that flashlight on and give away our approach," West growled.

I rolled my eyes and flipped West off, but I did put away my flashlight. We eventually came to Hull Street, the only actual road leading to the dock. We tucked ourselves into the shadow of one of the first buildings on the street and waited.

"How long does it take a new werewolf to change?" I asked.

"Fifteen to twenty minutes, and that's if they push through it. More than likely, it will take them thirty minutes to an hour. Any that survive will be exhausted or frenzied," West said.

"Can you control them? Keep them from going nuts?"

West held his hand out to illustrate that it was still raining. "It will be difficult in this. Water disrupts even werewolf magic," he said.

"What?" I asked.

West tilted his head. "You did know that magic could be hindered by moving water, right? Rivers, whirlpools, fire hoses…rain! You knew that, right?"

*No*, I wanted to scream but didn't. "I thought werewolves wouldn't be affected since you were able to transform."

"It makes it harder. Speaking of which," he said as he turned his attention to the other two werewolves. "You two should get into wolf form now before moon rise."

Faith looked at me, and I nodded to her. While West was focused on her and Everett, I tapped the Bluetooth in my ear. "Did you know about the rain?"

"If I said no would it make you feel better?" the voice in my ear said.

"Yes, it would," I said.

"Oh, then yes, I knew about the rain. It's why they needed you to find Everett. I think every single non-mundane being in the city knew. All but you."

I wanted to say something in response, but I started sneezing. My eyes started itching and watering. My skin itched, and I could feel a headache coming on. I pulled a bottle of allergy medicine out of a pouch on my tool belt and downed a few pills. The effect was almost immediate, which was strange. It usually took a few minutes for my allergies to subside.

With my allergies toned down I could feel a drain on my body. There was an ache in my bones as well. This was the undertone of the feeling I had experienced when Faith had called on me to help her transform. So why did my allergy medicine…

I looked down at the bottle in my hand and then up at Faith. West's back was to me, and Everett, having already finished his transformation, was watching the street with Willy. I met Faith's eyes just as I opened my mouth. She growled out words from her half-human, half-canine mouth. "Shut your face, Michael!"

I bit off my words and shoved the bottle back into my belt pouch as West looked back at me. Our eyes met, and even though I could see he was just annoyed with me, fear shot down my spine. The werewolves, their transformation, was somehow akin to an allergy. I was willing to bet knowing that would be reason enough for West to kill me.

"Head lights coming," came the voice in my ear.

"We have incoming. Are you going to transform?" I asked West.

"When the moon rises. Until then this will do," he said.

Turning back to the road I could see lights in the distance. The lights, three pairs spaced about a hundred or so feet apart from each other, were moving steadily toward the street that led to the pier. I noticed orange and yellow track lights. I recognized them immediately as trailer lights. Why in the hell were there three semi-trucks rolling in? I turned my attention out to the river and saw the lights of a ship slowly making its way toward us.

"White, why are there three trucks. You gave us a count of a couple of dozen werewolves. Why do they need three trucks?" West asked.

My plan had been to intercept Quinn and his crew before they reached the docks. I expected them to be on foot or in a packed van. I had no idea that they would have a truck, let alone three. "Plans changed. Take out the wheels of the trucks then duck back," I yelled.

I dashed ahead of the group. The first of the trucks was just rounding the corner. A streak of black, then a streak of silver, and then a streak of red went by me. The werewolves were on the move. I kept running at the lead truck but couldn't match their speed. So, I watched from the side of the road as West leapt at the lead semi-truck. In his feral form, he swiped his clawed hand into the back wheels of the truck. There was a small 'boom' as the first tire blew out and another as the one behind it went the way of the former. The sound of broken steal threads whipping through the air was drowned out by the screeching of stressed metal as West ran down the side of the side of the trailer destroying the wheels of the moving vehicle.

I heard similar sounds coming from the other two trucks but couldn't see them. My vision was currently filled with the sight of a semi-truck making a left turn while losing the support of most of the wheels on the right side of the vehicle. The truck tipped over, crashing on its side and skidding right at me. I turned to run but bumped into Willy who was looking in the opposite direction of the truck. We both went tumbling to the ground. I grabbed Willy, dragged him up to his feet, and pulled him into a run. I looked back to see a wave of displaced street water and debris coming down on us. The force of the wave wasn't enough to send us sprawling to the ground, but the trailer a few feet behind it was going to flatten us.

On a whim and a prayer, I threw Willy forward. Then I flipped my shield down to my hands while turning to face the skidding trailer. I screamed "Abstoben," as I forced my will into the shield. This shield, like my ring, had been forged by a gremlin smith, but this one preferred the activation words to be in German. So, when I screamed the German word for repel while feeding the shield my will power, magic pulsed forth from the shield. I realized my mistake the moment I felt the magic begin to weaken. The rain was dampening it, and though the truck did slow it wasn't enough to keep me from getting flattened. I slammed even more power into the shield. I willed all of my strength into repelling the trailer. Again, it slowed but did not stop.

All three werewolves came over the toppled side of the trailer to land behind me. They turned and charged the truck. Everett and Faith were fully transformed and to either side of West in his feral form. He centered their line as they dug in their heels and paws. The trailer came to a halt just a foot away from me. I noticed the werewolves all had their heads turned away from me, so I stepped forward and quietly put my shield on the trailer and leaned into it. When West turned to look at me, I pushed myself upright and acted like I had been holding back the trailer as well. The werewolf alpha looked me over once more, but this time he had a look of respect in his eyes rather than contempt.

"Boats coming in," came the voice in my ear.

I motioned for everyone to retreat back to the cover of the building. We all began to move when the driver's door of the overturned semi blasted free from the downed truck and crashed just a few feet from Willy, who had his back to the truck. He didn't flinch or turn around at all. Something came flying out of the cab. My eyes couldn't follow it while it was moving, but when it landed on the side of the overturned truck I could see that it was a male werewolf in his feral form. The werewolf had Randal Quinn slung over his shoulder. He set the man down gently then focused his attention on us.

Quinn dusted himself off. Aside from a little blood on his lips and forehead, he looked pretty good for a guy that had just been in a truck accident. He was wearing sunglasses at night like an asshole. This time he wasn't carrying a belt in his hand. He had a rapier on his left hip and a gun on his right. He still wore the leather coat, and it looked awesome when a gust of wind had it bellow forward. That same wind pushed part of my cloak into my face, and I had to scramble to pull it out of the way.

"Mike!" laughed Quinn. "You survived the fire? Did the bitch?" Faith growled at him, and he turned his head toward her. "I guess she did!" He looked over our group and smiled when he saw West. "The son of Kodiak Black? Well, that is something I didn't expect."

"I take it that he is the pack master," West asked. Everett prowled forward with his teeth bared, growling. Faith also began to growl in response.

I checked over my shoulder to see if Willy was going to join us. The mad mage was still looking off in the opposite direction. My plan was still somewhat on track, so I decided to play things out. "Tell me something, Quinn? What did it cost you to get the Fairy Courts involved with your abduction of Everett Black?" I couldn't tell if Quinn was looking at me now, but I noticed West's eyes cut over to me and narrow. "I mean, it's been raining since you abducted Everett, and the path of the storm flowed all the way from the site of the attack to here. Not many beings could call up a storm, let alone keep it going for weeks. Even then, it would be a constant drain on a being's power, wouldn't it? So, what did you pay for this? What does it cost to buy a fairy powerful enough to do this? A first-born child?"

"On your left!" said the voice in my ear. I didn't look. I just threw up my shield. The sound of steel striking steel rang in the air and I backed away. I drew my Desert Eagle as Faith jumped between me and the attacker.

My attacker danced back from my werewolf friend and rested his katana across his shoulder. He was still wearing that long black coat over a hooded sweatshirt. The hood was pulled up to keep his face hidden. "Always running your damned mouth," he said.

This time I recognized the voice. It was a bit deeper, but it rang out clear in my head. I leveled my gun at him and narrowed my eyes. "Nice to see you too, Sosuke," I snarled.

The hooded man stood straight and lifted his hand up to pull back his hood. He had a narrow face framed by long dark hair. His eyes, always an oddity to me, were silver. He had high cheekbones and narrow lips. Handsome was the way anyone on this planet would describe him, and I knew that under those baggy clothes he was a sculpture of solid muscle. He didn't smile at me, but he did show his teeth when he clenched them together to snarl back, "Why are you always running your damned mouth, Michael?"

"You know him?" Quinn and West asked at the same time.

"Boat's docking now," my eyes in the sky said.

"Randal, I don't care what you do with the others, but this bastard is mine," said Sosuke.

"Sosuke, what's up man? Why the hell are you working for this asshole?" I asked.

"Not all of us are so fucking blessed as you, bastard. Some of us have to earn what you were given freely."

"Sosuke, what are you talking about? You are the next in line to inherit…" I didn't get to finish what I was saying. When I started talking, Sosuke was a good distance from me on the other side of a very protective werewolf. When he moved, it was so fast and fluid that I didn't realize he was right in front of me until he spun and brought the heal of his left foot around at the corner of my shield. My shield was knocked clear off my arm and went tumbling to the ground. Sosuke's spin came full circle, and I fell to the ground to avoid the katana slashing at my throat.

Faith came at Sosuke's back, but he jumped, flipped, and slashed his katana as he flew over her upside down. He landed in a crouch with his sword at the ready. Faith landed over me protectively. Her left ear fell onto my leg. I scrambled to my feet and found blood running down the side of Faith's face.

"Stay out of this, wolf," Sosuke warned.

"Talk about a fucking ace in the hole! Did you see that, Mike? This bloke moves like one of those Asian cartoon characters, doesn't he. The wolf bitch probably didn't see him move either time. I know I didn't," howled Quinn.

Steam rose around me as I glared at the young man I had considered my friend, my brother! I had memories of him—happy memories of training with him, learning from him, and bonding with him. I ground my teeth and lifted my gun to hold him at bay, even though that hadn't worked the first time.

"Stick to the plan, Michael!" came the voice in my ear.

I forced myself to do just that. I lifted my head to the sky and yelled, "I can only imagine how pissed Kodiak Black is going to be when he arrives. He is going to want to kill everyone involved in the abduction of his brother."

"What the hell are you talking about, Mike? There is no fucking way Kodiak Black is in Baltimore. He would have to be invited in by the local representative of the Church. Even you aren't that fucking stupid as to invite Kodiak Black into your territory," Quinn said.

All three of my werewolf companions were silent as Quinn began laughing at the absurdity of me inviting Kodiak Black into Baltimore. It was at this point that I started thinking Kodiak wasn't just the New York Alpha. It was Sosuke that dragged Quinn out of his laughing fit. He narrowed his eyes at me and said through clenched teeth, "You have no idea just how stupid he is!"

"Stupid? I'm not stupid. Stupid would be abducting the brother of Kodiak Black. Stupid would be torturing the brother of Kodiak Black. Stupid would be not killing me when I was chained up and helpless. Stupid would be thinking that, with West Black standing right here, that Kodiak wouldn't be far behind," I cackled. Then I baited the hook. "It's a good thing that he just wants to kill those directly involved in the abduction. If any of Randal Quinn's associates want to leave now, then your involvement can be overlooked if not forgiven."

"What the fuck are you prattling on about, Mike?" Quinn asked.

"Okay, why the hell is he calling you Mike? Don't you hate that name, and isn't it way to close to—" asked the voice in my ear.

I yelled, "Because I, Michael White, found Everett Black! I found him and returned him to his family! There is no point in drowning out his scent now! This is a waste of your power and your time! Withdraw now, and this slight will be overlooked for now! On my word as a knight, I swear this!"

Everyone froze. Seconds passed with nothing changing. Then the rain just stopped. It didn't slow. It just stopped. Heads turned to the sky. The constant sound of water striking the earth ended, and a silence fell over us. The clouds dispersed and the fog began to drift away.

Sosuke snarled as he stood straight. The water on the ground began to pool around his feet. Slowly it began to rise behind him. The rising water reached his shoulder before it began to take shape. It bulged, stretched, tightened, and constricted. As the liquid took form, it began to freeze. Within seconds, a frozen sculpture of a beautiful woman draped in steam stood behind Sosuke. The clear ice gained color, definition, and tone. It shifted into a young woman with long dark hair, fair white skin, dark glasses, and long thin fingers that rested on Sosuke's right shoulder. She wore cut off shorts, a baggy hoodie, and no shoes. Her lips moved without sound, and Sosuke turned his head to face West.

"My Lady would have your word, son of the Wolf Lord. This business, which was not personal, will be overlooked tonight?" he snapped.

West looked at me and grinned. He turned back to Sosuke and the newcomer and said, "To remove a player from the board with this much power? Yes. If you withdraw now, then yes, you have my word as my father's son that he will not retaliate against you on this the night when our power is at its peak."

The young woman's mouth moved again, and Sosuke shook his head. "She will accept that. My Lady and I will withdraw. Have your father send an emissary to her court if he wishes to discuss her roll in this further." He turned to Quinn and said, "Our business has concluded, pack master."

"Like fuck it has," Quinn yelled. "I paid you to keep the mutts from finding me. Now they're here, and you think you can leave me high and dry?"

Her lips moved again, and Sosuke spoke. "The wolves could not find you.

The knight found you, no doubt due to the foolishness of your chosen underlings. When he found you, you managed to capture him, but instead of killing him and the werewolf directly you left them to fire. Fire is an unruly tool for such an easy task. It was a foolish decision not to kill the knight by your own hand. This is your doing. My Lady's obligation is fulfilled. Thus, we are leaving."

The ground started to shake. It wasn't so bad that I couldn't keep my balance, but it was enough to make the structures around us groan. The water on the ground began to flow toward Sosuke and the young woman. Water, waves and waves of it rushed from the street, the alleyways, and from the roofs of buildings. It was as if a dam somewhere had burst as water came rushing onto the scene. However, it was controlled as the water wove around the buildings, the toppled truck, and even those of us on the ground. The sudden tide flowed over Sosuke and the young woman and then surged out toward the pier. I watched as every last remnant of the magical downpour was swept out to the river, including my former friend and his mysterious lady.

The werewolves and I all faced Quinn. "What were you saying about an ace in the hole?" I asked.

The pack master sucked his teeth and then whistled. Six more werewolves in feral form leapt up on the side of the overturned trailer. Five were the ones that Faith and I had originally fought after speaking with Willy. One was Drew. They were all muscled like body builders with rotten looking claws and fangs. Worse, they were all nude, and all of their nonlethal parts were dangling and swinging everywhere.

"Open the trucks," Quinn said. "I want them dead before the moon rises."

# Chapter 34

FOUR OF THE seven homeless werewolves moved at Quinn's command. They dropped off the trailer too swiftly for me to react. That, however, did not mean that my companions couldn't keep up with them.

"Stop them," West barked.

Everett dashed forward, and with a single powerful leap he went soaring over the overturned trailer after the four werewolves that were trying to let out the rest of Quinn's victims. Quinn shrieked and dropped flat on his back at the sight of the gray-white wolf flying over him. I could hear screaming and snarling the moment he dropped from sight.

Quinn's three remaining werewolves moved to shield him from the real threats. Faith and West came crashing down to the left and right of the three new werewolves. Faith lunged in from the left, while West came on from the right. Drew and the third feral werewolf moved to intercept Faith, while Eddy lashed out at West. Faith's paw batted the third feral werewolf aside like he weighed nothing at all. The poor guy went flying off of the trailer and onto the street.

Drew wasn't a push over. He ducked back to dodge a paw from Faith and then brought his arm around in a powerful swipe to smack against Faith's lunging maw. I couldn't understand the reasoning behind Everett and Faith fighting as wolves. Obviously the feral form was the superior form, as it gave you the option of fighting on two legs and employing the versatility of the human anatomy. On top of that, you had superhuman strength. So why would you ever fight as a wolf.

I just didn't get it, until I saw Drew's arm collide with Faith's head. Faith didn't budge. The blow had enough power behind it for me to hear it land, but Faith regarded it as much as I would being hit by a ping pong ball. She plowed into Drew and bit down on his shoulder. He didn't have time to react as she turned her head and flicked him out into the air. Drew screamed as he flew into the side of a nearby building. I saw him fall to the ground amidst a section of broken wall.

Eddy didn't fare any better. He threw a right hook at West, and the alpha werewolf caught his wrist. West pulled him forward and jammed a solid punch into his gut. Eddy doubled over and then stumbled back. He tried to growl but coughed instead. When he tried to attack again, West brought an elbow down on his shoulder. I heard a loud crack just before Eddy screamed and fell over.

Faith and West turned as one on Quinn. The pack master scrambled back away from them. It honestly looked like this one was in the bag. My two werewolf companions began to growl in unison as they closed on our foe.

"Stop!" Quinn commanded. I felt his power echo like a scream in an elevator. It was forceful and present but ultimately it was harmless. Except for the fact that both Faith and West had stopped growling and moving.

I saw Quinn scramble to his feet, and it hit me. "The rain was suppressing his magic too, wasn't it?" I asked.

"Seems like it," the voice in my earpiece said.

"Get those trailers open!" Quinn roared into the air. One of the feral werewolves came running around to the back of the trailer Quinn was standing on. She opened it, and nude feral werewolves came stumbling out.

Quinn turned his attention back to Faith and West. "Sit!" Quinn commanded. Faith slowly started to lower her back legs. She began to growl as she tried to resist. West began to growl as well and took a step toward the pack master. Quinn drew his sword and plunged it into West's gut. West howled in pain but did not go down. Quinn drove the sword deeper.

"Oh crap!" I said.

"Get your head in the game, Michael!" the voice said again.

I lifted my gun and put Quinn in my sights. I pulled the hammer back, and my finger froze half way. I could hit Quinn—I had been practicing my shooting, and I wasn't panicking like I was a few nights ago. I could shoot monsters with no problem. Quinn was evil and had just stabbed my companion. But he was human.

"The boats docked Michael. Are we moving to plan 'B' or what?" the voice in my earpiece asked.

Something whirled by my head before I could answer. I saw a hole appear in the overturned trailer. Then I was flying backward as the trailer exploded. Not with fire and smoke, but with a sound like a giant speaker with the base turned up to 100. Pure deafening sound whooped out of the trailer, ripping it in half and sending everyone flying. I hit the ground hard and couldn't orient myself as to which way was up. My ears were ringing, and my bones felt like they were rattling inside of me.

Slowly things started to come back together. I don't know how long I was on the ground, but when I managed to figure out which way was up I found Willy standing over me with his staff pointed at the decimated trailer. He looked down at me and said, "Hey Michael, did you know that magic was working again?"

I ignored Willy as he walked away to do God only knows what else. I focused on sitting up, and it took a lot of effort. I tried to take in my surroundings as I forced myself to sit up. Faith was sprawled out in the gutter. West was lying in the street in a pool of blood. The naked bodies of feral werewolves were littered everywhere around the trailer. I didn't see Quinn, Everett, or any of the lead homeless werewolves. My gun was on the ground near me, so I crawled over to it and put it in my holster.

"Michael, can you hear me?" asked the voice in my Bluetooth.

"Barely," I said. "Willy decided to drop the base on us."

"It was a spectacularly stupid idea to bring a street mage to a fight. Do we move to plan 'B' now?

"Not until plan 'A' goes sideways or the moon is about to rise."

"You have no idea how long you were on the ground, do you?"

I sneezed. Snot went everywhere. My eyes began to water, and my skin crawled from all the itching. A slow chorus of groaning and moaning began to fill the night air. I turned to look at the feral bodies on the ground as they writhed in pain. The sound of breaking bones set an unsettling rhythm. I looked up to the sky and saw the full moon shining down on us.

"Willy, we need to get Quinn now!" I said.

When Willy didn't respond I looked around for him. I found him in the alley squaring off against a cat that was standing on a dumpster with what seemed to be a wrapper from a sandwich shop in its mouth. I could see part of a sandwich sticking out of the wrapper, a fine prize for any feline…or homeless wizard. The cat hissed at Willy, and the mad mage hissed back. "That's my sandwich. I earned it, not you," Willy said as he brandished his staff at the cat. The cat leapt at Willy, and he blasted the spot the feline had been standing on with spell fire. Thus began the epic battle for the scavenged dumpster sandwich. Better known as the end of plan 'A'.

"Plan 'B'," I screamed as I tossed more allergy meds into my mouth. Luckily, I had brought a bottle of water just in case, because I needed a lot of meds right now.

I got to my feet just as Quinn came walking out of the wreckage of the ruined trailer. He had his sword in his left hand and his gun in his right. "It's over, Mike," he yelled as he leveled his gun at me. "The change is upon them! I win!"

"Not tonight," I said. I tapped my forehead and smiled at him.

"What's that supposed to mean?" he asked as he mimicked me.

"You do know he can't see the red dot on his forehead, right. Want me to put it on his chest?" the voice in my Bluetooth asked.

"Yes! Sorry, but this isn't over," I said as I watched the red dot move down to Quinn's chest. "Check out the red dot on your chest."

Quinn looked down at his chest and jumped back. He looked back up at me and snarled, "A sniper?"

"Yes, a sniper. Now drop your weapons and get on your knees. This fight is over," I said.

Quinn sucked his teeth again and turned his gun on Faith, who was still struggling to her feet. "No, Mike. If your sniper fires on me, then I put a few silver bullets in the bitch."

"Quinn, it's over. You don't want to die, do you?"

"Are you daft? I'm doing my best not to die. That's why you are going to back down your sniper. Because you don't want to see your bitch die. It's your call, Mike. Kodiak Black will kill me if he shows up like you said. But if I go, then so does your bitch. What's it going to be, knight?"

"We are dropping plan 'B'," I said.

"Michael, I have the shot!" the voice in my Bluetooth said.

"So does he. Stand by, I may need you in a minute. Pray for me?"

"I will. Don't die on me."

The red dot vanished, and Quinn smirked. "There's a good lad. Now get on your knees and put your hands behind your head."

I glanced over at Faith. She was struggling to her feet and wouldn't be in the fight any time soon, so I got down on my knees and put my hands behind my head. Quinn turned his gun back on me and pulled the trigger. I heard three shots ring into the night. All three hit West Black as he darted in front of me. The North Carolina alpha had recovered enough to get into the fight and had opted to save my life.

"Well fuck me," said Quinn. "I stabbed you with a silver sword, and then you go and take three silver bullets for this fool?"

West stood there with his arms down and his body shaking as he said, "This knight was willing to risk everything to save a single werewolf that I want to join my pack. I wouldn't be much of an alpha if I wasn't willing to protect him as well." He stumbled as if he were going to fall over, but he caught himself.

Then West threw his head back and howled. I heard a sound like a coin hitting the ground, and then I heard it again. Pieces of the silver bullets that had hit West were falling to the ground. I heard more gun shots as Quinn emptied his magazine into West. Each shot hit him, but West didn't stop howling. "Damn, damn, damn!" Quinn screamed. "I want every one of you bloody mutts to hurry the fuck up and transform!"

The feral werewolves began screaming louder. The sound of their bones breaking increased in intensity and pace. "No, no, no. No one told me he could command them to change faster!" I complained.

West was still standing in front of me with his back to me. He was more of a wolf now, but he hadn't fallen to all fours. Looking at his frame it still seemed more human as far as his upper body went, especially around the shoulders. Suddenly his muscles bulged, and thick black hair began to cover his body. A tail sprouted from his back. As I watched it grow I saw his legs extend, break, and heal almost instantaneously. His muscles kept bulging, pulsing, and thickening. His arms began to lengthen, and so did his fingers and claws. He wasn't falling to all fours, because whatever West Black was turning into walked on two legs. "I really need those darn books!"

The silver bullets that hit West Black fell to the ground in pieces as he rose to his full height of over eight freaking feet. He was covered in black fur except for his left hand, which was covered in white fur. I figured he was done transforming when he stopped howling at the moon and growled at Randal Quinn. West took three strides forward and then lurched ahead as he fell to the ground. He turned over onto his back, and I could see that he was covered in blood. The silver bullets had drilled holes into him that were healing, but slowly for a werewolf.

Looking at West something occurred to me. Lydia Black had told me that she taught new werewolves how to turn into the feral and wolf forms. She never said there wasn't a hybrid man-wolf form when I asked about it. She had just ignored me like a tactical politician. She hadn't lied to me, but she hadn't informed me either. Why hadn't she told me about this?

Quinn's laughter tore my eyes away from West to look at him. "I have never seen a wolf take more than one silver bullet. That Black mutt took eight of them and a silver sword to the guts. Tough as nails, but still just a dead mutt in the end," he gloated. "Your wolves are down, your wizard's fighting a fucking cat in the alley, and if you had the guts to let a sniper kill me you would have done it by now. This fights over, Mike. I win."

"No, it's not you bastard," I said as I surged to my feet. The new wolves were still in the middle of their change and Quinn was out of bullets. I drew my sword as I rose and charged the pack master.

Quinn saw me coming and squared his shoulders. He took a fencer's stance with his right foot leading. I wasn't sure of his skill, but I wasn't bad with a sword. I leapt at him to force him into a defensive position as I brought my sword around in a sidelong slash designed to knock his rapier out to the side and put him on his heels.

Quinn whistled. Something that felt like a sledgehammer hit my chest. I went flying back through the air and skipped across the ground like a stone on a pond until I came to rest on the street. Nothing was broken, I think, so I struggled up onto my butt and elbows. Standing in front of Quinn was another giant man-wolf thing. This one had dark brown fur and wasn't filled with holes.

The pack master stepped from behind this new monster. "Loup garou," he said. "This is the ultimate form of a werewolf. A form that can only be obtained when a mutt has stood above all others in a pack. A form that only an alpha can obtain. This is why I came here, Mike. To raise a pack so that I could have my very own loup garou. Look at him."

I did. He, and it was certainly a he because everyone was going commando tonight, was over eight feet tall. From neck to ankle, I couldn't see any excess fat on his body. His claws were each the same length and thickness of a thumb. Its fur was short and thick, designed for warmth but not to impede movement or offer a handhold to a predator. Looking at this loup garou, I wondered if anything could look upon it and still consider itself a predator in comparison.

Quinn turned the loup garou's head and pried open his mouth to examine its teeth. I could see them clearly in the moonlight. They were large, all canine and sharp enough to have their own infomercial. "Eddy here was a wonderful find. A once confident man, connected in his community of vagabonds, and a war veteran. He was old, homeless, forgotten, and unwanted by a country that he served. He jumped at the opportunity to be strong again, to be needed, and to be respected. To be feared. Now look at him. My alpha. The perfect beast, the perfect watchdog, and the perfect predator."

Quinn let Eddy close his mouth then he patted the loup garou's shoulder. "Want to see?" he asked. "Sick him, Eddy."

## CHAPTER 35

EDDY WENT FROM 0 to 60 in four seconds. He came at me like an Olympic sprinter. Each of his strides thumped like a sledge hammer hitting a cement wall and crushed the asphalt below his feet. I let myself fall backward and pulled my legs up to roll over my back and onto my feet. He was there in front of me the moment I lifted my head, but I kept pushing up with my legs. I brought my sword up in a vertical slash with both hands. Eddy skidded to a stop just short of being sliced in half from groin to throat. I did manage to nick the tip of his nose and he flinched back.

I jumped back and set myself into a fighting stance. Left leg forward, shoulders squared, sword in both hands, hilt level to my shoulders, and blade pointed to the sky. Eddy touched the tip of his nose and looked at the single drop of blood that was on his finger. Then he chuffed at me.

"First blood, Fido," I said.

Eddy stopped chuffing at me. His canine features hardened into a snarl. He roared at me, and I swear the force pushed me back a few inches. He bared his claws and fangs as he stalked forward. He barked, and each time he did, I felt the force of it slam into me.

I didn't care. Everett and Faith were werewolves. Eddy had turned into a badass super werewolf. Randal Quinn could command werewolves. Willy was an insane magus with more power than most professional wizards. Here I was in the middle of a battlefield of super powered beings, and all I had going for me was a magic sword that worked whenever it felt like it. I was the smallest dog in this fight, and it wasn't looking good.

But that's the job and I was on the clock.

"Bring it," I said.

I started inching back as Eddy stalked in. He roared again, and I quickly stepped away. Then he lunged at me, and again I quickly stepped away. I knew he was playing with me, trying to intimidate me. So, when he lunged at me with his clawed right hand I ducked back and came forward in a rush. I brought my sword across from right to left and met claw with blade. Eddy pulled his hand back, and I reversed my stance to keep up with his speed.

He came at me with a punch to my face. I ducked and thrust my sword forward. He retreated and slapped my sword out to my right. Another punch came in at me, and I dropped down to my right knee. I let the momentum of Eddy's parry turn

233

me as I kicked out my left leg. I hooked his right leg with my foot and kicked his leg out from under him. The loup garou toppled sideways but caught himself with his hands and scrambled away.

I sprang to my feet with my sword low as Eddy rose up and roared at me. He came at me throwing punches left and right. I worked the flat of my sword in a small window of blocks. High left, high right, low left, and low right sweeping from each position to fend off the next attack. Each blow sent a wave of numbness down my arms, but I gritted my teeth and endured.

Eddy kept punching. Each blow was punctuated by a growl of frustration and rage. He threw his right arm back and brought his fist around for a haymaker that would put a hole through me. I jumped back just beyond the extent of his arm. But Eddy opened his clawed hand to grab hold of my tee shirt and chain shirt. He pulled me forward and rammed his left hand into my face. The impact broke my nose and snapped my head back to my left.

That violently painful blow may have saved my life, because a second later Eddy chomped down where my head would have been. Instead, he bit into my shoulder just beside my neck. His teeth tore into my cloak, my jacket, and my shirt, and were halted by my chain shirt. I screamed at the pain of his bite. The pain was a shock, but it was nothing compared to when he grabbed my right arm with his left and tried to pull me in three different directions. I howled in terror as I thrashed against his grip.

Quinn was laughing his head off. Eddy was chuffing again. I was screaming. So, it came as a complete surprise to me when I went flying up into the air and crashed toward the ground head first. My hard hat, a gift from Kerri-Lynn, smacked off the ground, and I barely felt the impact of all of my body weight coming down on my head and neck.

Adrenaline, fear, and pain had me scrambling to my feet. I found Eddy stunned on the ground with a hole in the ground where his head had landed after West Black suplexed him, and me, into the ground. West was laid out with half healed bullet wounds all over his chest and stomach. Then of course there was the sword wound in the middle of his gut. He was working his way off of his back and onto his stomach as Eddy got to his feet.

Well, if the half-dead alpha werewolf was still in the fight, I guess the knight with a broken nose had to stay in it, too. I rushed Eddy from behind and brought my sword down to crash into his head. At the last second I saw his freaking ears flick toward me, and he sidestepped. He swung his left arm out and hit me in the chest. I went skidding back but managed to hold my footing. Eddy turned on me and brought his right hand around in a looping right hook. I dove forward under the blow and rolled past him to kneel at West's side.

Eddy rounded on me again but leapt at me this time. I rose slightly and then fell back as Eddy came crashing into me. I rolled onto my back and kicked him in the stomach as I did to send him flipping over me. Eddy hit the ground and popped back up to his feet.

"Can't you just act like something hurts you?" I groaned as I scrambled to my feet. West was still face down and struggling from his silver inflicted wounds. I nearly smacked myself in the head when I thought about West's injuries. I hopped over him and charged Eddy with my sword in my right hand but positioned across my left shoulder. I screamed as I slashed across at the loup garou.

Eddy dodged my sword slash easily. I expected it. He leaned back and let the attack pass him by, and then he came at me in a fury. Then he yelped as my silver survival knife slashed across his chest. He fell back, and I crossed my blades before me to let him see what he was up against. In my right hand, the Sword of Innocence gleamed in the moonlight, while my silver knife shined in my left hand.

I saw West stand up as a reflection on my blade. He howled from behind me and squared up for a fight. Eddy growled low in his throat as he began to stalk away from us. I darted to my left to cut him off and to give West a clear charge if he wanted to take it.

"What's the matter, Eddy? A half dead loup garou and a knight with a bloody, snot-filled nose too much for you? Don't like the odds?" I taunted.

"Really, Mike you need to look before opening your mouth," Quinn said. I glanced over at him, and my hopes shattered like a jackknifed glass truck. He was surrounded by dozens of fully transformed werewolves. At a glance I thought there were forty, maybe fifty wolves. "Time for my favorite command. Kill!"

As one the wolves came on. We were outnumbered, and I was out of tricks. Well, I had one trick left, but it wasn't going to work on that many werewolves. I gritted my teeth and decided to go down fighting. As the wolves barked and howled I screamed in defiance.

West roared. The ground shook, the buildings shook, and my knees began to buckle. The newly turned werewolves each did one of three things. Most fell to their bellies. Ten of them sat down with their heads lowered. Six, I'm guessing they were the ones that had been running with Eddy the longest, stopped charging and stood with their heads lowered.

I watched as West stalked forward and growled at them. All of the wolves began to inch back. Quinn screamed in frustration, "I told you to kill! Kill the knight! Kill that mutt! Your alpha is mine, and all of you are mine!"

"Guess you aren't as dominant as you thought, Quinn. Looks like West's got the big dick in the wolf pack," I said.

Quinn looked up at me and screamed, "He's half dead. How long do you think he can hold them back? The moment he falls, you die, Mike old boy. Eddy is the alpha, and he belongs to me. I don't care how dominant West Black is, he can't take this pack from me without a fight, and I put enough silver in him to kill a dozen werewolves."

My brain raced. I glared at Quinn and said, "So, it's all about the alpha?"

"Damn, Mike, haven't you been paying attention. This whole thing was about making an alpha. Everything about the werewolves is about the alpha!"

I smiled. "Then I challenge Eddy for the position of alpha!" I turned on Eddy, and he roared at me. All I had to do was take down a loup garou. All I had to do was kill a monster that combined the agility, speed, and versatility of a feral werewolf with the strength and virtual indestructibility of a werewolf in wolf form. It wasn't like it was impossible. It was just annoying that I had to do it with a runny nose and watery eyes.

Before we could go at it, Quinn hooted and laughed at me. "It doesn't work that way, Mike. Only a werewolf can challenge a werewolf for alpha. One of the Blacks could do it, but neither of them is in any condition to fight my new pet. Face it, Mike, you bet on Black and lost. Now you mutts get up and kill them!"

The wolves began to raise their heads. West growled at them, and they cowed once more, but the North Carolina Alpha shivered and dropped down to one knee. Several of the werewolves lifted their heads again, and West snapped his head up to glare at them. They all dropped their heads again. Eddy began to chuff when he figured out that it was only a matter of time before West couldn't hold them back. Or maybe it was just funny to him that West was holding back fifty werewolves while I was stuck fighting one loup garou on my own.

"Kill them!" Quinn screamed again.

West roared, but he began to cough up blood.

The werewolves of Baltimore all began to growl as they stalked toward us.

A roar silenced them all. Once again the werewolves lowered their heads. I looked past Eddy to see Faith standing between us and the wolf pack. She had her head high, and her eyes were focused on Eddy. She growled and began stalking toward the loup garou. I saw fire in those eyes. I saw defiance. I saw contempt. I saw rage. I saw resolve.

"Hey Quinn," I yelled. "Faith Kane, daughter of Jedidiah Kane, challenges Eddy for alpha!"

# CHAPTER 36

JUST FULL OF surprises, aren't you Mike?" Quinn growled.

I slumped down to one knee and started taking deep breaths. I had no idea how this was going to go. Since everyone was waiting for the music to start, I decided to do my best to recover. Eddy had beat me up pretty badly, and things were going to get worse before they got better. I leaned on my sword as I took a quick inventory of my situation. Both of my Desert Eagles were loaded and ready. I still had a trump card that I was saving for later. My sword was still sleeping. So basically, I had some guns and a knife.

"Can you shoot Quinn in the leg if I need you to?" I asked my Bluetooth.

"If I shoot it's going to be in the head or heart. Don't ask me for anything less," came the voice in my ear.

"Then just watch my back," I said. I opened my mind to Eddy and Faith. Magically they felt the same, but Eddy felt like more than Faith. Like she was a single toy block, but he was an entire building block set. I also felt something else. When focused on Eddy, I was drawn to the other new werewolves. I focused on West and could feel my attention being pulled far to the south. When I returned my attention to Faith, I found nothing but her, a faint hint of myself, and a little bit of Larry.

"If you try to interfere, Mike, I will start killing these submissive mutts. I don't need them anyway, but I bet you care about them, don't you?" Quinn asked. To prove his point, he took his sword and slashed down the back of one of the wolves that was lying on the ground. I heard the new werewolf yelp in pain. Faith heard it too and she growled in anger. When she turned to lock eyes with Quinn the pack master yelled, "Fight."

Eddy rushed in and kneed Faith in the head before she could turn back around. She hit the ground rolling and Eddy pursued, stomping his feet with every step in an attempt to crush her head. Each stomp cratered the asphalt as he missed. Faith kept rolling away from the loup garou until she could get her footing. When she did, she reared back so that Eddy stomped down in front of her. That's when Faith turned her head and chomped down on Eddy's leg.

The loup garou howled in pain, and Faith plowed forward. She ran past Eddy with his leg still in her mouth. He fell into a painful looking split, and Faith started dragging him, and consequently his balls, along the ground. Eddy somehow managed to keep his presence of mind as he howled in pain. He grabbed a chunk

237

of the broken ground and smashed it into the side of Faith's head. My friend yelped, let go of Eddy's leg, and then fell to the ground. Eddy clutched his wounded leg while Faith lay still on the ground.

"Finish her off, you blasted mutt," Quinn yelled. "Give your alpha your power so he can heal!" He kicked one of the new wolves, and I felt power, life, drain from that wolf. I felt it flow into Eddy and watched as his torn leg stopped bleeding. I watched him heal and heard the other wolf cry in pain.

Eddy climbed to his feet and picked Faith up by the scruff of her neck. He began punching her in the chest and stomach. Faith didn't whine when he hit her. She growled and coughed when she couldn't growl. Eddy started running and threw Faith into the side of a building. She smashed into a corner, broke through the wall, and came out the other side to land in an alley. Eddy howled in victory.

I sensed Faith before I saw her limp out of the alley. Her front right leg was broken, but she came forward with her teeth bared for battle.

"This bitch just won't die. Kill her, Eddy. Be a good dog and rip her head off," Quinn ordered.

Eddy walked forward snarling. Faith kept limping. Just as they reached each other Eddy lunged at her, and Faith slammed her broken leg down and vaulted at the loup garou. Eddy caught her, but she bit down on his shoulder. He managed to push her away, but she tore away a mouth full of flesh and muscle.

I heard more wolves whining. I looked over and found Quinn, with his belt in his hand, beating them. "Give him your power. He has to win, you fucking mutts!"

I turned my attention back to the fight, and sure enough Eddy was healing. But Faith wasn't giving him a chance to fully recover. She kept coming at him, viciously trying to bite him. He fended her off every time and usually landed a hard blow to stop her advance, but she was pulling away chunks of flesh with each charge. It was hard to tell who was winning. Faith was getting pummeled, while Eddy was being ripped apart.

But Eddy was healing. No matter what Faith did, she was on her own in this fight. She needed a pack. All she had right now was just Larry, myself, and my stupid sword. I looked down at the blade and saw a flicker of light on the metal. Faith had me, and I had my sword. The light became brighter. Faith had the Knight of Innocence on her side, and my sword had helped her once before, when she wanted to help those poor people that were hurt and scared. I remembered her power, and I remembered where it came from.

My sword glowed with white light as I drew upon its power. I opened my mouth and bellowed out Truth. "Werewolves of Baltimore, hear me! You are not mutts. You are not meant to be slaves to anyone. This fight will determine your alpha, but there is another way. You may choose your alpha!"

Quinn looked at me with hate in his eyes. "Kill him! All you lot kill him!"

The six wolves that were still standing charged at me. My brake was over anyway. I stood up with my weapons low and at the ready. "Drop the wolves but don't kill them," I said into my Bluetooth.

"That I can do," said my back up.

I held my ground, and when the lead wolf leapt at me I spun backward and brought my knife and sword around to slash across its side. My sword cut into the werewolf's side, and I shoved my knife into its shoulder and pushed out with both blades. The wolf cried out in pain as I spun to meet the next attacker.

One wolf's side erupted in blood, and it fell to the ground. My sniper was good, and it helped that none of the new wolves were anywhere near as resilient as Everett. Another wolf came from my right side, and I met its fangs with the steal of my sword. The flat of my blade struck its muzzle to parry a bite to my leg. A third wolf came at my back, and I had to turn before slashing at it with my knife. The silver edge raked across its face and sent it sprawling to the ground with a torn mouth and nose. I turned back to the second wolf to keep up the dance but found it rolling over with a bullet wound to its side as well.

The werewolves were healing, and now they were aware that someone was taking shots at them. Moreover, they were afraid of getting cut by my knife. So, they circled and looked for an opening. I prowled around at the ready and spoke again with Truth. "It is your choice who you follow. It is your decision alone. The pack master would have you believe that you are just dogs to be ordered about, beaten, and sacrificed at his whim. Faith cares for you, she has cried for you, prayed for you, and now she fights for you."

One of the werewolves charged from my back but went down with another gunshot to the shoulder. The sniper was momentarily distracted with that shot, so the other five attacked. I struck one in the face with the flat of my sword, kicked one with my boot, and stabbed one in the back with my knife. One wolf, a blond colored one, hit me in the back and knocked me over. I rolled and slashed with my sword thinking to fend it off. But a dull brown colored wolf leapt at me.

My sword hit its neck and sliced clean through. The head smacked off my helmet while the body landed on me. I pushed it off and scrambled to my feet. I saw the other wolves scrambling away with new bullet wounds. They would heal soon enough. This one, however, was dead by my hand.

Something inside me burned. My soul screamed, and a new sound echoed within me. I had killed fifteen beings that had souls with my sword, and I had now lost fifteen days of my life. It was something I would need to deal with later. Right now, I had work to do.

"Almost out of rounds kid. I am missing more than I am hitting. Hurry it up," my sniper said.

"Randal Quinn will not feel the loss your pack just suffered. He will not weep for you or yours. But Faith will. She weeps for you now, and she will protect you with her life," I said. The next words came from my memory, from Faith's memory. "Run with her! Hunt with her! Fight with her! Be hers and she will protect you. Be hers and she will teach you. Be hers and she will die for you!"

The werewolves that were attacking me all held their positions. The power of Truth faded from me, and during this slight reprieve I discovered that my right shoulder was bleeding. So were my left forearm and somewhere on my right leg because my pant leg was covered in blood. Eddy and Faith were still going at it, but Faith was darting in and out of Eddy's reach. Neither was committing, and both were bleeding badly.

One of the werewolves, the blonde one, rushed me. I dropped into a fighting stance to meet its charge. A brown-furred wolf dashed ahead of the blonde one and skidded to a stop between us. It bared its fangs at the blonde wolf and forced it to back off. I heard howling and looked to see many of the new werewolves with their heads lifted to the moon. Some were growling at one another. Others were barking wildly.

"What have you done, you bastard?" Quinn screamed. One of the new werewolves growled at him, and he slashed it with his silver sword. "What the hell have you done. These mutts were mine!"

"They aren't mutts. They're people. Werewolves," I said.

"Eddy, kill her now!" Quinn screamed.

Eddy charged at Faith and kicked her hard in the ribs. She went flying toward the pack of werewolves, and they scattered, allowing her to land on the ground. Eddy sprinted after her, leapt into the air, and brought his fists down on Faith like a sledgehammer.

"Faith!" I yelled as I watched Eddy slam his clenched fists into her so hard that the asphalt exploded beneath her. The ground around him was reduced to rubble for yards in every direction. "Faith," I whispered once more in confusion.

She had taken the blow by catching his claws in hers. She tucked her legs and kicked out, hitting Eddy in the chest and sending him flying backwards. Faith, a tall red-furred loup garou, sprang to her feet and went after Eddy. She was still bleeding and limped a little, but she was healing, I could see it as she gained speed with each stride. Eddy hit the ground and scrambled to his feet only to have Faith run right over him. She trampled him to the ground and kept going. He scrambled up again just in time to have Faith turn around and run him over again.

Eddy surged to his feet as Faith tried to overrun him a third time. This time he lashed out with a strong right cross, but Faith slid under the blow and kicked his legs out from under him. He hit the ground but surged back up only to take a claw along his back as Faith darted by him. He wheeled around to face her, but she was behind him again and raked both of her claws down his back.

Eddy had overpowered me and had been overpowering Faith. But with all that strength and power, he had been doing it all wrong. Eddy fought with his fists and stood his ground like a man. It's how he had learned to fight, just like I had. Faith had learned differently. She didn't fight like a man…er…woman. She fought like a werewolf. She kept moving, using her speed to hit her opponent fast and used her strength to make sure each hit caused enough pain to stun Eddy. By the time he reacted after each blow, Faith was already out of his reach and positioning herself for the next strike. Always ripping into vital areas with her claws and always looking for the next opportunity to put him on the ground.

Eddy was bleeding from a dozen wounds now, and his healing had slowed. By comparison, Faith's healing had sped up, and judging by how the new werewolves were squaring off, I would say that they were getting an even amount of help from the now two packs of Baltimore. So, Faith was winning and winning well.

"Michael, watch out!" yelled the voice in my ear. I turned just in time to see Quinn's rapier coming at my head. I lifted my sword and parried the blow. I set myself to fight, but he ran by me and kept going.

"Kill the knight and the bitch! Eddy heel!" he yelled.

Half of the werewolves looked at me and growled. West had been holding them back, but he slumped over and began taking deep breaths wheezing. On came the werewolves, and just as they came after me Eddy turned and ran after Quinn. Faith barked and the wolves that weren't coming after me, came forward, and started attacking the wolves that were coming to kill me. Faith turned to go after Eddy, but the five wolves that had been fighting me turned and went after her. They dog piled on her, and she started beating them off. The wolf that had been protecting me ran into that dog pile and started aiding his new alpha.

That left me alone with Quinn and Eddy getting away. I turned and ran after them. I even managed to snatch up my shield. Eddy was limping and struggling to heal. Faith had worked him over. Quinn had some distance on me, plus I was weighed down with a lot of armor and gear. "Can you shoot his leg?" I asked.

"Head or heart," my sniper replied.

"Dammit, I don't want to kill him. Just keep the big werewolf busy," I grumbled.

Quinn was closing in on the pier. I could see a gang plank lowered for him as well as dark figures aboard the ship. If he got there, he was home free. But there was a chance I could capture him and wait on back up from Faith. In a moment of desperation, I took my shield and flung it at Quinn's legs. My shield flew through the air, went right past Quinn, and skidded across the ground. I snatched up my shield again with the intention of throwing it once more.

"Behind you!" came the voice of my sniper.

I turned and threw my shield out to block just as Eddy came down on me. His weight forced me to the ground as his momentum carried him right over me. I forced myself back up to my feet as I drew my sword once more. Eddy rose up before me. I could see fresh bullet wounds in his chest. My sniper had tried to stop him, but he had shrugged off several shots that would have dropped just about anything else.

"Get out of my way, Eddy. I want the asshole that made you do this crap, not you. Move so I can save you," I said.

Eddy started chuffing at me again. He held out his clawed hand and made the universal hand gesture of curling his fingers to say, "come get some." I had realized that Eddy was somewhat of an asshole, but until this point it never crossed my mind that he might have chosen to do all of this.

"Hey Eddy, be honest with me. I'm feeling kind of dumb right now. Did you choose to become a werewolf, and are you following Quinn willingly?" I asked.

Eddy started chuffing louder. He slapped his knee with glee. Then he looked me in the eye and grinned a huge doggie grin with his tongue out. He nodded at me and beckoned me to come fight him again.

I watched this loup garou laughing at me. I had come to save him, to help him, and as it turned out he wanted this. He had been complicit in torturing Everett, turning the homeless, and murdering innocent people. This is why the pack had split in two. Because, like Eddy, some of them were in on this. Some were the bad guys, and I was the little boy that was playing hero just like Lydia Black had said.

I banged my shield with the flat of my sword and rushed ahead. Eddy readied himself for my charge. I leaned into my shield and shoved it forward. I let go of my shield so that it flew forward like I was charging behind it. Eddy smacked the shield away with a swing of his right arm and lunged forward to grab me. But I wasn't there because I had dropped low when I let go of the shield. I took a cue from Faith and thrust my sword at Eddy's knee to cripple him. He leapt straight up into the air, tucked his legs, and then kicked them straight down at me. I flung myself out to my left to avoid being crushed.

We both came out on even footing. I drew my knife and paced out to my left toward the ship. Eddy matched me stride for stride. I started jogging and so did he. Then I broke into a run. Eddy was still limping, but he kept up. I leapt at him with my sword leading. He backed away, so I pressed in with a slash of my knife. Eddy dodged then punched out at me. I ducked and slashed at his face with my sword. When he ducked, I kicked him in the leg. He shrugged it off and grabbed my leg with both his claws.

Eddy pulled me forward and I stumbled. I tried to stab him with my knife, but I was too off balance. He pulled on my leg again forcing me to fall forward. His fist punched out and hit me in the mouth. He pulled my leg a third time and punched me again. So it went for five or six punches to my face. Finally, he jumped back pulling me along, and then he let my leg go and surged forward to hit me in the gut with his fist. It felt like a bowling ball had hit me in the stomach. I dropped my sword and knife as I doubled over in midair. I landed in a fetal position and rolled over with my back to Eddy.

My cloak was wrapped around me as Eddy began kicking and stomping on me. Where Faith fought like a wolf, Eddy fought like a human. He was taking every cheap shot he could to win. I didn't blame him. I rolled over onto my stomach and covered my head with my left hand. Eddy reached down and grabbed my cloak. He turned me over, and his eyes went wide when my cloak flipped back to reveal my new snub-nosed revolver in my right hand. He hadn't seen me draw it with my cloak covering me.

I pulled back the hammer and fired. I fired from less than two feet away. I was aiming for his chest. I missed. I still hit him, but not in the chest. The bullet sank into his shoulder and went clean through. Eddy fell over and howled in pain. I rolled away and started working my way back to my feet. "By the way, I got some silver bullets, asshole," I said as I spit out blood. I had been saving this for Kodiak or West if they turned on me, but it was now or never at this point.

I got to my feet and took aim at Eddy once more. I had come here to save him, to do my job and protect him from Quinn. Then, after all of that effort, I found out that Eddy had wanted this. He wasn't a victim, and he didn't want my help. Eddy had helped transform innocent people into werewolves, had helped kill children, and he wanted to kill me. He wasn't human. He was a monster, and not because he was a werewolf.

Eddy looked up at me with hatred and rage in his eyes. He growled and roared as he surged back to his feet in an attempt to rush me. I pulled the trigger on my new revolver and a single silver bullet exploded from the barrel. Eddy's roar vanished as his neck exploded into a mess of blood and silver. He fell to the ground with his eyes still locked on me with all that hatred and rage still very much alive in those dead orbs.

I wished it was still raining so I could blame it for the tears running down my face. Eddy was dead by my hand, which meant I had failed to save him. Whether he wanted to be saved or not, it was my job to save him, and I had failed…in that part. I still had work to do. I snatched up my knife, shield, and sword then ran toward the ship. I still needed to get Quinn, and I was running out of time.

"Werewolves on your six," the voice in my ear said.

I didn't even have a chance to turn before my arm exploded with pain as a werewolf raked its claws over my forearm. I dropped my gun and dropped back as the wolf growled at me. It didn't attack me, but it did hold me there as three other wolves rushed by us. They flanked Quinn to the ship and up the gang plank as this one werewolf paced in front of me. One of the other werewolves barked from the ship, and the werewolf holding me back ran to the ship.

From aboard the ship Quinn started pointing at me and screaming. I couldn't make out what he was saying, and I didn't care. I started running again. The gang plank was still lowered, so all I needed to do was get aboard and knock Quinn overboard. That or just kill him, and at this point either would work for me.

Two thugs ran beside Quinn and lifted rifles. I yelled "Anziehen" as I balled up behind my shield. Magic surged out of my shield as a storm of bullets thundered out of their automatic weapons. My shield pulled nearly every bullet into itself sending shock waves through my body from every impact. Some bullets escaped the magic of my shield and hit the ground sending debris flying up around me.

The gun fire ceased, and I looked around my shield to see the boat pulling away from the dock. Quinn was still pointing and yelling at me. I dropped my shield as I started running. Drawing both of my Desert Eagles I opened fire in a desperate attempt to kill him. I emptied both magazines, but Quinn was still standing.

"Can you shoot him in the head?" I asked.

"Now you want me to shoot him in the head! Too late for that kid. He's gone and you have bigger problems coming from your six," the voice in my ear replied.

I looked behind me and saw the werewolves of Baltimore marching down the pier. I saw Everette Black ahead of them. Beside him I saw a blonde werewolf and a chocolate brown one. Ahead of them walked Faith Kane, and beside her limped West Black.

Ahead of them all walked a loup garou that was covered from head to toe in the blackest fur I had ever seen. It was darker than shadow, and each stride made it look like he was just that, a shadow striding down the street in the darkness of night. I opened my mind to this new beast and found nothing. I sensed no magic, no power, nothing at all. I felt power all around me, but in this werewolf I felt only an abyss devoid of existence.

Kodiak Black had come to the battlefield.

I looked back at the ship to find it pulling out to the river. Just like that the ship began to turn away. I watched as the bad guys began their escape. I had failed. All because I was trying to save the wrong people, or some of the wrong people. They were escaping. I didn't know how to feel at that moment. The fight was over, but Quinn, the cause of all of this death and grief, was getting away. What was I going to do? What was I supposed to do?

Kodiak Black stepped up beside me. He had left the other werewolves behind. He alone stood next to me. He was taller than his son. Broad of shoulder, he held himself with an ease that I had not seen in any of the other loup garou. He extended his arm to me and handed me my shield. I took it and saw something odd on his left hand. A simple ring was on his ring finger, and I could see wisps of smoke curling from beneath it. It was his wedding band, and unless I missed my guess it was made of silver.

I started to say something when my ear piece chirped, "Look up."

I did. There was a plane flying low over the city. Over the river really. From it came ten figures in those cool glide suits that you see on internet videos. They dove in over the ship, loosed their parachutes, and continued their decent toward the escaping boat. They were too high as they came right above the ship. That's when they did the unthinkable and cut their chutes. They fell a good 400 yards toward the ship, and before they ever hit the deck the night was filled with the sound of automatic weapon fire. I watched as they descended upon the ship and listened to the sound of snarls and howls mixed with the sound of gunfire.

I watched as battle broke out on the ship. From further down the river three speed boats came surging toward the fight. Two pulled up to the ship, and I saw grappling lines fired up at the deck. Armed combatants in black ops gear scaled those lines as easily and swiftly as their counter parts had dropped onto the ship. There was an explosion, and I saw bodies flying from the ship into the river.

As the battle raged on, the third speed boat pulled up to the dock. Seven black ops dressed individuals leapt onto the dock, guns at the ready, and approached us steadily. I shifted my shield in front of me and strapped it onto my arm. Then I spit blood from my mouth and got ready for a fight.

"I've got you covered," the voice in my ear said.

Beside me, Kodiak Black stood silently. When the seven black ops guys got to us, the one in the lead lowered his weapon and pulled off his hood. Long black hair spilled out to fall perfectly into place. Aaron tucked his hood into a pocket on his tactical vest and made a gesture with his right hand. The other black ops guys, probably vampires, spread out but lowered their weapons.

"Kodiak Black, I presume," Aaron said. When Kodiak didn't respond, he pinched his lips and nodded. "Ah, of course. You likely cannot talk in this form. That makes negotiation difficult. Luckily, there is nothing to negotiate."

There was another explosion over on the ship, and I could see fire spreading across the deck. Aaron stepped forward but stopped just beyond where Kodiak could strike him. I had heard my friend preach before, I had heard him tell people about medical hardships, and I had listened to him lecture me on both scripture and my health. But the authority he spoke with tonight was nothing that I had ever heard from him.

"By order of the Harlequin Vampire Court, you have twenty-four hours to take the werewolves you brought into Baltimore and leave. You will dispose of the werewolves created here. By the peace treaty between our people, you will honor our agreement or face retribution. Are we clear, Kodiak Black?"

We all stood there in silence for a long time. I watched as the burning ship floated down river and into the distance. Finally, Kodiak turned and started back toward the gathered werewolves.

I spun on him as I yelled, "You can't kill them!"

"Michael!" Aaron snapped.

Kodiak Black stopped walking away from me. He tilted his head to the side but did not look back at me.

"You can't kill them! They didn't ask for this…well…most of them didn't! Even if they did, they didn't know that it was against some treaty. They deserve to live!" I yelled.

"Michael, shut up!" Aaron growled.

Kodiak Black shook his head in the negative and started walking away again. He walked over to the gathered werewolves. Faith and West parted before him. The blonde wolf and the chocolate brown one separated from Everett. The new werewolves fanned out until they encircled the six elder werewolves.

Kodiak Black stepped before Everett Black and stood there. Here in the light of the full moon, when werewolves are at their most powerful, Everett Black lowered his head and tilted it slightly to expose his neck. I watched as Kodiak reached out to take his brother's neck in his own clawed hand.

My mind flashed back to what I had learned. The law was that no wolf could be turned in Baltimore. That meant that any werewolf turned here had to die. That also meant that any werewolf that turned a human in Baltimore had to die. Everett had turned people into werewolves and had killed those that he didn't turn. For there to be justice by their standards, his alpha, his brother, had to take his life.

Every werewolf except Everett and Kodiak lowered themselves to the ground. Kodiak lifted his head to the moon. I clicked back the hammer of my revolver and pointed it at Kodiak. The eyes of every vampire and werewolf except Everett and Kodiak were on me. The vampires, all but Aaron, lifted their weapons to cover me in red dots. The werewolves were growling at me.

"Michael, stay the fuck out of this!" Aaron told me.

"You might be the alpha where you come from, but not here. Here, in Baltimore, there is no alpha. There are only my guests. I invited you here as a guest, and by extension, as a member of your pack, Everett Black is my guest. You are not permitted to kill another guest," I said.

One of the vampires said something in a language I did not know, and Aaron responded in what I suspect was that same language. "Michael, you need to shut your damn mouth right the fuck now!"

As Aaron warned me to be quiet, Kodiak turned his head slightly toward me and raised an eyebrow as if to say, "go on." I licked my bloody lips and let my brain run ahead of my mouth.

"I was asked to find him, and I did. So, until he leaves Baltimore he is my guest. And as his host, as Baltimore's representative of the Church, I exonerate him of any perceived wrongs. He and these new werewolves have done no wrong by my word. They are welcome here as are all peaceful werewolves."

No one moved. No one made a sound. We all just waited there. It felt like hours, and damn this new gun was heavy. I didn't let it drop though. I just waited. Kodiak lowered his head to look at his brother. He let go of Everett's throat and nodded. Then he turned and walked toward me. He stopped a good distance away from me and knelt down. Using his claw, he scraped a message into the ground. 'Kate's at noon. Be there. We will talk.'

I nodded. Kodiak wiped the message away with his palm and stood up. He threw his head back and howled at the moon. Every werewolf lifted its head and joined him. The night filled with their voices, and the urge to run filled me. Not to run away with fear, but to run wild. To be free, stretch my limbs, to push myself, to live! Kodiak took off into the night, and all of the wolves followed him. I wasn't afraid that they would hurt anyone, but I had a feeling that there were going to be a lot of stories about giant wolves running the streets tomorrow. That would be just one more thing to add to my list of screw ups for this adventure.

I turned around to face the vampires, and Aaron slugged me in the face. I went limp at the blow, but before I could hit the ground my best friend grabbed me by the front of my shirt and pulled me up to face him.

"What the fuck did you just do?" he asked me.

"My job," I told him.

Aaron's voice was low and even. "No Michael. Your job is to keep the peace between the mortal and magical communities. You just broke a treaty older than the Union. You have no idea what you just did."

"I kept people alive. That's my job. If your new buddies have a problem with that, they can take it up with my management," I said as I pointed to the heavens.

"We will," said one of the other vampires. He had a rich Italian accent. "We have lost contact with the aerial unit, and the aquatic unit reports heavy casualties. The wolves and the pack master have all been neutralized, Lord Aaron."

"*Lord* Aaron?" I asked.

Aaron sighed and gritted his teeth. He spoke loud enough for his companions to hear him. "Michael, we will talk about this later, when I return from my trip with Emory." Then under his breath he said, "You really put me in a bad situation, Bro. You really fucked up."

He shoved me away, made a motion with his right hand, and then he and the black ops vampires turned and ran back for their speed boat. They were out on the water before I had time to realize what I had just heard.

Quinn was dead.

I gathered myself up and started walking back to the site of the trailer wreck. There were bodies everywhere. At least sixteen people had not survived the change. Their mangled frames had died somewhere between man and wolf. After checking my watch, I found that I had a good thirty minutes before my fight with the troll was supposed to kick off. So, I walked around to each body and said a small prayer for each one.

When I was done, I tapped my Bluetooth and said, "Thanks for having my back."

"No problem. Find a place to sit down and rest. This was the easy part of the night," my sniper said.

"Do you see all the bodies?" I asked.

"You can't save everyone. It's just not possible. Rest. You're going to need it," my sniper said.

I found some stairs next to one of the buildings near the wreck. I liked sitting on stairs, so I sat down and waited. It occurred to me that if I were an actual action hero the big bad troll might have arrived while the werewolves and vampires were still around. In fact, maybe Aaron would have gathered the vampires behind me and insisted on aiding me. Maybe the troll and Kodiak Black would have had a convenient history of conflict and they each would have insisted on settling their history with bloodshed tonight.

But I'm no action hero. I'm a carpenter that's out of work with a side gig as a P.I. So, I get to sit around and wait for the troll to show up to his appointment to kill me. I took the opportunity to make two phone calls. Then I pulled out my flashlight and practiced making shadow puppets.

Why? Because what else was I going to do before fighting a freaking troll?

# CHAPTER 37

A DELOREAN CAME flying down the road. It whipped around the wrecked trucks and skidded to a stop in the middle of the street. It was something out of the *Back to the Future* movies, completely tricked out to look like Doc Brown's custom design. The driver's side door lifted into the air, and out stepped a skinny man in a red jerk coat, or a sleeveless vest if you don't know better. He walked around to the front of his car and leaned against the hood. I took stock of his outfit, and sure enough he was dressed from head to toe like Marty McFly.

I stepped out into the street to face him, a little in awe of his ride and his choice of clothing. All of my weapons were sheathed but ready to go. My shield was on my shoulder again, and I had straightened out my cloak. As I squared up to the newcomer, I had to wonder if he was a troll or not. He was dressed far differently from his associates, and just watching him lean on his car told me that his mannerisms were different. His hair was short but quaffed to look like Marty McFly's. This troll, at least right now, would stand out in a crowd.

"Are you the knight?" he asked.

"Yeah," I replied. "Are you Goy?"

He reached into his back pocket and pulled out a brown wallet. He took a business card and flicked it across the forty feet of asphalt between us. I really wanted to learn how they did that. I caught the card but had to pull out my flashlight to read it. It read "Goy T. Roll, Property Management and Real Estate Brokerage." I slipped it into my wallet with the others.

"Where's the leprechaun?" he asked.

"Around," I said. "Is that a flux capacitor blinking inside your car."

"What?" he asked. He looked behind himself at the Y-shaped LED inside his cab. "Oh, yeah. Guess I should lock up before we fight, right?" He pulled out his keys, clicked a button, and I watched the cab go dark as the door closed itself.

"That is so awesome," I said.

He lifted his left arm and took a look at his watch. "Look, I have a thing to-night. They're showing all three *Back to the Future* flicks at The Senator tonight. I'm missing the first one, but once we wrap this up I can catch the other two. I hear you carry nunchucks on you. Is that true?"

"Sometimes, yeah. I'm a martial arts enthusiast. Do you mean the theatre on York?" I asked. The troll nodded. "How did I not know about that? Dang!"

"Focus, kid!" said the voice in my ear.

"Look, no hard feelings, Mr. White, but I need to kill you so I can get back before the first movie ends. It's bad enough that I am going to miss the enchantment under the sea guitar scene. I cannot miss the hover board scene. I might kill everyone in that theatre if I miss that. So, how do you want to do this? Do you want to flail around, show off some sweet martial arts moves, and bust out some holy power or something? Do you just shoot me until you run out of bullets? Maybe try and slay me with your magic sword? How is this going to go, because I want to get done with this as fast as possible," the troll said. "I could just rip your head off if you prefer. My brother wants me to pound you into a paste for the cops to find, but I hate it when he tells me how to do my job." He started taking off his clothing. He tossed his coat and shirt onto the hood of his car. Then he started taking off his shoes and pants.

I waited until he had his shoes off and was working on the buckle of his belt before I called out to him. "Hey Goy, later," I said. He looked up at me and I started running. My entire plan to fight this troll depended on me moving the fight to a location that I had already picked out. I didn't know he was going to strip, but I wasn't about to look a gift horse in the mouth. I watched as he started shoving his pants down his legs and figured that I could put a good bit of distance between us. I had a few blocks to cover, so I dug in and put my training to use. I ran like my life depended on it.

I was almost a block away when a dumpster came crashing down next to me. I leapt away from it and kept running. I looked back over my shoulder but didn't see anything. Track and trailer tires started raining down at me. They hit the ground, smashed windows, bounced off of buildings, and generally made running in a straight line impossible. I looked over my shoulder again but still didn't see my attacker. I kept running.

Bricks started hitting the ground all around me. Bits and pieces were pelting me in the back, but nothing solid enough to stop me from running. I looked back and finally saw the troll. He was between ten and twelve feet tall, running clumsily on two feet while holding what looked to be a chimney made of bricks under one arm. He ripped off part of the chimney in one hand, crushed it, then chucked it at me. He missed but he kept doing it. His aim was getting better with each throw, and I had to flip my shield off of my shoulder to cover my head.

The rain of bricks ended, and I looked back to see the troll looking for something else to throw at me. I had almost a hundred yards on him, so good luck with hitting me at that distance. Super strength or not, he wasn't much of a marksman. I kept running but slowed my pace a bit to conserve energy. I watched over my shoulder as Goy the Troll shrugged. Then he leaned forward and started running …on all fours…like an animal…a really fast animal! He was covering yards with each stride while I was covering feet. I kicked myself into high gear and yelled, "Feet don't fail me now!"

I didn't slow when I came to the corner. I grabbed the light pole to fling myself around and down the street. I looked over my shoulder to see Goy take a different tactic for making the turn. He slammed full speed into the building on the opposite side of the street and bounced off of it. Then he started chasing me again. I cut down a small alleyway and then sprinted down toward a dock area populated by shipping containers. I darted into one of the rows of containers and looked back to see if Goy was still on my trail. I didn't see him and thought for a moment that I had lost him. I turned and skidded to a stop. My heart was pounding, my blood was pumping, and I was worried that I had lost him. I needed to settle things here and now. This fight was happening, and I wanted it here instead of out on the street. I looked around frantically. How the hell did I lose a freaking troll?

I heard a thump to my left and then metal scraping across the ground. I listened, and another thump touched my ears. I turned to face the sound and looked into one of the alleyways made by the shipping containers. I didn't see anything, but again I heard a thump and scraping. I leaned over and looked on the other side of the rectangular container in front of me. Nothing again. Still, I heard a thump and scraping again.

The door of the shipping container exploded outward, and I leapt out to my left to avoid it. The contents of the container seemed to be golf balls as they pelted me and littered all over the ground. A large hand smacked against the right side of my body and flung me down the walkway. I braced against my shield as I hit the ground and used it to skid as far away as I could from whatever had hit me. As I slowed, I got my feet under me and got up to my knees. Then I wanted to lay back down and die.

I had seen glimpses of what a troll looked like. I had seen Goy at a distance. But here and now, with Goy standing right in front of me, I wanted to go back to fighting the loup garou. Goy was ten feet tall and as wide as the bumper of my truck. His dark brown skin sported warts the size of bowling balls and liver spots like Frisbees. He had wisps of reddish black hair above a broad forehead with a bulbous nose. His eyes were sunken deep within his face to the point where they stood out only because they were tiny and human-like in comparison to the rest of him. He was grinning, and I could see that his mouth started at the base of his ears with thick rectangular teeth that sported jagged tops to grind food against the flat tops of the bottom row. He had a black tongue like a giraffe. His face was framed by large round ears that stuck straight out like clocks on a wall or that most famous mouse with a similar name to mine. As it turned its head, I could see that his ears were double sided, so instead of having two ears it was more like he had four.

He had a gut to make a jolly old elf seem thin in comparison. His chest had flabby pectoral muscles. His butt stuck out with a small donkey-like tail hanging from between his butt cheeks. His arms looked like a body builder that had injected steroids directly into his muscles. Goy had troth-like claws just like Gung had. He was supported on wide hips and thick legs. His feet were huge for his body, easily five feet in length with balloon-like toes topped with thick cracked toenails.

The troll looked like something out of a children's cartoon made real. It was cartoonish in every way, but with terrifying features that reminded me that this was a very serious situation. Lives, mine and Larry's, were on the line. So, I readied myself for the worst. I couldn't have expected what came next.

"Where is the leprechaun," squeaked the troll. Its voice was as high as a toddler on helium. It was a giant covered in muscles, and it sounded like a mouse.

I laughed. I opened my mouth to say something, and the laughter just poured out. I couldn't help it. I was in a bad situation. I had been beaten up, blown up, pelted with bricks, and my rent had just gone up $50.00 a month. Now I was about to fight a giant monster with a squeaky toy for a voice box.

"This is why I hate humans," the troll said. "They always laugh when I talk. All the others have deep imposing voices, and I sound like a chipmunk!"

I tried to pull myself together. I stopped laughing, and that lasted all of five seconds. I laughed even louder.

"Keep laughing human. Keep laughing until I rip your limbs off and you scream. Then I'll be the one laughing," the troll said.

That got my attention and sobered me. This was a fight. Squeaky voice or not, this troll was here to kill me. It took a step forward on the golf ball covered ground. I could see it falling in my head, but of course that didn't happen. It just crushed the golf balls as it walked toward me. I stood up to ready myself for battle. Then I slipped on a golf ball and fell back to the ground. I heard the troll laughing as I rolled away to get to my feet.

I came up to a crouch with both of my guns out. I had filled them both with explosive rounds, and Goy was too big of a target to miss. I opened fire and watched as bits of flesh went flying in small explosions along his chest and stomach. He shielded himself with his arms and opened palms, and my ammunition blew small holes into his skin. His stride slowed but didn't stop.

When my guns clicked empty I holstered them and took note that Goy was bleeding but still coming at me. His skin was so thick that he had absorbed the damage from my explosive rounds with little negative effect. I pulled out the revolver with the huge silver bullets loaded in it. I took aim and put one in the troll's gut. Again, I saw the damage, the blood, and the troll slowed, but he still didn't stop. I holstered the revolver.

Putting my weapons away drew a curious look from Goy the troll. "Is that it? I was told you planned to kill me. Aren't you even going to try to kill me?"

I shrugged, said, "Nope," and then ran away. I took off to my right, down another artificial alleyway. Goy must have been surprised at my answer and sudden exit stage left because he didn't come charging after me right away. When he realized that I really was running away, he roared with the voice of a furious toddler. He came barreling after me, and I didn't dare look back. I leaned into the wind and put everything I had into running.

I weaved in and out of the artificial alleyways. I turned left at one point only to run past two containers to turn right and then right again to head back in the direction I had just come from. I could hear Goy slamming into and sometimes through shipping containers. Where I was diving forward and sliding to improve my maneuvering through the alley ways, he was just crashing through like a derailed freight train. He was gaining on me, but whenever he got close enough to tackle me I made a quick turn and sprinted ahead, turning down another alleyway. All the while he was yelling at me in that squeaky voice of his calling me everything from a cuckolded coward to a soy boy. I had no idea what any of it meant, and I wasn't about to stop to ask him.

After almost three full minutes of cardio, I saw the pier ahead of me and the red shipping container that I had tagged with yellow spray paint. The tag wasn't artistic or fancy in the least. All it said was "If you are reading this then you aren't dead yet so keep running!" I ran past the container, turned left, and ran alongside it. Once I cleared the length of the container, I was on a small side street just big enough for a single car to drive down. Just off to my right, barely ten yards away, was the end of the pier. The only thing separating me from the water was a rotting wooden board suspended between two cement posts.

I dropped into a baseball slide as I drew my sword. I came to a stop and lifted myself up to face Goy as he came at me on the open street. I charged back at him just before he cleared the red shipping container and came in low with my blade sweeping from left to right. He leapt to his left the moment he cleared the container but kept his eyes on me. He was standing near the middle of the short side of the rectangular container now, so I came at him from his right side and slashed down a little too far to his left to hit his shoulder. Goy darted to his left and squared off against me while laughing.

"You swing that sword like a half-blind novice. I thought you were a martial arts enthusiast," he taunted.

"I am, but you know what? I am also a motivational speaker. Aren't I, Larry?"

Goy looked confused as I held my left arm in the air and caught a sports bag that was thrown to me from somewhere behind him. He looked up and back just in time to see Larry Lipowski, a soulless, ginger, Jewish leprechaun dressed in a Boston Celtics warm up suit come leaping off the top of the shipping container behind him. Larry began screaming at the top of his lungs while swinging my baseball bat with all the strength he could muster. His battle cry echoed through the night.

"Taste my rainbow!" Larry yelled as he smashed Goy the troll right in the middle of his face, crushing his nose and knocking in his top row of teeth.

Larry hit the ground rolling to get away from the troll. Goy stumbled after him, which brought him even closer to me. I sheathed my sword, reached into my bag, and pulled out my shot gun. I chambered a round and took aim at Goy's left leg. I fired and watched as Goy's kneecap and lower leg cratered with holes. Goy screamed as his leg gave out and he fell to the ground.

"You know that not a single member of my order has been able to kill one of you guys. Trolls I mean, not specifically you Bridge Boys," I said. "But I figured that they all were trying to kill trolls. I don't need to kill you. Just beat you. So, I figured, since you heal from just about anything, how about I make that as painful as possible. These shells, for example, are rock salt coated in actual table salt and Blue Star Ointment for that extra burning sensation."

Goy looked up at me screaming like a mad troll. He rose to come after me but stumbled back down to one knee. He looked down at his leg, genuinely surprised that it hadn't healed yet. I ran in while he was distracted and yelled "Impact!" as I laid into him with an upper cut to his jaw. I felt bone break and saw several of his teeth go flying. Goy swung his right arm around in an attempt to smash me against his chest. I put my shotgun to his shoulder and fired. The troll howled once more into the night.

Around came Goy's left arm, and I fired right into his armpit. Then I yelled "Impact" again and smashed my fist into his other kneecap. Then for good measure I used my ring one final time and punched right through Goy's toenail and into his big toe. Goy screamed and flailed wildly. I tried to jump away, but as he thrashed he hit me square in the chest with his open palm. I went flying out to his right side away from the pier like a swatted fly. It hurt like hell when I hit the ground, but it was worth it. I got to my feet and started backing away from him while firing. I kept aiming at his arms and legs to keep him from pursuing me or escaping.

"My grandpa always tells me to win any way that I can. He always gives me such good advice, like this idea," I said.

Lights came on behind me. I watched with a sense of satisfied glee when, for the first time since meeting a troll, I was not the one that looked scared. The engine roared to life, and I pulled open the driver's side door to the Rust Bucket. Larry was in the passenger seat. I fired the last of my special all-pain shells at Goy's chest and then handed Larry the shot gun. I slid into the cab and floored it.

"All together now," I said to Larry.

"Bring it!" I yelled at the same time Larry yelled, "Taste my rainbow!"

The rust bucket hit Goy head on and slammed the troll through the wooden barrier. I slammed on the breaks, and Goy the Troll went flying out into the Patapsco River. I climbed out of the truck, shaken from the crash but with no additional injuries. None that I could see anyway. I stood over the water as I re-loaded my shotgun. Larry stumbled over to stand next to me. He was using my bat as a crutch.

"Goy!" I yelled. "I know that didn't kill you. Tell your brothers and your boss that Larry Lipowski is off limits. The score between he and Bob is settled. As for the Bridge Boys and me, I kept my word. Larry and I fought you alone and won. This is over!"

We waited there for five minutes in silence. We kept our weapons at the ready. Once we were sure that there wasn't going to be a reply, we stepped back and assessed the damage to my truck. The front end was impacted badly. When I popped the hood and managed to pry it open, I found the engine was now in the shape of a badly made horseshoe. With a sigh I pulled out my cell phone and made a call.

"Hey Drey. Bring the wrecker," I said when my cousin picked up the phone.

<h1 style="text-align:center">Chapter 38</h1>

DREY DIDN'T KILL me when he saw the Rust Bucket. He did punch me in the face and threw me off the pier, but he pulled me out when he remembered that I couldn't swim. Then he gave me a blanket, because that water was freezing. We all climbed into the cab of the wrecker. Larry sat in the middle. Drey didn't start the truck right away. He just sat there drumming his fingers on the steering wheel.

"So, are you going to tell me why you wrecked Grandfather's truck?" he asked.

I thought about it for a moment and shrugged. "Nope."

Drey glared at me with his perfectly human eyes.

"Hi, I'm Larry. I'm courageous now," Larry said as he held out his hand.

Drey shook his offered hand and said "Hello Larry. It's nice to meet you, and that's good to know. Do you want to tell me why my beloved cousin wrecked my grandfather's truck?"

Larry stared at Drey for a moment before looking back at me. Then he shrugged and said, "Nope."

Drey drove us back to the scene of the first battle. "Are you going to tell me why there are three wrecked trucks and a DeLorean over there?" he asked as I got out of the truck.

"Nope," I said. I rushed down to the end of the pier, hopped a fence, and climbed up the ladder of a silo. I came back to the truck and got in.

Drey pinched the bridge of his nose in frustration. Then he watched as I adjusted all of my gear in the cab. I was carrying a lot of hardware that I didn't have a few minutes ago. "I'm not going to ask about the rifle, the duffle bag, or the stack of porno mags. You probably wouldn't tell me about any of it anyway. But why is your old teddy bear wearing a tiny S.W.A.T. outfit?"

"Nope," I said.

"That's not even a valid answer to my questions," Drey said.

I shook my head. "Nope."

Drey put his foot down hard on the gas, and we took off into the night. "I'm not even going to tell grandfather. I'm calling your mother and telling her that you wrecked the truck. Better yet, I will call grandmother! Drag me out here in the middle of the damn night because you wrecked the truck again! You're lucky grandfather says that I am not allowed to kill you!"

Aside from Drey swearing and threatening me, it was a quiet ride home.

He let us out beside my apartment. "Someone from the shop will be dropping off a loaner for you tonight. I will get the truck back to you as soon as I can fix it. Until then, don't break anything else, little cousin, and if you do, don't call me." Drey didn't wait for my reply before he took off down the road. I waved goodbye to him and watched as my valiant steed headed off for repair.

Once we were locked up behind my wards, Larry stretched out on the couch. I put Horace on my bed as I stowed my gear. It was a few minutes before he sat up and started changing out of his tactical gear and into his overalls. I didn't say anything to him yet. I finished putting away my weapons and then went to grab the EMT kit from the kitchen. Aaron kept one here for anytime a mission got as bad as tonight's had. I poked my head into my room and asked Horace, "Ready for the next part?" My bear nodded. He grabbed a notebook and a pen then followed me into the bathroom.

I closed the door and opened the EMT kit. It wasn't a standard medical kit. It contained tools and meds for dealing with injuries that ranged from "first aid needed" to "make the guy comfortable while he dies." Looking in the mirror I was somewhere in between. My short hair was covered in dried blood. Both of my eyes were black and swollen but not closed up. My nose had been broken, and some of my teeth were missing. They would grow back, and it would hurt like heck. I hadn't even noticed the scrapes along my neck.

I dropped my cloak to the floor and gingerly removed my jacket. The inside was stained blood red. My Silver Surfer t-shirt was soaked through with blood. Horace, sitting on a stool I kept in the bathroom, handed me a pair of scissors. I waved them away. I would have to get the chain shirt off anyway, so there was no point in destroying my t-shirt. I gritted my teeth and pulled the t-shirt and armor off by grabbing them by their ends around my waist and lifting them over my head. I dropped them to the ground too. Next I pulled off my Kevlar. I was sweating now and happily cut off my undershirt.

My right collar and shoulder were swollen. They were colored an odd combination of blue and purple. The broken bones were healed but that was it. The rest would take time since it didn't prevent me from fighting. My tattoos didn't give a darn how badly it hurt. If it wasn't preventing me from fighting, I was on my own unless I pushed them to heal. I could see indents where Eddy's fangs had dug in. I looked down at my jacket and marveled that it didn't have a tear on it. I had to cut off my pants, and sure enough my legs were bruised and swollen. There were several bite and claw marks all around my legs. There were bite marks on my sides and arms. My back was bruised in some places, but there were no battle scars there.

I got in the tub and started the shower. Between screaming from the heat of the water and the pain of it touching my body I somehow managed to clean myself off. I stepped away from the water and began pouring alcohol onto any wound below my neck. I screamed the whole time. Then I let the water run over my body again. I screamed a little softer this time.

Once I was done, I sat on my toilet and began cleaning each wound with peroxide and then alcohol. I stitched a few of my wounds before bandaging them and others. The entire time I dictated my report to Horace just to keep myself from passing out from the pain.

It was past midnight when Horace and I climbed into my bed. I took my cell phone and sent a simple text. It said, "See you for our run in the morning."

"Thanks for having my back tonight, Horace," I said.

"No problem, kid. It felt good to protect you. It felt good to be needed," he said.

"So, I know you don't want to be here, but until we figure out how to send you home I could use some help. How do you feel about being my Bear Friday every day?" I asked.

"What does it pay?" Horace yawned.

"Room, board, and beer," I yawned.

"Almost everything a guy needs. If you throw in smokes and porn then you have yourself a deal," he countered.

"Fine, but can you do the porn stuff when I'm not around?" I pleaded.

"No promises, kid," Horace grunted before nodding off.

I blinked a few times as sleep settled in. I was tired and in pain. All I wanted to do was sleep for a month. The last thing I remember before dozing off was a distant sound. Somewhere in Baltimore the werewolves were running, and I could hear a howl in the night.

## CHAPTER 39

THADDAEUS AND I were not the only people running in the morning. There were maybe two dozen people running around Druid Lake. I guess since the rain stopped people had gotten back to their normal routines. It felt good to know that I had played a part in that. These people were able to go about their lives in safety because I had done my job.

"On your left," a tall thin man said as he ran past me.

"So, you managed to solve your cases?" Thaddaeus asked. We were almost finished with our jog. As usual he wanted to know more about me, and I didn't mind sharing as long as I didn't give away too many things that he probably shouldn't know about.

"Yep. I will tie up the loose ends with my client from out of town later today," I said.

"And the man you were protecting?"

"He's safe and sound. He also gets to stay that way if what I have been told about the thugs that were after him is correct. If not, I will handle them."

"On your left," a tall man with a thick frame said as he rushed by. He bumped into me but didn't stop to apologize.

"Well, that's good to know. You seem confident in your ability to do just that. Why is that?" Thaddaeus asked as we moved into the last stretch of our jog.

"Not to brag, but I'm good at my job, and I plan on getting a lot better," I said.

"I see," Thaddaeus chuckled.

"On your left," barked a man of average height and build as he stomped past us.

"So, Thaddaeus, we have been running for a few days now. All we ever talk about is me. What do you do for a living?" I asked.

"On your left," a skinny dude on an oddly familiar looking pink skateboard said. He glided by us and did a few tricks as he wove around people.

We had reached the end of our jog, and Thaddaeus started to chuckle. "Well, I do believe that all we have done is talk about you, haven't we? How about this. I will race you once around the lake. If you win, I will tell you my whole life story. If I win, then you let me keep jogging with you for the rest of your thirty days. Deal?"

"Sounds like I win either way. Are you sure you want to try running around the lake?" I asked in all seriousness.

"I feel like giving it a go. Who knows, I might win," he said.

261

I shrugged. "Okay."

We stood next to each other and asked his chauffeur to call it. He said, "Ready. Set. Go!" and we were off. I pulled ahead immediately. I left Thaddaeus behind and rounded the first turn with the wind in my face. I wanted to slow down to let the old guy feel like he had a chance, but that wouldn't have been very honest of me. Still, I did slow down a bit.

I was a quarter way through the lap when Thaddaeus came running up behind me. He was breathing hard, but he had a determined look on his face. "Don't slow on my behalf, Michael. I plan to win," he said.

Then he dug in and started to push past me. I let him get a bit ahead before I sprinted ahead of him again. Just as I passed him, Thaddaeus found a new gear and got ahead of me. I upped my speed and passed him on the next turn. We were in the third turn when he came up beside me again.

"Is that all you've got?" he asked as he passed me.

I was sore, but I wasn't hurt enough that I couldn't run. I gritted my teeth, pushed down the pain, and leaned into my full speed. I passed Thaddaeus and committed to finish the run at this pace. I was so focused on running that I didn't notice Thaddaeus was keeping pace with me until he chuckled.

"Maybe next time, Michael," he said as he effortlessly left me in his dust. He just pulled away and ran all the way to his car.

I was coughing and wheezing when I finally caught up to him. He was stretching in the parking lot in front of my loner ride. He ran in place a little as I approached.

"How did you get so fast?" I asked. He smiled at me but didn't say anything. When he didn't reply I pushed further. "I thought you couldn't handle a run around the lake?"

"Well, normally I wouldn't even try. I just felt like showing off for my boys," he said.

"Your boys?" I asked.

"Yeah, they came to run this morning, too," he said.

I looked around the parking lot at all of the cars and then to the walkway around the lake. I froze and looked back at the parking lot. There were a bunch of different cars, but one stood out. Far down at the other end of the lot were four extremely nice-looking cars lined up together. One was a tricked-out DeLorean.

I looked at Thaddaeus, and he must have seen the puzzlement on my face. He grinned and said, "Hey look, here they come now."

I looked back over my shoulder and saw the four men that had each said, "On your left," when they had passed me. They were walking side by side, well one was skateboarding, and they were chanting.

"Hung, Gung, Hoy, Goy. We're the boys Boss Fraul employs. Hung, Gung, Hoy, Goy. We're the boys Boss Fraul employs," they sang together.

"Guard the bridge," sang Hung T. Roll, the Investment Banker.

"Scratch our pits," sang Gung T. Roll of Architectural Distribution and Supply.

"Smash intruders into bits," sang Hoy T. Roll, the Transit Specialist.

"Smash and bash the little shits," sang Goy T. Roll of Property Management and Real Estate Brokerage.

"Hung, Gung, Hoy, Goy!" they all yelled in unison.

I was already breathing hard from my run, and I needed a bottle of water for my burning throat. I pulled the knives out of my pocket then put myself between them and Thaddaeus. As they came toward us, I tried desperately to catch my breath. I could barely hold my stance, and I really needed some water. Adrenaline was pumping through my system, but at this point it was all that was keeping me upright.

Thaddaeus stepped past me, putting himself between me and the four trolls in human form. "Thaddaeus get back. We have to get out of here. Where are your boys?" I asked.

"Why Michael, I know you are a little slow when it comes to social sub-terfuge, but you haven't figured it out yet? Truly?" he asked.

"What are you talking about?" I asked.

His chauffeur ran up beside him and handed him a business card. He held it out to me, and a chill ran down my spine. I took the card and read aloud. "Thaddaeus Fraul Roll, City Architecture, Design, and Planning."

The smile on Thaddaeus' face drained the blood from mine. I was exhausted from the battle the previous night and the run this morning. I slumped down to the ground in utter defeat. I had to plan out an entire trap and wreck my truck in order to beat one troll. How the hell was I going to beat five of them?

Thaddaeus…Fraul squatted down in front of me. He sighed like he was disappointed. "Is this it? I thought you would 'handle' my boys if it came to it?" he asked.

"You will never get your hands on Larry," I said. I didn't mean it, but I had to put that out there. Maybe they wouldn't bother with him after they killed me.

"That's fine. We don't want him. Never did. It was a job, one I didn't care for, but the boys wanted to tie up loose ends for their private endeavors. No, this isn't about Mr. Lipowski. This is about you, Michael White, the Knight of Innocence, Guardian of Baltimore, so on and so forth," he said.

"Me?" I asked.

"Yes. Well not just you. It was about my boy's reputation. They are very good at what they do, you see. Too good, actually. They're so accomplished that more lucrative opportunities in the magical communities rarely come to Baltimore for fear that we would charge too much for their operations in this city. See, there isn't a magical deal that goes down here without my say so. You see, Mr. White, success breeds profit, but it also breeds complacency. Frankly speaking, the magical community doesn't come here to Baltimore for business because they don't want us butting in and taking our cut. I have been looking for a way to change that. Then low and behold, here comes a holy knight, a protector of the innocent and the downtrodden." He smiled.

My stomach began to churn. "When you came along, the straights felt more inclined to set up shop here because they would have a protector. But the twists were skeptical, because we were here to extort, and you were here to shut them down completely. So, I told my boys to let me know as soon as your paths crossed. Low and behold it wasn't long. So, I asked each of them to do themselves a small service," Fraul pontificated.

He was quiet for a long time before he said anything else. His boys were standing just behind him now with their shadows falling over us. "I asked them each to lose to you." Fraul shrugged.

I looked from him to the other trolls. They were all grinning at me. All but Goy, who was grinding his teeth. I hadn't won a fight against any of them. I just hadn't lost in our confrontations. The truth of the matter hit me like a ton of bricks. Not only had they each been trying not to kill me, but they had let me think I had a chance at actually winning. Hell, Fraul could have killed me any time in the last few mornings. Hell, I had pretty much told him everything I was planning and even listened to his advice! He had played me like a fiddle!

"So, what now?" I asked. I gripped my knives as tight as I could.

"Now Michael? Now we go on vacation," Fraul said with a big grin.

"Vacation?" I parroted.

"Yes. See, you defeated my boys. Outmatched them in strength and wit. They have been vanquished, and thus they will retreat. Business will suffer for us for some time, but with holdings, investments, and savings both in the mundane world of money and the more traditional channels of power we will be just fine. So, congratulations Michael, you win."

I won? They were letting me win? The trolls were going to retreat when they had me dead to rights. I had to be missing something. "Why?" I asked. "Why let me win? Why not kill me? I don't get it."

"Politics isn't your strong suit, is it boy? I guess not. As smart as you are, you actually expect people to be honest and forthcoming, don't you? Alright, how to explain it? I know you young people have a word for it…" he said. The other trolls were grinning and snickering. "Oh yes, I remember. We are *trolling* you."

Now the other trolls were just openly laughing at me. Fraul cleared his throat and they stopped. He looked me in the eyes and grinned all the wider when I didn't turn away from his gaze.

"Trolling me?" I asked.

"Michael, there may not be that many trolls left in the world, but we are still a part of it. Hell, we put a man in the White House. But this isn't about world domination. It's about Baltimore and money…power! With my boys gone, word will spread about how the Knight of Innocence defeated them, and with them gone twists will try to fill the various vacuums of power within the city. In a couple of years or so, they will be comfortable operating here, and then my boys will come to…well…take their toll for allowing them to operate here in my city."

"This isn't your city," I snapped.

"Exactly Michael! It's your city. While I will still be operating in it, every single twist that comes in is going to think about challenging you. Some will, some won't, but every last one will think about it," Fraul said as he clapped his hands in mock celebration.

"Anyone that threatens this city would have to deal with me anyway," I said. I was scared, so of course I was just running my mouth.

"True enough. So, I have some advice for you, Michael. Get stronger. Finish your thirty days of running. Then keep running. Work out more. Eat better. Whatever it takes for you to get stronger. You are going to need to be stronger. Because one day I am going to tell my boys to come back from their vacation, and if you are still around I won't be asking them to let you win the next time your paths cross."

There was no staring contest, no battle of wits, and no shaking of hands. Fraul simply stood up and walked away. His boys followed suit. Five very expensive cars drove out of the parking area, and I was left sitting in the dirt.

I had faced five trolls, and each of them had let me walk away. I replayed the events in my mind. Hung could have slammed me against the ground instead of a car, or he could have just not walked away. Gung could have come crashing into the box car in full troll form or just ripped my head off any of the times he had grabbed me. Hoy didn't have to meet with me. Goy had let me lead him through that shipping yard. I had seen him crash through a shipping container, so why would he have to go through all those twists and turns? They had each pushed me to my physical and mental limit.

And they weren't even trying to kill me.

<h1 style="text-align:center">CHAPTER 40</h1>

I WENT HOME and slept. I woke up when Eden called me. I picked up the phone and asked, "Is this an emergency?"

"No Church boy, but…"

I cut her off. "I'm sorry, but I can't talk right now Eden. I will call you later." I hung up the phone and went back to sleep.

Horace woke me up next. I stirred as he shoved my still injured shoulder. When I finally opened my eyes to look at him, he said, "Its 10:30, kid. You better get going. Oh, and you got a text."

I looked at the text. It was from Faith. All it said was "Bring my stuff when you come." I got up, washed up, and woke up Larry. "Get dressed, Larry. We are going to meet the werewolves, and then I am taking you home," I said.

"Home? Is it really safe for me to go home?" the half leprechaun asked.

"Yes. I had a chat with Fraul. You are off the Bridge Boys' radar," I said.

"Fraul? Boss Fraul? When? How?"

"I don't want to talk about it, Larry. You are off the hook. Get dressed and get ready to go." I got dressed in dark jeans, a black t-shirt, and a red flannel shirt. I slipped on my black Desert Eagle and my new revolver. I grabbed my sports bag, put my sword in it, and on a whim clipped my silver survival knife to my belt. Larry was dressed in a black and green suit. He had all of his stuff packed but barely helped me carry it all out to the car. He took one look at my loner ride and whistled.

"Is that your new car?" he asked.

"For now."

"I like the color."

"It's Drey's favorite. Looks good I guess. Hop in," I told him as I loaded up the trunk with his luggage. I climbed in, and we drove off in my shiny new Pink Chevrolet Spark smart car.

When we arrived at Kate's, there were two buses in the parking lot. Kodiak, Faith, Lydia, and West were outside waiting on me. I took my sword from my bag and slung it across my back. Grabbing Faith's bag, I left Larry in the car and walked over to them. I stopped a few yards from the werewolves just to gauge the situation. Kodiak and West were dressed in fine black suits with silver shirts. Faith was dressed in a black suit and silver shirt as well but with a skirt. Lydia was in a red dress.

Kodiak lifted his head and sniffed the air. He turned to me and said, "I smell blood. Are you injured, Mr. White?"

267

"I'm doing just fine. How is your son?" I countered as I dropped Faith's bag to the ground. Horace had told me I should do my best not to show weakness in front of apex predators.

West turned to me and said, "I'm fine as well. Ready for round two with that interesting cousin of yours."

"He's busy, and seriously he would kick your butt with one hand behind his back. I am glad to see that the silver bullets and stab wounds didn't kill you, though." I smiled.

"We heal quickly under the moon," West said cheerily.

Kodiak stepped forward and looked me up and down. "You threatened my life last night, Mr. White. Is that how you treat clients?"

"Only when they try to kill people that are under my protection," I snapped.

"We have our ways, Mr. White. This will be questioned by my kind, but I will uphold your decision," he said with a tone of finality. Then he let out a long breath and said, "Thank you, Mr. White. You saved my brother from our enemies and from my own judgement. Had you not acted, I would have lost him."

Kodiak reached into his pocket and pulled out an envelope. He handed it to me, and I opened it. "This is $50,000."

"I cannot measure the worth of my brother's life to me. I figured this would be enough for your fee and for any expenses you may have had. But I owe you a debt, and that is no small thing," he said as he extended his hand to me. I put the envelope in my back pocket and shook Kodiak's hand. "Again, I must thank you, Mr. White. We now also have a new pack and a new alpha. They will be coming to stay with us as they will all need training. After that, we will find them a permanent place to settle down. Goodbye, Mr. White. If our paths cross again, I hope it will be as friends."

He clapped my injured shoulder, and I tried not to scream. He and West walked off toward the buses. Lydia walked up to me and gave me a warm smile. I returned it, though mine must have come off as a goofy smile because she laughed.

"A Silver Surfer t-shirt? For an instant, I was worried that I was wrong about you, Mr. White. You are a little boy playing hero…and for that, I am grateful. You saved my brother-in-law because you couldn't bear seeing someone die. Such an innocent. I hope, for your sake, that you temper your innocence with wisdom. Thank you, Mr. White," she said.

I tipped my cap to her. "You're welcome, ma'am." She smiled at me again and walked away.

Faith and I were left alone. She came up to me and folded her arms. We didn't look at each other for a bit. We each just kept looking everywhere but in front of us. I broke the silence. "So, you are an alpha now?"

"Because of you," Faith said.

"I didn't know it would work like that," I said.

"Neither did I," she said.

We looked at each other then. I cleared my throat. "You…you can always come back here. Once you are done with Kodiak."

"You wouldn't mind me and my pack being here?"

"No. I like having you around," I said. "In fact, to make it official I, Sir Michael White, invite your pack to remain here as it was formed here."

Faith blushed and looked at the ground. She snatched up her bag and cleared her throat. "I will think about it. I will talk it over with Kodiak and my second."

"Your second?" I asked.

She turned her head to look at the entrance to Kate's. Everett Black walked out alongside Marshal Thatcher. A young man followed them. He was thin with a full head of dark hair and a beard to match. Everett and Marshal walked past me, but this young man walked right up to Faith and then said, "Hey boss."

"Drew?" I asked.

Drew looked at me and said, "Hey, Michael. Sorry, I was talking to Faith."

I looked from Drew to Faith. She nodded to him and said, "Hey Drew. They all ready?"

"Fed and coming out now," he said.

Skinny but fit people began filing out of Kate's. They were all dressed in cheap sweatpants and t-shirts. There were dozens of them. Men and women that just days ago had been homeless, invisible to so many people, and sadly unwanted. Now they were werewolves, immortal, and more powerful than any of them had dared imagine.

"What will happen to them?" I asked.

"It's our law that every werewolf has to go to college and contribute to the pack in some way. So, most of them will be getting an education. This is after they learn to control their change, that is," Faith said.

"It's your law that they have to get a college level education?" I asked.

"Yeah. Our laws are better than yours," Faith said.

"Wait, so you have a degree?" I asked.

"A bachelor's in economics, thank you very much."

"Cool," I said.

"I's an educated hillbilly!" Faith laughed.

One of the new wolves wandered away from the line toward us. He had broad shoulders, a muscular chest, and dark hair all over his brown skin. He had long hair up top and a thick beard. He shambled toward us like he was in a daze.

"Michael White," he said.

I recognized his voice. "Jermon Hernandez," I said. I was so happy he was alive and well that I moved forward to hug him.

Faith grabbed me and pulled me back just as a clawed hand swiped across my nose and lips. I screamed in pain as Drew slammed into Jermon and put him into a head lock. Jermon was bigger than Drew, which put Drew off balance and allowed the taller man to plow ahead while dragging him forward. Faith stepped past me and roared at Jermon. He growled back at her but dropped to one knee.

I was wiping blood from my torn nose and lip. "What the hell was that, man?"

"You killed my family!" he roared. The other werewolves all turned to me.

"I…di…I didn't… kill…" I began to sputter, but he cut me off.

"You told me to go to that shelter, and that wolf ate my children!" he growled. Jermon tried to get back to his feet, but Drew pulled his arm behind his back and leaned down on him with his free hand.

"Jermon…I'm sorry. I was just trying to help," I said.

"Help? You sent us to a death trap! My children are dead, and now I'm some demon!" he said. The other new werewolves were still moving toward the buses, but several turned to growl at me. "At first I blamed the wolf that attacked us, but now I know the pain he was in when he transformed. No man could keep his sanity after that. But you. You knew they were targeting the poor, and you sent my family to be slaughtered."

"I didn't know that they were going to attack Code Blue!" I yelled.

"But my wife and I survived. We endured. And even though we managed to live, you decided to finish the job last night!" Jermon cried.

"Jermon, I was fighting for everyone, to save you and your wife," I said.

"You cut her head off!" he yelled as he leapt at me.

My thoughts flashed back to last night and the wolf that I had decapitated. It was the only wolf I had killed, and it must have been Jermon's wife. I had sent her to Code Blue to be safe, and of course it had become a war zone. Then after she had survived that, I had stepped in and taken her life.

Jermon lifted Drew off the ground as he began to shift into a wolf. The arm Drew had forced behind his back broke loudly during the shift, but he was still flying at me. Drew let go and fell to the wayside. I was frozen. I couldn't react. He was right—I had killed his wife, and his kids were dead because I had told him to go to Code Blue. I waited for his jaws to rip into me.

Kodiak Black stepped in front of me and caught Jermon by the throat. Jermon growled, but Kodiak silenced him with a roar that shook the ground. Car alarms went off in the distance, and every werewolf around dropped to their knees. I felt confused. I wanted to run and hide, but at the same time I wanted to fall to my knees and be counted among his pack.

"Shift back," Kodiak whispered. Jermon did just that and slumped to the ground amidst the remains of his ruined clothing. Everett, Marshal, and Drew took hold of him and escorted him toward the buses. "He will become part of my pack until we can place him somewhere suitable. He may blame you, Mr. White, but you were defending yourself. I trust you did not know who you were fighting?"

"No…" I said.

Kodiak nodded and walked away. Once again Faith and I were alone. She stepped up to me and hugged me. "I am going to miss you, Michael. You take care. If you get the chance, call and tell me more about that girl of yours. Say goodbye to Mr. Bear for me," she said with a smile.

I smiled back at her. It's all I could do with the knowledge that the fifteenth soul I had killed with my sword was a woman whose kids I had sent to be slaughtered. Now her husband wanted to kill me, and I couldn't blame him.

"Bye-bye, Michael," Faith said before grabbing the back of my head and pulling me into a kiss. She bit my lip, kissed me again, and then whispered into my ear, "You saved all these people, whether they realize it or not. You saved this city. You also saved me, and I will never forget that. I hope the next time we meet your scent will have changed. Tell Mr. Bear I said bye-bye."

"See you Faith. Alpha of the Baltimore Pack," I said.

She walked off, got on the second of the two buses, and just like that she was gone. Faith was gone, and I was standing alone in the parking lot of Kate's Bar and Grill. I walked over to my loner and said nothing as I drove Larry home.

Traffic wasn't too bad on the way to Larry's apartment. Of course I carried his bags up for him. Larry pulled out a wad of money from a deep pocket and handed me $1000.00. "One hundred bucks a day. Plus, double for teaching me to be courageous," he said.

"Larry, you didn't have to pay me for that," I said. Larry's hand moved back toward the wad of cash, and I pulled it away. "That's just an expression, Larry. You tried to give my arm to a troll!"

"I still think it was a good deal," he said with a shrug. I just rolled my eyes and walked out of the apartment.

Larry walked out behind me to wave goodbye. I realized something as I was walking away and said, "Taste the rainbow isn't about Lucky Charms. It's about Skittles.

"I'm keeping it," Larry said. I gave him a thumbs up, and he smiled before closing his door.

My phone rang just as I got back to the loner car. It was my standard ring tone. "Hello," I said.

"You wanted to talk to me?" Sir Liam Keegan asked.

"Yeah, that gun your squire carries, what is it?" I asked.

There was a pause before he said, "A Taurus Judge. Why?"

"Because I went and got myself a Smith and Wesson Governor so that I could fire the bullets you left behind," I said.

"Was that why you wanted to speak to me, Sir?"

"Nah. It was more about his choice of bullets. Silver, right? Is that standard issue? Or is it a special round that he carried just to come to Baltimore. You know, because werewolves aren't supposed to be here, and silver rounds are so expensive, plus they don't do jack to anything but werewolves," I said with a laugh.

Again there was a pause. "That is a bold accusation, boy?"

"It's Sir, not boy. I am not sure where you stand in the order, but I am pretty sure I am at least equal in rank to you, Sir Liam. I am filing my report today, and I will be passing this information along to my Lord Commander. I suggest you keep a close eye on your squire," I said before hanging up.

I pulled off and my phone rang again. I answered, "Aaron, whatever it is can it wait until you can leave your coffin?"

"It's not Aaron, its Emory," Aaron's boyfriend said.

"Emory, what's wrong?" I asked.

"Aaron called me and told me to call you and tell you that there were going to be more vampires in Baltimore once he gets back. You should tell Eden and Kate. I have to go. See you when we get back."

Emory hung up. Great, now I was going to have more vampires to deal with. At least things couldn't get any worse.

Horace was waiting for me when I got home. He had a cold beer and two liters of Mountain Dew ready for me. I showed him the cash and he went nuts.

"I am thinking big screen TV, and we spend the rest on strippers," he said.

"I am thinking we buy a moderate sized TV, pay rent for the next few months, and then donate the rest to Code Blue so they can rebuild," I said.

"I hate you, kid," he said just as my phone began to play the theme from *Bewitched*.

I took another drink before answering the phone. "Hey Eden. What's up?" I asked.

"Are you done with the troll's and werewolves?" she asked me.

"Pretty much," I said.

"Good. Michael, do you remember that chalk I had you draw a circle with?"

"Yeah, the color changing chalk. That stuff was cool."

"About that…Michael, it wasn't color-changing chalk, at least not like you thought it was. It changes color to show the amount of magic released when someone uses it. Specifically, anywhere from white to blue."

I thought about what she said. It didn't make sense. "So, it was blue because?"

"Because we subconsciously expend magic when we draw, paint, or write. When we create something, put forth effort, we can't help but inject a little of ourselves into that work. It turned blue because the magic you subconsciously expended was on par with most magi that aspire to become wizards."

"Which means what exactly?" I asked.

"It means, Michael, that we need to teach you how to use magic before you go completely insane and kill us all," Eden said.

"Nope. I don't do magic," I said as I hung up the phone.

"What was that about?" Horace asked.

I looked at my teddy bear and realized that only an insane person would talk to a teddy bear. An insane person might also justify talking with the teddy bear by saying that it was magical. Furthermore, this insane person could further justify this interaction by saying that no one could prove that it wasn't real because the bear became lifeless whenever anyone else was around. But again, these actions would be those of a fractured mind.

"Nothing," I said. "Turns out I am the chosen one gifted with the power of a hundred wizards, and I have to master my gifts by next Tuesday or the Black Council will win the war for magic and plunge us into a thousand years of darkness."

"You suck at being an asshole," Horace said.

"Eden thinks I am a wizard, and I don't care. Why the heck would I want to learn magic?" I asked.

Horace shrugged as I went back to drinking my soda. "Well, it makes sense. Your mother and grandmother are two of the most powerful wizards in the country."

I spit out my soda at his words and yelled, "What!"

Horace just looked at me and sighed. "Do you know anything about anything, you freaking idiot? You can't be that much of a shut-in that you didn't know about your family being made up of wizards!"

"Wait? My family? Like more than just my mom and grandma?" I asked.

Horace dropped from the couch and went to the kitchen. "I am going to need a lot more beer," he said.

My name is Michael White. I won't tell you my whole name because that can get you killed. I am the grandson of a Paladin. Apparently I am also the son and grandson of two powerful wizards. I am the owner and once again soul employee of White Knight Construction. I am a part-time private investigator. I am a Knight of the Crucifixion. When you have a problem that seems too big for you, when you think the police can't help you, when the shadows are surrounding you, or when you hear something go bump in the night, just ask for help. I will be there.

### The Altered Manuscript
*Ellen Taylor*

The accidental discovery of the narration device completely changed entertainment and proved too dangerous to use without strict laws in place. Junior understood the reason behind these laws, which is why Bree does not know she's a character in a story. When a rogue narrator hacks into the system and begins creating chaos in Junior's story, does Junior continue to follow the laws to keep herself safe, or does she risk it all to protect the characters she loves?

### The Entropy of Knowledge
*Mark Dellandre and Britton Learnard*

We've all had moments when we felt like we were surrounded by idiots…
Babylon Briggs feels that pain every day because his town, his planet, even his galaxy, is jam-packed with the most thick-headed simpletons imaginable. So when his home world is invaded by a group of equally clueless conquerors, it's up to Babylon to save the day. The only question:
Is he smart enough?

**Time Starts Now**
*Michael Walsh*

Professor Cal Sutherland's research on time travel elicits only snide remarks from fellow philosophers and rejection notices from journals. Even Cal would admit that time travelers probably aren't real—until he encounters one inside his neighbor's burning house. Cal soon learns that, while the past cannot be changed, there is much a time traveler can do in the past. Unfortunately for Cal, this includes the possibility of dying there…

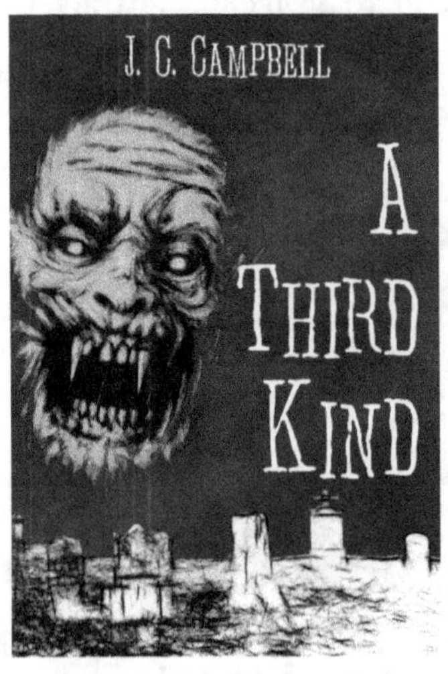


**A Third Kind**
*J. C. Campbell*

He was to have been an immortal undead, to have power and strength like he'd never known in mortal life. The Vampyrs lied. When he awoke he was some- thing else, a creature so foul they abandoned him to die alone in a crypt. When the local ruling Vampyr clan realizes what is living in their midst, they come in force to destroy Kaleb and wipe every last trace of his existence from the face of the earth.

# The Adventures of New World Dave
*Chris Cervini*

In the spring of 1519, Hernán Cortés arrived at the shores of Mexico to conquer the Aztec Empire and claim its gold for the glory of Spain. That's what the history books tell us. But sometimes, right in the middle of the history we know, somebody goes and does something to change one important detail, and the world is never the same…